SIEGE AND SPARROW

GUILDS OF ILBREA BOOK FIVE

MEGAN O'RUSSELL

Ink Worlds Press

WHITE MOUNTAINS
Royal Palace
Map Ma...
Palac...
BARRENS
Ilara
Arion Sea
Frason's Glenn
Barrens Bay
Ian Lioche
Harane
Ian Mithe
ILBREA
Ruthin Mountain
Ian Ayres
Southern Citadel
Mountain Road
Pamerane

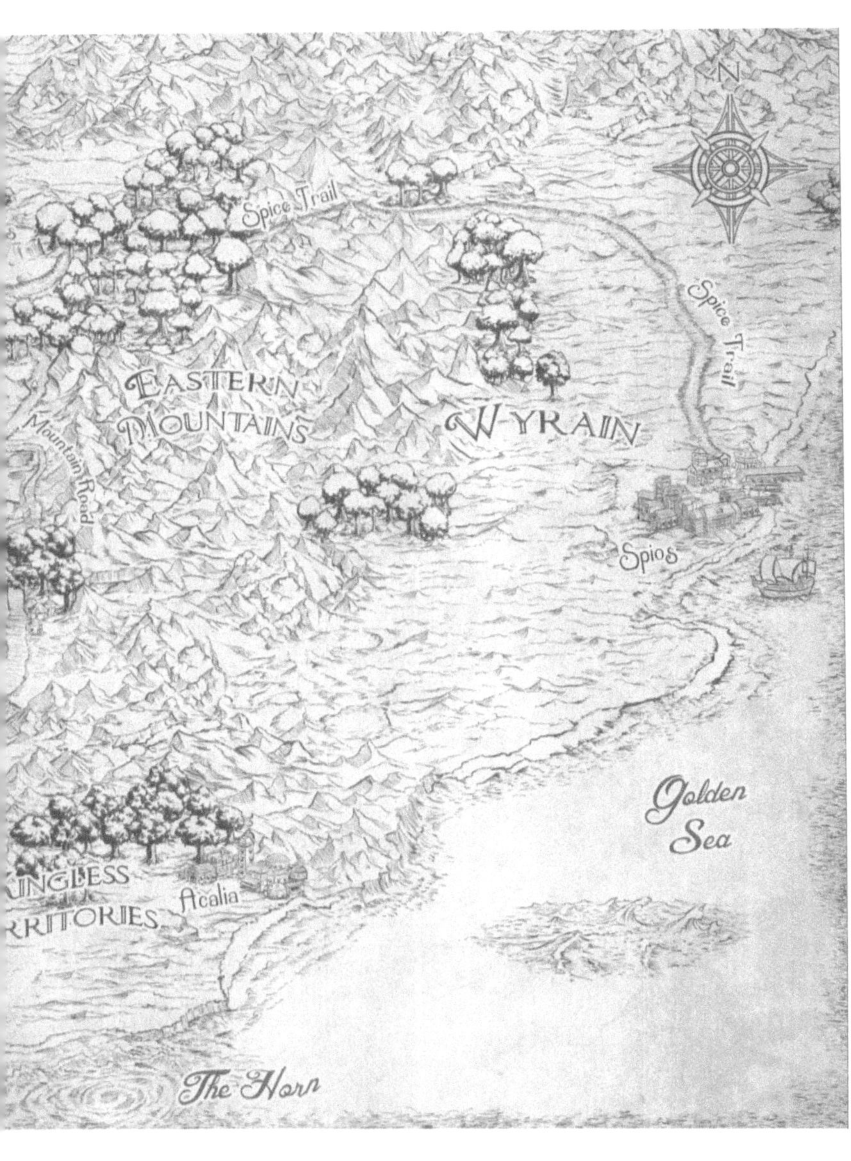

N
Spice Trail
Spice Trail
EASTERN MOUNTAINS
WYRAIN
Mountain Road
Spios
Golden Sea
JUNGLESS TERRITORIES
Acalia
The Horn

SIEGE AND SPARROW

1

———

ENA

The red of the sunrise bathed the doomed city, the hue tainting the white stone of the library as though the sky itself wanted to prove it understood the bloodshed to come.

The trickle of people appearing on the streets did not heed the sky's warning.

Faint mumbles carried up to the attic window as the fools headed toward the cathedral square. Whether wanting a good view of the Guilds' display or drawn by the promise of chaos, what lured them on wouldn't matter when a blade drove through their chest.

Fools rarely consider their own lives might be forfeit to the violence they crave.

"Soldiers have already arrived at the library, the docks, and that Map Maker Traim's house." Harrell stepped toward me.

Alane matched his movement, her hand on the hilt of her dagger as her gaze flicked between Harrell and me.

Attie and Kace closed in on either side of the window where I stood, both reaching for their blades.

Harrell's boots scraped against the grit on the floor as he inched back.

"I know." I held Harrell's gaze, waiting for him to glance away before continuing. "The Guilds have lined up all their pretty little soldiers in tidy little rows."

"Which offers us an opportunity to—"

"Leap into a trap?" Alane cut in.

"They don't know how powerful we are," Harrell said. "The Guilds, even the Sorcerers Guild, don't come close to understanding stone magic, if they've even figured out it exists."

"No." I looked back out the window.

The red glow of the library had paled, painting the stone a less menacing soft pink.

"Solcha, one trueborn in the square is all we'd need to attack the Guild Lords," Harrell said.

"And endanger my husband?" I pushed away from the windowsill.

"A crop of paun to be reaped," Harrell said. "That's what they're offering up."

"So you'll offer up whatever trueborn you send to attack as a martyr?" Alane said.

"There are those willing to accept the risk," Harrell said.

"You mean willing to die," Alane said.

"For a chance to strike the Guild Lords, yes." Harrell rounded on Alane. "They've yet to realize a trueborn's strength. We can take advantage of their arrogance."

"There will be no Black Bloods near the square today," I said. "There will be no chaos or magic near the square today."

"Solcha, the safety of one man—"

"Has been promised." I tilted my head. Attie and Kace drew their swords. "If a whisper of harm comes near the head scribe, the one responsible will die with my blade in their gut."

"Solcha—"

"Black Blood, underground, paun, I don't care." I let my wrath dance through my eyes. "The one who harms the scribe will not have a gentle death."

"I'll make sure he's not targeted," Harrell said.

"Not good enough."

"We can't give up a chance to strike at the Guilds to protect one chivving paun!" Harrell's breath came in quick pants as panic and fury filled his face in equal measure. He licked his lips and swallowed hard before speaking again. "I'm sorry, Solcha. But your husband—"

"Is protected." I stepped closer to the fool, watching the sweat bead on his forehead before leaning close to his ear.

The Brien stank of filth and fear.

"Your elder gave her word," I whispered. "Do you want to be the one to break Bryana's vow?"

Harrell's breath caught in his throat.

"One drop of the scribe's blood spilt, and the Brien who brought violence near him will have betrayed Bryana. Will you betray your elder?"

"No, Solcha." Vivid splotches reddened Harrell's cheeks.

I stepped away from him.

The slitch dragged in a shaky breath, as though reminding his lungs of their purpose.

"There will be no Black Bloods near the square today." I sank back to the window. "The Guilded beasts will bleed soon enough. If any others are too thirsty for paun blood to stay in their dens, remind them of your elder's vow, and who she made that promise to."

"Yes, Solcha." Harrell's quick footsteps thumped against the hollow floor as he fled down the stairs.

The door at the bottom of the steps banged shut behind him.

More lights flickered to life in the library's windows, their feeble glow barely visible in the sunrise.

"We should go," Kace said. "If Harrell rallied the courage to summon you, others will whisper as well."

"Let them."

A light appeared in the scribe's window. He'd lit the lamp beside the bed.

"If the whispers grow, they could become a distraction," Kace said. "We can't afford dissension from the Brien in Ilara. There are too few of us as it is."

A shadow passed by his window, moving toward the sitting room.

"The beasts of the Guilds are not the demons of the eastern mountains," I said. "We need better weapons than swords and stone magic."

Lights began flickering on in the sitting room, one after the other, as though someone were dashing to light every lamp.

A sharp pain twisted in my gut.

"They'll understand soon enough," I said. "Let the whispers grow until then. It'll only strengthen their faith in us when the storm begins."

"In *you*," Alane said. "They'll cling more to their faith in you."

"They can believe whatever they like, as long as they fight beside us."

A silhouette appeared in his window. The sun glinted off the glass, blurring the figure.

"We still need to go," Attie said. "The crowds in the streets will only grow."

"One more moment." I pressed my palm to the cold glass as the silhouette disappeared.

2

ALLORA

The line of staff led out of the parlor, cutting between the guards stationed at the door and stretching down the hall.

Another gift appeared in Allora's hand as a young maid stepped in front of the platform.

She curtsied, the dip of her chin not hiding the glee near bursting from her face.

"Thank you for your service." Princess Illia handed the maid a small, cloth-wrapped package.

"It's an honor, Your Highness." The maid curtsied again then moved on to the King, giving him an even lower curtsy before moving on to Allora.

The maid bit her lips together as she curtsied a fourth time.

"Thank you for your service." Allora gave the maid her gift.

"It is my honor, Your Majesty." She gave a fifth curtsy, this time with a bit of extra bounce on the way up, and hurried out of the parlor, her gaze fixed on Allora's package.

Allora's choice of fine fabric for the wrapping hadn't been a plot to impress, merely a detail to bring a bit of beauty to the gifting ceremony while using the spare bits left over from the creation of her many gowns.

Efficient and cheerful.

That the glinting of the gold woven through the fabric brought such delight to the staffs' faces was an offense for which she would have to beg Princess Illia's forgiveness…if the line of staff ever ended.

An older woman received her gifts next, the glee in her eyes better concealed, though very much present.

Allora watched her scurry away, allowing herself a moment to fully focus on the woman's joy—on the brief flutter of happiness she'd brought to someone's life.

Another gift appeared in her hand.

A young man bowed his way through the three royals.

"So many on the staff," Illia said as another young man approached. "It's hard to believe we'll get through them all. Thank you for your service." She placed her gift in the man's hand.

"Thank you, Your Highness." The man gave Illia a second bow before moving over to bow to his King.

The King gave the man a nod. "Maintaining the palace requires many hands. Thanking each of them individually is bound to be a time-consuming task."

The man bowed to Allora.

"Thank you for your service." Allora handed the man his gift.

"It is my highest honor, Your Majesty." The man bowed again and strode away.

I should have kept a tally of curtsies and bows.

A dangerous game, Allora. Kai's voice bounced with laughter as he whispered from a far corner of her mind. At least, far enough from the pain of his loss she could smile at his words rather than weep that they'd been whispered by a ghost.

"Thank you for your service." Illia handed a young maid her gift. "But if everyone on the staff is waiting in line for our thanks, and it takes ages to get through them all, they'll fall behind on preparations for tonight's party." Illia spoke over the maid's soft, "My honor, Your Highness."

"The staff will catch up." The King gave the girl a nod.

"But what if they can't?" Illia said. "What if this stupid line ruins everything?"

"There's no need to fuss," Allora said. "There are still staff hard at work."

The maid curtsied to Allora.

"Work in the palace stops while the gifts are given," the King said.

"Not all the staff are in line." Allora handed the maid her package. "Thank you for your service."

The maid gave a quick, "It's my honor, Your Majesty," under Brannon's sharp, "Yes, wife, they are."

Illia's voice gained a tense tone on her next, "Thank you for your service."

"At Winter's End, we thank every single person on the palace staff for their work throughout the hard months of winter." Brannon kept his gaze pinned on Allora, ignoring the man bowing before him. "These are my family's traditions that have been passed down through the centuries my family has ruled Ilbrea. Never presume to know better than a Willoc."

"Thank you for your service." Allora gave the now wide-eyed man his package, allowing the poor fellow to flee. "Unless the lower staff are all kept to the end of the line, or given uniforms specifically for receiving our thanks, menial tasks are still being performed at this moment by those deemed unfit for the occasion."

"Do you truly find wisdom in questioning me?" Brannon's tone honed to an even sharper edge.

"My apologies, Your Majesty." Allora curtsied to Brannon as a woman curtsied to Illia. "I was not intending to question you. It was a mere observation."

The woman bowed to Brannon and stepped in front of Allora.

"If you please," Allora said before the woman could curtsy. "Will all the staff pass through the line this morning?"

"It is an honor, Your Majesty." The woman dropped into a low curtsy, using the motion to angle her body slightly toward the door as though preparing to flee without receiving Allora's gift.

"Please do answer," Allora said. "I am the Queen of Ilbrea. You cannot be blamed for a question asked by me, and an honest reply would gain my gratitude."

"I—" The woman's neck tensed. "As I know it, there are a few kept below, Your Majesty. Those who aren't fit for royal halls."

"No," Brannon said. "Everyone is in line."

The color drained from the woman's face.

"An easy misunderstanding." Allora kept her tone light. "And one with a simple remedy."

"I cannot afford to stand in this line any longer," Illia said. "I've a party this evening, and the delegate from Wyrain could still—"

"I promise no more of your time will be taken." Allora held out the woman's gift, not letting go as the woman grasped it. "Please get a count of all those kept below and give it to one of my maids. I'll be sure the omitted staff receive a proper token of our gratitude."

"Yes, Your Majesty."

"Thank you for your service." Allora let go of the woman's hand.

"It is my honor, Your Majesty." Clutching her gifts to her chest, the woman near bolted from the room.

"And the problem is solved." Allora gave Brannon what she hoped appeared a sweet smile.

Brannon's jaw stayed clenched in the same way that had made him grind his teeth like millstones for the past two nights.

"I am the mistress of this house, husband," Allora said. "The duty of caring for the staff is mine. It's natural you wouldn't notice the absence of those everyone tries so hard to keep out of sight."

Brannon's chin barely dipped as he acknowledged the next man in line.

Allora pushed her focus away from her brooding husband, shifting to the task at hand.

The man blushed and accepted her gift.

She needed to think of a new token of thanks.

A gift that would ensure the staff kept below knew they were appreciated without making the rest of the staff problematically jealous.

Giving them the gift the upper staff had received with the addition of a gold coin would be the simplest, and presumably, most appreciated option.

But even rich men were wont to lose their heads knowing a piece of gold had gone into another man's pocket.

The heads of staff appeared in line before Allora had settled between either a staff banquet held in their honor or a new set of clothes.

"Finally," Illia muttered as the housekeeper stepped into the room and no one filled in the gap behind her.

A heavier gift appeared in Allora's hand.

"Thank you for your service." A true smile filled Illia's face as she presented her last gift.

Brannon gave a proper nod, and, though loath to admit it, Allora couldn't deny the touch of joyful relief that bought her lungs just a little more room in her chest.

The royal guards, who hadn't been included in the gifting, either, closed the doors behind the housekeeper, leaving only seven pairs of eyes to stare at the royals.

Allora turned away from the door and the guards beside it, fixing her gaze on the fireplace, sparing herself the sight of Brannon's temper-etched face while still keeping the guard with the pale blond hair out of view.

"Exhausting," Illia sighed. "Perhaps the tradition should be changed."

"To writing letters of thanks?" Allora said. "Your hand would freeze around your pen and be stuck for the rest of your life."

Illia laughed as she sank into the chair nearest Allora. "I'm just grateful I'll never have to do it again. Next Winter's End, I'll be dressing for my wedding."

"And what a beautiful bride you'll be," Allora said. "The most breathtaking Ilara has ever seen."

"That's impossible," Illia said, with only a faint touch of sullen envy in her voice. "Nothing I do will ever allow me to compare to you."

"Nonsense." Allora claimed the seat beside Illia. Her gaze caught on the blond guard for a moment, just long enough for heat to rise in her chest, threatening to surge pink to her cheeks. "I'll be entirely forgotten in the wonderment of your wedding."

"Do you think so?" Illia clasped Allora's hand.

"I'm certain of it."

"Your wedding will not excuse you from expressing your gratitude." Brannon stepped in front of Illia and Allora, his face stern as he towered over them as though they were no more than petulant children.

"Brannon—" Allora began.

"But brother"—Illia stood, keeping Allora's hand clasped in hers, yanking Allora to her feet—"a bride should not have to think of anything but her wedding as she prepares for the ceremony."

The muscles in Brannon's neck tensed.

"As it is, if I had to go to the square with you today, I'd have no chance of being ready for the party on time," Illia said. "I absolutely won't be able to greet a horde of servants and prepare for my wedding in the same day. I just won't."

"Your wedding will be held by my grace," Brannon said.

"And it's a year away." Allora squeezed Illia's hand, angling to place herself between the Princess and the King. "Let's not allow today's joy to be tainted by worries that are so far off. We have a mob of Ilara's finest coming to the palace this evening. All other concerns can wait."

"Fine." Illia squared her shoulders. "I can convince my brother another day."

Allora gave Illia a quick smile, keeping her cheer pinned in place as she turned to Brannon.

"How soon will you leave for the square?" Allora asked.

"He shouldn't be going. But I suppose it would be wrong of me to question my brother even in regard to his own safety." Illia strode toward door, barely giving the guard—the blond guard—

Don't, Allora.

—a chance to open it.

The guard bowed as Illia passed, returning to the stone-like stance of the other guards as soon as he'd closed the door behind her.

"She's right." Allora made herself meet Brannon's gaze as the thumping of Illia's guards' boots faded. "Going into the square is dangerous."

"Your point?"

"There are rebels in Ilara, Brannon. You could be attacked."

"Don't bother with false concern."

"It's not false concern. You are Ilara's King. If I had no reason other than that, I would fear for your safety. But you are also my husband. I don't wish my husband to come to harm."

"The King's safety has been assured." Gillien stepped out of the corner where she'd waited so quietly, Allora had almost fooled herself into forgetting the sorcerer lurked behind her.

Six guards, one sorcerer, seven sets of eyes always watching.

Watching me fail.

"If the King will be so perfectly protected, why am I not going to the square with him?" Allora fought not to flinch as the sorcerer touched her shoulder. "I am the Queen of Ilbrea. It is my duty to greet Ilbrea's people on Winter's End."

"The Lady Sorcerer wishes you to stay within the palace," Gillien said. "While King Brannon will be protected, we cannot guarantee there will be no commotion."

"Commotion?" Allora said.

"There is nothing you need worry over," Gillien said, "and no reason for you to leave the palace."

"Will you allow Lady Gwell to keep your wife from standing beside you?" Allora stepped closer to Brannon, freeing herself from the sorcerer's touch.

"Frankly, I don't care," Brannon said.

"As Queen, avoiding any potential danger is in your best interest as well as Ilbrea's," Gillien said.

"Ilbrea has no use for her." Brannon turned for the door. "She'll never carry a Willoc heir."

Jagged fear cut from Allora's heart to her throat as he stormed from the room.

His guards began to file out after him, the blond one joining the line.

"You, wait." Allora stepped closer to the door, beckoning the guard—the blond guard.

Kenrick.

He stepped out of line, taking a breath before bowing to Allora, lingering as he stooped low, as though buying another moment for the rest of his fellows to march out of earshot. "Your Majesty."

Allora glanced to Gillien as a fool's hope for privacy bubbled to life and immediately popped. "The final touches will be ready before the guests arrive. If the King shows any signs of leaving the party, you must try to delay him until I reach you."

"I've entrusted a friend who'll be on duty with me tonight," Kenrick said. "Not given any details, but he's been warned that if I make an odd request, I truly mean for it be done."

"Good." Allora nodded for her own comfort. "This would have been so much simpler in my father's home. I never considered how difficult living in a different place could make pulling off grand plans."

"The resources the palace affords are without compare," Gillien said.

"Which makes keeping a secret all the harder," Allora said. "The Map Master's Palace is undeniably grand, but there are far fewer eyes peeking around every corner."

"If you need help—" Gillien began.

"No," Allora said too quickly. She forced the corners of her lips up in the closest she could manage to a smile. "I want to surprise Brannon without the aid of any magic."

"As you wish, Your Majesty." Gillien bowed. "Only know my aim is to assist."

"If you truly wish to help, help me hide my foible," Allora said. "The lower staff and the royal guards were both overlooked today. I can't bear the idea of that mistake marring my first Winter's End in the palace."

"The first of many, Your Majesty." Gillien's smile sent a wave of nauseous loathing through Allora's gut. "I will personally see to those excluded."

"Thank you." Allora turned back to Kenrick. "You may rejoin the King's guard."

"Yes, Your Majesty." Kenrick bowed. As he stood, he met Allora's gaze, a hint of a smile lighting his deep blue eyes. "And thank you, Your Majesty. Your consideration will bring the royal guards much joy."

He bowed again, restoring his perfect guard's mask as though he hadn't just dared to meet the Queen's gaze, and left, abandoning Allora to the sorcerer.

"Come, Allora. You've a busy day ahead."

The smile curving Gillien's lips raked icy dread down Allora's spine.

3

KAI

Ink could not properly portray the face of the monster.

Kai recognized him, the runaway scribe. He'd seen the beast in the cathedral before. In a few taverns too if he forced his mind to recall all the times he might have ended the demon's life with a slash across the throat before the foul, chivving, sodden, loathsome, murdering, bower-breaking beast had dragged such pain into the world.

"Kai." Isla thumped her mug down onto Kai's hand, shocking him out of his bloodlust. Or, at least, distracting him from his plans for vengeance long enough to hear her words. "If you've lost interest, I'm happy to leave."

"You'll have to forgive me for being distracted by the murderer's picture staring at me from the bar." Kai sipped his ale.

Isla leaned back in her seat, peering around the balcony's column to the crowded bar below.

The notice had been tacked up on the wall, twice as large as those around it, displaying a frighteningly lifelike face.

Missing
Scribe Travers Gend

—were the only words Kai could read from his seat, but he didn't need to be able to see the text below for the mere glimpse of the notice to tighten his muscles as his body begged him to attack.

Tear the monster apart. Let his blood bathe the streets.

Scribe Travers Gend had honored the Guilds by orchestrating the capture and eventual death of the head scribe's common wife and her unborn child. Scribe Travers Gend's dedication to protecting the Guilds against the vile danger posed by the common invader had proven him among the most dedicated of the Guilded.

Information on his whereabouts requested.

No reward for his return offered.

A second piece of paper had been tacked over the top corner of the notice.

Demon loose in Ilara.
Reward for butcher's capture ~~six~~
~~*Seven*~~
~~*Nine*~~
Fourteen silver and growing.
Beast need not be breathing for coin to be claimed.
Donations to reward accepted.

"You can work on vengeance tomorrow," Isla said.

"And if someone kills him in the meantime?" Kai pointed to the notice. "The wrong soldier catches wind of common folk daring to defend their own, and blood will be spilt. And not the blood of the demon who deserves a painful introduction to Death. That barkeep is risking the noose, and we're drinking ale."

"The barkeep's drinking frie."

"It's different and you know it."

"Fine. It's different." Isla leaned toward Kai, planting her hands on the table. "But if you distract yourself with one bee, you'll lose sight of the hive. Do you prefer vengeance or freedom, Kai?"

Vengeance.

The scream roared through Kai's mind.

"Every minute you fight the Sorcerers Guild blind keeps Drew in danger," Isla said.

A swoop of breath-stealing fear broke through the scream. "I'll start on vengeance tomorrow."

"Good." Isla sat back. "Are you sure the head scribe will leave the party early? He's got nothing to go home to."

"Because that chivving murderer stole his family." Kai jabbed a finger toward the notice.

"Kai."

The bell on the bar rang.

In one swift surge, the crowd below bolted to the bar, cheering for the man who'd just rung the bell.

"Frie for all!" the man shouted.

The barkeep gave the man an exhausted yet delighted *huzzah* as he set to work pouring frie for the men and women who shoved their way forward.

Only four patrons Kai could see hadn't leapt up for a free drink.

One, a man who'd been passed out face down on his table for the last hour, didn't so much as stir at the racket.

A woman had also stayed in her seat in the far corner. Hands locked together on the table in front of her, she kept her gaze nailed to the front door of the pub, the anger seething in her eyes making Kai pity whatever poor fool she waited for.

The other two were barely in view.

Merial sat at the back of the bar, eating a massive piece of roast meat with an unfamiliar look of joy filling her face.

Near the front of the bar, Drew had claimed a table with six chairs.

No one had dared to join him.

Given the way Drew used his sailors knife to whittle the stick he'd brought with him, sharpening it to a vicious point as though preparing to gouge out someone's eye, Kai couldn't blame them.

Merial set her knife and fork down to take a drink of ale.

Drew set his sailor's knife down to check the point of his stick.

"Subtle," Isla said.

"As subtle as your man ringing the bell twice in the last hour," Kai said. "How much are your people spending to get the crowd spinning drunk?"

"It's not your concern."

"That you're spending a common man's fortune so we can meet in a chivving tavern? I didn't think you'd been sent to Ilara with coin to burn."

"The Karrons aren't the only ones with too much gold in their pockets."

"So Ilara's Brien have found an Ilbrean patron?" Kai sipped his ale. "Are they common or Guilded?"

The handle of his mug grew unpleasantly warm.

"Unnecessary." Kai took a deeper drink.

"Stop blathering and distracting," Isla said. "We're spending a lark's ass on frie because you've a job to do. Either you help, or I leave."

"Fine." Kai tightened his grip on the handle of his mug, holding Isla's gaze. "Adrial will wait ten minutes after the dancing properly begins, then leave."

"Ten minutes?"

The stinging heat of the mug's handle faded.

"Unless Allora forces him to stay, but as she's the Queen of Ilbrea now, I doubt she'll have the time."

"How do you know it'll be ten minutes?" Isla narrowed her eyes, studying Kai's face.

He let his attention scour his mind for a moment, searching for any hint of Isla drilling into his thoughts.

Not that he could be sure such a thing was possible.

Not that he'd have a chivving chance of stopping Isla if she resorted to using magic on an ally.

"Kai." Isla thumped her mug on his free hand again.

"Does the *why* matter?" Kai shook out his fingers and tucked his throbbing hand into his lap.

Closer to your blade anyway.

"Every detail matters."

Risking his unhurt hand, he took another sip of ale, failing to swallow the sour his impending betrayal shot into his throat. "It's his bad leg. Adrial doesn't like to sit in public, not when others are standing. He worries people will see him as weak."

"They would."

"So he'll make himself stand." Kai downed more ale. "He'll hide his limp as best he can, which will cause him pain I don't think most could bear, then he'll stand and watch the dancers, trying not to let the sweat from masking the agony bead on his forehead."

Isla finally drank.

"Adrial will make himself stay for ten minutes, the minimum span of a respectable appearance as proclaimed by Allora years ago, then flee. He'll make sure his driver knows he plans on a quick departure." A thick, weighty fatigue settled on Kai's chest. "Adrial shouldn't be worrying about standing or hiding his limp on Winter's End.

"The whole Karron lot should be together. Allora should have made sure we'd have too many seats, stealing any reason Adrial might have dragged up to stay standing. He should've sat while we drank and laughed, and not even thought of counting minutes. It should have been one of those nights so beautiful, time stops so you can revel in perfect joy.

"But Niko is dead, and Adrial lost his wife and child. Allora is the Queen, and I'm meant to be a corpse. The luckiest of us all are Mara and Tham. They're up in the white, beautifully unaware of how much our family has lost."

"Don't envy the absent. At least you've been here to try and protect the little your Karrons have left. Your friends will come home to find everything gone and never know if they could have found a way to stop it."

The sour in Kai's stomach snapped away, leaving a cruel void behind. "And I get to know they're alive."

"But they'll think you're dead. They'll mourn for you as the Queen and head scribe have. They'll have nightmares of your ghost trapped deep beneath the waves and shout to the gods, *why, oh why did the sea not deliver our Kai home?*" Isla sipped her ale. "I can keep pushing you into morbid despair, or you can tell me everything else I need to know so we can both do something better with our time than ache over things that can't be changed."

If you gave Adrial the choice, he'd take the risk.

Kai dug his knuckle into the growing pain in his temple. "He'll probably be alone in the carriage."

"Probably?"

"He'll try to slip away without being seen, but if someone asks to travel back to the library with him, he won't refuse."

"Would it only be scribes who might be in the carriage with him?" Isla glanced down to her man at the bar.

"I can't see why anyone else would ask to share his carriage, but the weather's worse than the season should offer."

Isla stayed silent.

"If rushing is too risky, we can find—"

"The head scribe will be taken tonight."

"And if someone else is in the carriage with him?"

"It changes nothing."

Someone at the bar gave a cackling laugh.

"A second person in Adrial's carriage could put him in danger." Kai's fingers tensed as a mortally foolish instinct screamed for him to grab his knife. "You said you would ensure he makes it through this gods-cursed nightmare. That was the deal."

"We agreed you'd help me take him without hurting him. If you don't help me, there is no deal."

"It would be a lot easier to help you if you'd explain why you've got to kidnap Adrial at all." Kai's chair rasped as he stood, planting his hands on the table, leaning over Isla like he chivving longed for a painful end. "Whatever foul plots are festering within the Brien have nothing to do with him."

"Sit."

"If you want something from Adrial, let me get it from him."

Kai's chair slid forward, whacking him behind his knees, knocking him back into his seat.

Isla didn't so much as flinch as Kai gripped the hilt of his knife. "If you want Adrial alive to see tomorrow's sunrise, stop puffing and wallowing in your own chivving guilt and give the help you promised. What else do I need to know, Kai?"

Bang!

The sound almost covered the cracking of the wood as the tavern's door flew open.

For a breath, less than a breath, everything went silent.

Then the screaming began.

The crowd at the bar surged toward the back of the room, fleeing the stream of black-uniformed soldiers pouring through the tavern door.

Isla grabbed Kai's arm, yanking him away from the table.

He gripped the rail, holding tight, ready to vault over the edge and grab the common folks' offer of a reward for the demon Gend before a soldier could spot it.

The handwritten notice had already disappeared.

Still, the soldiers pressed in around the crowd.

Drew.

Not at his table. Not standing blade in hand before the soldiers, either.

A sharp shock jabbed through Kai's hand, loosening his grip on the rail.

Isla jerked him back, slamming him against the wall, planting her hands on either side of his shoulders as three soldiers thundered up the stairs to the balcony.

Kai drew his blade.

"Don't," Isla whispered.

The soldiers' gaze slid right past them as they paused at the top of the steps.

One of the soldiers nodded to his fellows, as though giving them permission to imitate a child's ruinous tantrum.

The men tossed aside the empty chairs, knocking over tables as they searched for the only two people who'd been on the balcony in the last hour—the very two people jammed against the wall, barely breathing as a ginger-haired soldier came within inches of them.

The stench of last night's cheap liquor seeped from the ginger as he wiped the sweat from his freckled forehead with his sleeve, bellowing, "Empty up here."

The crash of breaking glass came a moment later.

A woman below screamed. More screams rose in response.

A man's voice joined the noise. A horribly familiar man's voice.

Kai kicked away from the wall.

"Don't."

A force pressed against Kai's ribs, pinning him in place as rigidly as if iron had bound his chest.

The rolling crash of a hundred glasses breaking came from below.

"Silence!" A man in a black uniform leapt up onto the bar, sword in hand, smile on his face.

With one final, defiant rumble, the crowd went quiet.

"Happy Winter's End." The man on the bar bowed.

The shifting of the light caught on the faint purple trim along his collar.

"How pleasant to see so many gathered together on this day of celebration." The man looked to the barkeep, who cowered in the corner, glass in one hand, barrel cork in the other, as though either might serve him as a weapon. "An ale, if you please."

The barkeep nodded, his head continuing to bob even as he dropped the cork and poured the drink.

Neither commoner nor soldier spoke as the man on the bar waited for his ale.

He smiled as he accepted the glass, letting the silence stretch as he took a drink and licked his lips. "What a winter we've had. So many trials Ilara has endured. And yet, we're still here. Still the living heart of Ilbrea. Yes?" He raised his glass.

The soldiers cheered.

The crowd joined in.

"Are you proud Ilbreans?" the man shouted.

The crowd cheered.

The man stomped.

The crowd cheered louder, rumbling the wood beneath Kai's boots.

"Will you celebrate the start of a new season with your fellow Ilarans?" the man shouted.

The crowd roared. Someone started pounding on a table. Others joined in, growing the racket until the entire wall behind Kai shook.

The man threw his glass, smashing it against the bar.

Silence snapped through the crowd.

"Then why are you drinking away Winter's End in this pathetic excuse for a pub?" The man kicked a chunk of broken glass at the barkeep.

The barkeep shielded his face, trading a slice on the hand for the salvation of an eye.

"To the cathedral square!" the man shouted. "If you are going to gather, it will be in the cathedral square. We will escort you to the festivities to celebrate as true Ilarans!"

The soldiers cheered, and the crowd joined in, fear tainting their whoops of joy as, hands on the hilts of their swords, the soldiers herded them toward the door.

Kai leaned sideways as far as the bindings on his chest would allow, trying to see the back of the horde as they filed out.

Drew was fourth from the last, the tension in his shoulders and neck making the smile on his face grotesque. He didn't swing for either of the soldiers flanking the pub's door.

The soldiers didn't shout that they'd found a sailor's ghost, either.

Merial was second to last. She glowered at the soldiers, not even feigning excitement as she slowed her steps, giving each of the men a long look as though memorizing the faces of the doomed rats who'd disturbed her meal.

One of the soldiers bared his teeth at her.

Merial's glower shifted to a grin as she gave the man a terrifyingly calm nod right before passing through the door and out of sight.

An older man with patchy hair and a cane took the back of the line.

He paused in the doorway, turning around to search the room, squinting into the shadows as though wanting to be sure he hadn't abandoned any common folk to deal with the paun on their own.

"Move." A soldier kicked the man's cane.

The old man stumbled, catching himself on the cracked door-frame. "Apologies." He hurried out of sight, the last of the soldiers filing out after him.

Kai held his breath, making himself listen for the sound of anyone lurking below the balcony.

Sounds on the street. His heart thundering in his ears. Isla's shallow breaths.

Nothing below.

He pushed away from the wall.

The band around his chest tightened, pinning him in place.

"Let me go." Kai kept his voice low, straining to hear any hint of screaming coming from the street. "Isla."

"You're not going after them."

Kai leaned his weight against her magic.

She gave no hint of noticing any strain.

"We can beat them to the square," Kai said.

"To do what?" Isla lifted her hands away from the wall.

The sounds on the street sharpened, gaining volume as though Kai's ears had popped.

He tried to step forward. The band around his chest tightened again, cinching hard enough to bruise.

"If you run to the square, you'll do what? Weasel in to stand next to Drew for whatever hell the tilk are being herded toward?" Isla pulled the mass of her hair away from her face and a string from her pocket. "You certainly won't be able to get Drew away from the soldiers. Not without putting only the gods know how many common lives in danger."

"If I can't find a way to get Drew and Merial out, then yes, I will stand beside Drew for whatever doom has the soldiers driving people to the ceremony." Kai eased his hand toward his knife.

Isla froze, her fingers partway through tying her hair back. "You can't cut your way through magic with steel."

"Stabbing you in the leg might distract you long enough for me to run." Kai's hand locked up as though Isla had trapped it in stone. "That soldier had sorcerer purple on his collar. Whatever that means has got to be a chivving terrible thing. The Lady Sorcerer put her sails on our ships, and now she's marking soldiers."

"That seems the Lord Soldier's problem."

"And he will be furious. He will push back against the sorcerers. The sorcerers will attack, spreading panic. Panic spreads violence. And when the demons of battle swallow the city, I'm going to be standing beside Drew."

"Not if you want help from me or any of the Brien."

The pressure around Kai's ribs vanished.

"We are taking Adrial Ayres tonight. If you don't help and he gets hurt, that's on you. If your underground stays stuck spinning in circles, crumbling as you cling to your vague hope for freedom, mark this as the moment you lost your chance at any help from me." Isla leaned against the rail. "Run to Drew. Tremble before the Guilds' evil with your hand in his. And when you beg the gods for a swift death, remember to beg their forgiveness for the lives you've cost."

"We've fallen to threats?"

"No threat I can give could compare to Drew's wrath when he learns you torched the underground's hope for success for a useless, chivving romantic notion." Isla headed toward the stairs, yanking on the sleeve of her coat and tucking her hands into her pockets. "May you live long enough to earn his forgiveness."

Anger battered reason as every ounce of Kai's soul screamed for him to run after Drew and let the rest of creation meet its doom.

"Adrial will fight back," Kai called. "He's taken enough beatings in his life, he won't freeze."

Isla kept walking.

Kai forced his feet to move, trying not to hear the cry thundering through his mind with every step.

Drew. Drew. Drew!

4

MARA

The whine of Elle's yawn filled the silence as Mara held Captain Haxton's gaze, refusing to look away even as he bent over his desk, looming closer.

Tham's chair creaked as he shifted to stand.

Mara reached out, placing her hand on Tham's knee, squeezing hard in a silent plea for him not to interfere.

Tham's chair creaked again as he sat back.

Haxton tapped his desk without even glancing down at the map. "We are not sailing north."

"Oh good, we're talking again," Elver said.

"And there's not a chivving chance of my taking this ship anywhere near those demons," Haxton said.

"That was an awfully long angry silence." Elver kept speaking, yanking the captain's glare his way. "That particular sort of silence is exhausting. And we've too much work ahead of us to waste our energy with scowls. Especially when there are doomed people to save. Or try and save. Who knows how many Queen Ronya's already killed? And, even if we had a perfect plan, I'm sure she would slaughter a few thousand more before we even start driving her back to the white. If such a thing is even possible."

"Elver," Mara whispered.

"Please don't say we're going back to doing silent again." Elver sighed and bit his lips together.

"We're not," Mara said. "And we can't afford to waste time begging the captain to sail north, either."

"You've finally accepted I'll not sail my men to their deaths?" Haxton said.

"You saw what the Ice Walkers are capable of," Mara said.

"I think that's one of the reasons why he doesn't want to sail north," Elver whispered too loudly for Haxton to even bother pretending not to hear. "If you're going to ask him to go toward Queen Ronya and her monstrous army, you might be better off not pointing out how easily the Ice Walkers could kill the sailors, especially as those sailors are armed with knives. Just knives. And I think I saw a slingshot."

"It doesn't matter that Ronya's army has weapons. It doesn't matter that they have magic." Mara stood, planting her hands on the near side of Haxton's desk, leaning close enough to see the stubby hairs growing from the top of the tip of his nose. "We are sworn members of the Guilds of Ilbrea. It is our duty to protect Ilbrea and the Guilds. A foreign army marches through our home."

"A worse enemy has already claimed Ilara." The stale scent of Haxton's breath surrounded Mara as he spoke through his teeth. "Blood slicked this very deck as my men fought chivving sorcerers to reclaim our ship. The rest of the Ilbrean fleet is still held by the Sorcerers Guild. Whatever demons you dragged down from the white are on your head. My men fight for their own freedom."

"Freeing the sailors of the Sorcerers Guild won't matter when Ronya massacres everyone in Ilara," Mara said. "We're running out of time. You have to sail north now."

"Map Maker Landil, you're clinging to the false notion that storming into my office and demanding to be taken north constitutes a negotiation in which you might gain ground." Haxton pushed away from his desk to stand upright, letting his height devour all the space in his cabin. "If you truly want to help Ilbrea, quiet gratitude for our saving your lives would be infinitely more productive than your continuing to distract the crew and myself with your useless demands."

"I quite agree, actually." Elver tugged at a stray thread on the cuff of his coat. "We should be very grateful for your saving our lives. And, though being a prisoner isn't my favorite thing to be, being the kind of prisoner with card games and ale is much better than being chained."

"No one here is a prisoner," Haxton said.

"May we leave the ship?" Elver said.

"No," Haxton said.

"May I have a weapon?"

"No."

"Then we are prisoners." Elver furrowed his brow and frowned. "Though, as I said, the better kind of prisoner to be."

"Bring us to shore," Mara said. "We'll find our way north from there, and you can—"

"He's just said we're not allowed off the ship."

"Elver." Mara shoved down the rib-grating desire to scream.

"I won't risk you running right back to the chivving sorcerers to help put nooses around my sailors' necks," Haxton said.

"Oh, we're not meant to do that." Elver wrinkled his nose. "Definitely not going back to the Sorcerers Tower. The cakes are delightful, but we'd definitely be executed."

"You know he's right, Captain Haxton." Mara sank into the crooked-legged chair beside Tham as a heavy fatigue draped over her. "How we ended up on this ship won't matter. We found refuge with a crew that killed three sorcerers. We'd never survive long enough to touch the outer wall of the tower, let alone be given time to beg for mercy."

"You know the purple demons enjoy spilling blood yet speak as though you regret losing your place as Lady Gwell's pets."

"We need allies."

"Against the army with ice magic coming down from the north? You can't trust the sorcerers not to burn Ilara, but you want them fighting beside you against an enemy they're trying to pretend doesn't exist." Haxton sat in his own, much sturdier chair. "Our families are in Ilara. Our Guild Lord is in Ilara. All that matters is in Ilara. We will pry our city from the sorcerers' claws. Any attempt to interfere will be considered a declaration of your allegiance to the Lady Sorcerer."

"Leave the wolves at the door, there's a lion in the house." Elver nodded.

Mara shut her eyes, digging her fingers into her curls, yanking on the roots as she tried to drag one brilliant idea from her mind.

Just one.

There's a way to fix this.

There's a way to stop the Ice Walkers, and protect Ilara, and convince Lady Gwell—

"Let us help," Tham said.

Mara's eyes flew open.

Haxton stared at Tham, the familiar snap of attention filling his eyes that often appeared when Tham chose to speak.

"Help us skewer your friends the sorcerers and roast them on a pyre?" Haxton said.

"Help your men smuggle their families out of Ilara," Tham said. "We all saw what the Lady Sorcerer was willing to do to innocent children. What will she do to the children of the men who stand against her?"

Haxton's knuckles whitened as he gripped the arms of his chair.

Elle whimpered.

"We have Lord Karron's resources," Tham said.

"You mean the Queen's resources." Haxton sneered.

A blunt burst of outrage and shock kicked the air from Mara's lungs as her mind screamed for the hundredth time that it couldn't possibly be true.

Allora isn't married to the King. Kai and Niko aren't dead.

Think, Mara.

There's a way to fix this.

"Get the sailors' families out of Ilara. The sorcerers will look to the sea, but Mara and I can lead them south through the forest away from the mountain road. We've coin to keep them fed and set them on their way once they're far enough from Ilara," Tham said.

"On their way to where?" Haxton said.

"Anywhere the sorcerers won't find them," Tham said.

"Then we tuck our tails up our asses and run after them?" Haxton said.

"If you want to survive Queen Ronya, yes." Tham stood.

Haxton stayed in his seat, as though aware he had no hope of filling more space than Tham.

"Getting the sailors' families out of Ilara saves them from becoming victims of the Lady Sorcerer's vengeance and places innocents farther from the Ice Walkers' army," Tham said. "All we want is to stop Queen Ronya from slaughtering Ilbreans, even if we can only save the crew's families."

Haxton's knuckles whitened again as he glared at Tham.

"We can show your men a way into Ilara by land without using the city gate, and they can get their families out the same way." Mara stood, keeping her knees just a bit bent, balancing herself against the constant rocking of the ship. "Take us to Ilara, and we'll help you ferry dozens to safety. But if you find the courage to bring us north, you'll be saving thousands while buying your sailors' families time to run."

Mara stepped around her chair, holding her hand out for Tham to join her.

Elle smashed her nose into Mara's hand instead.

"I don't want to make anyone more angry," Elver said. "And I don't want to be demoted to the chained kind of prisoner, but maybe you should try scrunching your eyes to help you see better. The sorcerer shape and the ice walker shape, they fit together. There are other pieces, some of them darker than black and some so shining they hurt the back of my head, and those pieces, I can't make them fit yet.

"But the sorcerers and the Ice Walkers are locked together, tightening around us. You can't pull them apart or set one aside to only kill the other. Death walks beside both. Devoted. A loyal companion. Your head's blind if you don't see them coming." Elver stood, staring at Haxton for a moment, then nodding sadly. "You'll understand soon enough. I don't mind you thinking me mad until then." He turned to Mara. "I'd like to go back to my card game now. If my end by horrific, magical means is coming quickly, I'd like to win a few more hands."

"Dire warnings wrapped in ramblings will do you no good," Haxton said.

"They weren't for my good." Elver opened the door to the deck, letting a burst of chill air sweep through Haxton's cabin. "Fine morning to be at sea." He bowed to a passing sailor. "Best to enjoy the sunshine. May not live to see it again."

"Sheep-brained, chivving fool," Haxton said as Elver hurried away.

Mara clenched her teeth, holding her breath against her ever-growing need to scream as she strode out of Haxton's cabin, Elle nuzzling her backside marring her façade of powerful calm.

"Elle."

Elle left Mara at Tham's murmur, retreating to his side.

Mara needed to go below, find a shadowy corner to silently scream out her rage, then find a better plan with Tham.

A way to reach the north, or at least Ilara.

A way to contact Allora. Warn Ilbrea's Queen of the horrors to come.

A way to contact Adrial, have him tell the common folk to flee south, run as far from Ronya's path as possible.

A bird swooped past the ship, circling close to the gentle waves before diving headfirst after its prey.

Mara walked toward the bow, watching the bird carry its bounty away.

"Those details were missing." Mara gripped the railing. "In the tower, I could have heard the waves against the ship and the creaking of the planks, but not the voices of the crew."

Tham laid his hand on her back.

She sank into the touch.

"Flowers but no insects," Mara said. "Heights but no fall. Predators but no prey."

"Mara—"

"What if Haxton's right? What if Lady Gwell destroys Ilara before Ronya has the chance?" Heat pressed against Mara's eyes. "On Ian Ayres, the Ice Walkers couldn't have defeated Lady Gwell, but they had enough magic to at least try and fight her sorcerers. Saelk finding out about wild magic scares the Sorcerers Guild. Wild magic strong enough to defy them? Lady Gwell has got to be terrified. I don't know what fear might make her do."

She nestled close to Tham's side, letting the weight of his arm around her still the constant worry spiraling up her spine.

"Whatever magic threatens Ilara, we'll move as many away from that magic's path as we can," Tham said.

"It won't be enough." Tears cut through the cold of Mara's cheeks. "Ronya's already slaughtered Ilbreans. And the sailors killed Fergal. I can't blame them because he would have followed Lady Gwell's orders and helped burn Ian Ayres, but I can't convince myself I'm any better than Fergal because we left the children behind. They could be in the hands of the sorcerers or the Ice Walkers. They may be dead. And maybe Death would be their kindest keeper."

Tham kissed the side of her head. "We'll find a way to help."

"How?" Mara whispered.

Tham didn't answer.

Elle whined and leaned against Mara's legs.

"Mara," Elver called from across the deck, "I think the angry one is cheating again."

"Why am I being called the angry one?" Brady said.

Mara turned just in time to watch Brady leap to her feet, clutching six cards in her hands and glaring at Elver with a crackling sort of anger a child should never learn.

"I would have called you the cheater one, but I wanted to be sure you'd cheated first," Elver said.

Mara dug deep into her chest, seizing the flicker of humor brought by Elver tipping his head as he studied Brady, examining her as one might view an inventive toy rather than an animal ready to bite. Mara managed a small smile as she weaved through the sailors, ignoring the stares that somehow questioned her allegiance to Ilbrea's saelk and her worthiness of the title of map maker all in a few moments' walking.

"If you'd rather call me the one who gave you the black eye, I'd be happy to help, you braidic sod of a chivving slitch." Brady threw herself at Elver, ramming her shoulder into his throat, knocking him to the deck.

The cheers of half the sailors turned to boos as Mara dragged Brady off Elver.

There's a way to fix this.

There's a way to save everyone.

5

____

ADRIAL

His heartbeat strained against the rhythm of the dozen guards marching beside his carriage, thumping just too fast to match the sound of the guards' feet, driving the fear of falling behind deeper into Adrial's mind.

He straightened the cuffs of his robes, checking the black bands for wrinkles for the fourth time since they'd left the library. He checked his fingers, making sure he hadn't smeared any of the pale pink ink from his morning's work on his fingers.

You're not an ink-stained apprentice, Adrial Ayres.

Shutting his eyes, Adrial focused on the rumbling of the carriage's wheels, on the jostling of his seat, on the tang of the pungent scent left behind by the carriage's last occupant.

The sound of voices beyond the carriage grew nearer, offering indistinct words from the people they passed.

Closer. Keep your mind closer.

The damp chill of the day cut through Adrial's robes, leaving the constant tension of goosebumps across his skin.

"Clear the way," a voice boomed. "I said, clear the way!"

Adrial dug his fingers into his knees.

Ten points of pressure.

He lifted one finger at a time, counting down as the noise outside grew louder.

"Clear the way," the voice kept repeating as the carriage pushed forward. "Clear the way."

Clear the way so the head scribe could stand beside the sorcerers and face a horde as likely to attack as applaud.

The carriage slowed. So did the footfalls of the scribes' guards.

Fear wound around Adrial's chest, tightening his lungs.

You are not a coward, Adrial Ayres. You are the Head Scribe of Ilara.

Who is wise enough to recognize a deadly chivving mess when he sees one, Kai whispered.

A foreboding sense of calm allowed Adrial to take a full breath.

"We will face their worst. Whichever *they* shoves Ilara toward despair today." Adrial opened his eyes, folded his hands in his lap, and waited for the carriage to finally lurch to a stop.

The carriage door swung open. A guard reached in for Adrial before he'd stood.

Adrial tamped down his pride, allowing the guard to take his arm and half-lift him from the carriage. A second guard seized Adrial's other arm, the pair of them propelling him up the steps of the ruined cathedral. They pivoted south, toward Lord Gareth, Map Maker Traim, Lord Kearney, and Lord Nevon, not letting go until they had deposited Adrial behind Lord Gareth and, even then, only stepped back three feet to fall in line with Lord Gareth's guards.

"Happy Winter's End, Head Scribe." Lord Nevon looked to Adrial without a hint of cheer on his face.

"Nothing joyful in this." Lord Gareth shook his head, wobbling his ever-sinking jowls. Not bothering with discretion, he pointed out the sorcerers positioned on the roofs surrounding the square.

The common folk had noticed the purple-clad sentries as well.

Some of the horde kept their focus on the Guild Lords gathering in front of the still-shattered cathedral.

The Guild Lords' placement highlighted the monument to the deadly attack on the paun, as though the Lords were either begging to be killed or flaunting their confidence in victory against any foe. Both options offered equal odds of provoking an attack.

Don't give in to panic. You go out to sit with the common folk every day. There are guards and soldiers here to protect you.

Which only puts you in more chivving danger.

Most of the common folk who weren't staring at the Guild Lords watched the sorcerers on the roofs, or the lines of well-armed soldiers, who surrounded the square in a border of black uniforms.

A few brave souls edged toward the paths out of the square, as though preparing to flee.

But none of them, not a single soul in the common crowd, dared venture near the line of sorcerers arcing out from the bottom of the cathedral steps.

Fifteen sorcerers formed the blockade between the horde and the arriving carriages, each of them standing with their elbows tucked close to their sides and their palms facing the sky, all holding the pose as though basking in the glow of Dudia's blessing for the dark-skied day.

"I doubled the number of soldiers Lady Gwell requested to protect the King. We agreed to the sorcerers in front of the stairs." Lord Kearney gripped the hilt of his sword, the leather of his gloves groaning from the movement. "The sorcerers leering at us from the roofs is an unpleasant surprise."

"You can't be surprised when a viper bares its fangs," Lord Nevon said.

"But a viper must never forget it's not the only beast that can strike." Lord Gareth raised his voice as though wanting to be sure all prying ears would know he didn't care to hide his words. "The purple pestilence is creeping into every corner of the city. I had five of them in the square beside the library this morning. As unnerving as the sorcerers' retreat into their tower might have been, I much preferred being discreetly spied upon to having a sorcerer staring up at my window at all hours of the day and night."

A red-trimmed carriage rolled into the square, flanked by guards in red uniforms.

"Now you understand how the docks have been for months. Sorcerers grabbing for power that will never be theirs while putting my sailors' lives in danger." Lord Nevon raised his voice to match Lord Gareth's. "And the infestation has only gotten worse. The purple lady commandeered three of my ships for Dudia may not even know the reason as the sorceress has not seen fit to tell me. And when I demand information on the whereabouts of my ships and my sailors, I get a dozen more purple specters haunting my docks."

A red carriage stopped in front of the steps. A guard opened the carriage door, reaching in to collect Lady Byrd as his fellows turned toward the crowd, weapons in hand, ready to face Ilbreans as enemies.

Lady Byrd paused as she stepped out of her carriage, giving a nod to the guard who'd helped her, her gaze lingering for a long moment on the purple trim on the man's collar.

The hue of the purple fought the guard's red uniform, screaming its presence like the markings of a poisonous beast.

The Lady Healer wore a smug smile as she climbed the cathedral steps, showing no hint of anger. She gave the guard's collar another pointed look before letting go of his arm.

Four more healers' guards with purple trimming their collars took their place behind Lady Byrd with the other Guild leaders' guards.

"Happy Winter's End, Lady Healer." Map Maker Traim bowed.

"May Dudia's blessings bring us a bountiful spring." Lady Byrd didn't bow back.

"May the feet you kiss not kick out your teeth," Lord Nevon said.

Lady Byrd's shoulders stiffened.

"A pack of fools," Lord Gareth said. "That is what we've become."

Another carriage entered the square, escorted by a single guard riding a black horse.

The purple of the Lady Sorcerer's carriage seemed to glisten in the sunlight, glimmering in a way that implied more than paint and enamel in its decoration.

The sounds in the square changed as the carriage approached the cathedral steps, the noise of the crowd seeming to grow farther away, their voices dampened as though the Lady Sorcerer's very presence shielded Guilded from common.

As the carriage stopped, the arc of sorcerers all raised their upturned palms, just a few inches, a movement too small to hold much menace, but the air began to crackle.

Sharp tingles danced across Adrial's skin as a sheet of sickly blue-white light surrounded the platform, enclosing the gathered Guild leaders.

"Hmm." Lady Byrd's shoulders relaxed as she gave the grating sound of satisfaction.

The crowd drew back as Lady Gwell stepped out on the side of the carriage nearest the crowd.

Adrial eased sideways, beyond the front of the carriage, gaining a proper view of the Lady Sorcerer facing the horde.

No guard held her arm or propelled her up the steps. The Lady Sorcerer stood alone as her carriage and single guard left the square.

She watched the common folk for a moment, as though daring the crowd to taunt her.

A wave of unease rolled through Adrial's gut. He held his breath, waiting for one brave fool to test the sorcerer.

A flutter of movement disturbed the center of the crowd but stopped before it had truly begun.

Let it be. Don't throw yourselves into the demon's jaws.

Lady Gwell raised her hand, sending a mind-rattling clang echoing out over the crowd.

The thunderous thump of marching steps approached from the north.

"What madness have we wrapped around our necks?" Lord Gareth said.

Three long columns of royal guards entered the square, leading King Brannon's carriage.

"We're not the ones who've done the wrapping," Lord Nevon said.

Sunlight glinted off the gold of the King's carriage, but a different, paler glow tainted the sun's work.

The blue-white light of the sorcerers' spell reflected off the gilding, altering its gleam with a pallid hue that seemed to promise impending rot.

The carriage stopped behind Lady Gwell.

None of the royal guards broke rank to open the King's door. Instead, Lady Gwell turned toward the carriage, opening the door herself. She held out her hand, taking the King's, helping him down as though she alone bore the mantel of King Brannon's protector.

With another gong, the royal carriage departed, leaving Lady Gwell to escort the King up the stairs. She supported the King's arm with one hand while continuing to grip his hand with the other, holding on as so many well-meaning souls had tried to help Adrial before.

King Brannon kept his eyes front and jaw set as he faced

Ilbrea's leaders, giving them a moment to bow to him before relieving his arm of the Lady Sorcerer's hold and turning to face the crowd.

Lady Gwell shifted to stand on his right, barely an inch behind him.

Close enough to strike.

Breathe, Adrial, Mara whispered in his mind. *Spilling a king's blood is dangerous, even for a demon.*

Demons feed on danger and blood, Allora whispered. *Their claws are always ready to strike.*

"People of Ilbrea." King Brannon's voice rang out over the crowd, reverberating as though they stood in a marble hall rather than an open square.

The horde tensed, some trying to move back, others flinching or covering their ears.

A soft sound, like a swallowed laugh, came from Lady Byrd.

Adrial leaned his weight onto his bad hip and fixed his gaze out over the square, tamping down his desire to scream.

"We have reached another Winter's End," King Brannon said. "After a year of strife and suffering, a new season dawns in Ilbrea. A season of greatness that will not be sullied by criminals breeding violence in this city."

King Brannon stepped forward—whether threatening the crowd or fleeing Lady Gwell, Adrial couldn't tell.

"As the healthy flesh around a wound must sometimes be sacrificed, so the cleansing of Ilara will begin," King Brannon said. "I offer all Ilarans this final warning—no violence toward the Guilds will be tolerated."

Lady Gwell stepped forward, planting herself in front of the King.

Adrial held his breath, shifting his weight to his toes, preparing to defend Lord Gareth, though he had no idea how.

He reached toward the back of Lord Gareth's white robes.

A numbing chill washed over Adrial's body.

Grabbing Lord Gareth and dragging him back, Adrial planted himself between the Lord Scribe and Lady Sorcerer.

The cold surrounding Adrial gained a sharper edge, like the heat of a fire promising to burn his skin.

"Remove your magic from my flesh, sorcerer." Lord Nevon stepped toward Lady Gwell, gripping the hilt of his blade.

A flash of bright light burst around him.

The sailors' guards rushed forward.

Light flared around them as well.

"This stops now," Lord Kearney shouted.

Adrial searched the ground as illogical hope promised he might find a weapon there.

A stick. A rock. A pen with a sharp tip.

A scribes' guard yanked Lord Gareth from Adrial's grip.

The lights around Lord Nevon and his guards faded, narrowing into thin strands of gleaming white.

"The cat should learn when it needs the lion's protection." Lady Gwell held Lord Nevon's gaze as she snapped her fingers.

Pop.

The sound, no more menacing than the cracking of a log in the hearth, barely reached Adrial's ears over the commotion of the healers, map makers, and scribes' guards herding their charges away from the Lady Sorcerer, farther into the cathedral's rubble.

Hands gripped Adrial's arms, lifting most of his weight from his feet, pulling him to follow the others.

"Wait." Adrial shook his head, trying to stop them before his mind knew why.

The guards kept dragging back.

"No. Up there." Adrial jerked his arm free, pointing to the disc of light high above the tilk.

Glowing the orange of hot steel, the edges of the light shifted, stretching down toward the ground like honey drizzled on the dome of a cake.

Adrial opened his mouth to shout a warning but couldn't find any words.

A few brave people in the common crowd tried to alert their fellows before screams of fear drowned out every other sound.

The cold biting Adrial's flesh ebbed as the viscous orange light dripped down the arc of the magic-made shield that trapped the common folk.

The lessening of the cold didn't come as an absence of discomfort, but as a growing warmth caressing his skin as though he were standing in front of a fireplace on a frigid day.

The sound of the crowd's screams changed, their terror gaining the pitch of pain as the horde surged toward the center of the square, fleeing the edges of their cage as the orange light reached the ground, encasing the people in its now-rippling glow.

"Stop!" Adrial shouted, charging forward, knocking aside his guards' attempts to grab under his arms. "Stop! You're hurting them."

"Yet you are protected." Lady Gwell flicked her hand as though tapping her middle finger on a pane of glass. No sound accompanied the spell that silenced the crowd's screams. "I suggest you discover gratitude."

She nodded to King Brannon.

"Those who stand with the Guilds," King Brannon said, "obey the laws of the Guilds, and the laws I set forth as your King—you will be protected by your King and by the Sorcerers Guild. Those who forget where their loyalty is owed—"

The light encasing the dome pulsed a sickly yellow.

"—will not be granted such shelter."

The yellow brightened.

A woman on the edge of the crowd fell to her knees, her mouth open in a scream Adrial couldn't hear.

"Those who stand against the Guilds will be excised," the King said.

The horde fought, tearing through each other, trying to reach the center of the dome as they fled the still-growing light.

Horror clamped around Adrial's limbs, locking him in place even as every bit of his being begged to flee.

"Their families, their friends, their comrades in arms," the King continued, "any who may have been contaminated by disloyalty and insurgence, will share the traitor's fate."

A few of the common folk stayed at the edge of the crowd, their faces twisting in pain even as they yanked those who had been knocked down back to their feet, saving them from being trampled by the growing violence within the mob.

"My city will be cleansed. My country will be cleansed. If any should choose to ignore my warning, know this. All innocent blood spilt is born of your sins. The time for gentle justice has ended."

The glow brightened again.

"Please!" Adrial shouted. "Stop this."

"This is monstrous!" Lord Kearney drew his sword.

A flash of light surrounded him.

"In the coming year, I give the Guilds these tasks," King Brannon said.

The thick yellow gleam surrounding the common crowd faded, retreating as it dimmed, leaving the common folk's cage glittering with sea-blue light.

"A royal army will be formed for the protection of Ilara," the King said.

Lord Kearney's bonds grew brighter. His jaw tightened, pain filled his eyes, but he neither screamed nor questioned the King.

"The Scribes Guild will create a registry of all men in Ilara over the age of fifteen," the King said. "Those who voluntarily register for the King's Army will be rewarded. Those who delay will be considered enemies of the Guilds."

Some in the common crowd turned back toward the cathedral, their postures of pain morphing into fear that surged into anger.

"The Healers Guild will provide care to all those registered to the King's Army," the King said.

"An honor to undertake such an immense task." Lady Byrd's wrinkled brow gave the extent of her protest as she bowed to King Brannon.

"The Sailors Guild will surrender the burden of defending the docks to the King's Army, and of chartering all ships to the Sorcerers Guild."

Lord Nevon whipped his head side to side, failing to free his mouth from the light locked over his lips.

"Before sunset tomorrow, the Map Makers Guild will send three journeys into the eastern mountains," the King said. "Every map maker will be utilized. None of the journeys will return to Ilara until they have found a path to Wyrain."

"As you command, Your Majesty." Map Maker Traim bowed.

One of Traim's guards took his elbow as he straightened, the guard holding on as though afraid Traim might faint or flee.

"The Sorcerers Guild shall oversee all other Guilds' tasks. The Sorcerers Guild shall select the elite warriors given the honor of leading my army. The Sorcerers Guild shall continue to be the legion that protects all Ilbreans." King Brannon paused for an extra breath. "The Sorcerers Guild will affirm their pledge of loyalty to the crown and the Willoc family, their declaration to be witnessed by the Guild leaders and our Wyrainian allies."

Adrial glanced toward the Lady Sorcerer. Her face betrayed neither shock nor satisfaction.

Dudia protect your peaceful children from the demons' violent work.

"And I shall draw Ilara out of the darkness!" King Brannon shouted. "With a gentle hand or a blood-soaked fist, peace will be restored. May Dudia's wisdom fill your hearts and loyalty to Ilbrea hone your blade."

6

———

ALLORA

She'd placed the musicians perfectly, allowing the song of the quartet near the entrance of the palace to fade away just before her ears caught the first notes of the players in the ballroom.

Allora enjoyed having a true smile to brighten her face as she accepted the greetings of her guests. The relief of not having to feign cheer, coupled with the satisfaction of mastering the palace's acoustics, painted her thoughts with a crisper brightness than she'd managed in a long while.

Two women in healer red bowed to Allora. "Happy Winter's End, Your Majesty."

"Happy Winter's End." Allora tilted her head slightly to the side as she nodded to the women, ensuring the diamonds in her crown caught the light at an angle worthy of their beauty.

The healers paused for a breath, taking in Allora's gown, their attention catching on her bodice for a heartbeat longer than they'd admired her crown, before bowing again and bustling toward the ballroom.

Allora let her gratitude at not be subjected to polite conversation bring more life to her smile.

She wished a Happy Winter's End to a merchant couple, two scribes, another healer, and another merchant.

None of them begged to know the maker of her gown, hear of her rapturous joy at being Ilbrea's Queen, or needled her for some statement of fondness for Brannon.

The best party I've been to all year.

A steep wave of grief slammed into Allora's chest.

It had only been a year.

Her breath caught in her throat.

Without them, time had dragged past like brutal centuries. But she'd only survived a year since her final gathering with those she loved best. Mara, Tham, Adrial, Kai—all of them together and happy.

And Niko, giving promises of love she should have clung to.

"Mother."

The sharp whisper yanked Allora from the familiar spiral that dragged her soul into unrelenting despair for all she'd lost.

A merchant woman in an impractically ornate gown stumbled over her hem as she hurried toward Allora.

Red climbed the cheeks of the young man walking beside her as the two continued toward their Queen.

The least Ilbreans deserve is your grace.

Allora took a few steps toward the palace entrance, placing herself to hear the faint music of the quartet.

"Your Majesty." The woman dipped into a curtsy a full step before she'd reached Allora, leaving her to shuffle forward with bent knees.

Red reached the young man's forehead as he bowed.

"Happy Winter's End." Allora nodded to the pair.

"I beg a moment, Your Majesty." The woman curtsied again.

Sweat bloomed on the young man's brow.

"Of course." Allora fixed her gaze on the woman, giving the poor fellow a moment to reclaim a calm façade.

"My family has always been proudly, and outspokenly,

devoted to the Guilds and the Willoc family." The woman finally straightened her knees.

"The King and I are grateful for every devoted Ilbrean," Allora said.

"Devoted and loyal. We are loyal." The woman grabbed the young man's arm, yanking him to stand right beside her.

"Thank you." Allora nodded again, using the tilt of her head to glance at the passing people.

Not a single savior emerged from the crowd.

"The very moment I found out, I told my Uaine to run right to the scribes." The woman smacked the back of Uaine's neck.

Uaine whimpered.

Shock kicked warmth into Allora's cheeks as she fought the childish urge to giggle.

"Uaine," the woman whispered.

"Mother, please." Uaine winced as his mother smacked his neck again. "I understand my duty and will fulfill it."

The woman raised her hand, preparing to land another blow.

A tinge of pity tugged on Allora's heart as the young man's face paled.

"For the good of my family, I beg you to believe it was a moment of weakness. The last thing I'd ever want is my delay in choosing the honorable path to harm those I love."

His forehead wrinkled, and his lips thinned.

The poor lad had the face of a boy with skinned knees, closer to childhood than seemed fair for one left racing to the scribes for marriage papers to save the girl whose skirts he'd invaded.

At least he's trying to protect her.

"We weren't in the square today, you see," the woman said.

Uaine's pale face gained a grayish shade.

"Not because we didn't want to be." The woman's face paled, too. "A quiet day as a family seemed best."

"Discretion is a useful tool." Allora turned, blatantly searching the corridor.

Not a soul looked hopefully toward the Queen, silently begging for an audience, saving Allora from listening to the poor woman dig herself further into danger and disrepute by telling the Queen of the unfortunate fertility of her son's seed.

"I swear to you he ran from our home to the scribes," the woman said. "Quite literally ran."

"Then wisdom begs you to adopt silence on the matter. A wrong has been righted, let it be. Happy Winter's End." Allora took a step down the corridor.

Her guards stepped closer, gripping their weapons, all looking to something behind her.

She spun back around.

The woman reached for Allora, ignoring the guards.

"Please, Your Majesty." Tears streamed down the woman's cheeks. "If they think my Uaine tried to put off going to the scribes with the other men—"

"Other men?" Heat rose in Allora's cheeks.

"If he'd found out at the same time as the others, my Uaine would have been first in line," the woman said.

"Please, Mother." Uaine gripped his mother's elbow.

"I appeal to the kindness you've shown so many." The woman clasped her hands as though in devout prayer. "Don't let my Uaine be punished for not hearing the declaration, not when it was me who kept him from the cathedral square."

An off-putting blankness shrouded Allora's mind as she tried to pluck sense from the woman's frantic words. "What declaration in the cathedral square?"

The woman froze.

Allora's guards stepped closer.

A bead of sweat dripped from the young man's nose.

"The—ah—the—" The woman caught her heel on her skirt as she shuffled back. Uaine yanked on her arm, keeping her on her feet. "His Majesty's wish for good, loyal, Ilaran men, men like my loyal Uaine, to register."

Allora held up a hand, stopping her guards from following as she stepped toward the woman. "Register for what?"

"It would be wrong of me to try and describe his—the King's, I mean, orders, Your Majesty. As…as I've mentioned, word of it didn't reach me for hours. I only beg you to remember my Uaine if any whispers of disloyalty fly in my family's direction." The woman grabbed Uaine's arm, whipped him around, and dragged him away.

"What declaration was made in the square?" Allora watched the pair flee, the woman only tripping on her gown twice before they disappeared. "What declaration was made in the square? Do not pretend you can't hear me."

"Are you speaking to me, or your guards?" Gillien's voice came from too close behind Allora's shoulder.

"I don't care who answers," Allora said.

"Then I will oblige." Gillien stepped around to stand in front of Allora. "The King gave his Winter's End proclamation in the square."

"And what was poor Uaine late to register for?"

"Nothing worth that woman's stumbling." A hint of humor colored Gillien's voice. "The King wishes to create a register of loyal Ilaran men to be trained to aid in the protection of the city. Lasting peace will require the people's vigilance against any hint of renewed insurgence. The register will aid in that path."

"And because her son wasn't first in line, the woman allowed herself to blather to her Queen?" Allora turned away from Gillien, silencing herself before her questions grew thorns. She cut between her guards, venturing toward the ballroom.

Conversation muddied the music of the players, their melody adding just a hint of whimsy to accent the first of the dark violets dripping from the walls.

Sorcerer-wrought candles filled the sconces, burning with an unnaturally rich glow like gold-kissed moonlight.

The magic-born gleam gave depth to the woven strands of

tulips that reached overhead, their bands thickening as she neared the ballroom. The deep purple petals draping the ceiling and walls seemed to breathe life into the shadows, luring her onward to the twelve-foot-high arch of pale orchids that welcomed guests into a midnight garden whose beauty surpassed even Princess Illia's dreams.

No trace of white or gold had been left uncovered. Vines, flowers, candles, deep green moss—every inch of the walls and ceiling had been coated by the sorcerers. A deep blue glaze, like a pane of stained glass, covered the floor, leaving guests constantly glancing down to admire the sorcerers' answer to Illia's demand they mask every surface. Or, the guests may have been peeking to be sure the magic they stood upon wasn't about to crack, fail, or rise up to trap them.

Allora couldn't decide which as she made her way across the ballroom, nodding graciously to the bowing masses, heading toward the center columns and the only hint of silver allowed.

Gleaming as though woven of moonlight, even the golden sheen of the sorcerers' candles didn't taint the perfect silver of Princess Illia's gown.

Two young men bowed as they backed out of Allora's path, both ducking their heads unusually low.

Like children proving they've cleaned behind their ears.

Allora nodded as she passed.

Or are terrified of anyone thinking they're staring at their Queen's breasts.

They needn't bother with fear.

Where Illia's gown seemed woven to repel the candlelight, Allora's fed on the flames.

The golden fabric shimmered in the magic-made light, the glint shifting with every step in a way, as much as she tried, Allora couldn't help but find breathtaking.

That the plunging bodice of Allora's gown blatantly displayed the glistening powder dusted between her plumped-up breasts was an embarrassment she tried to ignore with a fervent, repetitious prayer to Dudia that the dim light might hide her blush.

The diamond that hung from the single strand of her necklace brushed against the bare skin just below the curve of her breasts, reflecting the light like a beacon bidding everyone present to memorize her chest with a series of less than subtle glances.

Every soul in Ilara would have to be struck blind not to see you blush, Allora Karron.

Willoc.

Queen Allora Willoc.

The musicians ended their song. A tense, teetering pause hushed the voices of the crowd.

A lone note rang through the ballroom, heightening the masses' anticipation before the players dove into the first proper dancing song of the party.

The tension shattered, the chatter returned, and dancers claimed the center of the floor.

Allora arced around them, nodding and greeting her way to the center pillar on the right side of the room where Princess Illia had been holding her own special court with the Ilaran youths who longed to be her dearest friend or secret lover.

Illia had already been swept into the dance by a young man in soldier black. She beamed as the soldier led her with the grace of one who'd been trained in the ways of the ballroom.

The Princess dipped her chin as she giggled.

Allora turned away, fighting the fresh surge of heat that raced to her cheeks as the feeling she'd been spying through a curtain slit swooped shame through her gut.

Let the child enjoy her fun. Secrets and shadows can wait for tomorrow.

The same pale orchids that graced the entrance of the ballroom had been used to accent the two pillars that flanked the center of the room. Starting with a single, waist-high bloom, pale flowers replaced the dark tulips, gaining more space with every tier, until the orchids reached the ceiling where a diadem-like circle surrounded a seven-pointed star.

Count the blooms.

Count the blooms until there's something useful to be done.

"Beautiful." Map Maker Traim stepped into the edge of Allora's peripheral vision. "I've never seen so many orchids at once."

"It couldn't have been done without the sorcerers' magic." Allora reached out, trailing her fingers through the petals.

No heat. No tingle racing across her skin. No instinct to flee from something more powerful than a sane person would dare touch.

No hint of magic.

"Thousands upon thousands of perfect blooms. Not even the gardens of the Map Master's Palace could supply so many," Allora said. "Though I suppose you couldn't know that, as your attempt to steal my father's home failed."

"Please understand—" Traim stepped toward her.

"Bow before you address your Queen." Gillien spoke from right behind Allora's shoulder.

"Apologies, Your Majesty." Traim bowed, lingering low for a moment as though wanting to be sure Gillien had seen the gesture. "I sometimes forget you've traded Karron for Willoc."

"Hard to forget the woman wearing the crown is your Queen," Allora said.

"Harder to believe the one I've watched devote her life to the Map Makers Guild no longer stands as the Lady Map Maker."

Rage singed the tip of Allora's tongue.

Gillien stepped forward, placing herself just ahead of Allora's shoulder like a guard dog called to heel. "Do not forget your place, Map Maker."

"Nor you yours," Allora said.

Gillien didn't move.

Allora cut around Gillien, pinning Traim between herself and the flower-coated pillar. "Never dare to question my devotion to the Map Makers Guild. I am not the rat who tried to steal the Lord Map Maker's home. I am not the beast who tried to have the head scribe whipped for the horrid crime of loving another, a burden I am sure is unfamiliar to you. I am not a thief, a traitor, or a coward. Those honored titles lie with you, Map Maker Traim. Now bow to your Queen and leave me be."

"Yes, Your Majesty." Traim bowed. "But I beg a favor of the Lady of the Map Makers Guild."

"Walk away, Map Maker," Gillien said.

"What do you want, Traim?" Allora allowed her anger to sharpen her voice.

"When your father returns, tell him I'm sorry. I've made mistakes, but I never betrayed my Guild." Traim stepped closer, not retreating as sparks danced across his neck. "Tell Lord Karron I knew the journeys were a blood-laden path. If I were him, I would have found a way to stop this. But I'm not. And I'm sorry."

"Traim." Allora reached for his arm.

Her hand struck something cold, and solid. The invisible force didn't even shimmer as she pushed against it.

"Traim, what journey?" Allora leaned her weight into her hand.

"Happy Winter's End, Miss Allora." Traim bowed and walked away.

"What journey?" The cold wrapped around her hand, anchoring her in place as Traim disappeared into the crowd. "Gillien, what journey?"

"The journey ordered by the King's proclamation," Gillien said. "As is customary at Winter's End."

"A journey to where?" Allora rounded on the sorcerer, twisting her shoulder as her hand stayed stuck.

"As a destination or purpose of exploration?" Gillien said.

"Trying to hide information from me does nothing but drive me mad." Allora raised her free hand, halting the passing people.

Two scribes, one merchant, one healer, and two sailors stopped.

"Happy Winter's End." Allora kept her hand up, not allowing the six to flee. "Unfortunately, I was unable to attend the ceremony in the square this morning. I would love for you all to tell me about it. What news greeted Ilara?"

The well-practiced grace of Allora's smile did nothing to ease the sheen of fear on the faces of the six.

"I heard something about the scribes being tasked with a registry?" Allora looked to the two scribes.

The merchant slunk back a step, tucking his hands behind his back like a guilty child.

"Your Majesty." The shorter of the scribes bowed. "I beg your forgiveness, but we weren't in the square today and left the library before the Lord Scribe's new orders for our Guild were posted."

"I've heard the Lady Sorcerer's carriage was a truly beautiful sight, Your Majesty." The taller scribe bowed.

"The same holds for me as well, Your Majesty," the healer bowed.

"The Lord Sailor will address us in the morning," one of the sailors said. "Apologies, Your Majesty."

"And the only whisper you've heard is of a carriage?" Allora fixed her gaze on the merchant, freezing him halfway through trying to slink back another step. "Were you absent from the ceremony in the square as well?"

The golden light tinged the shining red of the man's bald head a rotting shade of orange. "Your Majesty." He began to bow, twitched halfway down and popped right back up to standing. "Your Majesty, I have—have no desire to—have no recollection of any tasks being given."

"You were in the square but do not remember your King speaking?" Allora asked.

"I have"—the muscles in the man's neck tensed—"I've no excuse but that I've been drunk since dawn."

Allora shut her eyes for a moment, smothering the flare of anger in her chest. "Please do eat something hearty before you sleep tonight, and when you tell the men in the tavern of admitting your drunkenness to the Queen, do emphasize my gracious manner and sage advice."

He nodded as the red on his head darkened.

Allora turned away from the six, releasing them from the terror of speaking to their Queen.

"Perhaps you should dance, Allora," Gillien said.

"Gossip flies more quickly than arrows," Allora said. "What hellish thing has my husband done that palace guests are afraid to tell me?"

"This is a day of celebration. Focus on your guests. Spark delight in those around you and make the King remember what a treasure you are. There are no troubles worth distracting you from the safety of those you love so dearly."

A burst of anger she could not stifle flared in Allora's chest. "Fear not, Sorcerer Gillien. Protecting Mara and Tham never leaves my mind. Whatever disgusting thing my husband has done will not dissuade me from trying to bed him. I am well practiced at hiding my revulsion."

Allora cut through the crowd, ignoring the bows of the Ilaran masses made cowards by their King.

7

ADRIAL

—and their skin cracked with a thunderous sound,
   that shook the passage below the ground.
   The blood spilt from kin made stone—

"Happy Winter's End, Head Scribe." A merchant curtsied to Adrial.

He kept his pinky ticking in time with the words as he met the woman's gaze.

—the gods demand payment for a miracle forsaken.

The woman had caked her face in powder. A vain attempt to cover the red of the burn on her brow.

"Happy Winter's End." Adrial let his gaze linger on the woman's forehead before meeting her eyes. He poured as much care into the look as he could, wishing he could do more than prove he saw the pained pinch around her lips and the puckered skin on the backs of her hands.

—eyes stolen from stars—

"—who already have employment," the woman said. "Surely they couldn't be spared from trade long enough to be useful to the King."

Plucked from the cradle—

"My apologies, but any questions regarding the registry will either have to go to the Sorcerers Guild or wait until they've given the Scribes Guild insight into the registry's requirements," Adrial said. "They are in command of the King's Army. The scribes have been ordered to keep a record. The King and Lady Sorcerer control who's on it."

Born of the blood they had bred—

"You're a good man, Head Scribe," the woman said.

"Then believe me when I tell you I have no information beyond what was spoken in the square. I'm sorry." Adrial nodded to the woman and headed toward the arch of pale purple blooms that promised a chance of escape from the flower-shrouded party.

Cursed with long lives and blessed with—

He passed two columns before ducking around the third, placing himself out of the burned woman's line of sight as he watched the dancers.

You're the head scribe, Mara whispered in his mind. *Lead the frightened people. Don't hide from them.*

—specters watching those saved by stone.

He focused on the movement of his pinky, jumping forward in the lines to fix the timing.

Sworn to the black until bones become dust.

Princess Illia twirled past.

Her gown glinted silver in the light, its pallid hue as out of place as her beaming smile.

—beloved be bound.

The pinch in Adrial's chest eased as he finished the final phrase. He bowed to the young healer who'd been standing beside him, accepting her fumbled curtsy before trekking toward freedom as quickly as hiding his limp would allow.

The musicians had been placed in the corner, tucked behind a wall of blooms. Four guards blocked the shadowed path between the players and the party, as though the fiddler were the true threat to all the fools who'd been summoned to the royal palace.

Past the musicians, an elderly soldier gave Adrial a stiff bow. The man favored his right knee, the corners of his mouth tightening with every limping step as he headed toward a servant bearing chamb.

Sympathy distracted Adrial from his own pain for a dozen steps.

The players switched tunes. Sounds of delight bubbled from the dancers.

May Dudia always bless Ilara with laughter and joy on Winter's End.

The silent prayer bought him another few steps of distraction.

Purple accented the collars of six of the royal guards flanking the ballroom doors.

Adrial didn't recognize any of the men. Not that he'd ever claim to know all the guards of any Guild, even his own.

But there was something—something that scratched at his mind as he studied them.

Not the anger that rose in his chest at the very thought of sorcerer purple tainting the other Guilds.

Not the need to point to the guards and scream, *Don't you see how far we've fallen? Can't you feel the chains tightening around our necks?*

A glint of gold caught Adrial's eye.

Each of the marked guards wore an extra blade beyond the normal weapons of a royal guard. A golden, seven-pointed star adorned the hilts of the blades, the symbol of Ilbrea inlaid in a pattern of swirling purple.

The marked had been given prominent positions in the formation near the door.

Better armed. Placed to attack.

Panic-born pain ripped down Adrial's back as fear promised

the guards would grab him, pin him down while spikes tore through him.

The sound of whip meeting flesh screamed through his mind.

You've already walked through that darkness.

Adrial kept his steps steady.

You will not let that nightmare break you.

His heart battered his ribs as he passed through the gauntlet of guards and reached the next stage of his escape.

As the music from the ballroom faded, the dark blooms on the walls dwindled. Even the air cooled as he abandoned the chaos.

An apprenticed scribe hurried down the corridor, heading toward the ballroom.

Adrial slowed as he watched her approach, waiting for the moment she realized her doom.

Five feet away from him, the apprentice froze mid-step. Her eyes went wide before she dove between a pair of chatting healers, slamming her back against the wall as though hoping the spattering of flowers might hide her white robes.

As the flustered healers stormed away, Adrial tucked his hands behind his back. He held the apprentice's gaze, giving her a stern look he'd learned from Allora.

"This will be handled tomorrow." Adrial continued his flight, hoping the girl had the sense to make good enough use of the evening for it to be worth the punishment earned by attending the party even though the Lord Scribe had forbidden all apprentices from leaving the library grounds.

Lord Gareth's attempt to protect his people, while admirable, had no doubt been tossed aside by more than one apprentice.

Balancing Tammin's rage at the sorcerers with her wrath at the wayward apprentices would take a delicate hand. With that understanding, Adrial's duty to the Scribes Guild demanded he return to the library at once.

Any hint of shame in his departure fell away as light strains of music floated from the entryway, like relief had been given musical form to carry Adrial to his bed.

"Head Scribe." Allora stepped into the corridor, the gold of her gown glinting off the walls. "Happy Winter's End."

She nodded to each of the four people who stopped to bow to her as she crossed the twenty feet to reach Adrial.

"Happy Winter's End, Your Majesty." Adrial bowed.

Allora's guards loomed over her shoulders.

"I'm so pleased I didn't miss you, Head Scribe." Allora's smile stayed too perfectly in place, more mask than true expression. "I hate to beg your time on Winter's End, but if you have a moment?" She gestured to the doorway where she'd appeared.

"Of course, Your Majesty." Adrial bowed again and stepped back, letting Allora's sorcerer take the place in front of him, unwilling to give the sorcerer his back even for the short walk across the hall.

Allora stopped in the center of the parlor, not bothering to suggest Adrial take a seat. "I would ask you to leave us, Gillien, but I'm in no mood to fight."

The sorcerer didn't reply.

"Are you well, A—" Her name caught on the tip of his tongue. "Your—"

"Formalities be burned." Allora stepped around Adrial, shutting the door to the hall herself. "What registry has the King created, and why are mothers desperate to have their sons' names down?"

"Head Scribe—" Sorcerer Gillien began.

"No one else will answer me." Blazing anger shone in Allora's eyes.

"Ilaran men of age have been ordered to register for the King's Army," Adrial said.

"Head Scribe." The sorcerer's words clipped with a warning that didn't match the smile still twisting her lips. "There can be no wisdom found in spreading whispers that could upset your Queen."

"Will you burn me with your magic as the sorcerers did the Ilarans in the square?" Adrial said.

"What?" Allora gripped his arm.

"Will you bind me with magic? Steal my breath? Will you beat me with another spiked whip?" Adrial kept his gaze locked with the sorcerer's as Allora tightened her hold on his arm. "You already ripped my family from me. There is no threat left that can force my silence on the sorcerers' shame."

8

—————

NIKO

Crisp air crept in through the gap, its mud-scented freedom taunting Niko, filling his chest with a bubble that threatened to explode and destroy his heart and lungs if he didn't break out of the chivving basement to bask in the glory of Ilara on Winter's End.

Brushing his nose against the dirt-packed stone, Niko tipped his head, trying for a better view through the eye-level slit in the basement wall. Freezing muck smeared his cheek as he watched the feet of the passersby from the height of a common rat.

Some of the people hurried as though still fleeing the nightmare of the sorcerers' display in the cathedral square. Others strolled, as though either too foolish to fear the sorcerers or too worn down from the sorcerers terrorizing the city all winter to have any fear left to burn.

A horse passed. The rider sang, the words of his song too slurred for Niko to understand.

I should be drunk and singing.

Even as the imagined taste of frie teased Niko's tongue, he couldn't pretend being trapped in the basement with only a narrow slit to view the outside world was anywhere near the worst fate the Brien might have given him.

The scent of bread filling the basement came with actual bread sent down from the two Brien living in the home above. Masquerading as a young, prosperous merchant, the man often played his fiddle in the evenings to the delight of his false, ever-baking wife.

The music drifting through the ceiling offered a bit of cheer to complement Niko's perpetually satisfied belly. He'd also been given one of the four bunks in the basement, complete with better blankets than he'd dared hope for in a secret lair.

And, even when the Brien were speaking of secrets Niko couldn't be allowed near, they didn't lock him away.

Given a book and sent to sit facing the corner, silence would surround Niko, making his heartbeat unsettlingly loud in his ears, but causing no pain. Once the Black Bloods' meetings ended, sound returned, and he was free to wander back to the narrow slit to peer out at the street.

"One day." Ena leaned across the table, holding Deryn's glare. "Our agreement stands."

"The chivving sorcerers attacked their own people." Red crept up Deryn's sallow face. "They just tossed a massive *up your ass with the spikey end* at their own people."

"Lovely." Marlo leaned back in his chair, frowning as he ripped into his apple tart.

"The sorcerers have been tapping their blades on Ilbrea's throat for years," Ena said.

Niko waited for a surge of shock, loathing, or disgust to twist his gut.

He only managed a fatigued sense of vindication.

The sorcerers were monsters strangling Ilbrea. He'd known that for far too long.

Had never been given proper cause to question it.

Pity it cost so much pain for the masses to notice.

"The demons have stopped hiding their scales," Deryn said. "Their tactics have changed. We have to take a moment to think th—"

"Take your moment tomorrow," Ena said. "Today is mine."

Niko gave the muddy street a final glance before claiming the last, lowest seat at the table, leaving him a full head shorter than all the Black Bloods.

Marlo swallowed a laugh and pushed the plate of tarts Niko's way.

"Bloodlust doesn't outweigh the work we're doing," Deryn said. "We can't risk losing Black Bloods for—"

"For what?" Ena pushed away from the table. A hint of a smile lifted the corners of her lips.

The red drained back out of Deryn's face.

"For petty vengeance?" Ena said. "I am plenty capable of ending lives on my own."

Cold fear tensed Niko's muscles.

"The blood shed today will do more than bring me joy." Ena cut around the table, stopping right behind Deryn. "This is how the fire catches. If you can't see it, you've never had a hope of fighting the Guilds."

"Solcha, what we've accomplished—"

"I'll not throw stones at a giant and call it a fight. Get in my way, you become my enemy, Deryn." She climbed the steep wooden stairs that led out of the basement. "Happy Winter's End."

Marlo winked at Deryn and followed Ena up, joining whatever other guards had been escorting Solcha on her errands around the city.

Deadly errands.

Niko held his breath, waiting for a voice in the back of his mind to chastise him for being dramatic.

Why did Adrial have to marry a woman who talks of Death with amity?

Deryn waited for the door to close behind Marlo.

"Chivving, hell-bound—"

"Careful how you finish that. You're speaking of the Ilbrean chosen by the mountain." Attie spoke from the far corner of the basement, near the niche where Niko didn't dare look.

Niko bit into his tart.

"That chivving, mountain-loved, hell-bound, blood-slinging Ilbrean will have a noose around her neck before the Guilded slitches have slept off their Winter's End frie."

"Then you should be honored to hang beside her," Danu said.

Common instinct bid Niko glance toward Danu. He caught his movement at the last moment, wincing as his muscles pinched.

He turned his wince into a yawn.

"The stronghold has kept you naive." Deryn lifted the crate he'd brought with him, dropping it onto the table with a thump. "Enjoy your Guild-made blades. May they keep you fools alive until morning."

Deryn stormed his way up the stairs and out of the basement.

Niko held his pastry up to the light, fixing his gaze on the way the layers of dough had browned so perfectly.

Lorna dragged the crate closer to herself, pulling off the top as she stood. "Anyone want to claim first crack?"

"I'd take two daggers over a sword," Attie said.

"Give me whatever's left," Cillian said. "I'm shit with blades."

"Should I find you a stick?" Lorna said.

"Manners." Cillian flicked his finger Lorna's way.

She jumped as though he'd given her ass a solid thunk.

"Manners to you, too." Lorna pulled two daggers from the crate. Both bore the seven-pointed star of the Guilds on the pommel.

Mael scraped his chair through the dirt of the basement floor as he pushed away from the table and stood.

Niko tilted his head and shifted his focus to the hand-drawn map of Ilara on the table, keeping the hulking Brien solidly out of his line of sight, clinging to the fantasy that the trueborn didn't exist.

Besides the proportions of the map being badly skewed and the lines looking as though they'd been drawn by a farsighted babe, alleys and passageways had been randomly left out as though deemed unworthy of inclusion by the map's creator.

Definitely not a Map Maker.

He twisted the paper, pulling it closer to himself.

"I've no place to wear a sword," Danu said.

Not a Map Maker at all.

"Then make do with a cheese knife," Mael said.

No one laughed.

Slashes had been drawn through buildings either ruined by fire or attacks. Blacked-out patches marked buildings that had disappeared entirely.

A pain pinched between Niko's eyes as he tried to keep his mind from diving into counting the number of homes destroyed during Ilara's winter of terror.

The city he loved burned and broken while he'd been trapped by the Brien.

Mistaken as dead.

And the world sped on without him, stealing more than he'd known he could lose.

"My turn then?" Cillian said. "What weapons shall I decorate myself with?"

"Let me have a look." Niko slid the map aside and grabbed the crate.

Mael gripped the crate's other side, holding it in place.

"While acknowledging I've spent a good portion of the last two days facing a corner with my heart thumping in my ears, and admitting that, whatever chaos Ena is spawning, there are undoubtedly many levels I don't understand"—Niko kept hold of the crate—"I would strongly urge each of you to consider how desperately you want me to come along."

"Niko," Danu said.

The pinch between Niko's eyes eased as he held Mael's glare. "Not only am I a sworn servant of the Brien Clan who returned to Ilbrea to stand with the Black Bloods fighting here, I'm also a better chivving Map Maker than any Brien's ever been if you find this wiggly lined monstrosity acceptable."

"What do we need a map maker for?" Lorna's words bounced with poorly hidden laughter.

"Your escape routes are shit." Digging his nails into the crate with one hand, Niko tapped the southeastern quadrant of the map with the other. "There are alleys all through here. Tight as a finch's ass, but you can make it. And this dress shop"—he slid his finger north—"never locks their back windows. The shopkeeper is a lovely woman. Happy to give you a place to tuck yourself away in exchange for a few coins, and you can pop right out her front door and onto the street, once the man, or woman of course, out for your blood has passed.

"And here"—he planted his finger on what should have been their basement sanctuary if the streets had been drawn proper-ly—"a mere two streets north, there's a clear path through this line of stables. If you're truly desperate, there's a roof you can reach here." He moved further north. "It's an easy hop to get to the far end of the street with plenty of chimneys to hide behind if you need to wait it out."

"Wait what out?" Lorna gave in to her laugh. "Who under the stars have you been hiding from?"

"The only person I've met who knows the warrens and hidden paths in Ilara better than me is Kai Saso." The pinch between Niko's eyes redoubled as a weight dropped into his throat. "If you need a quick escape, you've chiv all chances without me."

"Maybe you can join for the next picnic." Cillian laid his hands on the crate, not going so far as to yank it away from Mael and Niko. "I'm not denying you might be helpful. But the plan's been set."

"I'm not—" Niko began.

"Let him come," Mael said.

Niko stumbled back a step as Mael let go of the crate.

A twitched finger from Cillian jerked the crate back to the center of the table, yanking Niko forward with it, bashing his hips against the wood.

"Solcha should not be stopped from serving his clan." Mael crossed his arms, a tiny, Ena-like smile curving his lips.

Niko's knuckles whitened as he tightened his grip on the crate, swallowing the scream his lungs promised would suffocate him.

"Niko shouldn't be on the streets," Danu said.

Niko's eyes flicked to her.

Fool.

She'd pinned her hair back. The sleeves of her purple robes were too long, almost hiding her clenched fists.

Niko forced his gaze away.

"If we want to use Niko aboveground," Danu said, "Deryn at least has—"

"Solcha is sworn to serve the Brien Clan," Mael said. "He's of no use hiding in this den."

"He'll be of less use if we all end up dead because we're dragging his sodding ass around when he's never been a part of the plan," Cillian said.

"Solcha comes with us," Mael said.

"Wonderful." Niko pushed cheer worthy of Winter's End into his voice.

"You get to tell Ena, Trueborn." Cillian released his hold on the crate.

"I had prepared three more excellent reasons why your success depends on me," Niko said, "but I'll gladly set the list of ways I could save you aside and accept the easy *yes*."

The pinching between Niko's eyes drove all the way to the back of his skull as he dug into the crate, choosing a weapon he prayed would never spill Ilbrean blood.

9

KAI

"You're twitching." The toe of Isla's boot dug into the back of Kai's calf, pinning his leg down.

"I'm not built for stillness." As Kai said the words, a burning need to stop chivving lying on the gritty floor, leap to his feet, slip out the window, and keep running until his limbs couldn't move, surged through his soul.

He drove his hips, toes, and elbows into the dust-scented wood, trying to siphon out the energy pent up from lying tucked beneath the attic's eaves for so chivving long.

The burning moved to Kai's chest, clamping around his lungs, amplifying his need to scream.

"Stop it," Isla said.

"I'm not twitching." Kai dug his nails into the floor.

"You're panicking, which would be annoying even if I hadn't been stuck here for so long."

"Sorry." Kai let out a long breath. "Sorry."

Isla lifted her boot off his calf.

Kai pulled himself forward, nearly pressing his nose to the window set right above the attic floor.

The cobblestones below glinted as their rain-made sheen

caught on the faint light carrying from either end of the street. The glimmering highlighted the thick shadows that grew together, kissing right in front of Kai's perch as though the night itself wanted to warn passersby of the lurking danger.

That danger shifted positions beside Kai.

He shifted, too.

The burning in his limbs returned.

"I'm worried about Drew," Kai said. "I should have found a way to get him out of the cathedral square. I don't know if he was hurt or burned."

"I'm sure he was."

"What?" Kai twisted, cracking his head against the window frame.

"If anyone was in danger, Drew would try to help them." Isla kicked Kai. "Watch the street."

Kai blinked away his head bashing-born tears and looked back out to the street.

"If the whispers about the square are true, I'm sure he's crisped as forgotten bread," Isla said. "But there's been no word of anyone dying."

Panic pierced the center of Kai's chest. "I need to see him for myself."

"If you've lost interest in helping me, crawl away. I've no more use for you."

"I'm not leaving Adrial with you." Kai pressed his forehead to the floor. The pressure dulled the growing pain in the back of his head. "He'll be here soon."

"Unless you don't know Adrial as well as you think and you've been wasting my time."

"Wrong on both ends." The faint remembered sound of carefully measured words ticked through his mind, easing just a touch of the tension that gripped his neck. "Adrial memorized the poem of the City of Death to time the ten minutes he had to stay at parties. He spent a week choosing the right poem and another practicing the timing."

"He didn't memorize a ten-minute poem."

"He did." Kai flicked Isla's arm.

He froze, the familial vengeance feeling suddenly deadly as Isla slowly turned her head to look at his fingers.

"A demonstration of my thunking Niko on the arm every time he suggested Adrial just count to six-hundred instead." Kai gave a smile that would have earned forgiveness from both Allora and Mara. "Apologies."

Isla looked back toward the street.

"He cut verses from the middle of the poem to perfect the timing. I spent a whole day staring at a clock while he tried removing different lines." A low laugh bounced in Kai's chest, easing the tension around his lungs. "I've caught him doing it at parties, too. He stands out of the way, watching the dancing, reciting the poem in his mind, keeping time with what's almost a subtle twitch of his finger."

He angled his hand in front of Isla, demonstrating the movement.

Two women walking arm in arm hurried along the street.

Neither slowed or so much as glanced up at the attic window.

Please, Adrial, make this easy.

Counting to six-hundred would have been easier, Niko whispered. *But our scribe's never been one for easy.*

"I think he needed the work of it. Memorizing the poem." Kai dug his fingers into the floor, letting his nails crack, wishing he could tear the wood apart just for the satisfying relief of feeling it break. "Pushing through the words helps keep Adrial's mind off the pain while he waits out parties, sure. But I think he needed the memorizing of it, too. Words are what he had. While the rest of us had trouble to race toward, Adrial had books. I think he chose the City of Death for a reason, too."

"To remind himself there are worse torments than pain and parties?"

"Because he never had parents." Kai pressed his palms to the floor, lifting his fingers as high off the wood as he could, making the muscles in the backs of his hands tremble from the effort. "Not even their names or a vague memory of their faces. He doesn't know where they were from or if he has any living blood relations."

"To some people, that would be a mercy."

"Not to Adrial. The man studies great histories but has no family line to trace." Kai let a silent moment pass. "In the City of Death, the fallen rise to protect all children born of their blood. An army of stone facing battle for the salvation of their progeny. I never told him I knew why he found the poem so appealing."

The rhythm of a single horse's hooves clopped nearby.

"He's lost his wife and child, Isla." Kai tucked his chin, keeping his head away from the window frame as he looked to Isla.

"Eyes on the street."

"Adrial has suffered more pain than any man should endure." Kai fixed his gaze on the glistening cobblestones. "And he's survived it all as a truly good person. That takes more strength than most of us have."

"I know."

"Whatever you're taking him for, he doesn't deserve it. He shouldn't be anywhere near this misery."

"He's on the Guilds Council. Adrial is deeper into this hell than either of us, and we're not powerful enough to drag him from the muck." Isla cocked her head as a laugh carried down the street.

Another laugh joined the first.

The sound faded away.

"He's late," Isla said.

"Then something's held him up."

"Or you lied in a chivving foolish attempt to stop me from

reaching Adrial. The head scribe will be taken tonight. If we don't stop him here, there's no chance of us capturing him without spilling blood. If any paun guards die, it's not the Brien who'll bear the weight of those souls."

"I'm not lying or wrong. Adrial will aim to leave the party as soon as the poem is done. He won't hurry out of the ballroom, it's easier for him to mask the limp when he goes slowly, and he won't want to look like he's trying to run. He'll smile and nod to all the right people as he flees, then vanish into the night without anyone wondering where the head scribe has gone. Adrial Ayres is an incomparable master in the art of disappearing from parties. Historically, I've found it quite annoying."

"Then why hasn't he come?" Isla nodded down at the street.

"He might have gotten trapped in conversation." Kai dug his elbows into the floor again. "He's too polite to toss someone off if they won't stop blathering. Or, his carriage driver could have wandered off to take a piss and ended up rolling a palace maid in the trees, completely forgetting Adrial's habit of abandoning parties."

"None of this is funny."

"I'm not joking. He's actually had that happen before, and I'd rather think of Adrial waiting for his driver to finish plowing a maid's fertile valley than Adrial being attacked by the Sorcerers Guild or whatever other beasts lurk in that godsforsaken palace."

He paused.

Isla didn't snip at him.

"Or, maybe this is the gods telling us to call this chivving nonsense off," Kai said. "You've given me your vow you're not going to hurt Adrial, so whatever you want with him, there's got to be a better way to do it than this."

She stayed silent.

"I still have contacts in the Guilds," Kai said.

The faint rattle of wheels caught Kai's ear.

"High ranking contacts." The tightening around Kai's lungs

returned. "Whatever it is you want Adrial for, my contacts can help us find another way."

"You can't."

"Please, I swear to you—"

"She wants him." Isla eased the window open.

The thumping of boots joined the rumbling of the wheels as the carriage neared.

Fear hollowed Kai's chest.

No tightness. No air. No heart to beat.

No.

Words, he had to speak words.

"We can't do this," Kai said. "I can't let you drag Adrial into the Brien's horror."

A sapphire spark flared to life in Isla's palm.

"He's a good man," Kai said.

The carriage came into view.

Twelve guards led the carriage with another twelve following behind. Swords, daggers, spears—the guards had been armed well.

"There are too many weapons." Kai reached for Isla's wrist. A burst of heat warned his hand away before he touched her skin.

The first of the guards passed the window.

"Isla, please."

The spark vanished.

Crack! Crack!

Debris shot through the darkness as the wooden shafts linking the carriage to the horses shattered.

The horses' fearful snorts joined the snap of the axles breaking and the crash of the carriage body striking the ground.

Still tethered together, the terrified animals charged away, knocking over two of the scribes' guards who'd spun toward the ruined carriage.

"Defend the head scribe!" The command carried over the

shouts of the guards as they scanned the darkness, searching for the source of the attack. "Get him out. Now!"

A guard yanked Adrial from the carriage, gripping him under the arm with one hand, holding his sword in the other.

Two more guards closed in around Adrial.

Leaning on her elbows, Isla lifted her hands, blowing across her palms as though scattering dust.

"Go. Go!"

The rest of the guards clustered around Adrial, some facing away from their charge, shuffling backward as their swarm pushed onward toward the library.

The glistening of the cobblestones vanished as haze thickened the air.

Fist-sized stones shot from the alley in front of the guards, forcing them to retreat toward the carriage as the haze darkened to a deep purple smoke that shrouded the scene below entirely.

"The head scribe. Protect the head scribe."

"Back. Move back."

"I've got you. Sir!"

"Head Scribe!"

The clanging of steel joined the shouts below.

Isla pushed herself to her knees, turning away from the window.

"Where are you going? What have you done?" Kai dove behind her, blocking her path, paying for his audacity with an invisible force banging against his stomach and knocking him away.

"I've kept my promise to shed as little blood as I can." Isla crawled out from under the eaves, keeping hunched over as she got to her feet and hurried toward the trapdoor.

"Where are you taking him?" Kai scrambled after her.

"Your end of the bargain is done, Kai. Stay out of it." Isla hoisted the door open.

"I thought I could stay out of it, but now that you've actually kidnapped a member of my family, I find I'm not capable."

"Not my problem." She started down the ladder.

"If my part of the bargain is done, what about yours?" Kai bounced foot to foot, watching Isla descend, waiting for her to step off the bottom rung of the ladder before gripping the edge of the trapdoor and swinging himself down to land on the floor below in one smooth movement. "Information on the Sorcerers Tower, that's what I was promised."

"I remember." She cut down the hall of the darkened house, heading toward the stairs that led to the bottom floor.

He dashed ahead of her, bracing himself against the walls as he blocked the steps.

"Move," Isla said.

"Keep your end of the bargain."

"The best I can give for now is a warning." She stepped close to Kai, an unnatural light dancing in her eyes as she held his gaze. "Get belowground, saelk, and stay there till morning. The gods didn't build you to survive a night like this."

"But they did Adrial?"

"I'm trying to protect you. Let me."

"Take me wherever Adrial is going."

"No." Isla smacked the air, pivoting Kai away to slam chest-first into the wall. "Even if I could, there are some things outsiders aren't meant to see. Get back to your burrow, Kai. If Ilara still stands in the morning, check the Tiller's Tree. I'll leave word of where we can meet."

"Isla."

She cut past him, disappearing down the stairs.

"Isla!" He tried to push away from the wall. "You're a sodden slitch, Isla!"

He pushed again, gritting his teeth from the effort. "Chivving, sorcerer, cheat."

He stumbled back, slamming into the opposite wall as the force pinning him disappeared.

10

———

KAI

"Fire-haired"—Kai sprinted back to the ladder, racing up to the attic—"fink-fisted, ghost-wooing, horror-tainted"—he shoved himself under the eaves—"magic-wielding chivving monster."

Twisting onto his back, he grabbed the edge of the window, pulling himself halfway through before switching his grip to the outer eaves.

Praying the gods would grant him a quiet landing, he slid himself the rest of the way through the window and swung himself sideways to land on the roof.

The gods obliged.

He rolled to his knees and scrambled to the roof's ridge.

To the north, the scribes' guards had just begun to stumble their way out of Isla's purple smoke.

Lights flickered to the west, but none traveled fast enough to be fleeing with a kidnapped scribe.

To the east, a cluster of shadows moved together, their shapes intertwined as though the silhouetted figures had become one heinous monster.

Pushing himself to his feet, Kai took three long strides down the slant of the roof before leaping to the next building.

The shouts of the scribes' guards didn't change to warnings of a man in the sky.

Kai leapt again, crossing north, mimicking the path of the shadow monster, then cutting farther east.

His boots skidded on his next landing, costing him a precious moment when the shadow nearly veered out of sight.

"Chivving Brien." Catching hold of the chimney, he swung himself to the other side of the roof, using the turn to build momentum as he leapt cattycorner, chancing a jump over the widest part of the road, paying for the shortcut by bashing both knees as he landed.

He pulled himself up to the ridge of the roof, gritting his teeth against the throbbing in his legs. "Let's not tell Drew about that."

Trusting the chimney's shadow to hide him, Kai searched the streets below.

The shadow monster had vanished.

"Don't do this to me." Kai shut his eyes, giving them a moment of total black before searching the street again. "Come on now."

A sudden dimming of light caught Kai's eye as, to the north, a stable door slid shut.

The gap to the stable roof was barely five feet. An easy jump to make.

Hard to keep quiet.

"I am coming back for you," Kai whispered to his boots as he pulled them off and rammed them beside the chimney.

He glanced down at the street again.

A hint of movement on the western side.

Maybe a guard. Definitely not the scribes' guards coming to reclaim their stolen charge.

Keeping on his toes, Kai ran and leapt, exhaling as he neared the stable roof, keeping his limbs loose as he landed in an impressively catlike manner, swallowing the groan born of the pain shooting from his knees to his hips.

He didn't wait to see if he'd been spotted before crawling sideways, away from the guard, heading toward the hayloft door.

The sound of muted shouting came from inside the stable.

Kai drew his knife, using the tip to ease the door open.

"You were told he wasn't to be harmed," a woman said from inside the stable, her words sharp under the muffled yelling.

"We've done our best," a man responded.

Keeping his knife in hand, Kai twisted himself off the roof.

"He keeps tossing himself around trying to escape," a second woman said.

As Kai swung into the stable, the back of his thigh grazed the door. His heart jammed up into his throat at the hinges' tiny squeak, but the muffled shouting below had grown louder.

"If we tie him tighter—" the man began.

"Let him go," the woman said.

"It's not safe," a low-voiced man said.

The stables' hayloft was barely chest-high, and from the stale scent, the storage space, scattered with half-broken crates, hadn't been used in some time.

Kai crouched low, creeping between piles of splintered wood to reach the edge of the loft.

"Let him go!" the woman shouted.

"Yes, Solcha," the first man said. His silver hair caught the lantern light as he nodded to the two beasts of men who held Adrial between them.

The beasts let go.

Adrial stumbled forward, falling to his knees, barely avoiding smashing his face into the filth-covered ground with his hands tied uselessly behind him.

A woman with pure black hair, like a raven's wings, stepped toward Adrial.

The massive man beside her grabbed her arm.

Everyone in the stable but Adrial seemed to freeze.

The two beasts who'd let Adrial fall tensed as though preparing for battle.

In the far corner, tucked so deep into the shadows the darkness nearly masked her hair, Isla froze, too, her hands midway through tying her hair behind her, like a rabbit frozen mid-chew.

The only other person Kai could see, a well-armed woman, was the first to move, wrapping her fingers around the hilt of her sword.

The raven-haired woman held the man's gaze.

Burn scars crept out of the man's collar, reaching up to his jaw. The tight skin of the scars shifted as the man's neck tensed.

Adrial bent double, dragging his forehead across the ground, trying to free himself of the sack over his head.

The raven stepped closer to the burned man. "Don't."

He let go of her, keeping his eyes locked with hers for one moment before nodding to the two beasts.

He backed into the shadows as the beasts lifted Adrial to his knees and ripped the sack off his head.

Blood seeped from a wound on Adrial's temple. Sweat slicked his face, and anger reddened his cheeks.

The beasts yanked the spit and blood-soaked gag from Adrial's mouth.

He coughed, dragging in gasping breaths.

The color drained from his face.

The beasts gripped Adrial's shoulders as he swayed, his breath suddenly silent as though Death, not the raven, approached.

She stopped just out of arm's reach.

"Hello, scribe."

11

ADRIAL

The throbbing in his temple pulsed in time with his screams.

Help. Help. Someone help!

He rammed his tongue against the cloth gag shoved into his mouth, trying to spit it out. The thing wouldn't move. The ropes binding his wrists wouldn't give, either.

Help! I am here! Help!

The shouts of his guards had disappeared as the demons dragged him away from his carriage, but there had to be someone, *someone*, who could hear.

He kept shouting.

"Quiet." The man gripping Adrial's right arm squeezed harder.

Adrial screamed as loud as he could.

"Stop—"

Adrial kicked the man on his right before he'd finished speaking, catching the man in the leg, managing one step before the man on his left swung Adrial back in the kicked man's hold.

Adrial twisted farther to the right, lunging toward the kicked man, plowing his weight into the man's side.

"Just walk chivving nicely." The man on his left jerked Adrial to face front again.

The ground beneath Adrial's feet changed, losing the round-ness of the cobblestone, becoming the flat surface of a wooden floor.

Adrial screamed as loudly as his lungs could manage, ignoring the taste of his own blood moistening his gag.

Someone will hear. Someone will come.

This is not how you die, Adrial Ayres.

Help will come.

He kept screaming, ignoring the angry voices around him.

If they put him in a cellar where he couldn't be heard.

If they took him out of the city.

He bucked forward, trying to break free again. The men's grip didn't loosen.

If he could see.

If he could run.

The men let go of his arms.

Adrial tripped forward, crashing to his knees, rocking back to keep his head from smashing against the ground.

The voices around him fell silent, leaving only his own desperate cries for help.

Stay alive. Someone will come.

A cold blade to the back of the neck, surely that was to be his fate.

Keep trying. Don't let panic speed your doom.

Still screaming against his gag, he bent forward, doubling the throbbing in his temple as he dragged his forehead across the ground, trying to rid himself of the bag over his head.

The floor smelled of dust and filth. The worn wood gave no texture for the fabric to snag on.

This will not be my end. I will not abandon the ones I love.

Hands grabbed Adrial, dragged him up to his knees.

Dudia, protect those I leave behind.

Hair ripped from his head as the bag yanked free.

A dim, empty space.

Armed men flanking him.

The man on the left yanked the gag from his mouth.

Adrial coughed, gasping in air, trying to fill his lungs enough to give one, final cry for help before Death claimed him.

But Death had already arrived, bringing a ghost, a wraith of the woman he'd sworn to protect.

No. Not her. Please, not her.

Ena stood before him, her skin paler than it had been in life, her ghost clothed in mourning-black.

Death had stolen the rainbow of her hair, framing her face in deepest darkness.

Pain stole Adrial's breath.

He had no words to rage at his god, no pleas for mercy to pry her from Death's grip.

Fear flickered through the wraith's eyes as she met Adrial's gaze.

Her eyes held the same soul-soaring blue Ena's had in life.

Adrial swayed as sorrow carved through his heart. He leaned into the pain, greeting his end with gratitude.

His captors wrenched him back to his knees as the wraith drifted closer.

He'd failed Ena, hadn't protected her, hadn't saved her. She'd been snatched from this world, and he hadn't even been beside her.

But if Ena's ghost had come to him in the moment before death, if some part of her soul waited for him, and forgave him—

The wraith stopped just out of reach.

"Hello, scribe."

A sob shattered Adrial's chest, doubling him over as though the wraith herself had struck the fatal blow.

"Untie him," the wraith said.

"We're not—"

"He is my husband," the wraith said.

"Ena." A voice, terrifying and familiar, came from the shadows.

"Untie my husband. Now," the wraith said.

A sharp yank on his wrist jerked Adrial upright, the pull vanishing with his bonds.

He tipped forward, catching himself on his hands, giving in to the pain that promised to tear him from the world.

"I'm sorry," he whispered through his tears. "I'm so sorry. Forgive me."

A gentle touch lifted his chin, trailing across his cheek as the wraith took his face in her hands.

"You're all right." The wraith spoke with Ena's voice, as her fingers—warm against his skin—moved to the throbbing ache in his head. "Who did this?"

"I'm sorry," Adrial whispered.

"We pulled him out of the carriage that way," the demon beside Adrial said.

"I can—"

"Don't touch him," the wraith said. "None of you will touch him."

The demons flanking Adrial backed away.

"You're safe here. I won't let anyone hurt you." The wraith lifted her hands from his face, stealing their life-like warmth.

Adrial made himself move, grabbing her hands, clinging to the wraith.

Her hands stayed solid in his.

And her face—the dim light cast shadows on her face, as though she were more than a heartbreaking phantasm.

His blood stained her fingers.

A barely healed cut marked the back of her hand.

"Ena?" The world froze as he whispered the word.

The light caught the tears brimming in her eyes as she nodded.

"Ena." Joy and hope and terror slammed through Adrial in equal measure. "Ena?"

Tears caught in his throat as he clutched her hands to his chest, clinging to Ena.

Ena alive.

Ena here.

Ena's hands in his.

"No." Adrial let go of her, scrambling back, searching the shadows. "I've done everything you've asked."

"Scribe—"

"No, please." He tried to push himself to his feet. His legs wouldn't hold his weight. He looked toward the deepest of the shadows.

There, his face barely visible in the darkness, the revenant who had haunted Adrial for months waited to strike.

Adrial crawled toward the shadows, using himself as a poor barrier between the beast and Ena. "I'll do anything. Pay anything. Please don't hurt her."

"They're not going to hurt me," Ena said.

"I won't let them." The heat of tears stung Adrial's cheeks. "Whatever it takes, I'll keep you safe."

"I asked them to bring you here." Ena took his hand, turning him to face her, giving his back to the revenant. "I asked the Black Bloods to bring you here."

Black Bloods.

A new sheen of fear muddied Adrial's mind. "I don't care who they are or what they want."

"The Black Bloods helped me escape the ship to Ian Ayres." Ena didn't fight as Adrial twisted away from her.

"You will not harm her," Adrial shouted into the shadow where the revenant had been.

"I'm not their prisoner. I never have been." Ena's touch grazed Adrial's wrist. "The Black Bloods sheltered me for months. I needed help, and they gave it."

A cold, heavy understanding forced its weight into Adrial's mind. "But him—" Adrial pointed to the revenant. The shadows behind the demon shifted. "He made me help him. He said they had you." Panic shoved the weight away. "And Lily."

He spun toward Ena, pressing his palm to the place the child had grown. Her stomach had gone flat. Empty. No longer a sanctuary for Lily.

Lily.

"The baby," Adrial said. "Where's the baby?"

"Lily is protected." Tears streamed down Ena's cheeks. "And healthy and perfect."

"Is she here?"

"She's far away from the Guilds." Ena pressed her hands over his. "In the safest place I can give her."

"Wherever you think is safe, you're wrong," Adrial said. "That man—"

"Would never harm my child."

"You don't understand. The things he asked me to do—"

"Had to be done." The fear returned to Ena's eyes. "And our work isn't through. *My* work isn't through."

"Ena." The revenant stepped out of the shadows.

"I need you to understand." Ena lifted Adrial's hands, holding them to her chest.

"You're out of time," the revenant said.

"Not yet," Ena said.

"You have to go," the revenant said.

"No." Adrial slipped his hands from Ena's, wrapping his arms around her, holding her close, begging Dudia for the strength to keep the demons from stealing her. "I won't let you take her."

"It's time." A girl with red hair stepped out of the darkness.

"Please," Ena said.

"I'm sorry. We've got to go." The girl stayed planted in sight like a guard ready to pluck Ena away.

Ena nodded.

"You can't go." Adrial brushed the hair from Ena's cheek. "Tell me what I have to do to keep you here with me."

She leaned her cheek against his hand, closing her eyes as though his begging brought comfort.

"The signal's come from the palace." A woman spoke from the shadows.

Ena took Adrial's hand, kissing his palm, then pressed her cheek to his, whispering in his ear, "Stay inside the library. Keep all the scribes inside as long as you can. Pull the guards inside the library walls."

"If you don't go now, you're done," the revenant said.

Ena pulled away and twisted Adrial's palm toward the sky. "If you need help, crush the stone, and I'll find you." She placed a dark stone in his hand. "The blacksmiths at the southern end of the docks, they can get me a message, but only one. They know to watch for you."

The redhead moved to the door near Adrial, pushing it open as though she had no fear of the night.

"Don't go." Panic gripped Adrial's throat. "Please. Please, you can't leave."

Ena closed his fingers around the stone.

"No. Ena, no."

She brushed her lips against his, a kiss gentle enough to tear through the thin veil time had laid over her loss.

She kissed his cheek, gripping his hand that held the stone as she whispered, "Harane, Marten, Lir Valley. Look there. Try to understand."

"Second signal's gone," the woman in the shadows said.

"Break the stone when you find it," Ena whispered. "Please."

She stood, striding toward the door, disappearing into the night, never looking back as the darkness swallowed her.

12

NIKO

Twenty. Thirty-five.

Niko stopped counting the crowd gathered in front of the healers' hall once he'd passed seventy-two. His tally had barely reached beyond the centermost of the three barricades that barred the common folk from reaching the massive iron gates protecting the healers' refuge.

Three torches burned on either side of the gate. Their flames flickered in the growing wind, casting the horde in a foreboding light better fitted for the mob the guards seemed to fear than the sick and injured Ilarans seeking aid the crowd truly held.

The healers' guards kept their ranks, heroically facing the desperate, unarmed Ilarans, rejecting every plea for entry to the hall.

Three full floors separated Niko's perch in the servants' quarters of the massive, lived-in yet somehow currently empty, merchant's home from the street below and any hope of escaping whatever hell the Brien had chosen to drag Ilara into.

Niko's assigned window gave him a view of the alley behind the merchant's home and the roofs of the lower built homes just beyond, which shadowed the wide road in front of the healers' hall's gates.

Even from a distance, a few maladies were easy to spot—the man with the bleeding head, the woman doubled over with birthing pains—but most of the gathered only looked defeated.

Shoulders hunched against the cold, hats, scarves, and hair limp from the unrelenting wet.

Some managed anger as they begged the guards at the barricade to let them through. But forlorn or enraged, the guards treated them all the same.

A raised hand and a firm no. Then a drawn sword. Then a slice of the blade.

Niko dug his knuckles in on either side of his nose, trying to drive back the seething anger in his gut that somehow worsened the pain in his head.

A carriage approached the gate, the driver forcing the horse into the crowd to reach the barricade.

The driver bent down, speaking to a guard.

The guard shooed the driver back, then shouted an order to his fellows. They picked up one side of the centermost barrier, pivoting the wood out toward the crowd, knocking a man over as they moved.

Two women saved the man, yanking him to his feet before the guards could trample him, dragging him out of the way as the carriage cut through the opening in the barrier.

The guards pivoted the metal-braced wood back into place as the proper gate opened.

Something dark flew from the carriage window and into the hand of the guard who'd ordered the barrier open.

Sour flooded Niko's mouth as the guards went back to turning the common folk away.

The man with the bleeding head abandoned the crowd, giving up any hope of aid from the healers. He swayed with each step.

Niko watched the man until he made it out of sight.

Worse not to say it.

Niko leaned back against the windowsill, nestling farther into the safety of the dusty curtains. "I'd aim for subtle grace, but this is a chivving terrible plan, and I can't think of a kinder way to say it."

"A terrible plan, eh?" Cillian kept tossing a black stone from hand to hand like a man waiting on tea rather than Death's arrival. "Did someone tell the pet Ilbrean the terrible plan?"

"Of course not," Niko said. "But—"

Cillian stopped throwing the rock and held up a hand, silencing Niko. "If a plan doesn't put your neck on the line, and you don't even know what the chivving plan is to begin with, silence is your safest path."

The grit of the dust grated against Niko's skin as he rammed his fingers into his hair. "That would make perfect sense if I only cared about my own sodding hide!"

"Breathe, Niko," Danu said.

She'd tucked herself into the corner again, as though hoping the shadows would remind Niko of the new customary distance between them.

He fixed his gaze back out the window. The common crowd had grown.

He moved his attention to the curtain instead.

Something had picked at the threads. A cat? An ambitious mouse?

A slitch who needed something to do with his hands.

"I can't agree to keep my mouth shut." Niko worried his thumb on a thin patch in the curtain's fabric. "If this goes badly, I don't want to live with the guilt of having kept quiet."

"You're absolved," Cillian said. "Done now?"

"No."

"You've nothing to fuss over, Niko," Danu said.

"I shouldn't fuss when you've looked like you're waiting for the sky to fall for days?" Niko pushed away from the window, daring to take two steps toward Danu.

She didn't react.

A cringe would have been better.

"You're smart, Danu," Niko said. "If you don't like the plan, it means it's shit."

"I trust Solcha," Danu said. "Fear doesn't change that. If she fights here, so do I."

"Don't start buying into a chivving myth."

"Because deciding something is worth fighting for is so awful?" Danu said. "I have a chance to help stand against the Guilds, to stop the pauns' evil before they claw farther into the eastern mountains. I believe Solcha can help the Black Bloods. That's enough for me."

"Right." Niko found the same spot on the curtain he'd been fiddling with before. Below the worn patch, someone had picked at all the pulled threads, weakening the fabric.

I'm not the only one who's brooded by this window.

It's not brooding if bloodshed will come before breakfast, Kai whispered.

Heat stung Niko's eyes, as though the pain in his head had melted into godsforsaken tears.

Don't crack, Mara whispered. *Not now.*

The fabric had a worn line down the middle, as though it had spent a long time folded before being reborn as a curtain.

A part of someone's skirt, perhaps. Not a bodice or apron.

The barricade shifted as another carriage arrived.

A ping of fear shoved all other thoughts aside as a sound came from the floor below.

Niko let go of the curtain, sliding his hand toward the knife at his hip.

The chair Mael had claimed gave a groan of relief as he stood, pulling a handful of pebbles from his pocket as he faced the door.

Footsteps hurried up the stairs to the attic, not slowing as they neared the closed door.

Cillian raised his hand, pressing his palm forward as though preparing to stop an invasion of beasts single-handedly.

With a green spark, the door's latch slid aside.

"I was worried you'd abandoned us." Cillian lowered his palm, going back to tossing his stone from hand to hand.

"I thought we weren't allowed to worry," Niko said as the door opened.

A girl with brilliantly red hair stood in the doorway, the mass of her curls framing her face as though the gods wanted to be sure no one could doubt that this was a beast to fear.

She took her time looking around the room, taking everyone in before speaking. "Mind your own." She flicked her fingers.

Cillian flinched and rubbed the tip of his nose. "I regret teaching you that."

Tying her hair back with a string, the girl entered the room, ignoring Niko as she headed right toward his window.

It took his eyes a moment to realize the darkness in the hall wasn't a shadow, but Ena, the black fabric of her hood hiding most of her face as she took her own turn checking the corners of the room.

"Do you have a clear enough view?" Ena closed the door behind her, sliding the metal latch into place.

"It's less about view, more about time," the redhead said.

"You'll have it," Mael said.

"If I don't, it's your head on a pike." The redhead peeked around the curtain opposite Niko. "The tilk?"

"Marlo and Alane will be there," Ena said.

The redhead nodded and tugged on the sleeve of her coat. The cuff had been worn away in places, as though, same as the chivving curtain, the fabric had been fiddled with too often.

Niko shoved his hands into his pockets.

The chair groaned in despair as Mael reclaimed his seat.

"Sodden, mountain-burned tit." Cillian gasped, dropping his stone which now shone a vicious red. "Do we have to brand a fellow?"

"We need to go." Danu left her corner, grabbing Cillian's arm, pulling him toward the door.

"I'd do better without a singed palm," Cillian said.

"Tend to it later," Danu said.

"Danu, be safe." Niko ran the few steps to the door, daring to place himself in Mael's path as he reached for her hand.

Cillian leaned out of the way, twisting his torso sideways as Danu turned, still gripping the arm of her fellow Brien sorcerer.

"Please." Niko kept his hand out. "Be safe."

Danu brushed her fingers across his, letting the touch linger as she looked into his eyes. "Save some of the decent frie for me."

"Of course," Niko said.

The corners of her lips twitched.

Niko stumbled forward, catching himself on the wall as Mael knocked him aside to follow Danu and Cillian out into the night.

"Lock the door," Ena said as the Brien's footsteps faded. "Niko."

"Right." Niko slid the bolt into place.

"How did you convince them to bring you?" Ena said.

"Used my charm." Niko couldn't smooth his tone into anything near appealing.

Ena lowered her hood, moving closer to the window.

"No quip about my not belonging here?" Niko asked.

"I'll not waste my breath on a fool who could very well be dead before midnight," Ena said.

"Turn out the lantern," the redhead said.

Ena moved to obey.

"I've got it." Niko lunged for the light.

The great false Solcha extinguished a tiny flame.

A thrilling triumph for the Brien.

Ena pulled four stones from her pocket.

At first glance, the stones all seemed to be pure black, but as Niko's eyes adjusted to the darkness, tiny hints of light appeared, hitching a reactive fear in his chest he couldn't have explained.

Each of the stones held a spark at its very center—blue, green, white, and black—trapped deep within.

Ena claimed Niko's former post at the window. "Are you sure?"

"If they give me enough time," the redhead said.

"That's not what I mean."

The redhead checked the string tying her hair back.

"Isla," Ena said. "Are you sure you want to do this?"

Isla, the redhead, looked to Ena.

The faint glow through the window silhouetted their faces.

For a breath, with the shadows hiding the grim set of Isla's mouth and the ferocity burning in her eyes, she looked almost like a girl caught on the edge of adventure rather than a Brien ready to face whatever horror Solcha had planned.

But so does Ena.

"Do you have a spare sorcerer waiting in the shadows in case I run away?" Isla said.

"No. But I'll not force a blade into your hand."

"It's a burden I'll gladly bear."

Ena nodded.

The fear in Niko's chest tightened.

"I see her," Isla said, just before the sounds from the street changed.

The cries of the people gained a higher pitch of pleading as a red carriage came into view. The common folk surged toward the carriage.

"It's her?" Isla asked.

"Yes." Ena lifted the black-spark stone from her palm, holding it between her fingers as she watched the healers' guards that had escorted the carriage force the people back, plowing their way toward the barricade.

Just as before, the guards pivoted the centermost section of the barricade, making an opening for the carriage to pass through.

Isla let out a long breath, pushing her shoulders back and tipping her head side to side, like Kai readying for one of his chivving feats of daring that plummeted Niko's gut into his ass.

The sharp swipe of grief barely cut through Niko's fear as Isla stepped to the center of the window, framing herself against the night.

Niko crept forward, needing to see whatever nightmare Ena had summoned.

As the carriage moved toward the open barricade, the common folk followed, stopping only when threatened by guards' blades.

A voice below shouted an order, and the barrier began swinging back into place.

Three of the common folk left the crowd as the bloody-headed man had, giving up any vain hope their pleas for aid might be answered.

The guards moving the barricade reached right back for their weapons as soon as they'd set the barrier down.

Ena let go of the stone.

Niko would have sworn to Lord Karron himself that Dudia slowed time as he watched the black spark fall.

The stone hit the wooden floor with a hollow thunk, and time cruelly sped, not giving Niko a chance to steal a breath before Ena crushed the stone beneath her boot.

Pop.

Niko stumbled back, waiting for deep black flames to devour Ena.

A crack shook the attic.

The screech of twisting metal sliced into Niko's ears as flames shot into the sky.

13

NIKO

Screams joined the horrible screeching as another crack shook the floor.

A gasp drove air into Niko's lungs as he finally looked away from the three stones still on Ena's palm to find the source of the soul-tearing sound.

Four pillars of sparking flames soared toward the sky, lighting the cloud of dust that surrounded the bent gate of the healers' hall.

Chunks of stone tore free from the walls on either side of the gate, twisting the metal further. The flying stones curved, downing two guards as though they'd been felled by a rock-hurling giant.

The guards in front of the gate fled toward the barricade, failing to find shelter as more stones tore from the walls, buckling the front of the gate, ruining any hope the fools might have had of escaping into the safety of the hall.

One of the four remaining torches fell from its sconce, leaving only three pillars of light displaying the chaos.

Ena dropped the green stone, crushing it beneath her foot as the guards tried to pivot the barricade open.

A blast of wood shot toward the guards as the carriage's shaft shattered, freeing the Lady Healer's horses.

"Begin," Ena said.

Isla let out another long breath and raised her hands in front of her chest, palms facing the ground, her fingers curved like claws ready to tear through flesh.

A sharper crack came from below.

Niko leaned closer to Isla, searching for the source of the sound.

Crack!

A jagged slice split the top of the carriage, ripping the shining red wood apart as though it were merely a victim of the rock-hurling giant's tantrum.

"Ready." Isla tipped her head, still dragging her fingers apart as the split in carriage roof grew.

Ena crushed the blue stone.

Fear wrapped around Niko's lungs, stifling his breath. He dug his nails into his palms. He couldn't feel the pain.

The top of the carriage tore free, falling in two pieces that struck the few brave guards fighting to reach whoever was inside.

"Ena." Niko shoved the word past the pinching in his throat.

Two figures appeared on the roofs of the shorter houses between their attic perch and the healers' hall.

Danu and Cillian.

Facing the terrified and angry guards, the two Brien stood like gods of judgment, light radiating from their skin, from the purple robes that billowed around them with an unnatural wind.

The guards spotted the Black Bloods and the perfect imitations of Sorcerers Guild robes they wore.

Alane's work in making the costumes hadn't been wasted.

A few of the guards called to Danu and Cillian, asking for aid, sure Ilbrea's sorcerers had come to save them.

The rest knew.

Not that Danu and Cillian were frauds. That no one in a sorcerer's robe would ever offer protection.

They've wrapped her in demon's skin.

Danu slammed her hand forward. A hail of stone flew from around her, striking the guards below.

One fell. She didn't flinch.

Not from revulsion at the blood seeping from the man's neck or the weight of the magic she'd used.

Light flared within the ruined carriage, glistening and shifting as though it were a living thing.

Half the guards ran toward the carriage, but the rest stayed beside the barricade—some still trying to flee through the growing crowd of common folk, most helplessly raising their swords against the glowing sorcerers.

The light in the carriage flashed gold.

Cillian knelt, pressing his hands above his head as though lifting a massive weight.

Four tendrils of gold rose from the carriage.

Cillian screamed as though pouring out the last ounce of his being to work his magic.

Isla's breath hitched.

Her skin had gone pale, brightening the blue of her eyes, as though Dudia himself had marked her a monster.

She pinched her fingers, lifting her hands.

The golden tendrils followed her movement, rising into the sky.

The horses screamed and charged the corner of the barricade, breaking through the narrow opening the guards had managed to create, forcing a path through the common folk.

Two of the guards tried to follow the animals' route to freedom. Stones ended both their lives.

The crowd filled in the gap, pressing forward for a better view of the bloody entertainment.

The torches dimmed as the tendrils lifted a struggling figure from the carriage.

Robes glowing red like Death's own beacon, the Lady Healer rose above the horde. The golden lights wrapped around her wrists and ankles, keeping her legs pinned together and her arms stretched wide.

Someone in the crowd cheered.

"Now," Isla whispered.

Ena dropped the white-spark stone.

Pop.

"One," Ena said.

Danu slashed her hand down.

The Lady Healer screamed as a blazing white light sliced down her chest.

"Two," Ena said.

Isla matched Danu's movement as she slashed her hand from left to right.

The Lady Healer fought against her bonds as another slice cut through her robes.

Arrows soared over the healers' hall walls, flying on either side of the Lady Healer, aiming for Cillian and Danu.

"No!" Niko lunged toward the window, crashing to his knees as something hard struck the backs of his legs.

The glow around Danu brightened, knocking the arrows aside as she sliced her hand left to right, sweeping up at an angle.

"Three," Ena said.

A new slice appeared, cutting from the Lady Healer's hip to her shoulder, mirroring Danu's movement.

Niko dug his fingers into the crack beneath the window, prying it open.

"Don't," Ena said.

Vague pain pierced the side of Niko's throat as something cold pressed against his skin.

Danu raised her hand, slashing from high-left to low-right.

"Four," Ena said.

Another gash of light sliced the Lady Healer.

All four cuts glowed brightly, displaying the seven-pointed star carved through the Lady Healer's robes.

The fabric around the wound didn't sag away. The tears in the cloth stuck to her skin as though seared to her flesh. Blood seeped through the glowing red, muting its light, giving a gruesome background to the golden star.

A fresh wave of arrows flew toward Danu.

Again, the light around her flared, knocking the arrows aside.

The pitch of the Lady Healer's screams changed as the top left arm of the star glowed brighter than the rest.

Ignoring the pain digging into his neck, Niko pressed his palm to the window, blocking out the light of the star.

Danu raised both her hands over her head, gripping her palms together.

A wave of stones flew from around her, downing two more of the barricade guards.

She ripped her hands apart.

"Five," Ena said.

The Lady Healer's head snapped to the side.

Her screaming stopped.

Bold cheers rose from the horde.

Arrows flew over the wall.

The tendrils of light binding the Lady Healer vanished as a burst of wind extinguished the torches, leaving only the star glowing against the night sky.

Guards clustered beneath her, reaching for her, trying to pull the Lady Healer down from where she hovered.

As if fueled by the guards' desperation, the Lady Healer drifted higher.

Her head lolled to the side.

Ten feet above the guards. Fifteen.

Two of the guards tried to lift a third to reach her.

One of the Lady Healer's fancy slippers fell from her foot.

A storm of stones pelted the cluster of guards.

They screamed.

"When you're through," Ena said.

The star flared brighter, burning the Lady Healer's robes, outlining the gold of the star in glittering black ash.

Then the Lady Healer fell, landing on top of the twisted gate, a jagged spike of iron piercing the center of the star.

Arrows flew over the wall.

Danu and Cillian had already vanished.

"And so the Guild war begins." Ena's footsteps moved toward the door.

The star faded, surrendering the Lady Healer—the former Lady Healer—to the dark.

"Can you make it on your own?" Ena said.

"Far enough." Isla's footsteps moved toward the door.

The lock scraped open.

"Thank you," Ena said.

"Pray I haven't just doomed us all."

She left. The sorcerer walked away as though the world hadn't been pinned in place by an unthinkable atrocity.

More guards climbed over the wall, finally reaching their comrades who'd been penned between the barricade and the gate. The common folk scattered as guards rammed the barricade open, a line of them bolting toward the homes where Danu and Cillian had stood.

"We're going, Niko," Ena said.

One of the guards dragged a box from the shattered carriage. They pulled it to the gate and climbed on top, attempting to reach the former Lady Healer.

"They will search this house," Ena said. "You're not savvy enough to survive lying to guards, and the Brien will not come to your rescue. Stand up. We're going. Now."

Gripping the windowsill, Niko pushed himself to his feet. "Why?"

"Because I've kept you alive this chivving long, and I don't want to have wasted the effort."

"Why would you do this? She's dead."

"That's usually the aim when you skewer someone through the chest." Ena grabbed his arm, whipping him around, dragging him through the bedroom door.

"She's dead." Niko tried to yank his arm free.

Ena gripped harder, pulling him to the stairs at the end of the corridor.

His limbs were too numb to fling her off. "You just murdered someone in front of a crowd of people."

"That wasn't murder."

He grabbed the railing on the stairs, using the leverage to jerk free. "The Lady Healer is dead."

"And Ilbrea is better for it." Ena turned on the steps, terrifying even as she looked up at him. "The Lady Healer stood with the paun who ordered my husband be whipped. She watched spikes tear through his flesh, gleefully waiting for him to die."

A different, sickening kind of numbness took the place of the fear that had deadened Niko's limbs.

"When I wouldn't let them have him, they condemned me and Lily, the child you claim to care for, to a fate worse than death." Ena stepped up a single stair. "The paun stole my family. For that and a thousand other horrors, they will burn." She turned, climbing down the stairs without him. "Die if you wish."

Dead guards by the barricade.

The Lady Healer screaming in pain.

The sound cut too far into Niko's mind, plunging toward memories he was too weak to bear.

"You didn't have to torture her." He ran after Ena, banging his shoulder against the wall as he took the corner too quickly. "You didn't have to kill her on the street."

"That's how the Guilds work, paun." Ena rounded on him, the black of her cloak swirling around her as though she'd become vengeance made flesh.

There, that moment, if he'd doubted before—questioned why myths had wrapped themselves around her—he'd never have the comfort of pretending the Black Bloods were hero-hungry fools again.

"Have you never seen one of your soldiers slaughter a child in the streets? Have you never watched a mother die shielding her babe from paun? I'll find mercy when the Guilds have burned."

"You're married to a paun. Would you see him burn with the Guilds?"

"You tread close to the cliff, Niko. Mind your footing."

She tossed open the front door and strode out into the night.

Niko chased after her, keeping as close to her heels as he dared.

Shouts came from a street away, but it hadn't stopped the people nearby from coming out to see what monstrous entertainment the night offered.

Five healers' guards rounded the corner, swords drawn.

Niko reached for Ena's arm a breath too late.

She ran toward the guards.

No! Niko didn't dare scream. *No! Run. Don't fight her.*

"Please!" Ena called as she neared the guards, her hands held out like a child begging for attention. "Please, I can't find him."

Niko stopped just behind Ena, keeping his hands slightly out to his sides, his mind scrambling to find any way he could survive throwing himself to the ground and begging for aid and mercy.

One of the guards stopped in front of Ena while the others charged past.

"What's happened? Did the demons snatch someone?" The guard's gaze darted between shadows.

"Right out the window," Ena wailed.

"The bastards grabbed someone through a window?" The guard took a step back, leveling his sword, ready to charge at nothing.

"I was sitting right by the fire, and then there were those terrible sounds and he leapt up and bolted out the window. I've been trying to find him, but now everyone's out on the street and I just know he can't make it on his own in the dark. He's an absolutely worthless beast, but I can't bear the idea of my poor cat alone and afraid." Ena's words hitched with tears.

"Find your own chivving cat." The guard cut around her, storming to the nearest house to scream at the people in the doorway. "The sorcerers, where are they?"

"Niko, darling?" Ena weaved toward the corner searching the shadows. "Niko? Where are you, you mewling little rodent?"

"Niko?" Niko called, chasing behind Ena, searching the same shadows she already had. "Niko, you saucy little tomcat, leave the ladies alone, you virile beast."

"Niko?" Ena rounded the corner. "Niko?"

"Niko, let the ladies line up to see you in the morning, you over-loved cad."

"Niko?" Ena slipped into a gap between houses, vanishing into the darkness.

Niko dodged in behind her, sidling blindly along.

A hand grabbed his arm, yanking him around a corner he hadn't noticed.

"A cat? You spill blood on the streets of Ilara then spin a tale about a cat?"

"Would you rather have died?" Ena kept hold of him, leading him further from the madness.

"I thought you'd have preferred to fight your way out, kill as many paun as you can."

"Let the paun slit their own throats. We've no need to dull our steel."

14

ALLORA

Imagining blood dripping from the musicians' fingers brought Allora a touch of sympathy-bred comfort for the pain in her feet as the Winter's End party carried on.

Illia had insisted settees be brought out and placed in the center of the dance floor, providing luxurious seating for her new entourage of closest and dearest friends. She beamed as she sat among them, basking in the wealth of their attention and adoration.

The tension in her company's shoulders and the nervous way their gazes flicked to the sorcerers positioned around the ballroom didn't seem to bother the Princess.

She's a lonely child.

You were once, too, Mara whispered back. *Lonely doesn't have to be a permanent affliction.*

Heat pressed against Allora's eyes.

She'd been worse than Illia, far worse, before Mara and Adrial were brought to the Map Master's Palace.

Pale, bruised, terrified—and the most wonderful gift Allora had ever seen.

Dolls to care for as she pushed them back out of the shadows.

Friends, once they'd both healed enough to laugh. Family, once she'd realized her heart would crumble without them.

We're Karrons. Karrons protect their own.

I will not fail you.

The poor musicians began another tune.

A cheer rose from the brave souls still dancing, the raucous sound proof of how much chamb and frie had been poured.

Keeping behind the pillars to give the dancers a wide berth as they maneuvered around the island of Illia's devotees, Allora drifted toward the far end of the ballroom where the less frolicsome party-goers had settled. At least, the resilient cluster that remained.

The last of the Guild Lords and Ladies had departed, as had the few merchants Brannon seemed less than agitated at being forced to endure, leaving only the desperate merchants and lower Guilded lingering around the King's dais, frantically clawing their way into his good graces, begging for his attention with every crook of their lips and bat of their eyes.

Brannon rubbed his thumb across the tips of his fingers, barely concealing his temper-tinged boredom as he watched the fawners preform their adoration.

Allora squinted into the depths of the shadows, only needing a moment to spot the golden light glinting off the pommel of a guard's sword.

She approached slowly, not stepping into the guard's line of sight until she'd checked his other hip for a purple-hilted dagger.

"I need you to fetch the King," Allora said. "Go to the dais and tell him he is required on a most urgent matter."

The guard's eyes flicked her way before he bowed. "Your Majesty, might I tell him what the urgent matter is?"

"The urgent matter is your Queen gave you a task," Allora said. "Will you refuse?"

His face paled.

"Fetch the King. Bring him to me," Allora said.

"Yes, Your Majesty." The guard bowed and strode toward the dais.

Bad form, Allora. You needn't torment the guards.

"Your Majesty." Two girls barely younger than she clung to each other as they stumbled into mostly successful curtsies.

"I beg you'll excuse my forward speech," the taller of the two said. "Your gown is absolutely fantastic, better than I'd dreamt."

"Dreamt?" Allora brightened the end of the word, hiding the laugh that bobbed in her throat.

"Yes, Your Majesty," the shorter said. "Dreamt."

"We'd been told of how daring you are, how you've made it your cause to change Ilaran fashion and bring something new and modern to women," the taller said.

"So much better than having gowns of the same cut my mother used to wear," the shorter said.

The taller whacked her on the arm. "My father owns a dress shop. He's never been busier."

The shorter whacked the taller. "Don't be crass."

Wrinkles formed on Allora's brow, pinching themselves into existence despite her valiant attempt at pleasant poise.

"And to decorate one's breasts with a hint of glamour," the taller said. "Brilliance."

Unbidden, Allora's gaze flicked down to the girls' chests. Both had caked a thick layer of shimmering powder between their breasts. Rivulets of sweat cut through the sheen like braided rivers leading toward temptation.

Dudia, do not let shimmering tits be my legacy.

"Every whisper of your wardrobe sends a thrill through Ilara," the taller said. "And seeing you tonight positively smashed aside every bit of gnawing fe—"

The shorter smacked the taller on the arm.

The taller smacked the shorter back.

The shorter smacked the taller again.

Allora bit her lips, refusing to laugh as the girls went through another round of smacks.

"Don't say gnawing in front of the Queen," the shorter whispered more loudly than a hissing cat. "And you're not supposed to talk about fear at a party."

The humor that had lightened Allora's soul crumbled, leaving the weight on her lungs sitting heavier than before.

"After the events in the square this morning, I couldn't fault you for being afraid," Allora said. "It seems a petty contribution from a queen, but if hearing of the gowns created by the palace seamstresses brings you joy, I'll be sure the *whispers of my wardrobe* continue to spread."

"She's gracious and beautiful," the shorter whispered.

"She is." The taller nodded. "She is—ah!"

The shorter girl curtsied, yanking on the taller's wrist as though trying to force her to curtsy as well. The taller's knees buckled. She tried stepping forward to save herself but pulled the shorter, who still clung to her arm, off balance, bringing the shorter tumbling right on top of her, leaving the two of them on the ground in a pile of drunken, soon to be regret-ridden, foolish girls.

"Is this the urgent matter?" Brannon spoke from right behind Allora's shoulder.

Catastrophically regret-ridden.

"If there are drunks on the floor, surely a maid can mop them up," Brannon said.

"Oh no oh no oh no no oh." The shorter dragged the taller up off the ground. "No no no no, Your Majesty. Oh no."

The pair managed something close to curtsies as they swiveled around and scampered away.

"If that's all," Brannon said.

"No hint of gratitude for rescuing you?" Allora turned to Brannon, tipping her head slightly, ensuring the light of the grand chandelier in the center of the ballroom caught the spot on her neck Brannon had formerly favored.

Brannon's gaze flicked to the single diamond hanging against the bare skin below her breasts, then to the carefully placed shimmer on her neck.

He met her gaze with the warmth of one beholding spoiled fruit. "My thanks for the rescue. You've served your purpose for the year."

He sidestepped to cut around her.

Allora batted aside the tinge of panic in her chest and blocked his path. "I'm afraid the unfortunately inebriated girls were not the urgent matter. Pity you thought it was a bluff. Is the guard I sent to fetch you now out marching through the muck?"

"Does my wife believe she knows me so well?"

A merchant pair bowed to their King and Queen then wisely hurried on.

"Do you know your wife so little?" Allora asked. "If you would like peace from me, give me ten minutes of your time. Then you may do just as you said and ignore the sorcerers' attempts to foist me upon you for the rest of the year."

The well-tended loathing on Brannon's face didn't lighten.

"Brannon, please."

"Do not feign affection."

"Do not pretend your foul mood has a thing to do with me." Allora stepped closer to him, holding his gaze, leaving barely a foot between them. "I am not a shelved doll. I know what happened in the square, and I am positive that, whatever your part in it, your hatred for me has barely crossed your mind today.

"I am asking the man I pledged my life to for ten minutes of his time with an urgent request and he would rather sneer than accept? Should I ask Illia to make the request on my behalf? Or must the demand come from the Lady Sorcerer herself?"

"How dare you?" Brannon took her hand, holding it in a tender pose, squeezing her fingers hard enough to hurt.

Scream. Kick him. Break his thumb.

"My apologies, Your Majesty." Allora bowed her head. "I spoke in anger and regret my words. But my request for your time does not change."

Careful, Mara whispered. *Please.*

"Though I'm sure you think little of my word, I assure you I was not trying to waste your time, Your Majesty." Allora met Brannon's gaze, staring straight into his teal eyes. "Though I'll mourn the wasted effort, I'll swallow my disappointment and not bother you again.

"I'd only meant to give Illia hope for an amicable marriage. She sees how things are between us. I don't want our example to follow her to Wyrain. My attempt was ill-advised. My apologies."

She curtsied and turned away, stopping when his grip on her hand yanked against her shoulder.

"You can have your ten minutes." Brannon kept hold of her hand as he moved to stand beside her. "We will leave this ballroom radiating with joy. You will spend an hour in the morning telling my sister how thrilled you are to be married to a king." He set Allora's hand on his arm. "You will drive any hint of marital doubt from my sister's head."

"As you say, husband."

Allora kept her head turned just slightly toward Brannon as she led him out of the ballroom, her pace slow enough to give the lingerers a chance to watch their King and Queen promenade together and quick enough to imply a purpose to their departure.

Brannon's guards materialized from the shadows as they neared the pale arch of flowers near the entry.

Gillien and Allora's guards stayed out of sight.

A mercy to have a smaller audience should things go badly. An extra pinch of nerves speeding Allora's heart as she wondered where the sorcerer was watching from.

The same set of guards flanked the ballroom doors, the

purple-accented daggers on the hips of the chosen few obvious as fire now that Adrial had warned her.

A monstrous king creating a new army, sorcerers digging their fangs into guards, and a queen playing at domestic bliss.

You're a fool. A foolish girl on a calamitous venture.

Brannon kept beside her, making a good show of not being led as she steered him down the corridor.

In the morning, all the flowers would have vanished. The white and gold of the palace would devour the midnight garden along with any lovers' hopes that had flourished in the shadows.

At least I'm not that much of a fool.

"I hope this isn't an attempt at seduction," Brannon said as Allora led him up the grand staircase. "Though if it is, I prefer it to your more lurid displays."

"Lurid?" Heat crept up Allora's neck.

"Don't pretend you haven't been displaying yourself like a cat suffering through heat. Every person at that wretched party stared at my Queen's breasts at least once."

She fixed her thoughts on the diamond brushing against her skin—the decoration carefully placed by the sorcerers to elicit the King's temptation.

"Funny"—Allora sighed a hint of a laugh—"you used to worship my breasts. Fervently, as I recall. Though I suppose you haven't grown bored of them. You did say *every* person at the party stared at them at least once."

Brannon's arm tensed.

She forced her fingers to relax, willing his arm to do the same as she turned down the corridor to the family's private quarters.

The thump of guards' boots kept pace behind them.

Slowing her steps as they passed a mirror with a jewel-laden frame, Allora chanced a glimpse at the guards.

Kenrick led the other men.

Dudia, let this be wise.

"Here, husband." Allora stopped in front of a door that would have led to one of her youngest children's rooms, if she'd ever been blessed with the burden of birthing more than six royal heirs.

One of the guards stepped around them to open the door. Purple marked the hilt of his dagger.

Allora tamped down the questions she longed to shout at Ilbrea's King.

The room had been arranged as she'd asked.

Two gold-ornamented couches sat in front of the crackling fireplace. A desk had replaced the bed on the far side, and where a wardrobe might have been, a cabinet had been filled with bottles of frie and chamb.

"Why are we here?" Brannon said.

"I still have more than five minutes." Allora led Brannon to the center of the room, waiting for the sound of the door closing behind them before looking over her shoulder.

Kenrick flanked the door with three others.

"If you would." Allora nodded to Kenrick.

He bowed and stepped away from his fellows, not hesitating as he reached the fireplace and twisted the golden rose embedded on the left side.

A panel of the wall slid open.

"Your safety has been assured, Your Majesty." Kenrick bowed again.

"A Winter's End surprise." Allora slid her hand down to Brannon's, leading him toward the panel.

He didn't jerk away from her touch.

"I wanted the whole thing done completely without magic." Allora accepted a lit candle from Kenrick. "And while I must admit a few moments of frenzy, the feat was accomplished."

She kept her candle at her side as she stepped through the panel and onto the darkened stairs, sharing her light with Brannon.

"What is this place?" he said.

"A hideaway of your late uncle's if the information I've gathered is true. I had to rely on rumors to find a suitable unused space. Whoever built the room, I'm grateful. I wouldn't have had a hope of success without them."

The stairs led to what would be the floor above, then higher still, angling all the way up to the very top level of the palace, on the same floor as the servants' quarters—a place Allora would never have otherwise ventured.

A plain door blocked the top of the stairs.

Allora slid the newly polished bolt aside and pushed the door open, letting the firelight accent her silhouette for a moment before stepping aside.

Not a hint of white or gold tainted the space.

The rich hue of the wooden floors and subtle green of the walls gave the room a warmth no other part of the palace could achieve. The thick rug in front of the fireplace had been woven of sumptuous shades of blue and green, and the generously sized couch upholstered in deep scarlet. All hints of gold had been banished, even from the lanterns on the walls.

"That door is the only way in or out." Allora backed farther into the room as Brannon stayed planted in the doorway. "There are no hidden panels or passages. No way for anyone to watch you or attack."

A bottle of frie had been placed on the table nearest the couch. Two glasses waited beside it.

She poured a glass and offered it to Brannon. "It's a small haven. But it's yours."

"The entire palace is mine."

"The palace belongs to the King of Ilbrea. There is no place for him in this room. This is the haven of a mere man. Set the burden of your crown aside and sit."

"The weight of ruling cannot be cast off like a cloak."

"But you can let yourself breathe. The load you carry is an exhausting weight even if you're born to bear it." She set the glass of frie on the table. "And the load isn't going to get any lighter, Brannon. Give yourself a moment to rest before your soul cracks."

"I'm sure it already has."

Allora delved for every trace of sympathy her heart could muster. "Perhaps souls are like bones. The broken places heal stronger."

He didn't even frown in response.

She reached for his hand as she crossed slowly toward him, giving him time to choose how best to thwart her.

The warmth of his fingers against hers made it easier to imagine him vulnerable as she led him to the couch, sitting him beside the table and placing the glass of frie in his hand.

He stared into the crackling fire.

"Happy Winter's End." Allora bowed and turned to leave.

"Such an easy defeat? The frie hasn't been tainted? Your gown isn't designed to fall off? After such effort, my wife simply retreats?"

"I am married to Brannon the King. This sanctuary is for Brannon the man. I have no place here." She stepped onto the staircase, closing the door behind her.

Darkness swallowed Allora. She'd forgotten her candle in Brannon's study.

Tumbling into the black offered more appeal than retrieving her light.

She shut her eyes, feeling for the next step down with her toe as she fled from Ilbrea's King.

King Brannon. Husband Brannon. Enemy Brannon. Monster Brannon. Murderer Brannon.

Poor, tired man Brannon.

She descended slowly, feeling for every step down, one hand on the wall, the other managing the skirt of her gown, keeping her beaded slippers from catching on the hem.

A pinch twisted at the bottom of her throat.

She bit her lips together, focusing on the feel of her teeth digging into her skin, rather than the way her lips started to tremble.

The dinner for the lower staff had been scheduled for tomorrow. Perhaps some of the flowers from the party could be salvaged for decorations. Unless the staff would find the use of flowers worth more than their salary offensive rather than cheerful.

Allora's breath caught against the pinch in her throat. Vicious prickles of heat burned her eyes. Her lungs shuddered as she tried to pull in more air.

"Your Majesty?" A familiar voice spoke in the darkness.

Soft footsteps hurried up the stairs.

"Are you all right, Your Majesty?" A touch grazed Allora's hip. "Apologies, Your Majesty."

"Guard Kenrick?"

"Yes, Your Majesty. Are you ill?"

"I'm fine, thank you." She leaned against the wall as the sudden need to curl up in a ball and never move again sapped the strength from her limbs.

"If the surprise for the King wasn't a success—"

"I'm sure it will be a great success. I set out to build my husband a sanctuary and managed to create the perfect place to bring his whores." The word hitched in Allora's throat, coming out with the unmistakable shudder of one in tears. "Though I suppose it hardly matters how he uses the haven. The intent of the gift was an offer of escape. The women the King beds must distract him from his worries. If this is where he brings them, at least there will be fewer witnesses among the staff."

The chill of the wall sank into Allora's back, dulling the illness churning in her stomach. "You'll be sure the King's guards understand the importance of discretion? The haven promises the King privacy, but the entrance must be guarded. The King's safety mu—must—"

She swallowed her words before they could become sobs.

"I'm sorry, Your Majesty." A faint touch brushed against Allora's elbow.

The warmth of his skin against hers fed the sobs, letting them crash against her ribs. She pressed her hand to her mouth, stifling the sound.

"Let's get you away from here." The air around Allora shifted as Kenrick stepped up onto the stair beside her. His fingers grazed her shoulder. The faint whisper of his touch traced along her arm until his fingers found hers. He lifted her hand away from her mouth and set it on his arm. "Can you walk on your own?"

"Of course." Allora felt for the next step down, gripping Kenrick's arm as her legs trembled.

Send him away. Just curl up in the darkness and let it all disappear.

So much easier to just crumble.

"The royal guards are all grateful to you, Your Majesty."

For being the most pathetic and useless Queen they could ever dream up.

"The order has been put in for us all to have fresh-fitted boots and an extra day off in the next month," Kenrick said. "Even the old stones of guards cheered for that."

"It's been arranged already?"

"Yes, Your Majesty. And the men know where the orders came from."

Allora let out a long breath, making sure she could speak without tears stealing her words. "I'm glad the guards have had a bit of extra cheer on Winter's End."

"It's more than that. You remembered us. Like the lower staff, you noticed we weren't in the line. None of us ever expected that from the Queen. But we should have, because that's who you are. And you are loved for it. Adored even."

Allora's fingers trembled as she brushed away her tears. "The best I've earned is pity."

"I never thought I'd dare correct a queen, but I promise Dudia blessed the palace the day he brought you here. Though I know it's unforgivably selfish, I am grateful to have a queen worth protecting."

Kenrick stopped.

Allora noticed a moment too late. Her weight already moving down to the next stair, she tried to step back, snagging her beaded slipper on the hem of her gown. She twisted sideways, tipping as she freed her foot.

A vise wrapped around her waist, catching her, slamming her not against the wall, but against the warm, solid safety of Kenrick's chest. He tightened his hold on her, the bare skin below her breasts pressing against the buttons of his uniform.

"Tha—"

The rasping of a blade clearing its sheath silenced Allora.

Quiet pressed against her ears.

Thump.

Kenrick shifted his hold on her, moving his hand to her hip as he stepped onto the stair below her.

Muddled voices carried from the bottom of the staircase.

Allora lifted the hem of her gown, preparing to run back to Brannon's haven.

"—doesn't matter if he's fucking the Queen or himself," a woman shouted.

"Screaming does not override—"

"I'm getting the King, you rot-brained fool," the woman shouted louder. "People are dying out there."

Allora pulled free of Kenrick's grip, trying to step down the stairs, barely catching a glimpse of the panel below popping open before her back slammed against the stone wall.

Sword drawn, Kenrick pinned her behind him, shielding her body with his as a dark shape hurtled up the steps.

"What's happening?" Kenrick called.

The woman didn't answer as she bolted past.

"I have the Queen, what's happening?" Kenrick called again.

"There's been an attack," the woman shouted down.

"Is the palace secure?" Kenrick said.

Bam, bam, bam.

"Your Majesty." The woman banged on the door at the top of the stairs again. "There's been an attack in the city."

"Is the palace secure?" Kenrick shouted.

"You're needed, sir," the woman said.

"We don't know," a voice called from the bottom of the stairs.

Brannon's door burst open, casting a warm glow around the King's silhouette. He gripped the doorway on either side, looming over the woman like a flesh-hungry bear. "Where's Lady Gwell?"

"Still in the palace."

Brannon shoved the woman out of his path and ran down the stairs. "Where was the attack?"

Kenrick leaned back, pressing himself against Allora to give the King a wider path.

Five stairs above them, Brannon slowed, his attention catching on Allora. "Get her to safety and keep her there."

"Yes, sir," Kenrick said.

"Bring me Lady Gwell." Brannon reached the bottom of the stairs and ran through the panel, the woman a step behind him.

A thunder of boots followed Brannon's voice.

Kenrick eased his weight away from Allora. "Your Majesty, are you hurt? I apologize for—"

"What kind of attack?"

He turned to face her, taking her waist with his free hand as though afraid she'd faint. "Your guards are in the corridor below. There are secure places within the palace. No one will hurt you."

Shadows caught on Kenrick's face, casting hard-edged lines that made him seem more art than man. His hips were only inches from hers. The dark shape of his mouth so close to hers the vague, time-shined memory of his lips caressing her skin pushed her fear aside.

"Are you steady enough to walk?" Kenrick tipped his chin down. The dim light hit his eyes, darkening their blue to the shade of an unlit criolas.

Allora nodded. "I'm better with true crisis than heartache."

"Unsurprising." Kenrick pivoted, letting go of Allora and latching her hand onto his arm in one quick movement.

He kept his sword drawn as they hurried down the stairs.

"Illia won't have let go of her entourage," Allora said. "There will still be guests in the palace."

"They'll be taken care of." He lifted her hand away from his arm, moving in front of her as they reached the bottom of the steps.

Half of Allora's guards waited in the bedroom, each of them seeming eager to hold their sword with one hand and hurl her to safety with the other.

"Has the palace been breached?" Kenrick said.

"No sign we've seen." A guard opened the bedroom door.

"Pray to Dudia that doesn't change." Kenrick cut straight out into the hall, glancing back every few steps to make sure Allora still kept close behind him.

A faint hint of something insidiously like relief flickered through Allora's mind as Gillien stepped out of the shadows in the corridor to walk beside her.

"What's happening?" Allora said. "And please do not think there is any hope of my drifting into ignorant tranquility."

"Ignorance is all I can offer," Gillien said. "A messenger arrived ranting about an attack on the healers' hall."

"What?"

The guards herded her out of the family's wing and past the grand staircase.

"Between the shouting and blather, all that seems clear is that the Lady Healer is dead," Gillien said.

One of the guards in front of Allora stumbled a step, rounding over as though trying to plow through a blow to the gut.

"This Lady Healer?" Allora said. "Lady Byrd?"

"Yes."

"How?"

"I don't know." The edges of Gillien's words crisped.

"I'm sorry." Allora forced her fingers to let go of her skirt. "You said as much. I just—I can't see how it's possible. No, I mean—I understand how a person dies, but Lady Green was murdered last summer. If Lady Byrd was killed in an attack, that's two Lady Healers slain within the year."

"It seems so."

The guards stopped in front of the door to one of the smaller private parlors Allora had never seen used.

"I need to know what's happening." Allora stopped, daring to retreat a step as a guard opened the parlor door. "I need to be sure the guests downstairs are safe."

"Your Majesty." Gillien moved to take Allora's arm.

Allora twisted out of reach. "Our guests are traveling home tonight. The Ilarans we invited to the palace are out on the streets. If they were caught in an attack—"

"Allora," Gillien said.

"The head scribe was out on the streets tonight." Allora turned away from the door, meeting a wall of guards. "I need to make sure he's all right. He might need my help."

"Allora."

"If people are hurt, it is my duty to offer aid." Allora stepped close enough to stand on the guards' toes.

They didn't break rank.

"The best way you can help is by staying safe," Gillien said. "Here, you can be easily protected. Which allows more guards to help others. Doing as you're told can be the noble course."

"If the head scribe's been injured, I can't let myself be locked away." Allora shoved her hands between the guards, her arms burning as she tried to peel them apart. "I will resort to violence."

"Go inside, Your Majesty." Kenrick pushed through his fellows to bow Allora toward the parlor door. "I'll find word of the head scribe and bring it right back. You won't be able to gather information faster than I can, and I'd be disobeying an order from my King if I left you before I was sure of your safety. Staying with Sorcerer Gillien while I search is your quickest option."

An angry shout carried down the hall.

Gillien grabbed Allora's arm, her fingers digging into Allora's skin as she yanked her through the parlor door.

"No." Allora lunged sideways, trying to break free.

Gillien held on.

A guard planted a hand on Allora's back, propelling her forward.

"Illia." Pain throbbed through Allora's shoulder as she twisted from Gillien's grip. "Has someone gotten Illia?"

A guard scooped her up, carrying her toward the tall stone fireplace.

Six guards flanked the fireplace, all standing close enough to the wall Allora couldn't tell which of them tripped whatever trigger swung open the back of the well-scrubbed hearth.

The guard ducked under the mantel, carrying Allora through the fireplace to lock her in the black stone room beyond.

15

ADRIAL

Harane. Marten. Lir Valley.

Adrial's foot slipped on the wet cobblestones. He tripped forward, catching himself on his bad leg, spiking pain through most of his body.

He didn't slow to catch his breath.

Harane. Marten. Lir Valley.

Ena alive, in his arms. Her lips against his. Her voice in his ear.

Harane. Marten. Lir Valley.

A warning? A promise?

Voices shouted up ahead, coming from near the library.

Ena's face had been thin. And pale. So pale against the black of her hair.

"If you're not in the party, get to the wall," a voice shouted. "To the wall."

She could be sick. He hadn't asked if she was sick.

Or what if she'd lied?

Harane. Marten. Lir Valley.

What if the Black Bloods had been hurting her? Torturing her?

Harane. Marten. Lir Valley.

What if they'd lied to her? What if Lily wasn't safe?

Harane. Mar—

"Head Scribe!"

The shout pounded through Adrial's thoughts.

"I've found the head scribe!"

He'd touched her. He'd been with her.

Marten. Lir—

"Sir."

Four guards surrounded him, propelling him toward the library.

"Sir, are you hurt?"

"What happened, Head Scribe?"

"We've got the head scribe!"

He should have clung to her.

He shouldn't have let her leave.

More guards joined his four, encompassing him as though expecting Death's own horde to spring from the shadows.

If Adrial had fought harder, refused to let the Black Bloods drag him back to be dumped near the library. If he'd found a way to stay with her…

The guards escorted Adrial through the library gate but didn't stop herding him onward.

"I'm fine." The rawness of his voice betrayed his lie. "I can walk on my own."

"We've got to get you to Lord Gareth," the guard holding Adrial's left arm said. "He'll need to see you're alive for himself."

"He thinks I've been killed?" Adrial surrendered to the guards' propulsion. "I was taken, but I'm fine."

"The Lady Healer isn't," the same guard said. "Word of her death arrived less than an hour after you were taken. We've all feared the worst."

"The Lady Healer died?" A vague, rolling prickle began in Adrial's chest.

"Murdered by sorcerers," the guard holding Adrial's right arm said. "Flayed and spiked like a fish ready for roasting. The runner from the healers' hall said the sorcerers attacked from nowhere. They tossed the Lady Healer into the air, batting her around like a cat while she begged for mercy. May the gods protect us all, Head Scribe, for I've never learned how to fight a demon."

Two guards flanked the door to the lower corridor of the library.

Adrial angled toward the steps leading up to the main level, but his guards aimed the other way, steering him to the kitchen stairs instead.

Lir Valley. Marten.

Marten.

"I want them all away from the windows now!" Lord Gareth's crackling shout carried up the stairs. "Go room to room and drag them from their beds if you must."

"Yes, Lord Scribe."

A line of guards ran up the stairs, not slowing as they nodded to Adrial before passing him.

"We have the head scribe," Adrial's left guard shouted down the steps.

"Adrial," Lord Gareth called. "Adrial!"

"I'm coming, sir." Abandoning hiding his limp, Adrial hurried down the last few steps.

On the rare occasions Adrial had ventured into the library kitchens, the sprawling space had bustled with workers.

The same number of people were in the kitchen now, but a near-snapping tension had frozen the library staff. Cooks, bakers, maids, two grooms, a few children so young Adrial couldn't reason through their purpose—all of them stood clustered against the walls, staring at the wide table in the middle of the room.

Lord Gareth took the centermost seat with a healer on one side of him and Friel, the head of the scribes' guard, on the other.

"Adrial." Lord Gareth moved to stand.

"Careful." The healer placed a hand on his shoulder, keeping him in his seat.

"I'm fine, sir." The lie colored Adrial's voice.

He'd kissed her. He'd held her.

Harane. Lir Valley.

"That changes nothing, Lord Gareth," the healer said. "The Sorcerers Guild attacked tonight. An unprovoked attack."

"We need to secure the library, sir," Friel said.

"You need to stand with the Healers Guild," the healer said. "The healers have long been closely aligned with the Sorcerers Guild, and Lady Byrd continued that tradition. The Sorcerers Guild openly murdered an ally and kidnapped your head scribe. How much deeper will you let their blade sink before you respond? Your Guild has been attacked."

"Do not provoke the Lady Sorcerer on my behalf." Adrial's guards deposited him into a chair opposite Lord Gareth.

"You were kidnapped, Adrial," Lord Gareth said.

"And the miracle of your survival does not negate the horror inflicted by the demon sorcerers," the healer said. "We must move against the sorcerers before they strike another Guild."

"The madness of contemplating sending guards to fight sorcerers," Lord Gareth said.

"Please, let's take a moment," Adrial said.

"You were attacked, Head Scribe," Friel said.

"Not by the Sorcerers Guild." The panic in Adrial's gut sharpened into blades that drove upward, slicing into his lungs. "I never saw anyone I recognized or any hint of a sorcerer."

"Your guards were trapped in an impossible haze, Head Scribe," Friel said. "There's no question. It was the sorcerers."

"Then send your guards to join ours," the healer said.

"No." Adrial stood, leaning against the table to steady himself as exhaustion threatened to buckle his knees. "You can't move against the Sorcerers Guild."

"We are defending ourselves," the healer said. "The Lady Sorcerer has gone mad."

"All the more reason not to respond with haste or violence," Adrial said. "We have only a vague picture of what happened tonight, and we haven't taken a breath to try and understand the why behind any of it. I dug a toe in against the sorcerers and it robbed me of my wife and child."

Harane. Marten.

The blades in Adrial's gut curved and twisted, tearing into the edges of the joy that had dared to glisten in his soul.

"Pull the guards inside the library walls."

"Sending scribes' guards charging into the night will only end with blood on our Guild's hands," he said.

If Ena knew. If she'd killed the Lady Healer.

"My work isn't through."

"If we huddle in our halls, Ilara could be in ashes by morning," the healer said. "There is a blade at your throat, can't you feel it?"

"I am begging you, Lord Gareth," Adrial said. "Keep our Guild away from this."

"Adri—" Lord Gareth began.

"If you have ever truly trusted me as your heir, trust me now." Adrial leaned across the table, taking Lord Gareth's hand. "Pull the guards inside the library walls. Use every resource we have to protect our home. We are a Guild of thought and reason. I cannot reason through a scenario where sending our guards into the darkness, pretending they have a hope of fighting sorcerers, is anything but madness."

Lord Gareth worked his pale lips together.

"Please, sir," Adrial said. "We can't throw our guards to their doom."

Lord Gareth's cheeks wobbled as he nodded. "We cannot afford to act rashly."

"Rashly?" the healer said.

"My men are prepared to do what is needed," Friel said.

"We have nothing but secondhand accounts," Adrial said.

"You were kidnapped." The healer leapt to his feet. "Magic was used."

"Which should make you all the more eager to not run blindly for the Sorcerers Tower," Lord Gareth said. "Guard Friel, send word to Lord Kearney. Tell him the head scribe has been found and that I eagerly await his insight."

"Thank you, sir." Dudia-blessed relief eased the blades from Adrial's lungs.

"Yes, sir." Friel nodded to the young guard beside Adrial.

The guard nodded and ran up the kitchen stairs.

May you survive the night.

The blades threatened his lungs again.

"What insight do you await? Must you examine the Lady Healer's corpse?" the healer said. "The sorcerers attacked."

"And this is how you respond? Marching your guards to the Sorcerers Tower in the dark," Adrial said. "What will your guards do? Try to crack through the stone with their swords? Wait for the sorcerers to choose when to attack the men the Healers Guild so nicely delivered to their doorstep to be slaughtered? Perhaps the sorcerers will send a bright flash of light into the night, blind your men so the demons can pick them off more quickly."

The healer slammed his palms onto the table as he leaned toward Adrial. "How dare—"

"Racing to face the sorcerers now will accomplish nothing but a thicker layer of Ilaran blood slicking the streets. We need to tell Lord Kearney—"

"We sent word to him right after the attack at the healers' hall," the healer said.

"And did you wait for him to respond? How does the Lord Soldier intend to proceed?" Adrial said. "What of the King? Did the sorcerers murder Lady Byrd or did the King order her execution?"

"Lady Byrd was a loyal servant of the Guilds," the healer said. "The King would never allow her to be harmed."

"The King ordered me to be whipped with spikes then had my wife dragged away from me." The pain Adrial had expected to ravage his chest didn't come. Fire, a blaze that soared beyond hatred or rage, becoming a burning want to tear a soul from the world—that venom dripped into Adrial's voice. "Tend to your own house before you drag ours into madness. We wait for word from the King or Lord Soldier. Until then, the Scribes Guild will remain as it should be, the beacon that searches for truth and reason when others crave only steel and blood."

"When you record the story of Lady Byrd's murder," the healer said, "be sure to include a passage on the cowardice of the scribes, who would rather hide than fight."

A scuffling came from the far corner of the kitchen.

The healer's jaw tightened, but he didn't look away from Adrial.

"Our choice to abstain from immediate violence will be noted just as the foolishness of the Healers Guild will be included in the passage detailing the deaths of all the healers' guards who fall tonight, downed by magic before they have a chance to swing their swords," Adrial said.

"Slitching bastard," the healer spat.

More scuffling came from the far corner. The sound spread around the room.

"Careful, healer," Friel said. "The library is filled with loyal folk."

The healer glanced toward Friel, his eyes widening at the sight of Friel's hand on the hilt of his sword.

"I've been called worse than slitching, and that I was born a bastard is a simple fact." Adrial pushed himself to stand upright, refusing to allow even a catch in his breath as his hip threatened to give. "Our deepest condolences on the loss of your Lady

Healer. Please send any requested wording for the announcement of her death in the morning."

"Your inaction tonight will be remembered." The healer stormed around the table, cutting toward the stairs.

"Memories are kept by the living," Lord Gareth said. "I pray you survive to remember this Winter's End."

16

NIKO

Another scream sliced through the crumbling wood of the warehouse, the voice too high, too panicked.

Not her.

Niko dug his fingers into the frozen rot, breaking pieces away as he clawed his self-loathing drenched fear into the wall.

You're allowed to have a person you're terrified for. Kai's whisper felt like Niko's mind's sodding sad attempt at a comforting punch on the shoulder. *Being relieved they're not the one in pain doesn't make you cruel. It means you chivving well care.*

Blood dripping from the sky, guards falling as stones tore through their flesh, the horses screaming like Death's own beasts as they fled the horror.

Danu had helped create that horror.

People, Ilbreans, had died.

The Lady Healer's screams echoed in Niko's mind, muffling the clattering of a carriage racing past.

Niko's throat burned. Not from the bile his stomach shot into his mouth, but from a remembered ache of overuse.

Ghosts of pain sliced all the way to his bones, pale shadows—no not even shadows…only faint wisps of old agony. His soul wouldn't let him relive the true feel of a knife cutting down to his ribs.

Weeks he'd survived it, over and over at the hands of the demon Brien Elder.

The knife, his mind blurred, but not the tearing in his throat as his screams echoed through the demon's throne room.

That memory stayed intact. A perfect preface, echoing all the way to greet the Lady Healer's screams.

Niko gagged as a fresh wave of sour filled his mouth.

"Oh no." Marlo grabbed Niko's shoulders, pivoting him away from the wall. "Aim for the corner." He shoved Niko into place just in time.

"Better sick than sobbing," Alane said from her crate-made perch below the warehouse's sole window.

"Get it out," Marlo said. "Best to heave all the venom at once."

Alane chuckled.

"Sorry." Niko spat. "Sorry."

"Ever been in a battle?" Alane asked.

"I'm a map maker." Niko returned to his nail-torn section of the wall, leaving his spatter of sick behind like a frie-drunk youth.

He tried to summon shame or humor.

He dodged back to the corner as his stomach rebelled again.

"My mother died when I was twelve," Marlo said when Niko had finished.

"I'm sorry." Niko's legs shook as he gave up on standing and sat on the crate at Alane's feet.

"It was a horrible loss," Marlo said. "And I was there when illness took her. I watched the life leave her, and I thought I'd seen Death. I knew his face and I wasn't afraid to meet him again when I was old enough to swing a sword. But Death wears a different mask on the battlefield."

"What mask does he wear to an ambush?" Niko said.

"An ambush is a battle that costs fewer lives," Alane said.

The crate creaked, as though she'd shifted closer to Niko.

Perhaps this is when it ends.

"Or would you rather Danu and Cillian have strolled up to the guards to warn them the Lady Healer's life was rapidly coming to a close?" Alane said.

"Don't goad the poor slitch," Marlo said. "He'll toss another round, and it smells bad enough in here."

The crate creaked again.

The rumbling clack of something dragging across the cobblestones passed the northern side of the warehouse.

"It's a big piece of wood," Alane said. "Not sure what it's for, but I respect the fellow's determination."

"A pyre?" Marlo said. "Barricade?"

"Could be," Alane said.

"Battering ram?"

"Wouldn't trust the strength."

"Doesn't mean that slitch is so wise," Marlo said.

Alane *hmm*ed her response.

"I'd just rather there had been no attack at all," Niko said.

"What?" Alane said.

"Fighting on the streets of Ilara should never happen," Niko said. "We aren't trapped in a siege-locked war like the Brien and the Hayes. There is no enemy army attacking the city."

"I'd place tonight's crew on level with an army," Alane said.

"Pity the chivving army," Marlo said.

"There are a few corrupt leaders poisoning Ilbrea." Niko dug his thumbnail into the top of the crate. "They're the problem. Get rid of them."

"I don't think he's been paying attention tonight," Alane said.

Niko dragged his thumbnail across the wood, forming a straight, though barely perceptible, line. "The Lady Healer could have been removed from her post and tossed from her Guild. She could have been imprisoned."

"For counting her coins while innocents died at her door?" Marlo said. "Innocents she'd given her vow to aid?"

"Then she could have been executed in the cathedral square. It didn't have to be"—Niko couldn't find the right word—"this."

"Do yourself a favor and keep your pity for the Lady Paun quiet in front of Danu," Alane said.

"It's not pity." Niko sawed his thumbnail along the track he'd made. "It's revulsion at a world where justifying such brutality is even possible."

"It's the only world we've been given. There will always be demons, just as there will always be warriors to slay them. Those spokes carry us round and round, and no man is great enough to stop that wheel from spinning," Marlo said. "This fight is inevitable, Niko. My best advice to you, make sure you're on the warriors' side. Allied with good, at least you've a hope of healing your soul."

Never. Never. Never.

Niko gouged the dent deeper, and deeper.

"How much longer can we wait?" Marlo said.

"A bit," Alane said. "There are still enough people on the streets."

Deeper and deeper.

"If they were caught—" Marlo began.

"Don't," Alane said.

"Their faces were seen," Marlo said.

The crate creaked beneath Alane's boots. "We go to Harrell's post."

Dark stained the track in the wood. Niko wiped the darkness with his finger.

Blood.

Blood dripped from the tip of his thumb.

"Late and limping, the lambs wander home." Alane jumped off the crate and slid aside the wooden crossbar on the warehouse door.

As Niko stood, Marlo shoved him back, knocking the Ilbrean behind the two Black Bloods.

Alane pulled open the door. "Sodding stars."

Niko cut around the crate to get a view.

Mael's hulking figure blocked out most of the night. But part of the silhouette—it didn't fit.

He cradled Danu in his arms.

She pushed against Mael's chest, a feeble attempt to free herself. "I'm fine."

"You're not fine," Marlo said. "Set her here."

Niko reached out, ready to catch Danu as Mael turned toward the crate.

"We need to keep moving." Danu twisted sideways as Mael set her down, getting her feet to the ground before Niko could grab her. Her elbows slammed against the top of the crate as her knees buckled.

"Where are you hurt?" Alane wrapped her arm around Danu's waist.

"Just burned out from being a shit sorcerer," Danu said.

"Then why is there blood on your hand?" Alane said.

"Danu." Niko scrambled on top of the crate, taking her face in his hands.

No blood on her head. None by her mouth.

She'd shed the faux Sorcerers Guild robes, leaving her in a bodice, shift, and skirt, giving Niko a clear enough view to be sure her chest hadn't been torn by blade or magic.

He pressed his fingers to the side of her neck, making sure her heart hadn't stopped.

"I'm fine." Danu took his hand, not fighting as he tried again to feel her pulse. "An arrow clipped my arm. I'll be happy to have Cillian tend to it, but it's just a cut." She tipped her head, meeting Niko's eyes. "I'm burned out. That's all."

Niko's throat cinched shut, blocking any chance he had of speaking.

He nodded.

"We need to keep moving." Danu held Niko's gaze even as she spoke to the Black Bloods behind her.

"Are you sure?" Alane said. "I don't want the death of the Brien heir's sister falling on my head."

"Danu builds her own doom." Mael gripped Danu's arm, reclaiming her from Alane.

"I can walk." Danu gripped the edge of the crate, her hand covering the streak of Niko's blood on the wood.

Mael lifted Danu away.

The blood on her palm smeared across the crate, drowning out the faint stain Niko had left behind.

"I'm carrying you." Niko knocked into Alane as he slid between Danu and the crate. "Please just let me do it."

"Have at it, paun." Mael dropped Danu on her feet, toppling her toward Niko.

He caught Danu around the waist, holding her close enough to feel her ribs move as she breathed.

"I can walk," Danu said.

"That's a chivving lie," Marlo said.

"Then Mael can help me." Danu tried to round on Marlo, but Niko held her tighter.

He couldn't make himself let go.

"You can't carry me, Niko. I'll slow you down."

"Arguing with you will slow me down more than carrying you." Keeping hold of her with one arm, Niko bent, snatching her up and cradling her to his chest. "Please, Danu." He tightened his hold on her, clinging to her warmth as though daring both Mael and Dudia to try and steal her. "I need to do this."

Danu wrapped her arm behind his neck. "As long as you keep up."

"After me then." Marlo slipped out through the warehouse door.

"You next." Alane pulled the door wider, making enough room for Niko to carry Danu through.

Begging his limbs for strength, Niko walked out into the night.

Marlo kept his pace slow as he led their parade through the darkened streets.

The frantic panic from the attack at the healers' hall had vanished. The sensible Ilarans had fled the last of the Winter's End festivities and locked themselves in their homes, abandoning the streets to the sorts who laid a far heavier fear over the city.

A few drunks didn't seem to have realized what was happening. Their cheerful stumbling wove through the fires burning in the streets, the contrast giving a terrifying accent to the anger and vicious joy of the ones feeding the flames.

Soldiers rode through the city, but not enough. Not nearly enough.

They charged their horses at the fires, scattering the gathered slitches then moving on without capturing the death-hungry horde or dousing the flames.

The fires needed to be put out. All of them. Immediately.

If they spread to a house, if the whole city burned…

You were there. You watched it. You stood by and watched her begin this madness.

Three soldiers rounded the corner, riding straight toward them.

Danu tightened her hold on Niko's neck, pulling herself up to whisper in his ear. "Drop me. Drop me and run."

Niko stepped to the side of the road, tipping his head in a bow as the soldiers neared.

The soldiers slowed, one stopping right in front of Niko.

Pain sliced across Niko's back, stealing his breath as stone tore through flesh.

"What happened?" The soldier nodded at Danu.

"Don't," Danu whispered.

The pain in Niko's back deepened, pushing against his ribs.

"Fainted when a slitch ran through the party shouting about assassins taking over the city," Niko said. "I thought if we waited she'd get her feet back under her, but everything we've heard keeps getting worse. I'm just trying to get her home."

"Wife?" the soldier said.

A spasm seized Niko's chest as *betrothed* fell from his mouth.

Danu stiffened in his arms.

"Get her inside," the soldier said. "And see she's not left on her own."

"I will." Niko gave the soldier another nod.

The pain in Niko's back ebbed as the soldier rode away, leaving five of the monsters behind the bloody madness to slip away into the dark.

17

MARA

Mist wrapped around the ship, hiding even the nearby shore from view.

Keeping the lanterns dim and their voices quiet, the sailors worked as though monsters lurked just out of sight.

The icy fear locked around Mara's spine swore the men were right to be afraid.

She watched as the sailors prepared two rowboats, one to be hidden on shore should their party need to retreat, the other to come right back to the ship, if the ship could be found in the godsforsaken haze.

Dudia guard our foolish journey.

The bitter taste of resentful anger soured Mara's mouth.

Dudia, Saint Aximander, and every other fable meant to protect map makers had abandoned their journey from the start.

The saints of a blistering will to live and a desperate need to protect innocents from monsters were the only ones Mara could see fit to thank for any aid in her survival.

Elle gave a lonesome whimper from the stern of the ship. The lantern light caught her white fur as she plastered herself against Tham's legs, attempting to merge her body with his.

Tham leaned over, scratching Elle's head as he kept talking to Captain Haxton.

Mara couldn't see the captain's face or hear whatever he said to make Tham's whole body tense.

She managed two steps toward the stern before Elver appeared in front of her.

"We may have a problem," Elver whispered, "and I refuse to be the one to solve it."

A herd of footsteps pounded up the narrow stairs to the deck.

"Like a rampage of rats." Elver ducked behind Mara as Brady appeared at the top of the steps.

Carrying Ian, the smallest of the children rescued from Ian Ayres, Brady stormed across the deck to the rowboats. The rest of the children followed, all of them keeping their gazes fixed front, ignoring the sailors' stares as though Brady had banned eye contact upon penalty of a bloody beating.

Brady set Ian on his feet. She held on to the back of his pants, gripping the fabric as though lifting with all her might to keep the boy's legs beneath him, a feat that would have been impossible for either of them a few short days ago.

Proper food, a bed, and warmth. A child shouldn't face Death for lack of such luxuries.

"You." Brady pointed at the nearest sailor. "Help Ian into the boat."

"What?" The sailor frowned down at her.

"Put Ian in the boat. The rest of us can climb in on our own." Brady leaned Ian against her, steadying him as she scooted him toward the sailor. "I'll do it myself if you're too much of a braidic, chivving letch to give me a hand."

"Brady, no one's putting Ian in the boat. You included." Mara tightened her hold on the blanket wrapped around her shoulders, as though the wool might serve as armor against the child's blistering wrath.

"Be useless then, paun." Brady nodded to the largest of the other children. "Blinkers."

Blinkers passed his blanket to Asher and bent over, ready to hoist Ian onto his shoulder.

Mara slid between the children and the rail, blocking them from the boat. "Blinkers, do not pick Ian up. None of you are getting in this boat."

"Should we ride in the other one then?" Brady passed Ian into Blinkers's care.

"Please don't be difficult," Elver said.

"You're all staying on the ship," Mara said. "Captain Haxton will take care of you."

"We can care for ourselves," Asher said.

"Captain Haxton can shove a splintered stick up his hole," Brady said.

"Watch your mouth, girl," the sailor Brady had tried to command said.

"A row over to shore," Brady said, "that's all we're asking."

"And what does this pack of half-starved mice plan to do when they get to shore?" the sailor said. "Finish starving?"

"Don't say it. Don't say it. Don't say it," Elver muttered. "Don't say it. Don't say it."

"We're going to find the other children from Ian Ayres," Brady said.

"And the boulder shatters the ice," Elver said.

"Chivving children." The sailor dragged his hands down his face.

"We are going to find the other children," Mara said. "Tham, Elver, and I, we're going back to Ilara. Whether they were taken by the sorcerers or the Ice Walkers, the best place to start searching is there."

"Which is why we're going to Ilara," Brady said. "You say nice things about finding the others, but I don't trust your word any more than a matron's."

A sharp flick of hurt knocked the air from Mara's lungs.

"Our lot is heading to Ilara." Brady planted both hands on Mara's side, shoving her away from the rowboat. "Get him up, Blinkers."

"Ilara isn't safe right now." Mara took Brady by the shoulders, pivoting her away from the rail.

"'Cause we're so used to safety." Brady stomped on Mara's toes.

White spots danced through Mara's vision as pain zinged from her foot to her ribs. "You are an impetuous, belligerent—"

Brady yelped.

Blinking the spots from her eyes, Mara gripped the rail, ready for another assault on her feet.

Brady dangled upside down, her knees looped over Tham's shoulder, her hands nowhere near reaching the ground as she clawed the air in a vain bid for freedom.

"Apologize." Tham's tone didn't change as his focus shifted to Elle. "Down."

Elle ignored him, rearing up to lick Brady's face.

"Chivving spit demon," Brady said.

"Apologize," Tham said again.

"I'm sorry I only got one of her feet," Brady said.

"We're trying to protect you," Mara said. "The Ice Walkers are coming south. Whether tomorrow or in a month, they will attack Ilara. And the Lady Sorcerer will be furious and terrified after the Ice Walkers dared to fight her at Ian Ayres. She'll want to hide the threat they pose to the myth the sorcerers have painted themselves into, and if that means killing saelk children, she'll gladly wield the knife."

"Which is why we have to find the others," Brady said. "We're not chivving well sitting on a ship just hoping the rest of the bastards haven't been murdered."

"Yes, you are," Mara said. "You're children. You may not understand it, but children are meant to be protected. This is how it should be. Stay with Captain Haxton, and I promise you, Brady, we won't stop looking until we've found the rest of the children."

"I'm not trusting their lives to a paun coward." Brady swung herself forward, grabbing for Mara.

Mara leapt back, dodging Brady, who squeaked as Tham bounced her back into place.

"We'll find a way off this ship," Brady said.

"None of you can swim better than a stone," the sailor said.

"Watch your staff." Asher leapt toward the sailor, punching the man right in his most vulnerable part.

Brady cackled as the sailor's knees buckled.

"Oh dear." Elver grabbed Asher, tipping her over, attempting to hold her as Tham did Brady, getting stuck locking her in both arms like a struggling eel.

"Toss the chivving children overboard," the sailor growled.

"We can't lock them below deck," Tham said.

"I didn't say lock them up," the sailor said.

"We can't stop them." Tham held Mara's gaze. "You know we'd have found a way to shore. We'd have made it to Ilara, too."

"We never ran toward an ice army," Mara said.

"We would have," Tham said. "If our friends were in danger, nothing could've kept us from reaching them."

The heavy weight of truth smothered every argument Mara tried to seize as her mind raced through the thousand ways they could be delivering children to their graves.

"They do stand a better chance of actually reaching Ilara with us. As they've never been anywhere but Ian Ayres and that island could be easily eaten by one rich getch's farm." Elver jostled the still-struggling Asher. "I'm agreeing with you, little rat. Stop fidgeting. Your elbows are bruising me."

"We can't lead children toward Ronya," Mara said.

"Better Ice Walkers than paun." Asher spat at the sailor she'd punched.

"Why would you do that when he already wants to drown you?" Elver said.

"What would I have done to reach you?" Tham said.

Mara ducked her chin, burying her face in the musty blanket.

They were just children, younger than Mara had been when she'd finally met Tham, far too young to be allowed to knowingly venture toward danger.

But they were Ian Ayres born, raised by rock and sorrow, strong enough to survive the bastards' island. Too scarred to accept easy shelter, too bold to be shunted aside.

Mara let out a long breath and squared her shoulders. "If you come with us, you travel by our rules."

"Sheep's shit, we do," Brady said.

"You will give your word as a survivor of hell or you will stay on this ship," Mara said. "You follow our rules, agreed?"

"And don't punch anyone else's tender bits," Elver said. "Make them promise that, too."

"Coward," Asher said.

"It's your way to shore, Brady," Mara said. "Accept or get locked in a cabin until we've rowed away."

"We'll follow your chivving orders," Brady said.

"Swear it," Elver said. "All of you."

"As a ghost of the bastards' island, I swear," Brady said.

"I swear." Asher stopped wriggling.

"I swear," Ian said.

The rest added their oaths.

"May the gods bless you for taking the demons away." The wounded sailor leaned against the rail, the sweat on his brow glinting in the lamplight.

"Now put me down, you sodding slitch." Brady yelped as Tham swung her up to hold her in both arms.

"You still need to apologize." Tham lifted Brady into the rowboat.

"Even if I'm not sorry?" Brady said.

"Never have I been more glad for a lack of women in my bed." The sailor shuffled aside, letting Tham do the work of loading the rest of the children then the bundles of supplies the captain had offered for their journey north.

Two sailors climbed into the boat before Mara, Elver, Elle, and, finally, Tham joined.

The ropes lowering them creaked into motion, jostling their boat as they began their descent into the mist.

18

ALLORA

A turtle, a tree, and a rather sad puppet—not perfect matches for the shadows on the walls, but as close as Allora could manage despite hours of staring at the frozen silhouettes cast by the criolas set into the black stone ceiling of her prison.

Shelter, Allora. Remember gratitude.

She wrapped her blanket tighter around her shoulders, letting the soft fabric brush against her cheek.

Gratitude for a well-made blanket, that was an easy thing to manage.

Gratitude for the dried meat and frie stored in her prison.

Shelter.

Gratitude for her bed.

Gratitude for the placement of Gillien's bunk against the far wall, the greatest distance her pri—*shelter* offered.

Gratitude for the guards protecting her shelter.

Gratitude for Kenrick's promise to find word of Adrial.

He won't forget.

Kenrick will come back. He'll tell you Adrial is fine. It's only taken him so long to bring word because of something foolish, irrelevant even.

The city's been attacked, you stupid girl.

A delay means violence, and wounded, and death.

Allora rested her forehead on her knees, trying to push the imaginings of blood-slicked streets and sword-torn bodies from her mind.

You're staying out of the way. You help most by letting the guards follow their orders.

"Are you well, Allora?" Gillien asked.

Allora squeezed her eyes shut. "Fine, thank you."

"From the sound of your breathing," Gillien said, "you seem to be panicking."

Fighting against the weight of her own head, Allora looked to Gillien's chosen station—the only chair in the room, set right beside the black stone door.

"I'm not panicking."

"Is it the size of the space?"

"I'm fine." Allora winced at the sharpness of her own tone.

"My apologies, Allora. But huddled up in such a way, you look like a frightened child. I can't help but worry over you."

Allora tightened her hold on her blanket, gripping until her fingers hurt.

She had no argument to make against the sorcerer.

A few hours, or what seemed like, after they'd been shut in the room, Allora had unpinned her hair, setting her crown beside the bottle of frie and letting the mass of curls her maids had created fall loose around her shoulders.

When sleep became inevitable, she'd taken off her golden gown, leaving herself in the intricate, delicate undergarments Gillien had insisted she wear with the foolish hope Brannon would choose Winter's End to finally give in to the sorcerers and attempt to thrust a child into his Queen.

Had she any other clothing, Allora would have shredded the underthings. But with only the sheer lace draped over the peaks of her breasts, cinched bodice, and thin skirt—incapable of hiding the shadows between her legs even in the dim light—available, she wore the humiliating garments in a vague façade of modesty.

Now wrapped in the blanket that had become her comfort, sitting with her knees pulled to her chest, Allora couldn't make herself doubt she resembled a useless child more than a competent woman, much less a queen.

"Allora?" Worry pinched Gillien's brow.

"We've been locked in this room for Dudia only knows how long. We've no idea what happened in the city to force us in here. We don't know what's happening now. I don't know where Adrial is. I don't know if he's safe. I don't know if Illia is safe. I don't know if Brannon is in the palace or even alive."

"It's past midday."

"What?" Allora pressed her blanket under her eyes, blotting her tears before they could fall.

"We've passed midday. You should eat again."

"Do you have some magic to tell the position of the sun?"

"Merely a well-practiced talent for knowing how much time has passed when the sun can't be seen." Gillien stood, crossing the seven steps to their cache of food. She picked up a piece of dried meat, holding it out to Allora.

She didn't accept it. "We should have been let out by now."

"It's a pity I don't have something better to offer Ilbrea's Queen."

"What kind of trouble in the city could last all night and into the day without being stopped?"

"Although, the longevity of food must be a priority in such situations."

"Gillien!" Allora's voice bounced off the stone walls, banging into the vague ache surrounding her skull.

"You are safe." Gillien set the meat down and picked up the bottle of frie. "You will continue to be protected."

"And what about everyone else?" The cold of the floor stung

Allora's bare feet as she stood. "My safety means little if Ilara burns."

"You are the Queen of Ilbrea. Your value rises above the fate of Ilara."

"Of the city?" Allora grasped the spark of anger in her chest as she held Gillien's gaze. "You cannot possibly be implying my safety could be considered comparable to the wellbeing of all the people in Ilara."

Gillien poured a glass of frie and held it out to Allora.

"Tell me I misunderstood."

"Your worth cannot be overestimated." Gillien stepped closer, holding the glass inches from Allora's hands as she still clung to her blanket. "A city can be rebuilt. A royal line cannot. If the Willoc line is broken, chaos will devour Ilbrea as any man with a hint of Willoc blood in his lineage tries to declare himself King. As much as you may regret marrying King Brannon, you are wise enough to understand how many lives could be lost if factions begin warring for the crown."

Allora took the frie, letting the burn of the liquor feed the spark of anger, cultivating crackling embers of righteous fury. "Lady Gwell would hand the crown to whomever she chose as the next King. May Dudia pity her new puppet."

"For the good of Ilbrea, if the factions grew too violent and Lady Gwell had to install a new monarch to ensure the safety of Ilbrea, she would fulfil the task required. As it has always been."

"As she will ever force it to be."

A sharp sting slammed through Allora's cheek. A poor replica of an actual slap.

"Speak carefully of the one who protects you."

"Protection defined as suffering constant threats? I believe you and I have very different understandings of the word." Allora downed the rest of her frie. "If I've been locked in this room for the *protection* of the Willoc line, you mustn't have a problem with my leaving."

Gillien stayed maddeningly still and silent.

"I'm not carrying a Willoc heir." Allora stepped past her, enjoying the heavy thump of glass against wood as she abandoned her cup beside the bottle of frie. "The King has openly declared I will never carry a Willoc heir, despite my best, painfully desperate efforts."

"Allo—"

"Unless the Lady Sorcerer has found some spell to force Brannon on top of me, I mean nothing more than the least useful pauper in Ilara." Allora wiggled her feet back into her beaded slippers.

"You've given up hope of repairing your bond with Brannon?"

"I never had any hope!" She rounded on Gillien, screaming just to hear the sound ricochet off the walls. "I try, and humiliate myself, and try again. I built my husband a place to hide from me, hoping a reprieve might fade his anger enough he'll fuck me out of pity, because your precious Lady Sorcerer has Mara and Tham locked in your demon-built tower.

"I will never succeed. I will never give Ilbrea an heir. But I will keep clawing through this desperate pursuit of Brannon as long as I breathe, because it is the only way I can protect Mara and Tham from the Lady Sorcerer. But, Gillien—please, Gillien—right now, Adrial is in danger, and the city I love may be burning."

"And you change none of that by placing yourself in harm's way." Gillien held the piece of dried meat out to Allora again. "You cannot open that door without my aid. And I will not open that door until the danger has passed. Now sit and eat. Brannon's temperament won't matter if you're not healthy enough to carry his heir."

"Too ill to carry a child. What a pity it would be for Brannon to lose a second queen that way." Allora waited for Gillien to flinch. "Not even a vague denial?"

The sorcerer didn't so much as frown.

Allora turned toward the stone door as the embers of fury faded away, leaving nothing but a vast darkness and a soft whisper that wove into every thought, promising falling into the black was inevitable and accepting her fate the only way to dull the painful edges that dug into her mind, slaying every flicker of hope before it caught hold.

She dropped the blanket, letting the chill of the air set goosebumps all over her skin.

"You are Ilbrea's Queen," Gillien said. "And you are a good Queen."

"Who has failed in her primary duty to conceive an heir." Allora pressed her weight against the door. "I shouldn't be locked in here. There's no reason for it." The door gave no hint of movement. "Every soul who works in the palace knows the King would rather ram himself into a filth-covered pig than his own wife."

"The King's continued refusal to couple with you will be handled," Gillien said.

"Will the Lady Sorcerer herself tuck him inside me?" Allora rocked her weight from one hand to the other. "Will she pin him on top of me until he's finished his kingly duty."

Not even a click of movement within the door.

"You needn't drift into such crass worries. Ilbrea will have an heir," Gillien said.

"What threat will you toss at Brannon?"

"The King of Ilbrea is not to be threatened."

Allora coughed out a laugh.

"You will continue your efforts, as I will continue to assist you," Gillien said. "Set aside any worries of our success. Even the King's preference in bedmates will no longer be allowed to endanger Ilbrea."

"Bedmates?" Allora pressed her forehead to the stone. "Such a gentle word from a serpent."

"If you'd like to insult me to pass the time, I will allow it, but only if you eat."

"Bribed to eat like a petulant child." Allora turned, leaning her back against the door.

The frigid stone burned her skin.

Gillien pressed the dried meat into Allora's hand.

"Let me out," Allora said. "I'll do whatever you please. I'll eat. I'll lie naked on Brannon's desk. I'll dress as one of his whores and trick him into spilling inside me."

"You're safe here."

"But I don't know if Adrial is." Allora slid down to sit on the floor. "Now that you've seen me so concerned for his safety, will he be the Lady Sorcerer's next pawn?"

"I don't think she'll need one." Gillien pulled her chair away from the door just enough to sit facing Allora.

"Because Brannon will give in, or because the palace will burn with the rest of Ilara?"

"The palace will not be allowed to burn."

A low, dry laugh rattled in Allora's throat. "Unless the Lady Sorcerer orders it." Shivers took over the bouncing in her chest, seizing the muscles in her back as her hands started to tremble. She pressed the backs of her arms to the door, letting the cold take them. "Would this room survive?"

"You are protected."

"From the hoard of black stones you've hidden beneath the palace?" Allora trailed her finger across the floor, tracing the places where the criolas light caught the shades of purple hidden deep within the dark stone. She rapped on the floor. "I can't imagine the Lady Sorcerer allowing such an invulnerable shelter to exist."

"There are some forces Dudia did not create even stone to withstand."

Allora shut her eyes, picturing herself tumbling into a void.

Such comfort in the darkness. In the act of letting go.

"I need you to trust me, Allora. You are safe in this room, and when I am able, I will let you out. It is my duty to protect you, but I also care for you and your happiness. I am not keeping you from news of Adrial or the city to torment you. Give me at least that much faith."

Heat pressed against Allora's eyes.

The weight of her blanket draped over her. She flipped the blanket aside.

"You're shivering," Gillien said.

Allora rammed the tips of her fingers against the floor as though clawing through the stone. The pain of her nails bending back joined the sting of the cold.

The blanket brushed Allora's feet.

"Don't," she said.

"You need it."

"No."

"Take the blanket."

"I hate the blanket. I don't want to be grateful for a soft blanket. I don't want to be grateful for your protection or care. I don't want to ever feel any hint of friendship toward you. I want to hate you and everything in this palace." Trails of heat cut through the cold of her cheeks. "Loathing is a mercy. It burns away fear and grief. Loathing keeps me from crumbling to nothing, and I hate you for trying to steal that from me."

"Then I shall have to hope that hatred is strong enough to keep you moving forward."

The blanket tucked around Allora's shoulders.

"Whatever waits outside this room, you'll be better able to meet it if you're not ill."

"Word of Adrial hasn't come. If he..." Allora couldn't make herself form the words.

"If news had already arrived, I doubt it would have been good. Word of a head scribe's death would travel quickly. Finding proof that he's alive and well is a more difficult task."

The weight of tears pressed on Allora's throat.

"Guard Kenrick swore to bring you word as soon as he could. Let yourself have faith in him."

Allora forced the tension from her hands, willing her heart to slow as she pictured Kenrick at the gates of the library, demanding to see Adrial on the Queen's orders.

The scribes' guards obeyed, bringing Adrial out to the square, too tired to hide his limp, but alive and unharmed. Tears of gratitude spilled down Adrial's cheeks as Kenrick promised that Allora was safe and had begged to come find Adrial herself.

Kenrick rushed back to the palace, freeing Allora to deliver the wonderful news, not fleeing as she sobbed tears of relief.

19

ADRIAL

Three dozen soldiers had joined the scribes' guards surrounding Adrial's carriage on the long march to the palace. More still had been sent to the library to form the sea of black uniforms protecting the Lord Scribe's carriage.

The well-armed mass had easily scattered the few common folk who'd dared cross the city to gather in front of the library, begging for scribes' aid. But the number of desperate tilk outside the gates would only grow if the chaos continued.

Birth records had to be maintained. Delays in marriage papers couldn't be allowed, either, not with Ian Ayres always waiting to seize more innocents.

Not Ena.

The island didn't steal her.

She's alive. She's here in Ilara.

He'd seen her, caught the scent of her hair, felt her lips against his.

She could be just beyond the solidly blocked carriage windows and he'd never know. Her voice could be among the throng whose shouting filled the streets as Adrial's party neared the palace.

Adrial gripped the edge of his seat, not allowing himself to throw open the carriage door and search for his wife.

It didn't matter. She wouldn't be shouting with the horde. Fighting, perhaps.

Or slipping through the shadows, dripping poison into cups.

If she hasn't already finished her work.

Dread settled in the bottom of Adrial's lungs.

If her hand began this whole bloody nightmare. If Lord Gareth is the next to meet her wrath.

"You're a man of reason, not panic," Adrial whispered.

Harane. Marten. Lir Valley.

He needed to find the names in the library records. He hadn't even had time to try and fight his way past the guards to reach the shelves where he needed to begin his search.

If Lord Gareth won't allow scribes into any rooms with windows. If Ena was a part of the attack. If she'd been hurt in the attack.

If this council meeting is as disastrous as reason promises it will be.

If Lord Gareth locks me deep in the library.

If she attacks the library...

Adrial's breath rasped in his throat.

The scribes couldn't afford to fall behind on burial papers.

A list of the twelve killed in the ambush had arrived from the healers' hall just after dawn. Eleven guards and the Lady Healer. Adrial would draw up the guards' burial papers. Lady Byrd's papers would be written by Lord Gareth himself.

"Dudia, let this madness end before more blood spills." Adrial pinched the bridge of his nose, failing to banish the dull ache of fatigue blurring his eyes. "Don't ask for the impossible. Kingdoms are not saved by whispered words."

Access to scribes' aid would have to be established. More runners bringing the requests of the common folk to the scribes huddled inside the library, hiding from whatever hell the night had unleashed on the city.

The night or Ena?

"Don't, Adrial." He scrubbed his hands over the stubble sullying his chin. "Don't pin your mind on the darkest path."

You've already thrown yourself off that cliff. Kai's whisper bounced with amusement. *You can't blame the ground when you hit it.*

The harsh bark of orders replaced the angry shouts of the crowd. The rhythm of the stones beneath the carriage's wheels changed as they reached the bridge leading to the palace gates.

Which are you more afraid of, Mara whispered, *that madness drove you to marry a bloodhungry demon? Or that you'd let the whole city burn to catch another glimpse of her?*

"Sorcerers attacked the Lady Healer." Adrial straightened the cuffs of his robe. "Magic was the weapon. Not a blade or poison."

"We move one at a time." The order came as soon as Adrial's carriage had stopped. "One at a time."

Adrial closed his eyes, listening for the thumps of a swarm of soldiers' boots climbing the palace stairs.

A swarm traveled down the stairs instead, halting for a moment before thumping back to the palace entrance.

The sound faded.

Adrial turned to the carriage door, preparing himself for the indignity of being seized by guards and propped up like a tot still learning to walk, all in the name of protecting the Guilded Cripple.

The number of voices behind his carriage grew.

Adrial shut his eyes again.

A distinct rumbling of carriage wheels traveled with the voices. The guards and soldiers already at the palace steps refrained from shouting any telling greetings or threats at the new arrivals, leaving Adrial's sleep-addled mind to imagine the scene around him.

Not a sorcerer, ruled out for lack of increased fear.

Not the Lord Soldier. There had been no sounds of welcome

between groups or any hint of relief with the coming of the new arrivals.

Map Maker Traim, perhaps.

A fresh swarm of footsteps traveled up the stairs, delivering the other occupant to the palace.

Not Traim, then.

Lord Nevon. It had to be.

Unless it's the new Lady Healer.

May their service last longer than Lady Byrd's.

Two sharp knocks rapped on Adrial's door as it flung open.

He held out his hands, not fighting as two scribes' guards pulled him from the carriage, gripping below his arms, propelling him forward before he'd gotten his feet beneath him.

He needn't have bothered trying to walk. The guards held under his arms too tightly for him to fall, and the pack of soldiers and guards surrounding Adrial was too thick for him to have toppled over, even without his arms being squeezed hard enough to bruise.

His herd didn't slow as they reached the top of the steps and entered the palace.

Black uniforms lined the walls, outnumbering the pale uniforms of the royal guards to a degree Adrial had never witnessed.

A scrum of guards and soldiers had caught at the corner of the corridor, forcing Adrial's herd to slow as they waited for, what seemed to be, Lord Nevon's party to squeeze between the two columns of royal guards stationed at the turn.

The flowers from the Winter's End party still adorned the walls. Violence and daylight hadn't ruined the blooms, but the beauty of the dark petals had twisted from an invitation to a warning.

Magic formed the blooms. Magic filled the palace. Magic would not bow to reason or steel.

"—will have silence," the King's shout carried down the hall. "A member of this council was murdered."

"And we've told you who—"

"Silence!" The King cut off the woman's words. "If all you can do is prattle the same frenzied accusations over and over, get out of my palace."

The woman didn't respond.

Adrial reached the entrance of the council chamber.

The first six of Adrial's escort stopped, forming a path for him. His minders let go of his arms, letting him walk alone through the alley, which was so tight, his shoulders nearly brushed the guards' chests as he passed.

A foolish flash of relief shot through Adrial's heart as he reached the end of the column and stepped into the wide chamber.

The room hadn't been packed with soldiers, and the skylight hadn't been barricaded against attack. With a mere ten guards in the chamber—two each for the King, sailors, soldiers, scribes, and healers—only the air of violent loathing betrayed the meeting as something worse than usual.

Lady Gwell hadn't argued with the healers' demand that no sorcerers' guards be allowed in the council chamber. Standing beside the table, a sneer curling her lips, Lady Gwell surveyed the rest of the council as though wondering which fool would be the first to learn why guards meant nothing against her magic.

The Lady Sorcerer's eyes darkened as she spotted Adrial.

"Close the doors." The King slammed his hand against the table. "This meeting begins."

"There are no map makers present." Lord Nevon pointed to Lord Karron's and Map Maker Traim's empty seats. "Hard to notice in all the confusion, but a full Guild is missing representation."

"Lord Nevon, you could easily find yourself missing from this council as well," the King said.

"With all summonable respect, that is not allowed, Your Majesty," Lord Gareth said. "Each Guild holds the authority to select their leader."

"Until that leader is murdered." A woman in healer red stood in Lady Byrd's place. Black had been sewn around the cuffs and collar of her robes, mimicking the marks of mourning Adrial still wore.

"Death does prevent one from ruling one's Guild," Lady Gwell said.

"Repulsive." Lord Gareth tapped his finger on the table. "Or have you forgotten a woman has died?"

"Death is Dudia's servant. Lady Byrd did not simply die, she was murdered. Tortured and slaughtered by the Sorcerers Guild," the healer said. "The Healers Guild demands justice."

"Your accusations will not be allowed to incite further unrest in Ilara," the King said. "Guards and soldiers haunting the streets has spread fear among the people."

"The impaled corpse of the Lady Healer sparked more trouble with the common folk than the cathedral collapsing on all our heads," Lord Kearney said.

Lord Nevon gave a growl-like, single laugh.

"The fear tipping toward violence isn't stoked by my soldiers. It's the sorcerers who terrify the people," Lord Kearney said.

"As it has always been," Lady Gwell said.

"Not every man cowers at the sight of purple robes," Lord Kearney said. "Both city gates have been closed."

"I gave no such order," the King said.

"Your approval is not needed, Your Majesty. When Ilara faces an attack, the defense of the city falls to the Soldiers Guild." Lord Kearney bowed. "If there is any chance the sorcerers who murdered the Lady Healer—"

"I did not think you fool enough to accuse my people," Lady Gwell said.

"I speak with full knowledge that you may choose, as you so

often have, to use your magic to threaten and control the members of this council." Lord Kearney paused, as though waiting for an invisible hand to squeeze his throat. "I do not accuse your people, Lady Sorcerer. I accuse you."

A crackle of sparks danced across the shining wood and inlaid gold of the table.

Adrial held his breath, waiting for the sparks to leap to his skin and singe his flesh. No pain came.

Lord Gareth tutted his disgust, while Lord Nevon went so far as to cough another laugh.

"Healer Seay, could Lady Byrd's murder and the ambush of her guards have been accomplished without magic?" Lord Kearney said.

"An absolute impossibility," Healer Seay said.

"Which leaves two options." Lord Kearney pinned his gaze on the King, ignoring the deadly hatred in Lady Gwell's eyes. "Either the attack was carried out by a member of the Sorcerers Guild acting under Lady Gwell's orders—"

"How dare—" Lady Gwell began.

"Or the purple lady has lost control of her demons," Healer Seay said.

The sparks on the table surged toward the healer, rising up into a wall that formed around her, stopping a breath above her skin.

"I came to this meeting prepared to die," Healer Seay said. "Though I hadn't thought you'd crumble into a tantrum so quickly."

The sparks brightened.

"An assassination arranged on the order of the Lady Sorcerer or rogue sorcerers tormenting the city," Lord Kearney said. "Those are the two horrors the people of Ilbrea are caught between. Loath as some commoners may be to admit it, the soldiers and guards on the streets are bringing comfort to the people. We are not the monsters who steal loved ones in the night. Ilarans are wise enough to save their terror for the evil of the sorcerers."

"How quick you are to accuse those with magic," Lady Gwell said.

"What other possibility can you offer, Lady Gwell?" Lord Gareth asked.

A freezing cold clamped around Adrial's throat. He swallowed hard, forcing his mind to accept that the rope tightening around his neck, stopping his words, stealing any hope he had of averting the storm, had been born of mere fear rather than magic.

"Did you order the attack, Your Majesty?" Lord Gareth said.

The King sat back in his chair, watching the sparks dance across the seven-pointed star in the center of the table. "No. I didn't."

"Have any of your sorcerers rebelled from your Guild, Lady Gwell?" Lord Gareth asked.

"Never." Lady Gwell's whisper echoed around the room, scraping across the back of Adrial's neck.

"Lady Byrd was murdered by magic," Healer Seay said.

"Though logic may be my doom," Lord Gareth said, "murdered by magic that, by your own account, Lady Gwell, has never been under the control of the Sorcerers Guild."

The crackling of the sparks filled the silence.

"If not magic commanded by you, and not magic rebelling against your command, I see no option but ungoverned magic. A threat the Sorcerers Guild has long claimed does not exist," Lord Gareth said. "If I am mistaken, I am most eager to be corrected."

"Logic without wisdom is a dangerous thing." Lady Gwell planted her hands on the table, letting the sparks climb her arms.

The light spread, solidifying as it dripped down her chest, spreading around her torso as though she were donning armor.

"The Healers Guild demands the sorcerers responsible for this heinous act be surrendered to the Soldiers Guild and dealt the Guilds' justice," Healer Seay said.

"A fair demand," Lord Kearney said.

"And what would a soldier do with a sorcerer?" Lady Gwell said.

"An arrow to the neck," Lord Nevon said. "My men hauled a sorcerer from the sea who'd died from a similar blow in one of the attacks my docks endured because you, Lady Gwell, have strayed so far from the purpose of this council, you believe it's your place to reign over us all."

"My people died protecting your docks," Lady Gwell said.

"You're admitting they died?" Lord Kearney said.

"Forced protection is nothing more than occupation." Lord Nevon leaned against the table, not even flinching as sparks singed the hairs on the backs of his hands. "Were the sorcerers who attacked the healers' hall under your command? Yes, or no?"

He pounded his fists on the table, spraying a burst of sparks over the council members.

Adrial patted out the sparks that landed on his robes, leaving black specks on the pristine white fabric.

"Yes or no, Lady Sorcerer," Lord Nevon said.

"Enough of this madness," the King said. "I will not listen to this council bicker while Ilara tumbles into chaos."

"Lord Kearney," Healer Seay said, "I issue a complaint against Lady Gwell of the Sorcerers Guild. I accuse her of impeding the Guilds' pursuit of justice."

"I will share the burden as second," Lord Gareth said.

Two threads of light grew from the center of the table.

"I will gladly die as proof of your monstrous guilt." Healer Seay stared at Lady Gwell, ignoring the light as it neared her throat. "Continue your demonstration for the council."

"I'm an old man." Lord Gareth shrugged. "After all you've done to those I hold dear, not even Dudia himself would forgive my cowardice if I didn't speak against you when an opportunity finally came. You're snagged in your own knot, Lady Gwell. Who is behind the attack? Give the council the truth. Your oath to the Guilds demands it."

The thread of light slid across the front of Lord Gareth's neck. He shut his eyes, screwing up his face as he silently endured the pain.

Scream. Let the sorcerer's wrath fall on me.

Warn them all not to test the demons, there are darker shadows to fear.

"Your complaint is heard, Healer Seay," Lord Kearney said. "The Soldiers Guild gladly accepts the burden of upholding the Guild's laws."

"This is preposterous." King Brannon stood, waving a hand at the sparking table. "Lady Gwell, please remove your threat from the members of this council. Lord Kearney, the safety of Ilbrea—"

"As Lord Soldier, I bid the council consider what they deem an appropriate sentence for defying the Guilds' pursuit of justice," Lord Kearney said. "While our decision is debated, I suggest Lady Gwell be removed from the council chamber."

"Stop this now." The King's shout echoed over Lord Kearney.

"Those in favor, say aye," Lord Kearney said.

"Aye." Healer Seay leaned closer to the light that still reached for her throat. She didn't wince as the gleaming thread blistered her skin.

"Aye." Lord Gareth tucked his hands behind his back, seeming to surrender to whatever torment Lady Gwell's anger wrought.

"Aye," Lord Nevon said.

"Lord Kearney you are a man of the sword," the King said. "You are too wise to renounce your strongest warrior."

"Aye," Lord Kearney said. "Lady Gwell, in accordance with the laws of Ilbrea, you will surrender yourself to be held in isolation until your questioning can begin."

Fear struck every other thought from Adrial's mind as Lady Gwell smiled.

With a twitch of her finger, the sparks and threads of light disappeared.

"Escort Lady Gwell to her carriage." Lord Kearney spoke over his shoulder. "She will be delivered to the soldiers' barracks and made comfortable in her cell."

"You hold no dominion over the sorcerers," Lady Gwell said.

"We are a council of seven, no Guild Lord above another," Lord Gareth said. "Will you surrender as law requires, or will you prove yourself a traitor to your vow to serve Ilbrea?"

Joyful hatred flared in Lady Gwell's eyes. "Sorcerers are servants to none."

"Lady Gwell—" King Brannon said.

"We are not occupiers, or entertainment, or shields to be thrown in front of ungrateful worms," Lady Gwell said. "If our protection is not appreciated, we shall abandon the docks."

"This cannot continue," King Brannon said.

"We'll leave the protection of the city walls in the hands of the soldiers," Lady Gwell said. "When the library burns, we'll not douse the flames. And when there is no one left to heal the healers, we will let your flesh rot."

"Such wonderful promises," Lord Nevon said. "I will thank Dudia once they are fulfilled."

"Lady Gwell"—the King turned to face her, setting his back to his council—"Ilara stands on the edge of disaster."

"Disaster swallows many kingdoms, Your Majesty." Lady Gwell studied the King's face. "Will you reject my aid in preserving yours?"

The King glanced toward the doors, his breath quickening as though his soul begged his body to flee. "The crown stands beside the Sorcerers Guild, as the Willoc family always has."

"You would stand with the sorcerers, murderers who've stolen ships and innocents while rampaging through the city, against your own people?" Lord Nevon said.

"I would rather rule over ruins than traitors," the King said.

"A demon's most beloved trick is twisting the soul of a once honorable man," Lord Gareth said.

"Do not insult your King." Lady Gwell slammed her palm toward the entrance, snapping the bolt that secured the doors, sending shards of white and gold-painted wood scattering across the marble floor. "I advise you to take your guards and leave the palace grounds."

"Will you allow this, Your Majesty?" Lord Nevon said.

"All soldiers will leave the palace grounds," Lady Gwell said.

The gray glow filtering down from the skylight dimmed.

Adrial glanced up, daring to look away from the Lady Sorcerer just long enough to see the black mist expanding across the ceiling. He grabbed Lord Gareth's wrist.

"Any found lurking on palace grounds will be considered a threat to the King," Lady Gwell said.

"Up," Adrial whispered as he tightened his hold on Lord Gareth's wrist, urging him toward the doors.

"Your Majesty," Lord Kearney said, "this is the legacy you choose?"

"Dudia laid my path." The King stepped back, leaving the Lady Sorcerer between himself and the council.

"May history remember the truth of this day." Lord Gareth pulled free from Adrial's grip only to grab Adrial's wrist in turn, dragging his heir from the council chamber as quickly as his aged body would allow.

"It is the soldiers' duty to protect the King." Lord Kearney's voice followed them out into the guard-packed corridor.

"Get the head scribe into a carriage." Lord Gareth forced Adrial into the hands of two scribes' guards. "I want him back in the library now. I don't care if royal guards try to stop you. Run them down, just get him across that bridge."

The guards gripped Adrial under the arms, carrying him too quickly for his feet to catch the ground.

"No. Lord Gareth." Adrial tried to turn back. "Lord Gareth!"

His guards didn't slow.

"Stop." Adrial twisted, ramming his heels into the ground, trying to break free. "The Lord Scribe must go first."

The guards kept moving, carrying him out of the palace.

"Allora." Adrial thrust his elbows sideways, failing again to gain freedom. "I can't leave without Allora."

The guards shoved him into his carriage.

"The Queen." Adrial scrambled back toward the door. "Someone needs to get the Queen."

The carriage lurched forward as the guard slammed the door shut, beginning the Guilds' flight from the palace.

20

NIKO

Two lines of guards blocked the library gate, each of them armed as though they understood fury herself had come to sack Ilara. All of them wore the same uniform, but some, the ones tucked in the back line, wavered in their stance. A few seemed young enough they could have been kitchen boys, handed a sword to give the scribes' guards a better show of strength. The other nervous warriors, grooms perhaps, or scribes who fancied themselves capable in a fight.

A wooden barricade had been placed along the side of the street opposite the gate, forming a pen where those in search of scribes' aid could wait, hoping to catch the ear of the single guard who moved along the barrier, taking notes in a little book. Every few people, he'd tear a page out and pass it to a guard in the line in front of the gate.

The second guard would pass the page through the locked gate to a third guard, who then ran the note inside only to return a few moments later to repeat the process.

Ena shifted, turning to lean her back against the window frame.

She watched the gate as Niko did, but there was a darkness in her eyes that made it somehow impossible for Niko to believe they were seeing the same thing.

Maybe she didn't see frightened kitchen boys and a guard bearing the shame of his common handwriting to pass pleas for aid to the scribes.

Bones, blood, corpses to stack, pawns to sacrifice in whatever demented game she'd set in motion—those were the sights the true Solcha must recognize.

The guard ran another paper into the library.

Ena shifted back to leaning her shoulder against the window frame.

"There's no reason they'd be done yet," Niko said.

Ena gave no hint of having heard him.

"The Lady Healer died. And by *died* I mean you and the terrifying redhead killed her in a way that could easily cause a council meeting to drag on." Niko pushed away from the window frame, stepping closer to her. "The city gates are closed. The healers have got to be reeling from the loss of their leader. You've got to be patient."

Slowly, soul-chillingly slowly, Ena looked at him.

A streak of fear shot from Niko's heart to his ass.

"I'm merely trying to assure you that Adrial not having returned from the palace yet isn't a reason to panic," Niko said.

"Don't stand in the center of the window, paun," Ena said.

"Right." Niko tucked himself back against his side of the window frame. "When will we go back to the basement?"

"Are you more concerned for Danu than the scribe?"

Niko glanced toward the stairs that cut down through the floor, leading to the story below. He didn't have the nerve to creep over and peer down the steps, searching for Brien lurking in the shadows, clinging to Solcha's every mountain-blessed word.

"I'm not more concerned for Danu than Adrial," Niko whispered. "But Adrial has a mob of guards protecting him. Danu has Mael, which I'm almost certain is worse than being on her own."

"It is," Ena said.

"Then we need to go back to the basement. Make sure she's safe. Cillian, too. He could have gotten hurt."

"We're not just here to watch for the scribe," Ena said.

"Is there"—another streak of fear speared Niko's ass—"will the redhead be joining us?"

"There's no need. We only have to make sure the flames caught."

"Flames." Niko dug his nails into his palms. "Please let it be metaphorical flames, or, at the very least, promise me you're not setting the library on fire."

"I owe my life to a child who lives inside that library. His safety will not be risked."

"Good." Niko scrubbed his knuckles over the scruff on his chin. "That's good. But I'm no less terrified to ask what you mean."

Ena looked back out the window, choosing the path of silence.

Niko followed suit.

He focused on the feel of the half-moon dents his nails dug into his flesh, picturing each of the marks searing with pain rather than let his mind fill Ilara with flames.

The guards relayed another note to the library.

And another.

A new guard carried a basket of scrolls from the library. The guard at the barricade called out names, distributing the papers among the penned-in crowd.

Niko watched the people on the street tense and turn north before he heard the sound.

A white carriage raced down the street, going as quickly as the scribes' guards surrounding it could run. Three guards fell behind the carriage, their stamina failing them as the carriage rounded the corner to the library.

"Open the gate for the head scribe," the driver shouted. "Open the gate."

Ena leaned closer to the window, her breath leaving faint fog on the glass as she watched the guards open the gate and slam it shut behind Adrial's carriage.

The guards reformed their ranks even as a second white carriage approached.

"We can go to your precious Danu." Ena left the window, heading toward the stairs.

"Does that mean the flames caught? Shouldn't we try to catch a glimpse of Adrial?"

"Did you notice the guards at the gate trembling with fear at the sight of a racing carriage? The sweat on their faces that promises they might shit themselves in terror at any moment?" Ena stopped on the top step and turned to Niko. "They aren't defending the library from tilk or even from the Black Bloods they're too chivving power-blind to know exist. The Guilds are preparing to fight their own. The blades those cowering guards cling to are meant to draw paun blood, and that, paun, is a glorious thing.

"If the head scribe's carriage had arrived slowly, with no hint of horror-born pallor on his guards' faces, I'd have needed to tap another crack into your precious Guilds before climbing back underground to greet whatever venom Deryn longs to spew my way. But the Guilds have never held any loyalty. It's easy to break the trust of evil men. They've only their own foul hearts as a measure of honor."

21

ALLORA

Gillien swirled her finger through the air, tracing a spiral of purple flames along the wall. "Still nothing?"

"Despite every hint of tact I can muster, I cannot speak anything but the truth. You are a terrible artist." Allora dipped her dried meat into her glass of frie, moistening the petrified cow enough for her to chew without pain in her jaw.

Gillien furrowed her brow, looking almost displeased for a moment before laughing. "There are some sorcerers who can claim great artistry. I am not one." She drew four sticks coming down from the circle-tipped oval still burning with purple flames.

"A pig?" Allora pushed away from the door, sitting up straight. "Is it a pig?"

"A pig indeed." Gillien waved her hand.

The purple flames flared red before vanishing, leaving no hint of soot behind.

"No more animals." Allora sighed. "Choose a different category."

"I would offer to try flowers, but my knowledge of blooms is as poor as my drawing."

"Then draw me your room."

"My room?"

"The room you grew up in." Allora tightened the blanket around her shoulders. "The place where you felt safe and warm and had never even considered the world could be dangerous."

"I didn't have a room like that." Gillien drew a rectangle on the wall. "Not as a child."

"I'm sorry."

"Some of us are forced to find our home." Gillien added three arches inside the rectangle. "When I finally found where I belonged, I never wanted to leave." Lines dashed through the bottoms of the arches, forming a row of windows. "I could have spent my whole life curled up in the warmth beaming down from above, studying magic and its place in the world." She added a figure standing in front of the windows. "But when you love something, you protect it, even if the separation breaks you."

"You protect your tower by being my shadow?" Allora leaned back against the door. "As wary as I am to admit it, having you lurk behind me is better than having your predecessor's claws wrapped around my throat. But you should return to the place you love rather than waste your days following me. There will never be any progress between Brannon and me, and whatever it is you're protecting your home from, I'm no threat to it."

"Exactly." Gillien smiled. "Sit up straight."

"Wha—" Allora tipped backward, falling into the parlor fireplace with a yelp as a voice shouted, "The head scribe is safe, Your Majesty!"

Allora gripped her blanket tighter as a guard knelt beside her.

"Are you hurt, Your Majesty?" The guard slid his hand under her back, sitting her up before she'd replied.

"Your Majesty." Kenrick appeared at her other side, offering his hand to steady her. Half of his top lip had swelled like a gorged slug. Dried blood streaked across his other cheek, as though he'd carelessly wiped the blood from the wound by his eye with the sleeve of his uniform. "I returned as soon as I confirmed the head scribe's safety. Upon my honor, I did."

"You're sure he's safe?" Allora reached for Kenrick's hand.

The guard behind her was quicker, threading his arm under her legs and turning to set her on her feet outside the fireplace.

Allora stumbled back, catching her heel on her blanket, yanking the fabric from her own grip.

Twelve royal guards lined the room with two sorcerers placed among them.

All of their gazes caught on Allora as she stood before them, her sheer underclothes on perfect display in the midday light, the single diamond of her necklace glinting as it dangled below her breasts.

She stepped back, getting her blanket farther beneath her feet.

"Your Majesty." Kenrick gripped her arms, lifting her away, planting her back against the side of the fireplace, covering her body with his. "Someone pick up the blanket."

He kept his hands planted on either side of her shoulders, the curve of his neck a breath from her lips as he glared at the guard who grabbed the blanket. Kenrick yanked the blanket from the other guard's grip and held it over Allora's chest, keeping it in place as she tucked the fabric in beneath her arms.

"They would not grant me entry to your shelter to deliver the happy news," Kenrick said. "I apologize for your prolonged worry, Your Majesty. I beg you to believe I fought to obey your command, but they would not unlock the door until after the head scribe had left the palace."

"Adrial was here?" Allora said. "You saw him?"

"Only a brief glimpse." Kenrick eased away, finally glancing down, making sure Allora had covered herself before stepping aside and slipping into his rigid guard's stance. "He was on his feet, tired definitely, but I only noted one bruise from his capture."

"Capture?" Allora gripped Kenrick's sleeve. Blood crusted the cuff.

"Her Majesty is to be escorted to her rooms," the guard who'd caused her exposure said.

"A moment." Kenrick dipped his chin, snapping the words at his fellow. "I would have told her sooner if you hadn't laid me out flat and kept me pinned away from the door. As you have only now allowed me to reach her, I will take the time to deliver the report your Queen commanded."

Red-faced, the other guard backed a step away.

"Thank you," Allora said.

"The head scribe's carriage was attacked last night." Kenrick took Allora's forearm as she swayed. "The villains tried to kidnap the head scribe. He escaped and returned safely to the library."

"That's why they locked me in that room?" Allora said. "Someone tried to capture Adrial?"

Panic punched through Allora's chest as Kenrick hesitated.

"More than that, Your Majesty," Kenrick said. "I don't understand the extent of what's happened well enough to offer information."

"Then you are wise to remain silent." Gillien took Allora's other arm, holding on as though supporting an invalid. "The Queen's jewels and gown are in her haven. See they are returned to their proper places."

"Yes, Sorcerer." Kenrick bowed, then eased his arm away from Allora's grip, moving slowly as though she were a cracked glaze of ice over a puddle, ready to shatter from the smallest weight.

He's right. If I'd lost Adrial—

"Where is my wife!" Brannon's voice echoed down the hall.

Allora opened her mouth, ready to call *I'm here*, but she couldn't make her lips form the simple words. Freeing herself from Gillien's support, Allora lifted the bottom of the blanket and strode toward the door.

"Where is the Queen?" The anger in Brannon's voice deepened.

"She is here, Your Majesty," Gillien called. "She is well."

Allora leapt back, barely avoiding a blow to the face as the parlor door flung open.

Brannon loomed in the doorway. His hair out of place, sweat on his brow, and rage filling his teal eyes, filling all of him, making him tower larger than any man should as he shifted his glare to each corner of the room, as though searching for demons, before finally looking to Allora.

"You will not make me your monster." Brannon snatched Allora's wrist, yanking her from the room.

Without the parlor's carpet, the cold of the marble floor stabbed pain into her feet, shocking her fear into a sharper focus than her sleepless mind had managed.

"Brannon." She jerked back, trying to free herself, but Brannon kept walking, still dragging her behind him as though he hadn't felt a thing. "Brannon, let go."

"You will not paint me as the monster sent to destroy Ilbrea. That will not be the legacy my children inherit."

"Brannon, you're scaring me."

"Why am I the one you should fear?" Brannon stopped, rounding on her, lifting the wrist he held as though begging her to dare and slap him.

Allora didn't hide the tears that slipped down her cheeks. "Because you're hurting me."

"Come." He loosened his grip and headed toward the stairs, now keeping Allora right beside him. "You love the Guilds, you love your family, you love Ilbrea."

"As I should."

"Your precious Guilds don't understand that ruling a country isn't about keeping the people happy."

"*Our* precious Guilds. Ilbrea is built upon—"

"The strength of the Willoc family."

Allora lifted the front of her blanket, keeping it away from her feet as Brannon ran down the steps to the palace entry.

"When it all burns, you will not blame me. A horse, now!" Brannon shouted the command, to whom, Allora couldn't tell.

"Brannon, why do you need a horse?" Allora slowed her steps, leaning her weight back as they neared the palace doors. "Where are you going?"

At a wave of Brannon's hand, two men opened the doors.

"Brannon, I'm not dressed. I can't go outside." Allora yanked her wrist, stumbling as Brannon let go.

He scooped her into his arms before she could flee.

Pinning her to his chest, he strode out of the palace into the frigid mist. "It is a king's duty to ensure there is a country left for his heirs to rule."

"Please put me down, Brannon." Allora braced her hand against his shoulder. "We'll go inside. You can tell me what's happened."

"The Guilds have broken from the crown. They betrayed our covenant."

"What?" Allora clung to the front of Brannon's jacket, anchoring herself to the only thing she could as the world began to tip.

A groom ran toward them, leading a pure white horse.

"All of them. Five mewling children turning against the very power that promises survival."

Brannon tossed her up onto the horse.

She yelped as she tipped back, slipping to the horse's other side.

Ignoring the feel of her blanket falling loose, she grabbed the front of the saddle, saving herself from crashing headfirst to the ground.

Brannon climbed onto the saddle behind her, his boot tearing her blanket away as he grabbed her elbow to yank her upright. He wrapped an arm around her waist, locking her against him as he kicked the horse, charging the poor creature to the palace gates.

Allora huddled close to him, hiding the near bareness of her chest as the wind stung her skin.

"They wrote their fate." Something like pain twisted Brannon's face. "They abandoned their oath to Ilbrea. They turned away from their King."

"Brannon." Allora touched his cheek. "Please. I'm afraid and confu—"

"Open the gate," Brannon shouted to the guards on top of the palace wall.

A guard echoed the order to a fellow.

The two sorcerers on top of the wall only watched the King approach.

"Whatever hatred you have for me, do not take me into the city," Allora said. "I've already been humiliated in our home. Don't parade me through the streets."

The King rode through the gate before it had fully opened. He yanked on the reins.

The horse snorted, stomping to a stop just before the bridge that led out to the city.

"You will not name me your monster. Not for this." Brannon reached up.

Allora's heart froze as the King of Ilbrea slashed his hand down.

Silent.

As though Dudia had bid the world to pause and watch all men be damned.

The stones of the bridge made no noise as they fell away. Not even to splash as they hit the water far below.

In two breaths, the entire bridge had crumbled, leaving a chasm between the palace and the people of Ilara.

A commoner on the far side screamed. Another joined. And another.

Shouts of panic and rage shook Allora's lungs as Ilarans greeted their abandonment.

"They forced us all onto this bloody path. I will not carry the weight of their doom." Brannon turned the horse back toward the palace.

Kenrick waited just outside the gate, riding a horse still wearing a carriage harness. He held his coat in his hand, leaving his sweat-dampened shirt clinging to his chest as he stared at the empty place where the bridge had been.

"Your Majesty." Kenrick dipped his chin, holding his coat out to Allora as Brannon passed. His fingers caught hers in the exchange.

He looked up, meeting his Queen's gaze, offering her the only comfort he could as the King of Ilbrea ordered the palace gates locked.

22

KAI

The candles placed down the center of the table might have been a step too far, but as Kai re-strewn the flower petals between the lights for a fourth time, he wished he'd brought more trappings to the rendezvous.

"You're absurd," Merial said.

"You're humorless," Kai said.

He settled back into his seat between Merial and Drew and laced his fingers together, resting his hands on the table in his best impression of a merchant preparing for an important transaction.

The dim glow of the lantern in the stables below cast enough light for Kai to properly see the sole entrance to the meeting place he'd chosen.

The door didn't open.

Kai squeezed his hands together, banishing a touch of the heat that surged through his limbs begging him to run or fight or do anything but sit patiently and wait.

The candlelight glinted off the frie glasses on the other side of the table. A fingerprint marred the center glass.

Beginning to stand, Kai reached across the table.

Drew took Kai's elbow, keeping him seated, and let out a too-long-to-be-natural breath.

Kai mimicked the exhale.

His heart punched at his lungs with every beat, reminding him in no uncertain terms that the fate of Ilbrea could be forever altered at that very petal-strewn table.

Kai slipped his elbow from Drew's hold. Careful to avoid the rawest of the sorcerer-inflicted burns, Kai brushed a whisper of a kiss on the back of Drew's hand and stood, snatching the offending glass and polishing it on his sleeve.

"The part of my youth where conversations didn't involve more fists than words was spent in a palace." Kai held the glass to the candle, twisting it back and forth to catch different angles of the light. "Important things happen in important places. And yes, this stable reeks of fermenting horse shit, but that doesn't stop Allora Karron's voice from chattering in my head, promising the perfect setting can make mountains move."

"If you were going to fret over hosting the perfect *do we have a chivving chance or have the gods doomed us* party, I'd have preferred a venue that allowed a few dozen men protecting our backs," Merial said.

"I'd rather look a fool than shout wisdom and be tested," Kai said.

"There is no *look*," Merial said. "You *are* a sodding fool."

"Isla wouldn't charge in and attack us." Kai sat, digging his heels into the aged floor of the hayloft to keep his legs from bouncing.

"If she wanted us dead, she'd never enter the building," Drew said. "I doubt we'd even know what had happened when Death arrived."

"It depends on the situation."

Fear dropped Kai's gut as Isla's voice came from the shadows in the corner nearest the stable door.

"Do I want you all dead or only one?" Isla said. "Do I care if people know it was me? Do I want you to suffer?"

"Did you want the Lady Healer to suffer?" Kai stood, leaning across the table to gain a better view of the floor below.

Pure black lurked in the back of the shadow where Isla hid, the darkness too complete for him to spot a hint of her form.

"I assume it was you. Or hope, rather," Kai said. "If there's a second sorcerer of your ilk in Ilara, I'd very much like to meet them. Use my charms to convince them not to carve me up before impaling me in front of an enthralled crowd."

"Careful, paun." A man stepped out of the shadows where Kai had been sure Isla hid. "For the well-trained, it only takes a flicker of magic to end a life."

"How fortunate you're not well-trained," Merial said.

"How fortunate I don't care enough to want you dead," the man said.

"Cillian." Isla stepped out of the same shadow, her gaze fixed on the man.

The man lifted his eyebrows, pursing his lips as though asking why he wasn't allowed to play with his meal, before stepping back into the shadow.

"Wait!" Kai grabbed the bottle of frie from the center of the table. "All faces in the open and we'll toast to the soul who ends the sorcerers' tyranny."

Isla narrowed her eyes at Kai, then turned her glare on Drew.

"I hope you've enough faith in our sanity to believe we'd never attack you," Drew said. "It's a drink with three saelk, Isla. You're in no danger. Just give Kai his way or we'll never get on with it."

"It's the best frie I could find." Kai held the bottle over a candle, letting the flickering light glint through the amber liquid. "That's not promising much these days. But it is a far sight better than the watered-down piss half the taverns in Ilara serve."

"A toast to the fall of the Lady Sorcerer." Isla nodded to the shadow.

Cillian stepped out to stand behind her right shoulder. A woman appeared to stand behind her left.

"You actually brought two with you." Kai poured frie into all six glasses as Isla led her party up the ladder-like stairs against the stable wall. "I said you should bring two so it wouldn't seem unfair for me to have Drew and Merial with me, but somehow I didn't think you'd actually do it."

"You're rambling," Merial said.

"Better than screaming for answers," Kai muttered.

"I told you I'd give you all the information on the tower I have, and I'll keep my word." Isla pulled out the chair across the table from Kai. "And you'll wish you'd never made the bargain."

"Lovely." Merial downed her whole glass of frie.

Isla waited until her companions flanked her to sit.

The woman took her glass of frie right away, sniffing it, then taking a sip. Cillian watched the woman take a second sip before touching his own glass.

Kai pushed Isla's drink toward her.

"What do you want to know?" Isla didn't acknowledge the frie.

"How to get into the Sorcerers Tower. How to fight the sorcerers. How to destroy the tower," Kai said.

"I think you grabbed the soggy end of this deal, Isla," Cillian said. "The paun asks a lot after doing such a small favor."

"Betraying my friend—"

"Had to be done." Isla spoke over Kai.

Cold shocked through his hand everywhere his skin touched his glass, though the glass itself didn't appear to have frozen. He tried to let go, but his fingers wouldn't move.

He met Isla's gaze.

Her glare softened. "I needed your help and I'm grateful you gave it. All of us are."

"That's not a promising tone," Merial said.

The cold faded from Kai's hand, leaving his fingers numb.

"There is no way to breach the Sorcerers Tower," Isla said. "Not by stealth or strength."

"But if you got out, there's a way back in," Kai said.

"That's not how the tower works," Isla said. "Out isn't the same as in, and even if the gods broke a crack in the tower wide enough for the whole underground to storm through, it wouldn't do you any good. If the tower doesn't want you roaming through her halls, she'll trap you in the black and leave you to starve."

"You're talking about a massive stone rod as though it were a living thing," Merial said.

"The tower might as well be," Isla said. "There is a heart of magic that protects her. No saelk weapon can penetrate that stone, and even if I had every free sorcerer standing beside me, I can't promise we'd so much as scratch her shine."

Kai downed all the frie in his glass, letting the liquid burn away his need to scream.

"Outside the tower, your doom's less certain," Isla said.

"I'll accept any improvement." Kai poured himself another glass of frie.

"Saelk can fight sorcerers with the gods and knowledge on their side. It takes power for a sorcerer to truly shield themselves. Keep it up for too long and you'll burn out," Isla said. "When a sorcerer's gone that far, they're lucky to lift a blade, let alone manage battleworthy magic.

"But don't even dream of facing the sorcerers in the sort of battle the paun prefer. If you place your fighters in nice little lines while the sorcerers are fresh, none of your people will survive the first hour."

"Your advice?" Drew said.

"Fetch a fresh bottle of frie and find a rooftop with a nice view of the Sorcerers Tower," the woman said. "Take bets on how quickly the sorcerers will pick the saelk off once they've grown tired of the mob of guards and soldiers surrounding their home."

"An ambush would be the simplest answer," Cillian said

without glancing the woman's way. "Waves of attacks coming from every direction forcing the sorcerers to shield themselves on all sides. Luring them into a pit of fiery blades is also appealing. The only problem is their impenetrable tower."

"Anything can be broken into." Merial fixed her glare on Cillian. "Those who think otherwise lack imagination."

"I wish I had secrets to give you, Kai," Isla said. "I lived in that tower, and I've spent years going through it in my mind, trying to find a way to break in or get more people out, but there's nothing."

"No." Kai slammed his glass against the table, cracking the bottom. "The sorcerers do not get to hide in their tower, looming over Ilara as they wait to spill our blood."

"Their hiding could be for the best," Isla said. "The supplies, the tradesmen who've disappeared, if the Lady Sorcerer did take them, she did it for a reason."

"To torture innocents," Kai said.

"To prepare her stores," Isla said. "To isolate the sorcerers from Ilara and keep them living happily in the tower while they ignore the rest of the world. We want them to ignore us. If the sorcerers abandon Ilara—"

"It gives you freedom to target the other Guilds," Kai said.

The woman gave a low laugh.

"Removing the sorcerers from the fight saves lives," Isla said.

"Until they swarm out of the tower to slaughter us all." Kai refilled his glass.

"The palace bridge has fallen. The King has cut himself off from Ilara," Isla said. "The sorcerers have stopped stealing people, and the sailors have been celebrating freeing their docks from the sorcerers' grip since last night. Let this be its own victory."

"Victory is finding out what happened to the three chivving ships the sorcerers stole last week," Kai said. "Victory is finding those sailors and punishing the sorcerers behind any pain they suffered. Victory is making sure the sorcerers can never harm Ilbrea again."

"Then your odds of victory are nil," the woman said.

"I helped you kidnap Adrial," Kai said. "We put him in danger."

"Did he suffer so badly?" Isla held Kai's gaze, true questioning in her eyes.

You tossed him off the edge of madness.

Didn't you watch him shatter?

Kai dug his fists into his hips, clenching his teeth, measuring his breath, everything he could to keep from screaming.

"This is a chivving waste of time." Drew rammed his fingers into his hair.

"Not if the underground takes our bargain," Isla said.

"What bargain?" Merial snatched the bottle of frie from Cillian's grip. "We made a bargain, and you pissed on it like a sodding slitch."

"I promised Kai information, and I gave it," Isla said. "Don't blame the strength of the Sorcerers Tower on me."

"Serpent," Merial said.

"Watch it." The flame of the candle in front of Cillian flared six-inches high.

"I offer a meeting with someone far more dangerous to the paun than me," Isla said.

"I don't believe such a beast exists," Merial said.

Cillian's flame crackled. "Doubt us and see how long you survive."

"You need to do this." Isla ignored the sparks singeing the table, keeping her gaze locked with Kai's. "But it can't be just you three. Bring the leader of your underground here tomorrow night."

"What?" Drew coughed a laugh.

Merial's chair scraped against the floor as she stood. "The healers are trying to declare war against the sorcerers and I'm listening to this? Once you've realized that the chaos you've rained upon the city will drench you in gore, too, don't beg the underground for a washbasin."

"We survived the southern mountains together." Isla leaned closer to Kai. The candlelight flickered in her eyes, painting her as a fire-born demon even as unnatural cold flooded Kai's hands. "You saved my life, and I saved yours. You've trusted me before, Kai. Do it again now."

"It can't be done," Merial said.

"A meeting with your leader, that's all," Isla said. "Accept the offer."

"That sounds like a threat," Drew said.

"Handsome has sense," the woman said.

Cillian turned, distinctly facing only Drew. "There is no question of *if* the meeting will happen, only how cordial it will be. Come back tomorrow night. Bring your leader if you can. Pray for mercy if you can't."

"Find a way." Isla stood, nodding the others toward the stairs.

"Even if I wanted to, it's not possible." Kai swallowed his gasp as stinging cold throbbed up his arms.

"You won't be given another chance to meet her," Isla said. "You can't afford the kind of regret failure will bring."

23

THAM

Decaying leaves tumbled from their branches as Asher plowed her way back onto Mara's chosen path.

The girl held up a thorned twig. "This one?"

"Winter-dead blackberry bush?" Mara said. "Telling the difference between plants is much easier with leaves."

"Or it can't be done and you're a sodding liar." Asher dove back into the thickest patch of nearby dormant plants.

"She's not," Sailor Buckley laughed, still holding on to his humor as he carried Ian up a fourth slope. "The window box my wife grows cooking herbs in holds a dozen kinds of plants. All different and all delicious…usually."

Buckley bounced Ian, earning a laugh from the child.

"There are more edible plants in the world than you'd ever have time to find," Sailor Seward called after Asher. "Stop sprinting away, girl."

"She won't listen," Blinkers said.

Seward muttered something too quiet for Tham to hear.

"Paun." Brady rammed Seward in the ribs with the latest stick she'd taken to carrying. "If you're too afraid say it loud, best not let the gods hear you whisper it."

"I was begging Dudia for the strength to not crack and tie you little monsters to a tree," Seward said. "Abandon you to the wild beasts and shed an irritating burden before facing Ilara."

"No one's being tied to a tree." Mara reached back, offering Blinkers her hand before the boy even began to cry. "The length of the journey is already behind us."

"That walking for days has made some people surly is not nearly a dire enough offense to warrant abandoning children to be eaten alive." Elver tutted at Seward.

Blinkers's shoulders shook as he coughed on his tears.

Asher burst back onto the path. "And this one?" Asher kept pace beside Mara, holding a twig in front of Mara's face.

"A rotting chivving stick," Brady said. "Just walk, will you?"

Asher slowed, drifting back behind Mara, then Brady, then Buckley, to take the spot beside Elle just in front of Tham.

Elle bashed her head against Asher in welcome.

The front of their line kept the same order—with the rest of the children clustered behind Tham, and the sailors making up the back of their party—until they reached a half-frozen creek. Then the children took turns throwing stones, trying to hit the moving water as Mara led them north, getting lessons from the few sailors not determinedly ignoring the children.

Finding a safe place to cross the creek took an hour.

The Ice Walkers could have done it in a minute. A hint of magic from Ronya, and they'd have a path strong enough for an army to surge across the water.

A storm of flames to melt the ice. A way to contain Ronya's power.

Two things beyond reach of the Soldiers Guild.

Hot tar over the city walls.

Not boiling water, that would only feed Ronya more weapons.

Prepare the woods north of Ilara to easily ignite.

They traveled in silence as they neared the mountain road.

Even Asher followed Mara's path, forgoing scrambling through a wide thicket, obediently slowing as a rumble of voices came from the east.

Tham cut past Asher, making his way to Mara.

"That's not the gate," Tham whispered.

Mara shook her head. "We're at least two miles too far south, probably closer to three."

The voices gained distinction. Mostly male. All angry. None screaming in pain.

"We can cut west," Tham said. "Cross the road farther north."

The corners of Mara's eyes wrinkled as she frowned. "Chances of us convincing Brady to stay behind if you and I go see why people are gathered on the road?"

"I'll go and you keep Brady behind," Tham said.

A sharp jab struck the back of Tham's ribs.

"Sheep's shit I'm being left behind," Brady said.

Mara stopped, not managing to free herself from Blinkers's grasp as she rounded on Brady. "Yes, you are." She spoke through clenched teeth.

Blinkers let go of Mara to slide behind Tham, clinging to the back of Tham's coat.

"You agreed to travel by our rules," Mara said. "That means staying where you're told when we're trying to figure out why people are gathering on the mountain road."

"I'm not Elle. I won't sit and stay," Brady said.

"Brady." Blinkers gave a warning whisper.

"I'm trying to protect you, Brady," Mara said. "That's how it's supposed to work. You're a child. You stay safely behind while the grownups do the dangerous things."

"Usually preferable," Elver whispered behind Tham's shoulder.

"Five minutes," Mara said. "Stay with the others. Tham and I will be right back."

"I'm coming as well." Seward passed the remains of his supply bundle to another sailor. "There's nothing to be heard that applies more to you than us."

"I could make several arguments against that," Elver said.

"It's fine," Mara said. "Let's just go and be quick about it."

"Stay with Elver." Tham scratched Elle's head.

"Yes, stay," Elver said. "Brady, you could watch Elle to try and learn how to properly stay."

"You braidic, corpse of a—"

Tham followed Mara, slipping away while Brady quietly raged at Elver.

Ahead, the ground dropped away at a steep slant that stretched down to a line of crooked trees whose roots had been exposed by the eroding slope. The trees' bare branches offered a clear view of the mountain road just beyond.

Tham took two quick steps, dodging behind the tree closest to Mara's chosen shelter as a rider passed, heading south on the road.

Mara looked to Tham, mouthing *north?*

Tham nodded.

He pulled the sailors' blade from the sheath at his hip, focusing on the cold of the knife's hilt rather than all the ways a better weapon could change their fate in a fight.

Traps for Ronya's wolves. Possible to build. Harder to bait.

Ballistae for the giant birds if a perfect shot could be made.

A glint of silver caught Tham's eye as a cluster of travelers came into view.

Six soldiers blocked the road, facing two carts and a group of seven men.

"—to fulfill his bidding." One of the cartless men knelt before the soldiers. "His orders, I mean."

"Turn around, you fool," a soldier said.

"I've a cart of food," a woman said.

"We've told you all the gates are closed," a different soldier said. "Closed to food. Closed to fools. Now sod off before our good will's spent."

"But we've come to join the King's Army." A second cartless man knelt in the mud beside the first.

"Do you live in Ilara?" the first soldier asked.

"No, but we—" the first cartless man said.

"Then the King's order doesn't even chivving apply to you," the second soldier said.

"We're loyal men ready to fight for our King!" the first man shouted.

"Do you even know who the King is fighting, you slitch?" The first soldier loomed over the man.

"It doesn't matter." He tucked his chin, bowing before the soldiers, exposing the back of his neck as though begging for a swift slice from a sword. "I've come to be marked as loyal to the King. I fight for King Brannon."

The soldier stepped forward and kicked at the same time, catching the bowed man in the teeth, pitching him backward into the mud.

24

KAI

Ena.

Surely, that was Isla's ominous *she*. If the gods had finally handed Kai a bit of fortune.

A chance to meet Adrial's wife. A chance to ask her what in all the chivving, madness-wrought hells had happened to his family while he'd been gone.

Dead, Tham whispered. *To us. You're dead.*

Kai kicked the stable wall, sending pain shooting up his toe as the wood gave a cracking thump. He clung to the pain, twisting his fear into anger and piling it all on his throbbing toe.

"Sit, Kai," Drew said.

"He's not capable of it," Merial said.

Kai paced a lap along the lip of the hayloft.

Drew poured frie into the metal cup he'd brought to replace the one Kai had cracked.

And if Isla wouldn't let Kai speak to Ena because he hadn't brought Lord—

Kai didn't even want the name in his head.

"We didn't have to come here." Merial kept writing in her notebook as she spoke. "We could have stayed well away from the demon's impending fury when she realizes we didn't bring the person she demanded to see."

"If she demands the impossible, she'll have to settle for as well as I can chivving do." Kai shook out his hands in a pathetic attempt to fling the anxious energy from his limbs.

"None of us are leaving this loft alive," Merial said.

"Of course we are," Kai said. "Isla may be a terrifying sorcerer, but she's also a friend."

Merial gave a grunted tsk.

"Drew?" Kai prompted.

"He's right," Drew said. "She's not the type to slit throats for fun."

"Are you?" A man with daggers on his hips stepped out from below the balcony.

"Not for fun," Merial said.

"You're not going to attack?" The man narrowed his eyes at Kai. "Pity."

"How long did you lurk in the shadows waiting for the perfect entrance?" Kai asked.

The man smiled. "You look like birds huddled on a perch, hoping a cat won't notice you. Do you think she can't reach you?"

"A cat from your view is a mouse chittering in a cellar from mine," Kai said. "Where's Isla?"

"She'll not be coming," the man said. "Then your leader didn't come either, did he?"

"He sent a nice note in his stead." Kai pulled the letter from his pocket.

"Too afraid or too arrogant?" the man said.

"Too wise," Merial said.

"Pity he wasn't wise enough to show up," the man said.

"Isla gave us shit for information on the Sorcerers Tower," Kai said. "She owes us, and she knows it. Tell her the note is the best I can do, and let our meeting begin."

"I'm your gatekeeper, and debts Isla owes mean shit to me."

The man rested his hands on the hilts of the daggers at his hips. "Rules will be followed. You'll leave your weapons here. If I find so much as a sharp stone in your pocket, I'll use it to end your life. Inventively. If a whisper of her filters into your underground—"

Kai's heart pummeled his throat.

"—I'll take it as an invitation to come into your tunnels and slit as many throats as I chivving well please," the man said.

Drew stood, his hand drifting toward his own dagger.

"You're going to come down those stairs and follow me," the man continued. "You'll follow silently, for as long as I chivving well please. If you speak, I'll silence you. If you fall behind—

"You'll leave us?" Kai said.

"I'll leave you to the ones you can't see." The man gave what could have been a smile, if a beast intent on tearing through one's throat chose to smile in the moment before ending one's tormented life. "I was chosen as your guide because of my charm. The ones watching"—he shrugged—"not fond of polite conversation. I don't fancy your chances with them."

"Some of the greatest nights of my life have begun with far worse warnings." Kai tuned to Drew, meeting his gaze, trying to convey *yes, it sounds threatening and yes, I'd enjoy punching the slitch as well, but I've been keeping something from you, and I'd very much like you to just go along with me on this one, and I promise I'll explain everything and find a way to earn your forgiveness* with only a widening of his eyes, before bending into a sweeping bow. "Long ago nights of my wandering days, of course." He kissed the back of Drew's hand. "I'd rather sleep with you in a bed of pig shit than revel in a palace without you by my side."

"May the gods soothe my temper." Merial pushed her line of daggers across the table. "And give me strong enough bowels to stomach the pair of you."

"I didn't think I'd have to warn you not to linger." The man frowned.

"Apologies." Kai pulled his knife from his belt. "Assuming you don't end up murdering us, would one of your shadows mind bringing the weapons along? If you're going to march us endlessly through the streets, I'd rather not have to walk all the way back to collect our blades."

"Kai," Drew hushed.

The man's frown flipped back into that predator's grin.

"I'm glad you find me amusing." Kai pulled the blade from the ankle of his boot and set both his weapons onto the table.

"Like watching a bone-assed slitch fall on ice." The man turned, walking toward the stable door without waiting for them to follow.

Drew reached the stairs first, hurrying down and running to catch up to the slitch with Kai on his heels. Drew held out an arm as they reached the door, blocking Kai's path, firmly inserting himself as a barrier between Kai and the man.

Drew stayed in the doorway, looking over his shoulder, not moving until Kai whispered, "Fine. If you must."

The man's path aimed straight south, giving Kai, Drew, and a glowering Merial ample time to catch up before he cut through an alley heading west.

Clouds stretched from the Arion Sea, shrouding all but a few faint stars to the east. Almost every home had their windows covered, and even the shops that had dared light the lamps by their doors had long since closed for the night, leaving the streets as dark as they'd been in months.

The shouts of anger and panic that had terrorized Winter's End didn't shatter the night. Only the footsteps and murmured speech of passing Ilarans filled the quiet.

Most traveled in little clusters, as though clinging to the naïve notion that safety in numbers might apply if faced with a murderous sorcerer.

A trio of men. None wore uniforms. All carried swords.

Sorcerers aren't the only monsters for the soldiers to fight, Tham whispered.

May the gods keep those blades from innocent throats.

Kai rubbed his empty hand against the empty sheath on his hip.

A rock, a boot, a bottle—chivving useless, bladeless slitch.

He eyed every shadow they passed, searching for a weapon to grab or a person waiting to attack or whatever other hell this farce of a quest for answers slung them toward.

An instinctive lightening eased Kai's worry as they moved closer to the docks. He studied the buildings they passed, making sure familiar paths hadn't been destroyed, searching for places easy enough to climb even Merial could scamper up to a roof.

The man cut south again, then west, then south, not as though weaving their path to avoid being followed—he hadn't even bothered keeping to the shadows as he strode through the night—more akin to a man who knew what streets smelled worst and had found the least rancid route home.

A group of young women flanked by two armed men rounded the corner, heading north.

Kai slowed his steps as the women neared, letting short-legged Merial pass him as he listened to the women's whispers.

One of them began to giggle. The woman nearest her smacked her on the arm. The giggler smacked back. Two of the others swallowed their laughter.

Kai picked up his pace, cutting around Merial to reach Drew.

Drew held out a hand, stopping Kai from walking beside him.

Kai grabbed Drew's fingers, giving them a quick squeeze before obediently dropping behind him.

Even through the layers of his coat, the tension in Drew's shoulders crisped his silhouette. His gait had an unfamiliar stiffness as well, as though with every step his whole body prepared for attack.

May the fool who springs that trap have settled their accounts and prepared to meet Death.

But if they weren't attacked.

If the tension trapped in Drew's body wasn't wrung away in a bloody fight…

Focus, Kai.

Footsteps approached from the east.

Drew turned toward the sound, his stance steady, his hands raised and ready to defend.

All the gods couldn't save you from the wonder of that man.

Get your chivving mind together, Kai.

Four women crossed their path, heading east. One holding a lantern, the other three, club-like sticks.

One of the women turned, guided by another while she walked backward, watching Kai and Drew until their party moved out of sight.

The man turned west again, then stopped at the stone building on the far corner.

Built in three stories and wide enough to fit two modest merchant homes, the house offered rooms for rent.

Candles flickered in three of the front windows, but no rumble of conversation floated out to the street.

The man leapt up the house's two front steps and leaned against the doorframe, his arms crossed over his chest as though he hadn't a care in the world.

Drew stopped ten feet away from the stairs, angling his body to keep Kai behind him.

But he makes it so chivving hard not to think about him.

Kai tucked away the radiating spark in his chest that shot heat to his face, preserving the wonderment to be studied at a safer time, as the man nodded for them to come closer.

"As skilled as I may be at drawing blood, I'm not overly fond of it," the man said. "Save us all some trouble and don't become my enemy. My blades are freshly cleaned. I'd rather not have to dirty them a second time today."

"A request I'm most happy to oblige," Kai said.

The man flattened his lips and shook his head, as though declaring Kai would probably fail, as he reached back and knocked on the door.

The scrape of metal on wood came from inside.

The man stepped out of their way as the door swung open.

A woman, better armed than the man, kept one hand on the door as she studied Drew, then Merial, then Kai.

"Kai." She shifted her gaze to Drew. "Drew." A smirk lifted her lips as she finally looked back to Merial. "And the angry little one who's always writing in her little book."

Kai tried to hide his laugh a moment too late.

"Is that what your redheaded sorcerer calls me?" Merial shoved past Drew. "Tell the demon to add *vengeful* and *resourceful* to the title."

"Could you write that down for me? Just tear a page from your tiny book." The woman stepped aside, bowing them into the corridor.

Candles had been lit in the two sconces just inside the door, but the warm light coming from the room at the far end of the hall rendered the pathetic flames unnecessary.

The woman allowed Merial, Kai, and Drew to enter then bolted the door, shutting the man out on the street.

Kai peered up the staircase as the woman led them toward the brightened room, searching for whatever guards hid in the shadows making the man who'd been locked outside unnecessary to their host's protection.

Or to prevent her escape.

If she lied to him. If Ena is a Brien prisoner—

The heart-tearing memory of the pain and panic on Adrial's face as Ena left him in the stable drove the last hints of distraction from Kai's mind.

Then you rescue her and be done with it.

A crackling fire greeted them, the scent of its smoke complementing the aroma of roasted meat and freshly baked bread that filled the kitchen. Four lanterns hung from the ceiling, casting their glow on the feast-laden table.

Candelabras flanked the cakes, cheese, soup, and frie—a glorious bottle of fine frie the likes of which Kai hadn't been near since his world had shattered—arranged in the center of the table. Three settings with ceramic plates, real cutlery, and crystal glasses waited for the slitches from the underground who'd been collected from a foul-smelling stable.

Kai's stomach gave a resonant growl as he tore his gaze from the feast to focus on the woman sitting across the table.

The inviting air of the kitchen had not extended to *her*.

Ena, Adrial's Ena, stayed silent as she studied each member of their party, her black hair cascading around her shoulders, framing a face the gods seemed to have carved in a bid for perfection, her bright blue eyes betraying neither welcome, nor fear, nor anger.

The need to speak had begun to itch Kai's tongue before Ena finally nodded to the woman. "Thank you, Alane."

The woman, Alane apparently, raised her eyebrows at Ena.

Ena tipped her head.

Alane lingered for a moment before stepping out of the kitchen and closing the door behind her.

Three unnaturally long heartbeats passed.

Kai willed his body to relax as he stepped forward and bowed. "Ena Ayres, we meet at last."

25

KAI

A murmur of "What?" and the sound of a muffled smack came from behind Kai.

"Kai Saso," Ena said, "they were right to keep searching for your ship."

Kai ignored the flare of pain in his chest. "The ship is gone. Drew and I are the only two left."

"I'm sorry." Ena looked to Drew. "Walking with that many ghosts behind you is a heavy burden."

The pain in Kai's chest slithered higher, climbing up to squeeze his throat.

"Thank you," Drew said.

Ena opened the bottle of frie, pouring into her own glass before the three across the table.

She set the bottle down, pressing her palms to the tabletop as she watched Kai.

Run. Run.

Grinning, Kai tossed the instinct aside and took the seat opposite Ena. "Always good to start with a drink. Pity these aren't better times. If we'd met in public, I could have made some excellent *three dead Ilbreans walk into a tavern* jokes."

Ena didn't so much as furrow her brow.

"Thank you." Kai lifted his glass of frie. "I wasn't expecting a feast."

"You prepared so well for Isla," Ena said. "It's only right I repay your hospitality."

"With rude chivving guards?" Merial thumped down into her seat.

Ena sipped her frie.

"It's a pleasure to meet you." Drew claimed the last chair.

"To tilk surviving in the Karrons' world." Ena tipped her glass toward Drew.

Kai downed his frie. "I know Adrial knows you're alive."

He gripped Drew's leg, sending a silent plea for forgiveness.

"Chivving madness," Merial muttered.

"And I'm thrilled to know it, too," Kai said. "Adrial is a good man, and the depth of his grief for you tore at my heart."

"But he has no idea you're alive, though you've been back in Ilara for months," Ena said, "living in holes beneath the street while he grieves for you."

"I hate it." Kai grabbed the bottle of frie. "I'm a ghost in my own city. But alive, I'm a danger to everyone around me. Dead, I can help the underground."

"How have you helped?" Ena asked.

"By working to pro—"

"No," Ena cut across. "What have you actually done? Caught a handful of sorcerers on fire? Bravely flung a few arrows their direction? Is throwing pebbles at a giant worth hiding underground?"

"Sorcerers are beasts," Merial said.

"The Sorcerers Guild will drown in the blood it's shed." Ena leaned back in her seat. "Your hiding in tunnels does nothing to speed that end."

"We're standing against sorcerers. It can't be done quickly. Not if we want to be alive to greet the next battle. We spend every day fighting the beasts." Kai loosened his hold on his glass. "Or at the very least searching for a way to chivving well fight them."

"Yet they've only now retreated from your precious docks," Ena said. "The sorcerers have gone into hiding, the King is cowering in their skirts, and the rest of the Guilds are ready to tear the sorcerers apart and the King too for siding with the demons."

"The sorcerers fleeing the docks has been a great relief. But the"—Kai swallowed the word *Brien*—"but Isla attacking the healers' hall only drove the demons into their tower. The Sorcerers Guild is still a threat. They're not dead."

Ena refilled Kai's glass. "Is a tally of the dead the measure you cling to?"

"I can see how it might be difficult for three of the people in this room to understand, but in most circles, the dead tend to stay dead," Merial said. "Killing a sorcerer permanently removes them from the fight. All we have now is a hive of chivving furious sorcerers who could spring out to attack at any moment."

"And they'll be greeted by a thousand soldiers," Ena said. "Will that be enough dead for you to count?"

"The sorcerers will slaughter the soldiers," Kai said.

"And there will be fewer paun in Ilbrea," Ena said.

Run. Just chivving run.

Cold trailed down Kai's spine as his every nerve promised him the predator across the table had scented his blood.

"Have you seen the soldiers surrounding the tower? Or the guards from the five rogue Guilds piled in behind them?" Drew said. "The sorcerers will have to climb over corpses to reach their next victims."

"Paun aren't victims. They're oppressors," Ena said. "Murderers who thrive on the pain of the innocent. Ilbrea will be free of the Guilds."

"There is no Ilbrea without the Guilds," Kai said.

"Careful, paun," Ena said. "If the head scribe weren't fond of you, you'd have died before you crossed the threshold."

Kai set his glass gently on the table. "Not an end I'd considered. Murdered on the orders of Adrial's wife."

"No orders," Ena said. "I'd have done it myself."

Drew stiffened.

Ena kept her attention fixed on Kai. "The Guilds will fall. The more the sorcerers thin the ranks of the soldiers, the fewer paun the tilk will face in battle."

"Battle?" Merial said.

"After the paun have picked each other off," Ena said.

"You're mad," Kai said.

"Then my madness will burn Ilara." Ena leaned toward Kai.

He dug his fingers into the wood of the tabletop, refusing to flinch even as the tiniest ghost of a smile curved her lips. "Does Adrial know his wife craves Guilded blood?"

"He knows I'll not allow my daughter to live in fear of the Guilds," Ena said.

"And therefore condones the terror that's spread through Ilara? Just handed off the burial papers for the guards who died at the healers' hall to an apprentice? Adrial Ayres would never accept bloodshed as necessary."

"Lady Byrd's healers pinned me down to examine me. Held a blade at my stomach to keep me still while they judged the age of the child in my womb. Lady Byrd gleefully watched my husband whipped before condemning me to Ian Ayres. Now Lady Byrd is dead." Fury blazed in Ena's eyes. "The scribe forgave my poisoning the last Lady Healer at our wedding. His soul won't suffer for my part in ending Lady Byrd."

"Both? You killed the last two Lady Healers?" Merial reached across the table, pulling the platter of cheese toward her. "Let's drink frie with someone who's murdered *two* Guild Ladies. We'll ignore how our chances of being hanged have exploded just by glancing in her direction."

"Black Bloods don't favor hanging," Ena said.

"Black Bloods?" Merial's glare snapped to Kai.

"Yes." Drew spared Kai from speaking.

"Black Bloods. Of all the chivving, hell-carved pits to let chivving slitches drag you into." Merial claimed the bottle of frie. "The murdering redheaded demon is a Black Blood?"

"Ilbrean born," Drew said. "But yes."

"And you?" Merial pointed at Ena while topping off her frie. "Are you a Black Blood as well? Another rogue sorcerer? A chivving pixie?"

"Merial," Drew whispered.

"The gods have doomed Ilara, and I fought my way to the head of the line for torment," Merial said. "I should have kept to smuggling and tossed every bleeding-heart sympathy I've ever suffered into the chivving fire."

"Don't blame the gods for terrors dragged upon our heads by the savagery of men," Kai said.

"Paun only call it savagery when tilk fight back. My husband loves you, Kai. For his sake, my blade isn't pressed to your throat. Because he trusts you, I'm offering you a path that will not open again." She sat back in her chair, her shoulders relaxed, the fire in her eyes muted. "The underground will join the Black Bloods. You will fight under our command."

"There's not a chivv—" Kai began.

"The Sailors Guild will break with the other Guilds and join the Black Bloods," Ena said. "If not, the Ilbrean fleet will burn."

Kai leapt to his feet. "I will not listen to you threaten our ships."

"I would have told Lord Nevon myself," Ena said. "Pity he decided not to join us."

An echoing ring filled the space in Kai's mind where the words should have made sense.

"Though I suppose with all the trouble in the city, being the

Lord Sailor and the leader of the underground has got to be exhausting." Ena sipped her frie. "Poor chivving paun."

"You must be confused," Drew said. "Lord Nevon is a fine man and has no love for the sorcerers—"

"Don't. Sputtering wastes time and makes you look a fool. Lord Nevon has terrible taste in servants and locks." Ena pointed to the bottle in Merial's hand. "But excellent taste in frie. Next time I visit his study, I'll have to ask which distillers he prefers."

The echoing in Kai's mind reverberated down into his chest, making it harder to pull in air. "You went into his home?"

"Don't worry," Ena said, "his wife and children need never know I was there."

Merial's knuckles whitened as she gripped the bottle. "You've threatened the Ilbrean fleet and now you're threatening the Lord Sailor."

"I'm offering Lord Nevon the chance to survive while protecting the sailors he pretends to care for," Ena said.

"Do not insult the Lord Sailor," Drew said.

"He storms on about protecting his men but lets the sorcerers control the docks," Ena said. "Calling him a coward would be a compliment."

"You've no idea what we've been through to protect the Sailors Guild." Kai planted his hands on the table, leaning toward Ena.

"Protect the men, not the Guild," Ena said. "Attacking the docks is easy work for the Black Bloods. It's an open space with too few guards, and the Ilbrean fleet would be a joy to burn. But there are tilk working the docks and ships. Some think the common sailors traitors who deserve to burn with the paun."

"Common sailors aren't traitors," Kai said. "They serve Ilbrea. All sailors serve Ilbrea."

"By working the ships that carry women to Ian Ayres?" The fury in Ena's eyes flared again. "Every sailor who's made that voyage is a murderer, and the tilk are worse for tormenting their own people. But even collaborators have families. I won't allow tilk children to starve because we made them orphans."

"Hypocrite." Merial downed her glass. "If working for the paun makes you a collaborator, what does fucking the head scribe make you?"

"My scales are balanced, smuggler," Ena said. "Are yours?"

"Is this why Isla brought us here?" Kai said. "Not so I could meet Adrial's wife or gain some hope of fighting the sorcerers, just to be threatened?"

"Your hope of standing against the sorcerers begins and ends with the Black Bloods. Devotion to a seven-pointed star won't protect you from a blade or magic." Ena stood and tucked her chair back into the table. "The next time I visit Lord Nevon's home, he'll know I was there. Best you deliver him my offer tonight, and encourage him to choose wisdom."

"Sodding stars." Merial swigged her frie.

"We fight for freedom. Fight with us, or run." Ena strode out of the kitchen, leaving the three members of the underground in an abandoned house with an untouched feast and half a bottle of Lord Nevon's finest frie.

26

ADRIAL

Feathered lines swept up the right-hand side of the map, forming the shape of the eastern mountains.

The long line of the mountain road followed the range, never straying far from the massive forest that began in the foothills and stretched farther east than most Ilbreans would dare venture even with ghosts gnawing at their heels.

Harane.

A little dot marked the village, the writing beside it so small, the script itself seeming to imply it was a place better forgotten.

Adrial traced his finger north, reaching the marking for Nantic, then, further up, the walled city of Frason's Glenn drawn as a square nestled between two rivers.

North of the Frason's Glenn, a different road cut away from the mountains leading to Marten before stretching all the way west to the Arion Sea.

Lifting his finger from the parchment, Adrial skipped over a wide stretch of farms, meadows, and wilderness to reach the Lir Valley where a shaded patch promised a wide, sweeping detail in Ilbrea's landscape.

Adrial tapped his finger on the valley, moved it back to

Frason's Glenn and traced all the way down to Harane before leaning back in his chair, giving himself one moment to close his eyes and wallow in exhaustion and confusion.

"Are you all right, Head Scribe?" A gritty voice came from across the room.

Adrial opened his eyes, forcing himself back into the reality of the corner of the kitchen the Lord Scribe had declared Adrial's office.

An older man stood facing Adrial, kitchen knife in hand as he stared at the head scribe, seemingly unaware of Adrial's guards all gripping the swords on their hips.

"Fine, thank you," Adrial said. "Just rattling thoughts into order."

"Best you have more tea then," the man said.

"That would be much appreciated," Adrial said. "Thank you."

Adrial rolled the map back up and tucked it into the smallest of the three well-lined baskets currently serving as most of his desk. Selecting a scribe's journal from the second basket, Adrial consigned himself to once again digging through the records of the head scribes whose assigned territories included Harane, Marten, and the Lir Valley.

Vital research for Princess Illia's vellum. At least, vital to the newly conceived pages dedicated to the southern expansion of the Guilds and the joyful acceptance of their rule by those already living on that land.

Each of the journals had been written by the head scribe of their territory, detailing both the head scribe's work as well as the work of the scribes laboring beneath them.

Adrial turned back to his place in the journal of the head scribe nearest Marten.

While she had noted her complaint against the number of soldiers in the area, the entry was years old and only accused the men of excessive drink, poor sanitation, and annoyance.

All the other passages offered nothing of interest or intrigue worth whispering about, let alone worth the fear in Ena's eyes.

"Think, Adrial Ayres," he whispered.

He opened the records from Harane.

An increase in the sale of land. A harsh winter with a fever cutting through town.

"That's not how he takes his tea."

Adrial looked toward the central kitchen table.

Tege stood, chin up, hands balled into fists as she faced a servant four times her age.

"Go scrub something," the older woman said.

"The head scribe is particular about his tea, and you're doing it wrong." Tege glanced toward the stack of crates in the corner of the kitchen. "Thank you."

"What?" The older woman set the teapot down and turned fully toward Tege.

Tege looked to the crates again. "You're making it too sweet. So if he could…if I could just take the cup—"

"Why do you want the head scribe's cup?" One of Adrial's guards moved toward Tege, angling his hips to squeeze between two of the other scribes' desks that had been packed into the kitchen.

The guard's scabbard clipped one of the scribes' desks, which caught the scribe's elbow, jostling his hand just enough to drip ink from his pen onto the center of the parchment he'd been laboring over since his morning's work had begun.

The scribe's chin dropped to his chest.

"Move away from the table, girl," the guard said.

"Tege." Adrial pushed himself to his feet, letting the legs of his chair scraping against the stone floor emphasize his use of her name. "It's kind of you to worry about my tea, but I'm grateful for whatever I get."

"Of course, sir." Tege's leg began to bounce.

"Thank you for your protection." Adrial nodded to the guard. "Tege regularly delivers things from the kitchen to my office. Which is strangely more complicated with my office in the kitchen."

He gave the guard what he meant to be a good-natured smile, but what may instead have seemed more the grimace of one aware they are tumbling down a slope with nothing to cling to but a hope they'll find something soft at the bottom and a rueful gratitude they've yet to shatter any bones.

As the guard sidled back through the desks to rejoin his fellows, the scribe with the unspoiled parchment set her pen aside and steadied her inkwell, saving her work from the guard's scabbard's assault on her desk.

Tege backed away, heading toward the crates.

"Tege." Adrial waved her to his desk.

Wrinkles pinched between Tege's eyebrows, matching her shoulders creeping up toward her ears as she carefully weaved between desks to reach Adrial. "Yes, sir?" Her leg kept bouncing as she curtsied.

"Are you well, Tege?" Adrial sat back down, placing himself closer to eyelevel with the girl.

"Yes, sir."

"It's been a frightening time for us all," Adrial said.

"I'm fine, sir. Thank you, sir." Tege's neck tensed as though she were summoning every bit of will she had to not glance to the crates for a third time.

Adrial bit the inside of his cheek, banishing the first urge to laugh he'd felt in…far too long.

"Tege, I spent my formative years with three brothers by home who could cause more trouble in an hour than most could manage in a lifetime and two sisters who were somehow worse," Adrial said. "What's behind the crates?"

Her eyes went wide.

One of Adrial's guards stepped toward the crates, grasping the hilt of his sword.

The man with the gritty voice and kitchen knife stumbled back, knocking into the table, causing the older woman to shriek as she spilled Adrial's tea down her front.

The scribe who'd already had his work spoiled once jumped so high in his seat he knocked his inkwell over, letting loose a little stream of ink that spilled right onto his white robes.

The scribe's bellow of rage and despair snared the attention of everyone else in the kitchen just in time to watch the guard's sword clear its sheath, launching the staff and scribes into utter panic.

"Don't murder me!" The shout carried over the chaos as two of the crates fell, dumping potatoes onto the floor and revealing Taddy, his back pressed to the wall and his face stark white as he dropped the dark fabric he'd been clutching as though praying Dudia might have kept Adrial from noticing it.

"Enough," Adrial shouted the order.

All but the guard froze.

"Please don't kill my apprentice." Adrial sat back down.

The ink-spattered scribe stormed out of the kitchen.

"Should your apprentice be escorted out of the kitchen, Head Scribe?" the guard said.

"After I speak to him." Adrial waved Taddy over.

Taddy bit his lips, pulling them entirely into his mouth as he leaned back as though attempting to force his body through the wall.

"Now, Taddy," Adrial said.

Red crept up Taddy's cheeks as he slid out from behind the crates and picked his way around the strewn potatoes and livid scribes to reach Adrial's desk. He stopped, giving a jerky bow to the guards before facing Adrial. He paused for a moment, then inched over to plant himself just in front of Tege as though trying to block her from Adrial's view. "I'm sorry, sir."

"What for?" Adrial laced his fingers together, laying his hands on top of his desk.

"Pretending I'd gotten assigned away from Scribe Tammin so I could follow you down here, sir," Taddy said. "And pretending I worked in the kitchen so I could get past the guards."

"You did what?" the guard with the still-drawn sword said.

"But I'm your apprentice, sir," Taddy said. "It's my job to help you."

"Working with Scribe Tammin does help me, Taddy."

"Not enough, sir." Red devoured the rest of Taddy's face as tears glinted in his eyes. "You were kidnapped, sir. You could've been killed and I wasn't there to help you. I'm not making that mistake again."

Guilt sharpened the gratitude that pinched the front of Adrial's throat.

"You are a far better apprentice than I could ever deserve. But it is not your job to protect me. And"—Adrial pressed on as Taddy opened his mouth to speak—"even if it were, the library is guarded."

"Only, not really, at all, well, sir." Tege stepped forward to join Taddy.

"Don't," Taddy whispered.

"It's my fault, sir," Tege said.

"It's not." Taddy puffed up his chest. "I accept full blame."

"I've been using one of the old corridors to reach the stacks of ruined books in the library," Tege said. "I only touch the damaged ones that have already had copies made."

"The library doesn't even keep those books," Taddy said.

"And the path I've been using, sir, there aren't any guards on it," Tege said. "I could run an attack from the main library to the basement and not meet a single guard once I'd reached the damaged book stacks."

"What old corridors have you been using?" The guard still didn't lower his sword.

"If you cut past the laundry, there's that funny old door partway up the wall like there used to be steps there. It looks like a closet since there are hooks on the wall inside, but the wall's another old door and that leads to the back corner of that funny old office no one uses because it always smells of week-old meat, and a second door that goes to the closet of an office someone does use, but that door is blocked by shelves on the outside.

"If you go through the door to the rancid office, then you just have to cut around the corner to reach the shelves in the far back of the library where the ruined books are." Tege's hands trembled as she pushed the stray hairs away from her face. "I didn't think there was any harm in using the corridor, sir."

"We didn't," Taddy said. "Not until you were taken. I hadn't told anyone—"

"We." Tege dug her elbow into Taddy's side.

"And mentioning that we knew a secret path through the library but hadn't told anyone about it seemed like a foolish thing to do after you'd been taken," Taddy said.

"I was afraid of losing my position here, sir," Tege said.

"I realized you were in danger when they brought you down here to the Lord Scribe after you'd been kidnapped, sir. And we've been keeping guard whenever you're in the kitchen ever since," Taddy said. "Extra eyes to make sure no one slips through the corridor."

"Chivving children." Sword still drawn, the now boiling guard stormed across the kitchen, his empty scabbard knocking into three previously unscathed desks as he headed for the laundry.

"I'm sorry, sir." Tears spilled down Taddy's cheeks. "I hope you'll believe I'd never try to hide something that might endanger you."

"I'm the one who showed him the doors," Tege said. "If there's any punishment to be given, it's mine to take."

Adrial sat back in his chair, slightly furrowing his brow in his best impression of a disappointed Allora. "Taddy, an apprentice may not choose to abandon his post, even if the cause is rooted in good intention. This will be noted in your record, and extra duties will be assigned to make up for the time owed the Scribes Guild."

"Sir, I—" Taddy began.

"Tege, the books in the library, even those damaged beyond use, are only to be handled by those granted permission by the Scribes Guild," Adrial said.

"I know, sir." Tege's voice cracked as the shaking of her leg became a full body tremble.

"The ruined books are carefully catalogued to ensure every text has been copied before being released from the scribes' collection," Adrial said. "Moving a book to the wrong stack could cause an uncopied text to leave the library's care."

Taddy hiccupped on his tears.

"I'm so sorry, sir," Tege whispered.

"It will take more than an apology for the Lord Scribe to overlook your lapse in judgment," Adrial said. "Tege, you will report to the keeper of texts. You endangered the library's collection, it will now be your duty to aid in its maintenance and protection. The keeper has an eagle eye and talons to match. She will be giving regular reports on your training. Your first duty will be a thorough cleaning of each shelf in the ruined book section. I trust you'll not disappoint me again."

"No, sir." Tege swiped the tears from her cheeks as excitement blended with the fear still filling her eyes.

"Taddy," Adrial said, "you'll begin repaying your time to the Guild by checking the catalogue against the shelves of ruined books. This will be done on top of your normal duties."

Taddy didn't so much as blink.

"If either of you knows of another path that isn't guarded, or any other dangers to the library, tell Head Guard Friel at once," Adrial said.

"Yes, sir." Tege curtsied.

"You're dismissed." Adrial sat forward in his seat, dragging his mind back to the records of Marten's head scribe.

"No, just leave it," Tege whispered.

Adrial looked up to find Tege gripping Taddy's arm with both hands.

"Sir," Taddy said.

"Taddy." Tege leaned back, trying to drag him away.

"I don't understand, sir," Taddy said. "I think you've left out part of my punishment."

"Not all lessons have to bite in their learning," Adrial said. "Please do bring me a cup of tea before you report to Scribe Tammin. You're quite right in my preferring only a dash of sugar."

Adrial dipped his chin, hiding his smile as Taddy broke free from Tege's grip and bolted to the teapot.

"Thank you, sir." Tege nigh on bounced out of the kitchen as she took the proper path up to the great room.

The guards had deemed the massive space with its myriad windows unsafe for scribes, leaving only library staff with the ability to access the collections. Perhaps, if Tege did well, she could act as Adrial's runner, deliver requests for texts, carry the texts to his kitchen office.

You shouldn't send a child into a space deemed unfit for you, you thoughtless getch.

Adrial dragged his hands down his face as though that could somehow mash his thoughts into order.

Let the guards fear monsters, Ena whispered. *The child is safe from me.*

Warmth—undeniable, soul-soothing warmth—filled Adrial as the sound of her voice kissed his thoughts.

Let them find joy while they can. Grief filled Ena's voice. *The world is too broken for such light to last.*

"That's not true." Adrial gripped the edge of the desk.

"What, sir?" The man with the gritty voice set Adrial's tea onto the little table beside his desk.

Adrial barely caught a glimpse of Taddy's white robes disappearing as the apprentice fled the kitchen.

"Sir?" the man prompted. "Anything else I can fetch you?"

"No," Adrial said. "Thank you."

"That was kind of you, Head Scribe." The man sidled over to stand right in front of Adrial's desk. "But if you might consider having someone keep an eye on those two. Tege is a good girl, but attention from a Guilded fellow? That can turn a sensible head. I'd hate to see her ending up, well, ending up taken to the bastard's island, sir."

A flare of the fear Adrial's own birth had carved deep into his bones squeezed his lungs, making him work to drag in air. "They're practically children."

"Doesn't stop a seed from taking. You've every right to sack me for speaking so boldly, but my conscience couldn't abide silence, and I've faith you're a compassionate man of reason. And that's—well that's all I've got to say, sir." The man bowed. "Thank you, sir."

He turned away, squeezed between desks, and went back to his place at the table. Two of the women nearby had stopped their work to watch him. He picked up his knife, checked the blade, and began chopping a carrot.

They're children. Adrial pinched the bridge of his nose. *Practically infants. They've probably just learned to tie their boots on their own.*

You know better. The sound of Ena's laughter filled his mind. *Fear makes fools, and the gods don't stop dropping babies into the world, no matter how dark times get. See that Taddy doesn't father one of those panic-begotten babes, scribe.*

A sickening sense of dread settled into Adrial's stomach as he dove back into the journal from Marten, letting his second dissection of the poorly kept notes distract him from planning the lecture he'd never considered having to give an apprentice.

27

MARA

Lord Karron endured whispers of everything from madness to vanity upon his petition to purchase all the land atop the cliffs just east of Ilara. Unreachable by horse, the plateau had, as long as the scribes had recorded, been home to only criminals, hermits, the impoverished, and a small company of soldiers watching over the city from above.

But service to the Guilds had earned Lord Karron a boon from the council, and his bounty from the northern barrens journey had easily brought enough gold to offer the King a fair price for the land and to build an estate worthy of Lord Karron's bride.

A haven for the Lady Map Maker with a view of Ilara no other home could boast.

The King gladly accepted Lord Karron's request. Granting the boon, the King also bid the Sorcerers Guild build a road leading up the cliffs, and as an added token of the Council's gratitude, ordered the Lord Soldier to see the land cleared of squatters.

At his wife's pleas, Lord Karron sent men to the plateau, offering coin to any who cleared the cliffs before the soldiers arrived to force their departure. Most left peacefully with a poor man's fortune in their pockets. Soldiers drove out the lawless squatters.

But a few brave souls hid, staying in the woods on the plateau even as the sorcerers finished the switch-backing road up the cliff and the construction of the grand Map Master's Palace began.

After every sighting of a lurker in the trees, soldiers came up the cliff, searching for hidden dens. Even the addition of a high wall running along the eastern side of the plateau where the cliffs were less than completely sheer did little to drive away the people in the woods.

A terror for the father of a little girl. An opportunity for endless exploration for that little girl's wayward friend.

Lairs built beneath the roots of upturned trees, a stone-lined pit deep enough for a person to stand in with lashed beams and fallen leaves as the ground-level roof, nests built high in the trees, a hollow rock cairn with the dirt scraped flat for sleeping—a dozen secret fortresses for an orphan to claim.

Lord Karron noted each of Mara's discoveries, always sending men to hunt for whomever had created the den, always leaving her prizes intact once searched.

Mara had never asked why. She'd been too afraid of calling his attention to their survival, sure the slightest whisper could change Lord Karron's mind and all her lairs would be torn apart.

She clung to her discoveries, treasures even greater than Adrial's books, for each served as a fortress if the matrons ever came to steal her back. With her sanctuaries, she could protect Adrial, too, and Allora if Lord Karron died and they tried to send her to Ian Ayres as an orphan.

On the morning Mara found the refuge, she chose to lie.

Not while she dug her way through the thicket concealing the entrance, or as she climbed through the woven branches bracing the trapdoor.

Even the rotting curtains hanging across the openings of the eight niches along the dugout corridor seemed excellent artifacts to show Lord Karron when he returned from his latest journey.

But each niche had a hole in the ceiling leading up to a patch of light, the openings above carved through tree trunks or hidden in piles of stones. And at the end of the tunnel, wooden beams supported the walls of a wider chamber, where the forest dwellers who'd called the place home had left stools made of stumps and a roughhewn table. The occupants had even dug a clever little firepit on one side of the room with a little vent diverting and hiding the smoke.

And the window! How the dwellers had managed it, Mara could only guess.

A slit through the cliff offered a view of Ilara almost as perfect as the one from Lord Karron's favorite bench on the estate.

The Sorcerers Tower rising above the city, the bright white dome of the Guilds' cathedral, the glittering of the Arion Sea—all displayed as though Dudia had built the city just for her.

And—far more important than any beauty—twisting sideways, Mara could easily climb out the window. Rope and a well planted anchor would give her a chance at escape if the matrons ever cornered her.

Watching Ilara through her window, Mara sat for hours on a stump-made-stool, weighing all the ways lying to the man who'd rescued her was wrong, never finding an argument that made the lie an unworthy sacrifice.

Taking the tools she needed to make a proper climbing anchor didn't bring any guilt. Neither did stealing the rope for her window escape or the three old cooking pots.

Allora discovered Mara's plot and became the chief thief from the trunk of blankets onward, adding everything from pails for collecting water to proper forks and knives.

Everything a terrified orphan could want when running from demons.

The new children from Ian Ayres didn't agree.

There were enough blankets for all and better food stolen from the Map Master's Palace's root cellars than the children had ever eaten, but their view of the city far below shattered the feel of perfect safety the refuge had offered Mara for so long.

Blank patches of mud dotted the city where the sorcerers had destroyed homes and businesses as though plucking weeds. The Guilds cathedral still lay in ruin like a monument to the start of Ilbrea's end.

And, looming over the nightmare Ilara had become, the Sorcerers Tower glinted in the sun, unblemished by the evil wrought by the monsters hiding within.

When she finally forced the children to sleep, Mara covered the window with waxed fabric, promising herself she was blocking out the chill rain rolling in, ignoring the whispers in her mind that mocked her childish attempt to hide from the demons living in the tower.

28

ALLORA

The frie in Allora's glass hadn't warmed, though she'd been gripping her drink as a sad tether to salvation for the past ten minutes.

"Of all your faults, I never believed you heartless," Illia said.

Allora dug her heels into the ground, fighting her overwhelming desire to knock over her chair and flee.

"Six men," Illia said. "Is that what my happiness is worth?"

"Your happiness?" A soft thump came from Allora's right as Brannon set his knife on the table with far more restraint than the anger dripping from his voice implied him to be capable of. "Is this your new plea?"

"I shouldn't have to beg at all," Illia said.

Fionnaula barked from below the table.

"You are the one who declared I marry Prince Dagon," Illia said. "I am trying to do as you commanded."

The palace walls rumbled in the pounding sleet, promising life beyond the windowless study-turned-dining room still existed if only Allora broke free.

"A party has been sent to greet the Wyrainian delegate," Brannon said. "Nothing more can be done."

"The delegate should have been here well before now," Illia said.

"I am aware." Brannon paused between words as though giving Illia time to absorb the meaning of each.

"Then something's gone wrong," Illia said.

Allora sipped her frie, concentrating on its burn as it washed down her throat.

"Or they've reached Ilara, seen the anarchy that has seized our city and run right back to Wyrain," Illia said. "If they're hurrying home to tell Prince Dagon not to marry me, you've got to stop them."

"Bar a delegate from returning to their home?" Brannon said. "I'd prefer they had frozen to death in their foolish attempt to cross through the mountains in winter."

"But what if they did freeze?" Illia slammed her palms against the table.

"Then blame Dudia, not me," Brannon said.

"And if Wyrain blames us?" Illia said. "If the King changes his mind and doesn't want Dagon to marry me?"

"Then you would be a petulant child for whimpering about your petty woes while Ilbrea loses an alliance it's taken our family a century to foster."

Allora set her glass aside. Her fingers ached, begging not to be moved from the position she'd gripped them in for so long.

"Love isn't petty, brother," Illia said.

"Don't think so highly of your heart, sister," Brannon said. "You're not in love with Dagon. You've never met him, you don't know him, and you wouldn't recognize him if he crawled into your bed."

"I wish your lewdness surprised me," Illia said. "But your desperate attempts to prove yourself a foul-minded beast have been too successful."

Allora locked her hand back around her glass, downing the rest of her frie.

She reached for the frie bottle.

Gillien got there first.

"I know Dagon in the best of ways," Illia said. "He's shown me his heart in his letters."

"Letters most likely never touched by Dagon's hand," Brannon said. "You could very well be swooning over the words of a toothless, flaccid, old advisor."

"How dare you!" Illia leapt to her feet.

Fionnaula dove out from under the table, circled around the nearest guard, and leapt up onto the table, knocking Illia's plate to the floor and smashing her chamb glass.

"Get that dog out!" Brannon shouted.

Fionnaula growled, the sound instantly becoming a whimper as she stepped on shattered glass.

"My sweet." Illia grabbed the whimpering dog around the middle, hoisting her into her arms. "You're all right, my dove. I promise." Illia hurried away, pausing as she reached the dining room door. "You've let our kingdom crumble, brother. You're a king hiding from his own people rather than ruling over them. I always feared I would be the one to damage the Willoc name, but I may give that worry to the wind now. I will never sink as low as you."

Illia strode away, seizing the freedom Allora couldn't summon the courage to attempt.

Gillien refilled Allora's glass.

"You agree with her," Brannon said.

Allora sipped her frie.

The burn of the frie had dulled, as though even her throat had finally gone numb.

"Answer me, wife," Brannon said. "Do you think your King is a coward?"

"No, husband," Allora said.

"Am I a monster then?" Brannon said. "Have I finally twisted into the demon you've declared me? Is that why you won't look at me?"

Allora pushed away from the table, keeping hold of her glass as she stood.

"Allora, answer me," Brannon said.

"I don't believe you're a coward."

"Only a monster."

"Not even that." Allora made herself look at the man who controlled too much of her fate.

His skin had gone a pale gray. The dark smears under his eyes and stubble coating his chin made him seem almost ill.

A creature to be pitied.

Sour rolled through Allora's stomach.

"The palace has been my cage for months, but you've brought the walls closer in. I feel people staring at me all the time, and I can't tell if it's real or if I've only been so humiliated that madness has convinced me every person in this palace has memorized the details of my body."

A gentle hand touched Allora's elbow.

"I don't know what scared you into locking us away from the city, but I'm certain it's not a petty fear," Allora said. "You're many things, Brannon, but you're not a man to run from a fight he thinks he can win."

The hand on Allora's elbow led her toward the door.

"I am protecting our future," Brannon said.

"May Dudia bless your endeavors."

Gillien kept her pace slow as she led Allora down the corridor, parading between the columns of guards that stretched from Brannon's newly declared dining room to the study that hid her black stone tomb.

Six guards flanked the parlor fireplace.

Panic burned in Allora's chest as her mind promised the guards were staring at her breasts, imagining Brannon dragging her through the grounds displayed for all to see.

Their gazes raked over her flesh, claiming every piece of her.

They're looking at the wall. They aren't looking at you.

The wavering voice in her mind couldn't drive out the panicked scream begging her to run.

Allora shook her head, pulling away from Gillien's grip, backing into the hall.

Gillien followed, not arguing as Allora cut farther down the corridor, keeping her gaze fixed on the floor as she fled to the small balcony at the very end.

Two guards flanked the door. Neither tried to block her path. They both bowed. One even opened the door for her, letting her step out into the sleet that pounded down as the sky's own attack upon Ilbrea.

The cold of the sleet stung Allora's skin for only a moment before abandoning her to an unnatural warmth.

"Don't," Allora said.

"I'm not going to let you fall ill standing in the rain." Gillien closed the door to the hall.

The scratching at Allora's flesh eased. She stepped into the back corner of the balcony, where neither of the guards could peer through the glass in the door to watch her. The sensation faded away as the night shrouded her with merciful darkness.

She leaned against the wall, letting the weight on her lungs ebb.

"Would you like a chair brought out for you?" Gillien said.

"You're not going to force me right back inside?"

"I can keep us warm." Gillien moved to the corner opposite Allora, placing herself where she could watch the corridor inside.

"You'll protect us, too?"

"The storm won't harm you."

Allora looked up, meeting Gillien's gaze.

"No storm will harm you," Gillien said. "It is my duty to protect you, and it will be done."

"We're cut off from the city, and Brannon is still afraid. He should be doing everything in his power to ensure the Wyrainian delegate's safety and not just for Illia's sake. But he only sent six men north, men who needed sorcerers' aid to cross the chasm that stands between me and freedom."

"No one is trying to deprive you of your freedom."

"Intentions mean little when you're trapped."

"Even if the intention is your protection?"

"I'd rather be in Ilara facing whatever horror Brannon is hiding from than stay protected in his palace." Allora finished her frie and set her glass on the balcony rail. "No comforting words promising I'm imagining Brannon's fear? Have you given up on your Queen's placidity?"

Gillien watched Allora, her brow furrowed in a perfect picture of concern.

"Brannon's had nightmares the past two nights." Allora turned, pressing her palms to the palace, letting the ice that covered the stone freeze pain into her hands. "I'm sure whoever is watching from inside our bedroom walls has already reported it. The King of Ilbrea has woken himself up screaming twice."

Gillien swept her hand toward the door. The light from inside faded as the glass darkened.

"I've always hated sleeping beside him. Pretending to find peace in his presence feels like the worst of lies." She pressed her forehead to the ice. A shiver shook her shoulders. "I know he's a monster and the demons that stalk his dreams were crafted by his own hands, but what did he do to bring them now?"

Allora shut her eyes, waiting for Gillien to answer. A wave of shivers shook her spine.

The cold of the ice disappeared, leaving the warmth of the midday sun filling the stone.

Allora pushed herself away from the unwanted comfort of the heat. "Five of the Guilds abandoned their King. Why?"

"They turned against the Lady Sorcerer. King Brannon chose to stand beside the Sorcerers Guild."

"Why?"

"Ilbrea's King is wise enough to recognize his strongest ally."

"Why does he need an ally against his own people? Why drop the bridge? Is Brannon afraid Lord Kearney will bring soldiers to attack? Or is it the commoners who want their King dead? Did Brannon truly fail to realize that demanding the conscription of unwilling soldiers only builds an army of men who despise their King?"

"You're convinced the King is to blame?" More wrinkles furrowed Gillien's brow, as though she'd asked a true question.

"I can't bring myself to believe Brannon didn't earn the wrath of whoever has driven him into hiding."

"You paint the King to be the worst of all monsters. May Dudia help me protect that naivety."

"If you have a better monster for me to hate, please do share. Give me an easier target for my loathing than the man I married."

Gillien's brow smoothed. She laced her fingers together, assuming a pose of perfect calm. "You are safe, Allora. Let that be what matters."

"Brannon has summoned demons upon us, hasn't he?"

"You are driving unnecessary worry through your mind."

"And you're digging it in deeper." Allora left the pitiful comfort of her hidden corner to stand right in front of Gillien, where the dim light still filtering through the darkened glass displayed her silhouette for anyone patrolling the grounds to see. She crossed her arms over her breasts. "You promised to always tell me the truth, and despite myself, I believe you have. Why are you weaving around my questions?"

"Your safety is my priority." Gillien's calm didn't waver.

Allora took Gillien's face in her hands, bearing the scraping of imaginary eyes devouring her flesh as she held the sorcerer's gaze. "Is my husband spiraling toward madness?"

"No."

The pang of panic in Allora's chest had no edge to slice through her lungs.

The blade has cut too many times before.

"Adrial," Allora said, "is he safe?"

"I haven't heard mention of the head scribe in days. All scribes in Ilara have retreated into the library. It seems they are avoiding rash actions in favor of safety."

Allora closed her eyes, nodding to herself in a desperate bid to accept the sorcerer's veiled comfort.

"How long will we be trapped in the palace?" Allora asked.

Gillien's jaw tensed. Her fingers were warm as she took Allora's wrists, lifting Allora's hands from her face.

Forever.

The single word echoed through Allora's mind. She squeezed her eyes shut again, banishing the heat of tears.

"You need rest," Gillien said. "You've exhausted yourself with worry. We'll get you to bed, and all will be well in the morning."

Allora slid her wrists from Gillien's grasp. "I'll sleep in my stone tomb. Let the guards lock me in for the night."

"You are safe sleeping in your room with the King." Gillien laid her hand on the door handle, blocking Allora's path without any effort.

Where would you run?

"If I'm going to stay trapped in this palace, I'd rather hide from my humiliation. Every person's eyes dragging over me stings like a fresh blow, and I am too battered to keep pressing through the gauntlet." Allora swiped a rogue tear from her cheek. "Please let me hide in my tomb or lie down in the storm and freeze. Either freedom or isolation. Give me one."

"I may be able to arrange daily seclusion on the balcony to soothe your anxious mind during these trying times. But you will not abandon the King's bed. A queen's duty to her people is too important to be washed away by a storm."

"Thank you." Allora leaned against the wall, sliding down to sit on the floor of the balcony. She pulled her knees up to her chest and tipped her face to the sky, imagining the freedom of trudging through the pounding rain.

29

ADRIAL

The center of the staircase offered as much privacy as Adrial could hope for. He glanced to the top and bottom of the long steps, making sure the guards in both positions were out of sight, before slipping the cloth that held the little stone Ena had given him from his pocket.

Laying the cloth on the step above his feet, he unwrapped the stone.

Have the courage to do what's right.

The spark inside glimmered red as he stepped up with his good leg, breaking the stone with an unexpectedly loud crack before he could doubt himself.

The sound of running boots came from both ends of the stairs.

Adrial jumped down two steps, paying with pain spiking up to lock his jaw, and grabbed the cloth and stone shards.

The guard running down the stairs stopped four steps above him, hand on the hilt of his dagger.

I've doomed my wife.

"Head scribe, what happened?" the topmost of the three guards below Adrial asked.

Ena.

I've doomed Ena.

"Sir, are you hurt?" The scribes' guard above Adrial stepped closer, reaching for his arm.

I'm sorry.

"Not hurt, no." Adrial showed the guard a glimpse of his handkerchief before tucking it into his pocket. "Just prone to fumbling today. My mind and my body don't seem eager to work together."

"I understand, sir." The top guard stepped out of Adrial's way, holding his arm out in a less than subtle offer to help Adrial up the stairs. "A few nights' solid sleep would be my mother's first direction for most everyone in the library. Funny the things you don't think of until they become luxuries you can't afford."

"Your mother sounds to be a very wise woman." Adrial stepped past the guard.

"Thank you, sir." The guard let Adrial walk a few stairs in front of him.

Adrial gripped the fabric bundle in his pocket, letting the sharp edges of the broken stone press into his palm, their sting keeping his mind from wondering if the guard behind him climbed with his hands held out, ready to be a savior should the cripple scribe crumble.

They're trying to help. All the guards want is to keep you safe.

He passed through the cluster of four guards at the top of the steps.

I've called Ena into a hoard of waiting blades.

Dudia, save my reckless heart.

Adrial hurried down the last, short corridor leading to the Lord Scribe's newest temporary office—out of the basement where Lord Gareth had found it hard to breathe—tucked in an interior crook in the library's structure that made the room's one tiny window an inconvenient route of attack.

Adrial nodded to the Lord Scribe's guards as he approached,

giving them the calming sort of smile he'd been perfecting for days.

You could be dooming innocents.

Too many innocent lives have already been lost.

Adrial knocked on the Lord Scribe's door before the weight of his conscience could freeze his hand.

"Yes?" the Lord Scribe called through his door.

Adrial let go of the bundle in his pocket, tucking his hands behind his back as a guard opened the door.

His heart rammed against his ribs. The rhythm pounded all the way up to his ears.

"Adrial." The Lord Scribe waved Adrial in, giving him a far better version of a soothing smile than Adrial had yet to produce. "There's been no news from the siege at the tower." Lord Gareth pointed to the chair nearest his desk. "And Lord Kearney's message said all was calm at the gates today."

"A happy improvement." Adrial sat on the edge of his assigned chair.

The lamplight glinted off the window behind Lord Gareth's shoulder, accenting the starless night.

"Every word Lord Kearney writes is tinged with his anger at having a flock of common Ilaran men demanding they be trained into the King's Army," Lord Gareth said. "But the decree was given. And the men did register."

"And without a new decree from the King, the Scribes Guild cannot retract such orders." Adrial dug his nails into his knees. "I fear Lord Kearney may be grateful for his common flock all too soon. If the sorcerers do attack, the more trained men, the better."

"And by Dudia's blessing, the registered are being brought under Lord Kearney's command and not the King's. Though Lord Kearney must pray Dudia delivers an unexpected wealth of resources to train and outfit Ilara's newest warriors," Lord

Gareth said. "Badly trained men with dull swords will only lead to more burial papers for us to file."

"I know, sir. All the scribes do, and it worries me. The hopelessness that's rampant in Ilara is spreading through the library right alongside the cough that's bouncing from one apprentice to another with alarming speed."

"Scribe Tammin said as much." Lord Gareth tapped his chin. "Deprive children of sunlight, they wither."

It's true. You're only encouraging truth.

"Living every moment of the day as though the library is under attack has been straining to the sturdiest of scribes," Adrial said.

"We are at risk every moment of the day."

"Yes, sir. And we could remain so for a very long time. Too long to keep our people sleeping on floors and working in windowless closets."

"We've got to be ready for an attack." Lord Gareth tapped the letter from Lord Kearney still on his desk.

You are not allowed to fail, Adrial Ayres.

"I agree, sir. I'd actually come to speak to you about switching to a system of evacuating scribes to their assigned shelter upon any guard's command, while allowing the option of scribes returning to their normal quarters at night. The apprentices have been sleeping in one long corridor. Putting them back in their dormitories would slow the spread of the cough at least. And allowing people to rest in their own beds—"

Adrial searched for the right words, something to prove to his own mind that he hadn't slipped into a terrible nightmare. "The siege of the Sorcerers Tower could last months. Years, if the sorcerers don't choose to emerge. Sleeping in a proper bed, having that bit of normality, I think it would be an investment in the scribes' ability to keep trudging onward for however long this schism lasts."

"The loosening of precautions would stop the unending

misery leaking under my door." Lord Gareth's tapping finger stilled. "But there are too many windows, too many unguarded places." His hands began to tremble. "The library wasn't built to keep out sorcerers."

Don't let go. Keep the line taut.

"If the sorcerers want to attack, lack of a window won't stop them," Adrial said. "Cowering in fear is wringing us all to exhaustion. Let the scribes return to their own quarters. Whatever we face, we'll greet it better well rested and calm."

"The young should not have to reason through such things." Lord Gareth's wrinkled jowls shook as he nodded to himself. "The skylights in the great room are a blatant invitation to attack. The space must remain closed."

"Yes, sir." A tiny prickle of victory dared to grow in Adrial's chest.

"The guards can't be lessened, and the library gates will not be opened. Call the scribes together in the morning. Request volunteers to bolster the guards' numbers."

The victory vanished, leaving a bitter ache where it had been.

"I've no doubt many will be willing," Adrial said, "myself included."

"You're the one they'll be volunteering to protect." Lord Gareth shooed Adrial toward the door. "Go rest, Adrial. No guard can protect you from your own failing health."

"Thank you." Adrial stood and bowed. "Please rest as well, sir. I'll see you in the morning."

Adrial opened the door, stepping out into the corridor.

For the past several nights, the small rooms along the hall had been granted to older scribes as private quarters. Adrial had been assigned a private room as well and given a bed rather than a pallet on the floor. A far higher level of comfort than most others had.

Adrial would be hailed as a hero for convincing Lord Gareth

to release everyone back to their quarters. An easier feat than Adrial had imagined.

But if Lord Gareth had agreed because of his faith in the scribes' guards. If Guard Friel had blocked every unguarded path in the library.

You've doomed her.

If the sorcerers do attack through the windows. If someone is hurt because of me. If they hurt her...

The string of fears looped through his mind over and over as guards peeled away from their fellows to follow him up the stairs to the long corridor of scribes' quarters.

"Please tell Scribe Tammin to spread the news that we're allowed to return to our rooms." Adrial slowed as he neared his door. "And to warn the male apprentices to clean the portion of the corridor they made their den."

One of the guards behind Adrial gave a soft huff of a laugh.

"I promise," Adrial said, "the stench is even worse than you're imagining."

All four of his guards laughed.

Adrial joined in as he stepped into the darkness of his sitting room and closed the door.

He hesitated with his hand on the lock.

The protection of a barricade or the danger of a barrier.

I should know which is better.

He turned the lock and backed away, stopping before he ran into the chair, fumbling to light the lamp with his gaze still pinned to the door.

No screams of pain or terror came from the hall.

The lamp flickered to life, casting the room in a familiar glow that needled at the back of Adrial's mind as though the light itself were demanding Adrial take comfort in its warmth.

"You're a fool to hope." Adrial lit another lamp on his way to the window.

The metal of the window latch stung Adrial's fingers with

cold as he pushed it open, testing the window hadn't frozen shut before moving on to the next latch.

He checked the lock on the door to the hall, giving the handle two quiet tugs to prove its soundness.

The sitting room light spilled into the bedroom, casting jagged shadows from the furniture, giving Adrial's mind a dozen new fears to strangle his thoughts.

"There are enough monsters in this world. There's no need for you to imagine more."

He lengthened his stride as he walked into the bedroom, trading an extra throb in exchange for fewer opportunities to dither over each movement. He reached for the lamp as he stepped through the door.

"Leave it off." The whisper came from the corner.

Pain slammed through Adrial's shoulder as he banged into the wall.

He hadn't asked his feet to move.

"Lock the door behind you." Ena spoke just loudly enough for Adrial to be certain it was her.

He spun toward the door, forcing his hands to stay gentle as he closed it and slid the lock into place.

His breath rasped in his ears as he turned to the shadow that held her voice. "How?" He reached toward the darkness. "How did you get here so fast?"

"Are you grateful or afraid?"

"I was terrified you'd be caught. There are guards everywhere. There are guards outside the sitting room now." Adrial lowered his hand. "I had promised myself I'd never use the stone. I couldn't imagine putting you in danger by asking you to come into the library. But you told me to break the stone when I understood the names you'd given me. The very least I can do is honor your wishes."

You're doing what's right. Prove you're capable of that much.

A hollow formed at the center of Adrial's chest, the ache of it growing every heartbeat. "I couldn't see it at first. Harane, Marten, Lir Valley, none of them seemed important enough to be whispered about. And you'd sounded so afraid."

The darkest part of the shadow shifted.

"I dug into the library's records, but not even the soldiers' ledgers held anything of note." Adrial swallowed the pain in his throat and stepped away from the dark shape, pressing his back to the door. "I searched the scribes' records twice before noticing the pattern.

"All three places had a sudden drop in registered births. I'd seen a similar thing before, when an illness ravaged a town. But there was no record of an illness, not even a rise in requests for burial papers."

The shadow shifted again.

"So I dug all the way down to the tax records. In every place, names just disappeared between one year and the next. Far more people than would have been granted permission to sell their property in one year. Such a large, localized exodus could cause instability. The matter would have come before Lord Gareth.

"But the properties, they weren't sold, they were inherited. Left to the heirs of people who, according to the records, never died. And where there wasn't anyone to inherit, the land became the property of the Guilds, seized as though the penalty for unpaid taxes."

"Grave robbers," Ena whispered.

"One of those properties was in Harane. It had been recorded as the home of an inker." Adrial closed his eyes, shoving aside the pain that stretched from the aching void in his chest to his throat, growing every moment, threatening to tear him in two. "The notes include a ward living under the inker's care. An orphan listed as Ena Ryeland. Both names disappear from the records at the same time. Ena and—"

"Lily."

"Lily," Adrial breathed the most precious name.

"The soldiers hanged her. Put her on display while they burned her home."

"I'm so sorry."

"She wasn't the only one they murdered that day. I've watched paun slaughter a hundred more since."

"Ena." He reached toward her.

The shape in the shadows shrank away.

"I can't imagine the brutality you've witnessed and endured. I've always known the Guilds are far from blameless, but for more than half the people in a town to disappear? What kind of monsters quietly tuck massacres aside?" He couldn't keep the true questioning from his voice.

A quiet sound, like a breath fighting to become tears, came from the shadows.

He leaned his weight onto his bad leg, willing the stabbing in his hip to drown out the tearing in his chest as the void devoured more and more of his soul. "Now that I've seen where the names are missing, I can't understand how I never noticed before. I should have caught it. Someone should have found the gaps and brought the records to me."

"It's hard to find nothing if you don't know what you're searching for."

"It doesn't matter. I'm the Lord Scribe's heir. I serve Ilbrea, and I didn't notice my own people vanishing. And I can't..." The need to clutch Ena to his chest flared through his limbs.

He let the impulse fade. "I know there's nothing I can do to make up for the horrors you've endured at the hands of the Guilds, or the time I've spent, however unwittingly, ignoring the actions of fellow paun.

"Ena, I beg you to believe I am truly sorry. I know it's a petty recompense, but I will push for answers and make sure these deaths aren't ignored. Whoever is responsible for the fates of the fallen will be brought to justice."

"No." Ena stepped out of the shadows, reaching for Adrial's

arm. She stopped three feet away from him, hesitating as though unable to force herself any nearer. "Don't taunt ghosts when there's a blade at your neck."

"If my neck is the price, it's the least I can offer."

"No."

Adrial dug his knuckles into his chest, pressing against the pain. It didn't help. "If you don't want my aid seeking justice, then tell me what to do."

Ena tensed, shifting her stance as though preparing to run.

Do what is right.

Adrial stepped away from the door, clearing her path.

"I understand why you despise the Guilds. I understand there are depths to your loathing I can't comprehend. I understand why you sought me out." His words sounded too far away, as though spoken in some distant nightmare. "After all you've suffered, reaching someone near the heart of the Guilds would be a valuable enough opportunity to allow a paun to touch you."

"Stop."

"I can't attempt to deny you've made good use of me. Assassinated two Guild leaders, been in the royal palace, you have ways in and out of the library our guards can't find—you must have gained useful information from your time with me. At least I hope the information was useful."

She backed further into the shadows, hiding what little Adrial had been able to see of her face.

"Please believe I don't blame you for attaching yourself to me. The only regret I can muster is not being able to stop them from forcing you onto the ship to Ian Ayres. Being your"—the pain streaked up Adrial's throat, roughening his voice—"your husband, dreaming of being a father to our child, brought me more joy than I ever dreamt possible."

"Stop it."

"I understand you're a Black Blood and your blade belongs at my throat. I understand the Guilds are your great evil and I am your villain."

"Adrial, stop." She grabbed his wrist with one hand, knocking him back to pin his shoulder to the wall with the other. "Call me an assassin, husband. Cower in fear at the blood on my hands, rage at me for hiding with the Black Bloods, but don't you dare pretend I whored myself to you."

"You were fighting for your cause." Tears burned in Adrial's eyes. "I apologize for any shame giving yourself to the Guilded Cripple—"

"Don't—"

"I would never have taken advantage—"

"When I came to Ilara, I thought I'd never see a Black Blood or set foot in the eastern mountains again. They were ghosts to me, and I was alone. I climbed to that chivving balcony last Winter's End because I'm an inker and I needed coin to eat and I risked my neck taking you to a magic chivving flower because you were the only glimmer of anything hopeful or good in the world I'd seen in too long and if I couldn't make myself believe it was real then I'd have no reason to keep breathing.

"I married you to protect the child you swore to call your own." She pushed away from him. "I made a vow and I meant it. You're my husband."

"Not all sacrifices need to be permanent." Adrial forced himself to stand tall. "The Guilds have stolen enough from you. I won't keep you chained to me."

"My vow isn't a cage."

"You're fighting the paun, and that's what I am. I am one of your demons, and I'm setting you free."

"You're not the demon, scribe. I arranged the Lady Healer's death. I've done worse before, and my work still isn't done. It's not me who deserves freedom from a monster, it's you. Slipping into the shadows and making sure you never hear a whisper of me again is the kindest thing I could do."

The pain in Adrial's chest peaked, punching through him like a mortal blow.

"I'm not as good as you are, scribe. I can't make myself wish you away from me." Ena stepped closer. "Come with me. Out of the library. Away from Ilara."

"Whatever help I can offer your cause, I will give." Tears burned Adrial's cheeks. "Just please don't pretend. I've made myself understand my role in this tale. I am the tool, not the lover. Let me be of use, but don't lure me further into madness."

"Come with me into the eastern mountains. I promised Lily I would protect you. I promised I'd see you safely to her side." Ena laid her hand on Adrial's chest, just above the agony that threatened to destroy him. "I know you love the Guilds and Ilbrea and I know what I'm asking you to sacrifice, but I'm still asking. Come with me, husband. Come build a life with our daughter."

The void in Adrial's chest froze, the agony of it locking into his body as though some part of him needed to memorize the feel. Even his heart seemed to stop beating as his soul twisted and shattered, the cracks aligning in different places as the shards sprang back together as a painful new creation.

Ena lifted her hands away from him. She dipped her chin. A curtain of raven black hair hid her face.

He caught her wrist, wrapping one arm behind her back in an achingly familiar way, keeping her pinned close enough he could see her face in the faint starlight. "Promise me this is real."

"Nothing between us has ever been a lie." Fear-fueled pain filled her eyes. "You're the one I would defy the gods for. There is nothing more real."

She slid her wrist from his grip, freeing herself only to slip her hand into his, locking their fingers together.

He couldn't make himself tip his chin down as she rose up on her toes, brushing her lips against his.

She loosened her hold on his hand.

"If this is a dream"—he pushed the words past the spikes in his throat—"I won't survive waking up."

The fear in Ena's eyes dimmed, outshone by a glint of humor.

She pulled her body away from his enough to slide her hand down to his stomach. She kissed his neck and jaw, teasing her hand lower with each brush of her lips.

A throb of heat pulsed through him, promising bliss the moment before she bit his ear and squeezed his tender parts just enough to shock absolute awareness through every nerve in his body.

He gasped as she let go, returning her hand to the safety of his chest.

"This isn't a dream, scribe. I'm here, and I'm asking you to give up everything for me."

He tightened his hold on her waist, keeping her close as he dipped his chin, brushing his lips against hers.

She slid her hand up to his shoulder, removing the barrier between them as she teased his lips apart.

The taste of her swept aside every hope of reason. She shifted her hips, pressing herself against the undeniable evidence that rendered any attempt to pretend his mind had stayed fixed on dire matters utterly useless with every growing pulse.

A sudden cold surrounded Adrial as she backed away.

Panic crashed into his chest, knocking the air from his lungs.

She left only a foot between them as she unfastened the top of his robes.

Air rammed back into his lungs.

Think, Adrial.

He made himself grab her hands. "I can't—we can't—" The pulsing scattered his thoughts before they reached his mouth. "There are guards. In the corridor. Guards everywhere. You have to go."

"I can't." Ena unfastened the second closure. "I barely beat you and your guards to get in here. I've no chance of sneaking out with your door guarded."

"I can lead them away."

"Leaving your room just after arriving could make your guards suspicious. Lingering is safer for both of us."

She lifted Adrial's hands, placing his fingers on the knot at the top of her bodice.

"You shouldn't have come here. It was too dangerous. I never should—"

She kissed him, cutting off his babble.

Lacing her fingers through his hair, she steered him, her body still pressed against his, her kisses not stopping until his legs met the bed and he twisted his face, stealing his lips from hers.

"I don't know how to protect my dead, Black Blood wife from guards."

She unfastened the belt that held her knives. "I can defend myself." She held the blades up for Adrial to see, then pulled knives from the ankles of both her boots.

She laid her weapons on the foot of the bed, each blade catching the faint light from Adrial's window.

"I never want to put you in danger." He wrapped his arms around her, folding her into the poor safety he could offer.

The void in his chest drifted out of being, refilling his broken soul with a gentle, radiant warmth.

She tipped her chin up, meeting his gaze, not trying to hide the tear that ran down her cheek. "I wasn't sure you'd want to come with me. After everything I've—"

"I love you, Ena Ayres." He kissed her cheek, his lips gaining the salt of her tears. "Ena Ryeland." She closed her eyes as he kissed her other cheek. "I love the Black Blood and the warrior and the inker and the mother of our daughter and the miracle who climbed into my life and stole every part of me." He pressed his lips to her forehead. "I will gladly trade Ilbrea for a life with you. Wherever that life takes us."

He brushed her hair from her cheek. She leaned into his hand as though savoring the touch.

She kissed him, her lips barely grazing his, taunting him as she unfastened the last closure on his robe. "The gods may burn us all tomorrow. Let us have tonight."

She lowered her hands to his hips, gathering the fabric of his robes, raising the hem. She swallowed a soft laugh as he grabbed the fabric from her and ripped his robes over his head.

He kissed her neck, reveling in the softness of her skin as his fingers fumbled on the laces of her bodice, his hands' dexterity failing as his better parts demanded attention.

She moved his hands from the laces, giving him the easier foe of the buttons on the back of her skirt, getting her bodice untied and over her head before Adrial had dropped her skirt to the floor.

She pressed on his chest, pushing him back onto the bed.

Catastrophic joy thrummed through Adrial's every nerve as she kissed his ruined hip, trailing her lips up to the scars on his ribs, then the scar on his shoulder, taking in every broken piece of him before finally kissing his lips.

Her center pressed against him as he lifted the hem of her shift. He trailed his fingers up her thighs, drawing the fabric past the curve of her hips, teasing higher, his own pleasure pounding at her gasp as he reached the sides of her breasts.

He lifted the shift over her head, banishing the last barrier between them.

She sat up, taking his hands in hers. She kissed his fingers. "Ours is the path you choose?"

"Yes."

"Swear to me that will never change." She kissed his palm, then laid his hand over her heart. "Whatever comes, we greet it together."

"I will stand beside you until the skies crumble."

She lifted his hand from her chest and twined her fingers

through his, keeping their hands locked together as she buried him inside her, plunging him into radiant bliss that blocked out everything but her.

Her head on his chest as they lay tangled together, their breath still quick.

Her moan as she wrapped her legs around him, demanding to have him again.

Her tears as she pressed his hand to her stomach where the bit of their souls that was missing had grown.

Her warmth as he held her close, whispering words of comfort and promises of reunion he would defy Dudia to hold true.

Her fingers as she traced the scar on his shoulder as though wanting to make sure she hadn't forgotten the shape.

Her whispered instructions and warnings.

Her final kiss, gentle and fleeting, before she banished him to the corridor, sending him on a middle of the night stroll through the library halls, leading his guards away from the orphaned inker the Guilds didn't know they were hunting.

30

—————

NIKO

Ice coated the slit in the wall, offering Dudia-blessed relief from the cold seeping in through the street-level gap.

While the improvement in temperature couldn't be denied, the lack of feet to watch passing by had deprived Niko of his chief enjoyment, leaving reading—when he was banished to his corner of silence—and building impossibly complicated and dispiriting walls from bread scraps when allowed a seat at the table as his only pastimes while the Brien kept their second Solcha stored in the basement.

The true Solcha, whose affinity for blood even Mael seemed to appreciate, had been freed from the den.

Set loose on Ilbrea.

Niko glanced toward the stairs, ready for Death to dramatically appear at the mere thought of Ena.

"Waiting for someone?" Lorna tossed a chunk of bread across the table, pegging Niko in the forehead.

"I ordered new boots from the cobbler." Niko popped the bread into his mouth, winking at Lorna's grin. "Waiting for them to arrive. Better be worth the coin I paid."

Lorna laughed as she leaned back in her seat. "Have them

deliver something to eat besides bread, and I'll kiss those new boots."

"Would you like a roll?" Niko pointed to the plate in the center of the table. "A biscuit? A fruit tart?"

"You're a flirt."

"Dudia gave me the talent. I can't help but use it." Niko glanced to the far corner.

Danu didn't look up from her book, but the corner of her eye twitched in a way one could potentially interpret as a smile.

"Of course, there's little I can do trapped in a basement with bread as my only tool and half my time stuck in a corner with magic blocking my hearing, but"—Niko stood, catching Lorna's hand and bringing it to his lips—"but…" He winked and brushed a kiss to the back of her hand. "Give me one evening in a peaceful Ilara, and you will savor sweet memories of our time together for the rest of your days."

"Tempting. But…but…" Lorna flicked Niko's nose. "I've heard better."

Niko sat back down, rubbing his nose. "You've wounded my pride and my face."

He glanced to Danu again. She didn't look up.

Something hard and boot-like rammed into Niko's ankle.

He looked toward Lorna as she kicked him again.

Lorna widened her eyes at Niko.

He furrowed his brow in return.

Lorna tipped her head toward Danu.

Niko flattened his lips.

Lorna gave a pointed glance to the far side of the room where Mael lay on his cot, his feet hanging off the end as he slept.

Niko took a turn widening his eyes at Lorna.

Lorna kicked his ankle. Harder.

Niko shook his head.

"Danu, save me from the boring paun," Lorna said. "Come sit.

I haven't seen this kind of pastry before. We can take turns guessing what our cook is trying to kill us with now."

"It's savory chicken," Niko said. "We had them last night."

Another kick to the ankle.

"Danu, come save the paun before I stab him for being tedious," Lorna said. "We've been down here too long, and I'm starting to think stabbing could be a fun afternoon entertainment."

"I'd rather you not," Niko said.

Danu closed her book and laid it in her lap. "How shall I entertain you?"

"Tell me something delicious about your brother," Lorna said.

"The heir of the Brien Elder?" Danu raised her eyebrows.

"Your lack of consideration for my boredom has been noted," Lorna said. "Tell me something that will make Niko blush."

Heat raced to Niko's face.

"That was easy." Lorna sighed. "Niko, shall we make Danu blush? Has she told you the story about the weapons master?"

"You didn't get a true blush from Niko," Danu said.

"Really?" Lorna looked to Niko, her hair hiding her face from Danu as she winked at him.

"If you want a true blush from him, ask him about his first lesson with a sword," Danu said.

"Unfair." Niko leapt to his feet, grabbing the half-eaten roll that had been the gate beside his bread-made moat, lobbing it at Danu's chest.

She parried the roll with her book. "Lost the balance of his blade, got the tip lodged in the ground, tripped forward, and rammed the hilt into his tender parts."

Heat enveloped Niko's face.

"Almost sliced his bits off, too, when he toppled forward over the sword." Danu pursed her lips in a half-hearted attempt to hide the humor brightening her face.

"In my defense"—laughter bounced Niko's words—"the

sword was much heavier than I'd expected, and after mortally wounding myself, I didn't have enough control of my limbs to fall any other direction."

"And you kept teaching him?" Lorna laughed.

"I didn't trust anyone else with such a student," Danu said.

"And I am eternally grateful." Niko stood, testing his luck with a sweeping bow.

Danu didn't turn away.

He knelt beside her, taking her hand. The chill of the basement had sunk into her fingers as though they'd been standing out in the weather. He covered her hand with his as he pressed her palm over his heart, giving her fingers at least a moment of warmth. "Thou art the epitome of patience and grace, wrought by hands beyond mortal comprehension to salvage the fools of this world."

A hint of a smile curved the corners of Danu's lips.

"And I, the worst of all fools, would be hopeless without you."

Her smile flickered away.

Niko stood, keeping his hold on Danu's hand, pulling her to her feet.

Danu sucked in a sharp breath.

"Sorry. Bad arm." Niko dodged around her, taking her arm that hadn't been torn open by an arrow. "I'm a sorry chivving slitch, and yanking on your wounded arm is nowhere near the worst of it."

"A slitch? I'm shocked. The terror of it all." Lorna pulled out a chair for Danu right beside Niko's.

"'Tis far worse than terror. You should be mortified to have ever broken bread with me." Niko eased toward the table, guiding Danu inch by inch, as though he were leading a reluctant pup. "That wasn't the only time I tripped on my own sword."

"No." Lorna clapped her hands over her mouth, speaking through her fingers. "You can't have banged your bits with your own sword twice."

"He did." Danu's words bounced with a tiny laugh. "The second time, he bloodied his knees when he fell. Like a babe falling off their own stick horse."

Niko opened his mouth, closed it, and opened it again. "I have no retort."

Danu shook her head as she sank into her seat at the table.

Niko sat beside her, claiming the chicken tarts, taking one for himself, leaving the plate within Danu's easy reach.

"I've changed my mind." Niko pointed his tart at Danu. "I do have a retort. I've made it clear on more than one occasion that I do my best fighting while drunk, or well on my way. Danu banned frie from the training field."

"The ban didn't come from me," Danu said.

"You didn't have to enforce it," Niko said.

"Sounds like she may have saved you from chopping off your better bits by keeping you sober." Lorna laughed.

The heat from his face burned all the way down to his neck.

"And finally," Lorna said, "a perfect blush."

Niko grabbed the northern wall of his bread-built creation and chucked it at Lorna. "I improved rapidly."

Lorna didn't bother dodging Niko's attack, fixing her full effort on crying with laughter at Niko's expense.

Danu pushed away from the table.

"You haven't eaten." Niko grabbed Danu's hand. "The chicken tarts really are edible."

Danu slid her hand from Niko's.

Lorna's laughter stopped.

Danu cut behind Lorna as though heading toward the stairs, stopping before Niko could think of a better lure than chivving chicken tarts. She picked up the bit of bread Niko had thrown and returned to her seat.

She straightened Niko's eastern and western bread walls before returning the northern to its place.

She took a chicken tart from the tray. "You broke your palace."

A drop of cold sank into Niko's stomach, spreading to freeze everything in his gut as Danu broke off the corner of her tart, placing it where the bridge to the royal palace should have been.

"It feels like the paun are taunting us, doesn't it?" Lorna said. "Open air between us and the King and we can't just hop over and kill him."

"Doubting your fellow Brien?"

Niko jolted as Mael spoke, eyes still closed and feet still hanging over the end of his cot.

"Does everything you say have to sound angry?" Lorna said.

"You woke me up," Mael said.

Lorna grimaced, leaning close to Niko to whisper, "We mustn't disturb the great trueborn."

Niko grabbed a roll, shoving it into his mouth rather than feign a smile.

In the quiet, Niko heard a carriage pass with another right behind it. Merchants, most likely, continuing commerce as the King of Ilbrea locked himself away, hiding from his own people.

A man with a boisterously loud voice passed, guffawing at something.

Danu finished her tart and retreated to her niche.

She ate.

She spoke to you.

Let that be enough.

Niko scrunched his eyes shut.

You're a fool.

A planless, helpless fool.

The white spots dancing through the black twisted into a silhouette of the palace. He dug his knuckles into his eyes. The silhouette didn't change.

The problem wasn't in the bread palace or even the real palace.

It was the massive chivving fissure surrounding the palace that stomped out every spark of hope before it could catch.

Like a massive stone pillar rooted in water, the palace grounds didn't connect to the city of Ilara. Looking from a distance, the palace sat at an even level with the city, giving a fool the impression of being easy to approach on foot.

If, however, a fool wanted to reach the palace with no bridge, climbing down the city side of the cliff, swimming to the pillar where the palace sat, then climbing the pillar and *then* climbing the palace wall offered the only path.

If a fool could make the climbs without being spotted and killed.

Which a fool had a sodding sheep shit's chance of doing.

Niko grabbed another tart, chewing it with as much pent-up frustration as he could inflict on a pastry.

Lorna kicked his ankle. She furrowed her brow at him.

He shook his head and brushed his bread palace onto a plate.

There are sorcerers in the palace, Mara whispered. *Monsters protect their lairs.*

I don't care! Niko shouted.

Rushing into Death's embrace for a hopeless plot helps no one! Mara shouted back. *Patience, Nikolas. Something will change. You have to find the strength to wait.*

Niko dragged his hands down his face. *You're a getch when you're right, Mara.*

He imagined her frowning at him. Probably whacking him on the arm.

The thumping of footsteps carried across the kitchen floor right above them.

"More tarts?" Lorna whispered. "Bread? Rolls? Buns?"

"Perhaps we'll be lucky and get cake," Niko said.

A second set of footsteps crossed the kitchen.

"I never thought I would grow to hate bread," Lorna said. "I'm rather bitter about the development, actually."

Two heavier footsteps pounded in.

"To my corner?" Niko said.

Lorna nodded, pulling a knife from her belt as she stood.

"Don't let anyone murder me while I can't hear." Niko grabbed his book, reaching his corner before Danu. "Are you up to this?"

The door at the top of the staircase opened.

"Sit," Danu said.

Niko obeyed, humming to himself, vibrating his voice through his body to lessen the shock of the moment when every sound around him vanished.

He opened his book to the scrap of cloth he'd used to mark his page.

The sea called to her heart, every day, every night, begging her to have faith, for her lover would—

"Niko."

He leapt to his feet, banging his elbow against the wall as he spun around.

"Do you know a way past the city wall?" Cillian leaned on the back of Niko's chair, propping himself up as he panted.

"The city wall?" Niko asked.

"Yes," Cillian said. "Northern side and fast."

"I know three ways besides the gate," Niko said. "Only one could be called fast."

"We're going." Cillian grabbed Niko's arm.

"Cilli, what's happened?" Lorna ran for Niko's coat.

"Niko's not going anywhere," Danu said.

"Something's happening on the road north of the city." Cillian grabbed a roll from the table and stuffed it into his pocket. "No idea what it is, but it's got enough paun panicking we can't afford to ignore it."

Lorna tossed Niko his coat.

"He's not going," Danu said. "It's the middle of the day. He could be recognized."

"It's a necessary risk, Danu! Unless you know a way past the northern wall, he's coming." Cillian ran back up the stairs.

Niko tugged on his coat. "It's a pleasant day for a walk."

"Tell me where the path is," Danu said.

"Danu and I are coming." Mael pulled two blades from under his pillow.

"We're not having a chivving walkabout," Cillian said. "Niko, let's go."

"The paun's not one to survive a fight without help," Mael said. "Unless you'd like to shepherd the slitch on your own."

"Fine." Cillian tossed the door at the top of the stairs open. "But keep up."

Niko ran to follow, Danu right behind him.

The kitchen had emptied, giving Danu room to cut around Niko and grab Cillian's arm. "Solcha wouldn't want Niko out in the daylight."

"If she were here, I wouldn't need his help," Cillian said. "But Solcha the second was closer, and Ena would agree it's worth the chivving risk when a line of soldiers on horseback forms at the gate."

"And it's not Ena who's done something?" Niko squeezed past Danu and Cillian's duel of glares to open the door to the street. "This isn't like the healers' hall?"

He stepped out into the fresh air.

The freezing rain spattered his face, streaking cold down the back of his neck and ruining any hope he'd had of a burst of joy to celebrate his temporary freedom before he'd reached the middle of the street. He headed east, turning north at the next corner.

Cillian elbowed Niko in the side. "Word of advice for our fresh, little, warrior babe. If you're going to ask about a person the soldiers would like to hang, don't open the door and step outside before you've gotten an answer."

"Right." Niko squinted against the rain, searching for anyone lurking along the street. "But was it her?"

"Last I heard, she was back with Harrell's folks," Cillian said. "So the best I can offer is a probably not."

"The one with you," Niko said, "the other set of heavy footsteps in the kitchen. Did he go to Harrell to find her?"

"Close enough," Cillian said.

Niko headed east again, taking the corner wide enough to give him a chance to subtly glance back to make sure he hadn't left Danu behind.

She met his gaze.

Something between anger and fear filled her eyes.

Niko stopped and turned to face her.

She sidestepped to cut past him. A tiny shake of her head, so small it could have been a shiver, gave the only hint she had noticed him.

"Come on." Cillian looped his arm through Niko's. "If whatever's got the paun spooked happens to bring our doom, I'd rather not linger in the wet any longer than necessary before I die."

31

NIKO

Burrowing through the tunnel had been less pleasant than Niko had remembered. The cold, the wet, and Cillian's grumbling hadn't helped.

Cillian kept beside Niko as they cut through the forest, glaring at Niko as he smacked mud from his coat in a way that seemed to imply he'd much rather be smacking Niko's face.

Niko shoved his fists into his pockets, resigning himself to wallow in soggy filth until Dudia led them back to their basement.

Cillian flicked a mud glob from his shoulder. "If I'd known you were part mole—"

"You'd have waited for Ena to show you a path out of the city?" Niko ducked beneath a branch, gritting his teeth as a frozen twig dragged through his muddy hair.

"Ena wouldn't take anyone with her," Cillian said. "She'd climb over the wall and leave us all behind."

"Then you should be grateful for my tunnel."

A stick snapped behind Niko. He kept his gaze on the next branch waiting to scratch his face.

"What under the stars do you use that hole for anyway?" Cillian said. "Do you find yourself attracted to worms?"

"I used it to sneak out of the city to indulge in the wicked glories of youth," Niko said. "Admittedly, I did learn to bring a spare set of clothes."

Cillian murmured something that sounded like *chivving paun.*

Ungrateful stone blood.

Two sharp knocks came from behind Niko. He eyed the trees ahead, searching for the least unpleasant path.

Knock. Knock.

Cillian grabbed Niko's arm, spinning him around to face Danu and Mael.

Danu had fared well in the tunnel, her smaller frame leaving her far cleaner than mud-packed Mael.

She tapped her ear and pointed southwest.

Niko closed his eyes, tipping his head in that direction.

Voices, several angry voices rumbled beneath the constant patter of the rain, low but urgent—inconveniently close to the wall where the trees hadn't been allowed to grow as thick, leaving little in the way of hiding places.

Niko pointed to the voices, nodding to Danu then continuing west, giving them more time in the thicker trees before heading south.

The road came into view before the wall.

A cluster of people, worse off than Niko's party in terms of filth and wet, huddled in the middle of the road. Five children shared the backs of two horses. Six adults surrounded the horses, while two more kept in front of the group, facing the lines of soldiers blocking the gate.

"Just the children," the woman nearest the soldiers said. "They're frozen, wet, and hungry."

"No one enters Ilara," one of the mounted soldiers just in front of the gate said. "Notices have been posted, and our orders have been given. There are no exceptions I can make."

"But they're children," the woman said.

Niko kept low, grateful for the mud coating his clothing as he crept closer to the cluster.

"You won't go up the road to help the others," the common man near the gate shouted. "You won't let us in the city. You won't even bring food for children who haven't eaten a bite since they were almost stolen."

One of the children on horseback began to wail.

"Don't make things worse." The woman rounded on the man.

"Word of your request has been sent to our commander," the mounted soldier said. "If you don't like waiting for their response, you may turn around and follow the road north."

"Either wait here to die or run back into Death's claws?" the man said.

"Don't." The woman gripped his arm, saying something too soft for Niko to hear.

The man wrenched his arm free. "We were attacked!"

Niko dropped down as the soldiers in the line nearest the common folk reached for their swords.

"An Ilbrean village was attacked." The man stepped toward the gate. "My family was murdered."

Niko clenched his teeth against the sting of the cold as his hands sank into the freezing muck.

The woman grabbed the man's arm, trying to drag him back.

"I am sorry for your loss," the soldier said.

The man broke free and kept stalking forward.

The woman didn't follow.

"I didn't misplace my wife," the man said. "The demon-bound monsters that came with the ice, they killed her."

"Aren't all the paun busy in Ilara?" Cillian whispered, his hand meeting Niko's in the mud as he leaned close to whisper in Niko's ear.

"We have sent word to our comman—" the soldier began.

"Are you not listening?" The man stopped ten feet from the guards.

"As much as you loathe the Guilds, there are plenty of unguilded in Ilbrea capable of doing horrific things," Niko whispered back.

The woman backed toward the cluster around the horses.

"Their horde was traveling south," the man said. "Even running for our lives, we can't have stayed far in front of them."

"Thank the mountain I was born a Black Blood," Cillian said as the soldiers drew their swords.

"You aren't listening! The ice rose up to attack us," the man said, "blocking our path, penning us in to be slaughtered."

A marble of solid dread ricocheted through Niko's mind, shattering his thoughts into unusable fragments.

"And it wasn't plain men wielding swords." The man's voice cracked as he kept shouting. "They had magic."

Niko pushed himself to his feet.

Run. Quiet.

"Twisting the ice into weapons as they slit our throats," the man said.

Make his body run. Make the man quiet.

"And the demons fighting beside them wouldn't die," the man said. "How could I protect her from something that wouldn't die?"

Hide. Find them a place to hide.

Niko stepped forward.

A yank on his arm pulled him down as a sting sliced across his back, expelling the marble from his mind as pain surged awareness through his body.

"Demons with magic murdered my wife." The man spread his arms, offering his chest to the soldiers. "Any soul on this side of the gate doesn't stand a chivving chance when the ice horde arrives."

Ignoring the pain in his back, Niko twisted his arm free.

Mud clung to Niko's boots, slowing his every step as he ran for the road.

A warning pang twisted through Niko's ankle as Danu knocked him behind a tree, pinning him out of sight of the soldiers. "What are you doing?"

"I don't mind greeting Death before the demons come," the man said. "It'll be a better fate than your family faces when the ice breaks through the gate."

"We have to save them." Niko craned his neck, finding a view of the soldiers through a gap between trees.

"He's baiting paun," Danu said. "We're not charging into a fight for a fool who's begging to die."

"Take him," the soldier said.

"Am I to be arrested?" the man said. "Will that get me through the gate?"

"Any whisper of wild magic will get you killed in Ilbrea," Niko said. "Whatever other hell has seized Ilara, I will wager every coin I'll ever earn that quick route to the grave hasn't changed. At least I hope the ones the sorcerers choose to capture will die quickly."

"You are being arrested for defying a soldier of the Guilds, for agitation, and for disrupting the peace," the soldier said.

"I can head north," Danu said. "Pretend I'm another survivor and try to get them to follow me."

"There isn't time." Niko pushed against Danu's arm.

A force greater than her physical strength kept him pinned in place.

"And when the Guilds realize you should have listened to me, will they thank me before they put a noose around my neck?" The man kept his arms spread wide, not defending himself as the soldiers approached.

"If word of trouble at the gate reached the Brien, the sorcerers know, too," Niko said. "Locked in their tower or not, they've got to have better eyes on the city than the Black Bloods."

"Get your children out," the man said as a soldier grabbed his arms, yanking them behind him. "Whatever it costs, take them south. May the gods never let another babe be stolen by the demons' magic."

"The sorcerers know these people are here, they've had a nice chat about it, and now they are on their way to do horrible things," Niko said. "We can't watch that happen."

The force pinning Niko in place eased.

"All the way to the eastern end of the city, the cliffs behind the Map Master's Palace—"

A scream cut through Niko's words. High-pitched, terrified.

Niko's bonds vanished as Danu stepped back, her wide eyes fixed on the mountain road.

He shoved past her, fighting the mud with every step as he raced for the cluster of common folk.

They hadn't moved. Hadn't fallen.

The child kept screaming, but no one else joined.

Niko looked toward the man, expecting to see a sword through his gut.

But the man wasn't bleeding. Wasn't screaming, either.

Niko's boot caught on a root. He stumbled forward, slamming his shoulder into a tree as a woman's scream drowned out the child's.

A streak of movement caught Niko's eye.

On top of the city wall stood four figures in purple robes.

The soldiers on the wall raced toward the sorcerers. Barriers of blue mist curled into being, blocking their path.

Ignoring the branches tearing his face, Niko bolted for the children.

On horse, they might be fast enough. If they fled north—

A soldier launched a spear at a sorcerer.

The spear slowed as it cleared the top of the city wall.

The sorcerer the fool had targeted tore her hands through the air, shattering the spear into a dozen pieces. The shards shot down at the soldiers.

Niko ignored their screams, still sprinting toward the children who still hadn't run north.

Go. Please, go.

A sphere of light burst into being, surrounding the man who had been shouting at the soldiers.

The soldiers around him screamed as their arms, caught inside the spell—

Severed. A bloodless detachment.

Two streaks of bright, white sparks shot toward the cluster.

"Run!"

The bolts hit their marks before Niko had finished his shout.

The horses bucked. Three of the children flew off, crashing onto the road. The other two held on as the horses charged north.

Two more bolts shot toward the cluster.

Niko tipped his head down as instinct promised that would somehow save him from a sorcerer's magic.

Another spear flew toward the sorcerers.

Most soldiers had prepared their shields against the storm of fragments the sorcerers rained down on them in return. Two hadn't.

Shouted orders came from the city side of the wall as Niko fixed his gaze on a child trying to push themselves out of the mud.

Grab one. If you can save one.

A wave of purple light emanated a high, piercing shriek—the sound of Death's approach.

The soldiers didn't scream as the light consumed them.

The woman didn't scream, either.

Niko reached for the child, but they were far away, too far. He dove toward the road.

A force slammed against his gut, shoving him back the instant before something rammed into his side, knocking him into the mud.

His lungs had no air to scream as the purple light enveloped the survivors.

He clawed at the mud, trying to get up.

"No." Danu slammed him back down.

The light receded, rolling away from the people who'd fled to the safety of Ilara.

Their bodies lay on the ground. Not torn or burned. But fallen and still and unmistakably dead.

But not the children. The children weren't there.

Danu screamed, her body arching away from Niko's.

He knocked her arm out from under her, pushing her sideways, tossing his body over hers.

Her scream pitched higher for a terrible heartbeat. She bit her lips together, swallowing the sound as she rammed her hand against Niko's chest.

"Run, paun."

A hand grabbed Niko's arm, wrenching him to his feet. Cillian shoved Niko east, then seized Danu's hand.

Niko made himself move, following Mael's path through the trees.

He looked back, letting the branches slice his cheek, needing to see Danu behind him.

Cillian kept hold of Danu's arm, propelling her forward, staying by her side.

Behind them, on the road, three glowing orbs rose into the air, floating toward the wall like wind-caught bubbles.

Niko made himself keep running.

You couldn't have saved them, Mara whispered in his mind, her words barely audible over the rasping of his breath.

His ankle wobbled with every step, threatening to collapse beneath him.

Nikolas Endur, Mara whispered, *you could not have saved them.*

Mael slowed, letting Niko take the lead as they neared the tunnel under the wall.

The entrance burrowed down through a gap between the roots of two old trees, the shape of it more like a bear's den than anything meant for a person's use. A perfect thing for a soldier unaccustomed to the wilds to miss if they were sent prowling through the woods, searching for smugglers and miscreants.

Gasping for air, Niko leaned against the tunnel's southern tree, sparing his ankle as he reached for Danu.

She ignored Niko's hand as she pulled away from Cillian. Her legs shook before she'd managed a full step.

"What under the mountain happened?" Cillian locked his arm around her waist.

She swallowed a scream.

"Shit." Cillian let go, still holding his arms toward her as though she might fall.

"My back," Danu said.

Niko pushed away from the tree, rounding on Mael.

A hint of a smile crowned Mael's brutal indifference.

"I'm fine." Danu's tone backed Cillian away. "Some sodding shit of the sorcerers grazed me. Nothing frie and a bath won't fix."

"The mountain grieves the pain of each faithful black blood." Mael stepped back, clearing Danu's path to the burrow. "May your wounds be as small next time Death approaches."

32

MARA

A steady pattern of low murmurs with the occasional louder warning to be quiet or face Brady's wrath came from the hearth room of Mara's refuge.

Part of Mara, a very selfish part, wished she could leave the stolen papers behind to go bicker with the children. Better frustrated by young tempers than crushed by the weight of answers perched out of her reach.

Elver sighed and returned the letter he'd been reading to the pile on the trunk Mara had stolen long ago to protect her supplies.

And now you've stolen much worse.

Sneaking into the Map Master's Palace presented no problem for two of the Karron brood who had spent their more wayward years living in the massive house. And, while Allora could have picked the locks in Lord Karron's study more quickly, Mara had managed well enough.

But digging through Lord Karron's papers had begun a circle of guilt that had been churning through Mara's mind ever since.

She respected the Lord Map Maker, but she couldn't pretend there was no possibility of his hiding information from her, even if she and Adrial had more of a right to know the fate of the older children missing from Ian Ayres than even Lord Karron, with his seat on the Guilds council, could claim.

Lord Karron had been kind to her, raising her alongside his beloved daughter, but he had never rescued the other children from Ian Ayres.

How could he have seen Adrial's horrible scars and not stormed straight to the demon's island to steal the rest of the children from the matrons?

What if Lord Karron knew the fate of the missing bastards and it was too terrible for him to face so he'd just pretended the island had sunk into the sea?

He'd never do that, Mara, Allora scolded. *My father hides danger from us, not pain.*

Mara shoved her attention back to the journal in her hand.

Lord Karron had never been one for gushing sentiment. A peeve to Allora at times, a boon to Mara as she read through the entries following her rescue from Ian Ayres.

The boy's skin is improving, but the healers haven't made any progress on the deeper injuries.

Allora has started dressing the girl up like her own living doll. I've told Allora to stop, though have little faith in her heeding my warning. I fear my daughter may have to learn the rougher lesson from the doll herself.

The entry carried on with notes on preparations for a journey heading to map the changes in the southern coastline after the winter's horrible storms. Lord Karron wished he could do the work himself but didn't think it safe to leave Allora alone with the two new additions to the household.

The entry dates in the journal jumped ahead nearly two weeks, with no missing pages or scratched out passages.

Allora has shifted her attention to the boy, finally accepting Mara's rejection of her preening. A welcome change, though the window needn't have fallen victim to Mara's wrath.

Allora is determined to have the boy reading by the end of the month. I don't know if he's too terrified of her to plead for an end to the ceaseless lessons, or actually enjoying learning his letters. Either way, he's stopped hiding in closets.

The news beyond the household was a council meeting. The Lord Sailor and Lord Soldier had a spat over soldiers betting on how many sailors they could arrest in a night.

The next day…

The boy's lungs are infected again. The healers look at him as though I'd dragged a dying kitten home. Allora's heart will break if the boy doesn't survive. Damn the monsters who made a child suffer so.

Nothing beyond that.
Not for nearly two months.

Allora has determined Adrial will be a scribe. He still stumbles when reading simple words, but Allora has asked that I hire tutors to aid in Adrial's learning. I can't find it in my heart to say no. I don't think I could reject any request from the boy, either. I begged him to survive, and Adrial managed the task.

Mara has not settled into any of her studies. The only interest the girl has is digging through the trees. I don't know how to tame a reckless child as I have never learned to be content with my feet firmly planted. Dudia may have put too much faith in me when he placed Mara's fate in my hands.

Mara swiped the tears from her cheeks.
Tham laid his hand on her leg, assuring her of his presence

without abandoning Lord Karron's ledgers of coin spent in the months after saving Adrial and Mara.

The next entry in the journal came a few days after the last. Mara had finally become friendly with Allora again. A day after that, Adrial asked Lord Karron if the tutors might come more often.

Mara fell from a tree and terrified Lord Karron.

Adrial showed true talent with a pen.

Allora spent the afternoon helping Adrial walk longer distances, strengthening his legs.

Allora managed to braid Mara's hair without bleeding.

Treasure after treasure as Lord Karron recorded the birth of the clan. Each item a miracle for a child salvaged from hell. Not a single hint of his even wondering what happened to the older children of Ian Ayres.

Mara shut her eyes, letting them rest after hours spent reading in the dim light.

Finding nothing about Ian Ayres beyond Mara and Adrial was almost the best she could have hoped for—if he hadn't learned some horrible truth and ignored it, but had simply been easily turned away when the council ignored his condemnation of Ian Ayres.

"Are you done reading for now?" Elver whispered.

"Yes." Mara opened her eyes.

Elver knelt right beside her, his face inches from hers. "Good. I've had a thought. No, three thoughts."

"What are they?" Mara straightened up, stretching her back.

"First, I don't think you should have broken into the Lord Map Maker's study. This is all useless. You should have gone for the kitchens instead."

"I'm close to agreeing," Mara said.

"I'm not sure what all the initials in Lord Karron's ledgers mean," Tham said. "From what I do recognize, none of it seems odd."

"Hence, the kitchens would have been a better idea," Elver said. "My second thought is anger at the Ice Walkers for killing all the matrons instead of breaking them for information. Not even a solid day's worth of questioning. Pathetic."

"Elver," Mara said.

"My third thought is what if the older orphans never left the island?"

"We know they did," Mara said.

"Do we?" Elver frowned. "From what I understand, we know they were no longer living on the island, but that doesn't mean the matrons didn't kill the children to keep them from making children of their own and burn the bodies to make the crispy bits easier to bury."

Sour shot into Mara's mouth.

Tham dropped the ledger, wrapping his arm behind Mara's waist as she doubled over, trying not to be sick on the dirt floor. "They didn't kill the older ones."

"How do you know?" Elver said.

"Why would you waste food on a useless infant only to murder the child when they were able to work?" Tham said.

"Waste of resources. Fair point." Elver's frown deepened.

Mara let out a slow breath, willing her stomach to calm.

"That is a relief," Elver said. "Though it was the only guess I could think up."

"Any chance of your whispers helping us?" Mara said.

"No." Elver shook his head, stopped, then shook his head again. "This isn't what they worry over."

"Then what do they worry over?" Tham's arm tensed around Mara.

"Dark, dark things," Elver said. "Things children should never touch, but I suppose Brady has already seen worse."

A scream, a slap, and a muffled yelp came from the hearth room.

"Chivving, chivvers, chivvet, chivvinitte-chiv." Brady tore the curtain to their niche aside, ripping the fabric from the walls. "The city. It flashed up purple by the wall. The braidic sorcerers are going to burn the city."

Mara leapt to her feet, dodging in front of Tham, running for the hearth room.

Asher had Blinkers pinned to the floor. Ian had curled up beside the fire, covering his head. The rest huddled around the window.

"Let me see." Mara squeezed between the children, twisting toward the opening.

"The purple stopped," Bevvy whispered. "Does that mean we won't burn?"

"Where did you see the light?" Mara asked.

"Right," Bevvy said.

Mara looked north. The torn city sank heavy hatred into her gut, but she couldn't spot any hint of magic.

"There." Bevvy pointed. "Right there!"

A burning sphere rose into the sky above the northern gate. Glowing brightly enough to gleam in the daylight, the sphere floated higher and higher, drifting slowly south.

"More. More. More." Bevvy pounded her fist into Mara's arm as three faintly glistening orbs followed the burning sphere. "Does that mean burning alive, or no burning alive?"

"You're not going to burn," Mara said. "Whatever's happening down there, I won't let it hurt you."

All four balls of light glided toward the Sorcerers Tower.

"Maybe it means the Ice Walkers have come," Blinkers said. "And they brought the Daeduris—"

"Deadish." Asher punched Blinkers in the ribs.

Elle barked.

"Daeduris," Blinkers shouted.

"Mine's better!" Asher punched him again.

Tham lifted Asher off Blinkers.

"The Ice Walkers can't fly," Bevvy said.

"And you're sure how?" Brady said.

"The ice men who came to Ian Ayres said dead ice soldiers would help us." Blinkers swiped his tears away. "They promised an army against the Guilds. The *Daeduris* will—"

"Deadish!" Asher bucked free from Tham's hold, throwing herself toward Blinkers.

Brady elbowed Asher in the neck, knocking her aside.

"You're a fool of a braidicky letch, Blinkers. If any of the Ice Walkers you've met are still alive, they've chivving well forgotten you." Brady yanked Blinkers to his feet. "Don't go all soggy and hopeful. If the deadish are coming, it's not to help us."

The lights reached the dark stone tower and disappeared.

33

NIKO

Common men rode through the city, some ringing bells, some slamming metal mugs on metal plates, all of them shouting to clear the streets.

The rain had already kept the city clear of any idle strollers, making the men's work easier, but a few stubborn getches resisted their shouted pleas.

A woman hauling a handcart kept to a steady plod as she crossed Niko's path, her reddened face seeming more perturbed than frightened, as though the Sorcerers Guild murdering innocent common folk at the gate were nothing more than an annoyance.

Niko kept their course steadily south, ignoring the fools who ran toward the gate, poor weapons in hand, not allowing his mind to drift toward how many bodies the sorcerers could stack in the streets if a whim drove them to try.

You can't help them. You're not that powerful.

Start within reach.

Niko took two steps back, adjusting to walk beside Cillian. "We need to get warm."

"I wicked your clothes," Cillian said.

"It lasted all of a minute," Niko said.

Cillian clapped his hand on Niko's shoulder, his pace barely slowing as the wet crisped out of Niko's clothes, leaving him cold, but dry. "Best I can do. Keeping the rain off you entirely takes more magic than I can afford to burn through. Unless you want to huddle together in an alley. A canopy, I can offer."

"Cold and dry isn't going to be enough. We need to go somewhere warmer than that basement." Niko tipped his head, giving the tiniest glance toward Danu, who kept behind them, arms wrapped around her middle, from pain or cold, he didn't know. "An hour in front of a hot fire, something warm to drink. We all need it."

"Should we nip up to the Map Master's Palace?" Cillian said.

"If the Brien can't offer a fireplace, I say we chance it. I've survived too chivving much to die from cold seeping into my lungs." Niko stopped in the center of the next cross street. "We just watched sorcerers, Guilded sorcerers, murder innocent people."

"I can't believe that's uncommon," Cillian said.

"What's wrong?" Danu stopped beside Niko, her hands near the daggers on her hips though her voice trembled with cold.

"We just found out there's some kind of murderous ice rampaging through the north," Niko said.

"Which is why we've got to dodge back to our hole," Cillian said. "That's the sort of information we're supposed to share."

"Surely there's somewhere we can carry the news that's warm," Niko said. "That home near the healers' hall had a fireplace."

"We're not going back there," Danu said.

"I'm trying to get you warm," Niko said.

"I'm not a broken doll. I can care for myself."

"Not if you die of cold." Cillian dragged his hands down his face. "Sodding stars."

He cut down the road heading east.

Niko's heart banged into his throat. "Are we going to the Map Master's Palace?"

"I thought our goal was warm, not dead," Cillian said.

Niko kept his pace slower than Cillian's, dropping back to walk beside Danu. "How bad is it?"

Danu stayed silent as she pushed her rain-drenched hair from her forehead.

"I know you're not a doll," Niko said. "You're stronger and more capable than I could ever be. But I also know what it's like to have your back flayed from the inside out. You made me take care of my wounds. You've no sodding hope of me not doing the same to you."

"I'm not a slitch who's going to let their wounds get infected," Danu said.

"I'll let Cillian know you need tending then," Niko said.

"I will tear the sodding hair from your—"

"Then unless you've suddenly developed the ability to heal with your magic, I'm your choice. Tending to your own back takes more skill than it seems, and that is knowledge gained from hard-won success."

"If I need help, I'll ask." Danu picked up her pace.

"You won't." Niko caught her hand, holding it as though she were returning the poor offer of comfort even though her hand stayed as stiff as if it had truly frozen through. "I will kneel in the middle of the street and beg if I have to. We just watched sorcerers snatch the life from those people with a wave of chivving light. If there's a way to defend from an attack like that, I've never heard of it.

"And now we've no one to question about the danger sweeping down from the north. Between ice that kills and waves of purple death, I can't convince myself Dudia and all the gods haven't turned against us, and you're in pain. And your being in pain sinks a sharper panic into my chest than magic-made doom ever could. Your face is getting paler, and the panic is twisting deeper."

She didn't fight as Niko raised her hand, pressing his lips to her rain-slicked fingers.

"Please, Danu. Some salve on the wounds, and I'll leave you alone."

"You asked for heat, not salve. There might not be anything where Cillian is taking us. And I'm not—" Danu let out a long breath, as though fighting to keep her voice calm and low. "I won't bare my mark in the basement. I won't give that slitch the pleasure."

"I understand."

She wrapped her fingers around Niko's hand, the comfort lasting only a step before Cillian stopped near the servants' entrance of a fine merchant's home. Danu snatched her hand from Niko's, moving it toward the blade on her hip.

Low bushes surrounded the three-story house. Built of pale stone with blue shutters flanking the windows and ornate drapes visible through the panes, the home didn't give any impression of being a place where muddy, cold Black Bloods might find welcome.

"I'm burning through a good bit of grace and favor bringing you here. So best behavior." Cillian took two steps toward the door before stopping to look back at Mael. "And for the love of your trueborn blood, don't growl at anyone."

Cillian knocked on the door and shoved his hands back into his, assumedly dry, pockets while he waited for the door to open.

The edge of the curtains in the kitchen shifted, as though someone were peeking out at them.

"Come on." Cillian knocked again.

Niko glanced down either end of the street, searching for the wave of purple death that would surely catch them now they'd stop moving.

"Breathe, Niko," Danu whispered.

He dragged in a deep breath, forcing his lungs to accept air. The cold tightened his throat and swept through his chest.

He managed two more full breaths before the door opened.

A girl of around sixteen stood in the doorway—hands on her hips, feet planted as though preparing to attack—blocking their path into the house. She narrowed her eyes at Cillian.

"Kyley," Cillian said, "it's cold as a snow hare's fluffy dangles out here. Set us by the fire, would you?"

"I'll see if she's allowing visitors today." Kyley smiled as she flung the door closed.

Cillian blocked the doorjamb with his foot. "But we could wait by the fire. Let this be the day you grow a heart, girl."

Kyley kicked his foot out of the way and slammed the door shut.

"Charming child," Cillian said.

"We could be back to our quarters by now," Mael said.

"She'll let us in," Cillian said. "It wasn't bad enough for her to leave me out in the cold."

Niko shifted from foot to foot, preserving what little feeling he had left in his toes. "What wasn't bad enough?"

"That stays between Nora, me, and the ruby-eyed snake brooch."

Niko's cheeks had gotten too cold to give even the smallest grin to go with his chattered, "Ha."

"We've got to get word to the others," Danu said. "We can't just wait here."

"Nora can make sure the right people are told the right things," Cillian said.

A woman appeared in the kitchen window, bright blonde hair framing a face so perfect, she seemed more suited to a romantic fairy story than any nightmare involving sorcerers and Black Bloods.

Cillian waved.

The woman raised one, well-arched eyebrow.

"Upon the stars, I will behave," Cillian called.

The woman pursed her lips.

"Upon the safety of my manhood." Cillian clasped his hands together. "Please."

The woman shook her head, her curls bouncing gently around her face, and disappeared from the window.

"I may have to try and bribe the ruby-eyed snake for that story," Niko whispered.

"I'm not sure you'd want to know," Danu whispered back.

Kyley opened the door again. "She's a soft-hearted sap. Try not to forget some people in this house would love to shove their foot up your ass and wear your guts as stockings."

"Kyley," a woman said, "threaten Cillian once he's inside. You're letting in a draft."

Grinning, Kyley bowed the four frozen wretches into the house.

Cillian nigh on ran inside, whether to escape the cold or wanting to be sure Kyley couldn't slam the door in his face, Niko didn't care as he planted himself between Mael and Danu, making sure she entered the house next before following behind.

The kitchen smelled of roasted meat and fresh-ground herbs with only a hint of bread tainting the scent. A crackling fire filled the hearth.

Niko took Danu's hand, pulling her toward the warmth, ignoring the tsks of the older woman near the stove.

"We need to get your boots off." Niko pulled a chair from the table.

"Stop fussing," Danu said.

"I'm taking mine off, too." Niko set a second chair beside the fireplace. "Frostbite is a beast I prefer to avoid."

"All of you take your sodden, sopping boots off." The older woman slammed a kettle onto the stove. "I don't like mud in my kitchen. Filth up my floor, and if your toes have to be chopped off, I'll let Kyley wield the knife."

"With pleasure." Kyley grabbed a carving knife from the table.

"That knife is too large for toes." Niko yanked off his boot, his half-numb fingers slipping on the wet leather. "A good pair of shears would be best."

"I'll see what the gardener's tools can offer." Kyley strode out of the kitchen.

"You didn't have to give her an idea like that." Cillian hung his coat on a hook by the fire.

The glorious blond entered the kitchen the way Kyley had left, carrying a blessedly large stack of blankets.

"Nora, beautiful Nora, the stars rained all their glory upon Ilbrea the day you were born." Cillian yanked off his boots and socks, placing them inches from the fire.

Niko added his and Danu's sopping boots to the line.

Nora dropped the stack of blankets onto the table, clearing Niko's view of the round, jeweled brooch that accented the magnificent mounds of her breasts peaking above the low front of her bodice.

"Making yourself comfortable, Cillian? Did I not hear Kyley plotting something with shears?"

"We didn't end up frozen stumbling around drunk," Cillian said. "I'd have come today even if I was warm, rich, and full-bellied."

Niko hung his coat by the fire. Without the sopping layer, the heat of the flames finally reached his skin.

"It's bad, croimian." Cillian took Nora's hand, pressing her palm over his heart. "The sorcerers slaughtered seven tilk and stole three more."

Niko reached for Danu's shoulder, ready to help peel her coat away.

She gripped the front of the coat, keeping it on.

"Black Bloods or paun?" The words being spoken by a bejeweled Ilbrean grated against Niko's remaining shreds of reason.

"Paun," Cillian said.

"Cacting purple demon spawn," the older woman said.

"That's why all the men are banging around the streets?" Nora opened a tall cabinet, pulling down a bottle of frie.

"The slitches with bells are only carrying half the warning," Cillian said. "I need a few weighty flyers. We can't afford the time it would take to send runners to every den in Ilara, and word needs to go beyond the city walls."

"Sib"—Nora looked to the older woman pouring steaming water into four mugs—"have Kyley and Rowan close the shutters. Then make up four rooms for the night."

"Nora—"

"You just dragged muddy Black Bloods into my home, bringing word of something apparently worse than paun sorcerers murdering tilk in such a blatant manner men have been riding through the frigid rain to warn us all." Nora took over for Sib, pouring frie into the steaming mugs as Sib tutted her way out of the kitchen. "Night is about to swallow the city, and you've drawn the gods' eye to my door. There's not a chivving chance of you leaving me without your protection. If we're still alive in the morning, we can renegotiate your freedom, *croimian*." She scowled as she mimicked Cillian's tone.

"We serve the Black Bloods," Mael said. "Not you."

Nora tipped her head, her lips curving into an alluring, teasing grin. "You're Mael, aren't you?"

"Yes," Mael said from his spot by the door, his boots and coat still on.

"You're just as I imagined." Nora set the frie aside, approaching Mael with no hint of fear.

His expression didn't change as she leaned close, looking into his eyes.

"A giant brute as Bryana's pet trueborn." She patted his cheek. "Adorable."

A growl rumbled in Mael's throat.

"Shit," Cillian muttered.

"Quiet, little brute." Nora pressed her finger to Mael's lips. "If you'd like to accept my hospitality and have a nice bath and sleep in a warm bed, you will behave as a polite and gracious guest. If you'd like to run back into the rain to shiver in whatever filthy hole the Black Bloods have chosen for you, by all means go. It's Cillian's protection I want, not yours. If I wish someone to throw stones, I'll buy them a slingshot."

"If you—"

"I am protected by alliances wrapped in treaties and sheltered by blood oaths." Nora kissed Mael's cheek. "Even think of threatening me, and I'll have your balls made into pretty little earrings you can wear while you scrub my floor."

"Vivid," Cillian said.

"Now, would the brute like a bath and a bed, or will he crawl back to his hole?" Nora said.

"We're going." Mael sneered as he gave Nora a somehow disrespectful bow. "Cillian can set raising his mast above his duty to the Black Bloods. I serve my oath to the Brien Elder."

Mael turned toward the door.

"No, we have to stay." Niko stood, the cold floor stinging his barely thawed feet. "At least for a while longer, please. I haven't"—Niko didn't let himself glance toward Danu—"I need a night's sleep in the warmth. I wasn't born with stone blood. I'm at the edge of tipping toward illness, and none of us are useful trapped in bed, dying of fever. We've been offered a respite from the cold. We have to take it."

Mael's sneer sharpened. "As Solcha demands."

"You're that one?" Nora frowned at Niko.

"We'll only need three rooms," Mael said.

"If you're heading back to the den, I won't send a message to Lorna," Cillian said.

"I'm staying. Danu and Niko can share a room. They have so little time together, best for them to take advantage of every moment." Mael's tone held no malice.

Panic and fear twisted around Niko's spine, threading through his ribs, squeezing tight, not letting his lungs expand.

"We're acknowledging that?" Cillian said. "Why wasn't I told?"

Nora looked to Danu and Niko. "One room or two?"

Niko gasped as sharp pain tore through his back.

"One," Danu said.

"As you wish." Nora stepped behind Mael, opening the window and pulling the shutters outside closed, leaving the kitchen fire to light the room. "The mugs are mostly frie with a bit of hot water for show." She slid the latch on the shutters, locking them. "Sib will show you to your rooms. But do leave your boots here. The old love is vicious if you dirty her floors."

She closed the window and locked it as well.

"Take off your clothes and wrap in a blanket, Cillian," Nora said. "You're not ruining any of the parlor's upholstery."

"I wouldn't dare." Cillian unbuttoned his pants, dropping them to the ground.

Nora laughed as she strode toward the door that led to the rest of the house.

Niko waited until she'd stepped out of the kitchen before chasing after her.

"Niko," Danu called.

He walked faster. "Nora."

Nora turned, laying her hand on the polished wooden banister of the wide stairs that took up most of the corridor. "Yes, Solcha the second?"

"Do you have any bandages or ointment?" Niko asked. "Anything to tend a wound?"

"Is our little Solcha injured?" Nora leaned back, studying him from the ground up.

"Not badly," Niko said. "Got cut all to hell getting away from the sorcerers. There's a few deep ones I'd rather wrap before going back to our dirt hovel."

"Everyone suspects a rat, but no one thinks to doubt the blue jay. Why the Black Bloods think hiding from the paun demands wallowing in filth will never make sense to me." Nora sighed. "I'll have a box brought to your room."

"Thank you." Niko fled Nora's piercing gaze, dodging back into the kitchen as gracefully as his aching, still half-frozen body allowed.

He'd finished his frie and regained full feeling in his feet before Sib came to fetch them.

At a withering glare from Sib, even Mael took off his boots, abandoning them in kitchen.

The corridor and staircase Niko had seen before served as the center point of the house with doors leading to a dining room, a library, a morning room, and behind a closed door, Niko assumed, the parlor where Cillian and Nora worked spreading word that things in Ilara had somehow become unbelievably worse.

Lanterns had been lit throughout the house, making up for the shutters blocking out the gray dusk. Still, knowing there should be light coming in from the windows somehow made the intricate maroon swirls decorating the walls of the second-floor corridor a threat—the home's promise to snatch the life from his body before the Sorcerers Guild had a chance.

Six doors led out of the hall. Sib gave Mael the first room on the right, closing him in before giving Danu and Niko the first room on the left.

"I'll make stew for supper," Sib said in a low voice, keeping her eyes on the door of Mael's room as she barred Danu and Niko from entering theirs.

Ours.

Sodding, sheep-shitting, slitch of a demon-bred trueborn.

"Come down and eat your fill before you tell the giant there's food. Watching him scrape the bottom of the pot is my kind of revenge." Sib winked and stepped out of the way, waited for Danu and Niko to enter the room, then closed the door behind them.

34

NIKO

A fresh-lit fire crackled in the grate, beginning its fight against the chill in the room. Two chairs and a little table had been set beside it, the box on the table giving Niko something to fix his focus on that was neither the four-poster bed nor the massive tub that were the other features their quarters offered.

He checked the contents of the box. Three rolls of bandages, salve, and a bottle of tonic of the sort Ena favored.

"As good a supply as we'd have found in the bread den." Niko took one of the smaller cloths from the shelf above the tub.

"You don't have to help me."

He looked up at the pain in Danu's voice.

She pulled her coat to the edges of her shoulders, swallowing hard before dropping it down to her arms.

"I'm sodding well helping." Niko stepped behind her.

The sopping-wet sleeves of her shift clung to her coat as he gently slid it the rest of the way down her arms.

"You should have dried your clothes." Niko laid the coat beside the fire.

"It's harder magic than you'd think."

"Cillian could have done it for you."

"I didn't want the fabric dried into my back." Danu's fingers slipped on the knot at the top of her bodice. She turned her back to Niko, hiding her fumbling, sending a white-hot wave of rage thrumming through his veins.

Above her bodice, a thick streak of red stained her shift, its vivid color fading to pink as it spread down the white fabric below the highest of Danu's marks. The rain had turned the deep blue of her bodice black, hiding the rest of her wounds.

Niko twisted the tap on the tub, gratefully greeting the sting as the first hint of the water warming reached his hands. "I don't know how Cillian made friends with a wealthy Ilaran, but I am very grateful."

"I feels wrong to be here when—"

"The stars have chosen to rain demons upon us?"

Danu made a sound too near a whimper as she peeled her bodice from her back.

There were only two coin-sized patches of pale fabric left. The rest had been soaked with blood.

Niko shut the tap off, laying the cloth on the side of the tub.

"How deep did he pull from?" He banished the anger from his voice, making the words come out flat.

"I'm not sure how to tell." Danu unfastened her skirt, dropping it to the floor.

The rain had pulled the red of her blood all the way to the bottom of her shift.

"Could you…" Danu took a deep breath. "Could you bring me a blanket?"

Niko grabbed one of the three that had been left folded on the foot of the bed.

He set it on the chair beside her and closed his eyes for a moment, trying to pick the right words. "Do you want me to help you lift the shift away from your back?"

"It's not dried to the mark like your shirt is to yours." She raised the bottom of her shift.

"He can only rip at the part of my mark he drew. It's a nick compared to yours."

Danu took two more deep breaths. "Can you please help me peel off my shift?"

"We'll work it up slowly."

He stayed behind her, bunching the blood-stained fabric as he lifted it away from each of the slashes on her back.

Ignoring that his fingers were moving along her bare skin took no effort as an unfamiliar longing for violence dug its vicious claws into every niche in his mind.

The wounds on Danu's back went deep, ripping into her flesh as though she'd truly been whipped.

Niko's hands shook as he lifted the shift over her head and tossed the bloody garment by the fire. He kept his gaze lowered as he passed her the blanket.

She wrapped the heavy fabric around herself, letting it sag in the back to hang below her shredded mark.

The raw edges of the wounds had already turned an angry red.

At least the dirt they'd been crawling through hadn't reached her back.

At least Danu could get warm. At least the Sorcerers Guild hadn't killed them.

"Do you want to sit by the fire?" Niko said. "Would lying down be easier?"

"You sound like you think I'm going to break."

"I'd be shattering into sand if our places were switched."

"You know that's not true."

"Fixating on helping you is making it easier for me to not storm across the hall and do my best to cut Mael's throat even if he can just tear the stone in my mark through my heart and kill me."

"Don't say that." Danu gripped Niko's wrist. "Never say that. Fate fulfills such whispers."

"Mael is a monster."

"Mael is what Bryana asks him to be." She let go and sat in front of the fire, lifting her hair over her shoulder, silently granting Niko access to her wounds.

Niko gathered cloths from near the tub and knelt behind her. He hesitated for a moment, uncertain of where to begin.

She deserves better care than I can give.

Every touch as gentle as his shaking hands could manage, he cleaned the blood from around the highest of her marks.

Danu pulled her knees to her chest, dropping her head as Niko worked.

He moved on to the next mark down.

She gasped at his first touch.

"I'm sorry. I'm so sorry."

"You're helping me."

"I never want you to be in pain."

"Just keep going. Better to get it over with."

"I'm sorry," Niko whispered as she tensed at his touch. "It's torn deep. What madness made that barbaric, chivving monster rip through your mark while sorcerers were attacking?" He moved farther down her back where the wounds were wider. His stomach rolled, driving sour into his throat. "There is evil within the Guilds, but I promise you Mael can stand with the worst of Ilbreans."

"Leave it, Niko."

Niko rinsed the cloth, twisting his anger into the fabric as he wrang out Danu's blood. "Him tearing at my mark makes sense. I disobeyed. I ran to help Ilbreans. All you did was stop me from getting spotted by the sorcerers. If I'd made it out onto the road, we all could've ended up dead. Even by your demon elder's standards, that's forgivable."

"It wasn't."

"Mael's got to value his own life."

"But I saved yours."

"For the nine hundredth time."

"That's why he tore my mark, Niko. I didn't let you die."

Niko's mind weaved between her words, trying to form a bearable thought.

"Bryana gave the order." Danu dipped her chin, looking back, as close to facing Niko as she could manage. "She wants a martyr. Solcha murdered by Ilbrean Sorcerers as he tried to stop them from slaughtering their own people—a perfect tale for the Brien to cling to. Better than Bryana could have dreamt. I disobeyed my elder when I kept you from reaching the road. Mael gave the punishment I'd earned."

"If Bryana wants me dead, why not have Mael do it?" Niko snatched the bottle of tonic from the table. "I'm sure he'd revel in the pleasure of shooting a stone through my heart. Or is he the fallback plan? If the sorcerers don't end me, he'll torment and kill me then stage my corpse as a victim of the Guilds?"

"Not him. Me."

Niko's rage flipped into a cold, stone-heavy fear that filled his chest. "If the sorcerers don't kill me, you're supposed to."

"I couldn't stand in the trees and watch you die. I couldn't even make myself want to try." Danu's shoulders rounded, stretching her highest mark. She sucked a sharp breath through her teeth and straightened back up.

Niko's hands stayed steady as he set the tonic aside. "He tore your back because you disobeyed Bryana by saving me."

She didn't answer.

"What will he do if you disobey again?"

"Nothing for you to worry about."

"Danu, no." Niko crawled to kneel in front of her, placing his fingers under her chin, tipping her face up just enough for him to see her eyes. "What are Mael's orders?"

"I would never hurt you."

"That wasn't my question."

"Niko, just—"

"Danu!"

She closed her eyes, her breath shuddering as tears ran down her cheeks. "Bryana wants a martyr. Either one of us will do."

"You're wrong." A ripple of relief bought Niko a full breath. He took Danu's hands, kissing them both. "You're Bryana's niece. I'm sure she wants me dead, but she'd never hurt you. You misunderstood her orders."

"If the Guilds don't kill you, I have to. If I don't, Mael kills me and makes it look like the paun's fault. Bryana was very clear." Danu slipped her hands from Niko's to swipe her tears away. "I disobeyed. I was punished."

"No. No." Niko sat back on his heels, shaking his head as though his denial held some sort of defensive power. "No, if Bryana wants me dead, Mael can do it."

"He's been ordered not to kill you."

Sadness filled Danu's eyes. Not confusion, or fear, or anger, but so much pain.

"Right." A kind of calm that seemed to slow time settled over Niko. "Right." He turned toward Danu's knives in front of the fireplace. "Then you've got to kill me."

"Niko—"

"Does it have to be now? Could we—do I have a little more time?"

She laid her hand on Niko's before he could reach for a blade. "I'm not hurting you."

"Right." Niko nodded. "Fine. That's fine. Better for me really. We'll find a ship heading south. The Pameranian coast is lovely. And once word of the murderous ice spreads, there should be plenty of people fleeing Ilara. We'll slip out with the horde."

"I'm not running."

"Ilara can fend for itself and the Black Bloods can fight the Guilds without you. You're not staying here."

"I am."

"If we get far enough from Mael, he won't be able to feel or use your mark. I'll—"

"I can't leave the Black Bloods, Niko." Danu rose to her knees, taking his face in her hands. "I won't. Even if we could run fast enough to escape Mael, I have to stay in Ilara."

"No, you don't."

"My brother is the heir of the Brien Elder. If there's even a whisper my betraying our clan or abandoning the Black Bloods, it could turn people against Paiman's ascension. The clans are at war. The threat from Ilbrea grows. If any doubt is cast on my brother, it could begin a second war within the Black Bloods. I won't risk thousands of lives to save my own."

"You have to."

"I won't."

"You can't just say you're not going to save your own chivving life."

"I've carried this since we left the stronghold, Niko. I've thought through it a thousand times."

"Clearly not well enough." Niko knocked Danu's hands away, reaching for her blades. "I don't want to bleed on Sib's floor. We should go outside before you stab me."

She leaned sideways, blocking his hand, swallowing her gasp of pain. "I'm not going to hurt you."

"Then why did you save me!" Burning tears slid down Niko's cheeks.

"I couldn't watch you die."

"But I'm supposed to tuck my hands under my ass and sit quietly while we wait for Mael to kill you?"

"Niko—"

"You don't get to announce you're going to be Bryana's martyr and expect me to accept it. If you get to choose to die in my place, I get to choose not to let you."

"It doesn't work that way." Danu tried to take his hands.

He yanked away from her touch.

"I will lock you in this room, march to the gate, and spit in a tired soldier's face." Niko began pushing himself to his feet. A weight clamped around the back of his calves, keeping his shins pressed to the floor.

"You can't lock me up." Danu brushed the tears from his face with her thumbs. "And nothing will ever convince me to let someone hurt you."

"I thought you were angry with me. You should be. You should hate me." Niko took Danu's hands, locking his fingers through hers, clinging tightly enough to stop Death from dragging her away. "I thought you weren't speaking to me in the black because I was the reason you were trapped in the darkness with a mark on your back. And you got even more quiet when we reached Ilara, and I thought when you'd found out Allora—"

"Allora makes it easier." Danu gave the smallest smile.

Pain tore at the edges of Niko's soul.

He tried to speak. He couldn't push words past the desperation tightening around his throat.

"The woman you love is trapped in a palace with sorcerers and an evil king. Losing Allora destroyed you and now you have a chance to get her back. We can rescue the love of your life, Niko."

He could only manage to shake his head.

"You can't leave Allora with the King. So, we'll find a way to get her out. Chances of us both surviving are sodding shit. If one of us dies, Bryana gets her martyr. If neither of us makes it, she'll have two tragic deaths to rally the Brien."

Niko clasped their joined hands to his chest.

"And if we both survive getting Allora out, then Mael can have me."

"No." The word caught in Niko's throat. "No, he—he's not hurting you. I'll tear his spine out if that's what it takes to stop him."

"If Mael dies, Bryana will send the order for someone else to give her the martyr she demands. There's no way out of this. Not that I'm willing to take." Danu eased her hands from Niko's grip. "But I can choose for my death to be in service of something better than Bryana's vengeance. Reuniting a friend with the woman he loves, let that be my end."

A crack, no, a crevice wide enough to swallow a city, split through Niko's soul, slicing past grief, rage, or pain.

An endless darkness waited at the bottom, ready to embrace anyone who dove far enough down to find it.

He rose up on his knees, pressing his lips to Danu's forehead. "If we both survive tomorrow, we can fight about it again while I change your dressings."

"There's no fight to be had."

"I'll let you hold on to that comfort for tonight." Niko kissed her forehead again and twisted awkwardly sideways, grabbing for the tonic bottle with his shins still locked to the floor.

With a huffed laugh almost too faint for him to hear, Danu freed his legs.

He tipped sideways, barely catching himself. "Thank you." He wet a cloth with tonic and crawled behind her, forcing himself to face the wounds he'd caused.

Bile rose in his throat. He swallowed the sour.

"Better for us to focus on enjoying the most luxury we've had in ages. Normally, I'd be gracious and insist on sleeping on the floor so you can have the bed to yourself." He dabbed tonic on the topmost slash on her back.

She gasped in air through her teeth.

"But as I've been on a godsforsaken crooked cot as an improvement to the ground in the endless darkness, I'm going to be greedy and ask for the right half of the bed."

"You can have the left half." Danu dug her nails into the back of her neck as Niko kept working.

"I'm only a little sorry Mael took out his chivving mood shoving us together. If I'm going to wake at every sound ready for ice to slit my throat, I'm glad you'll be on the other side of my nightmares."

"He did it to taunt me." Danu dipped her chin, looking back, meeting Niko's gaze. "I ruined your perfect heroic death. Mael wants this over soon, and after today he thinks he'll get to be the one to end it. You tending my wounds, sleeping beside me? You're cleaning my corpse and visiting my grave before I've even greeted Death."

35

MARA

The list of impossible actions had grown too long to stomach.

Mara ran her finger down the three pages of parchment, making sure she hadn't forgotten a previous notation before adding *break into Lord Soldier's home* to the bottom of the third page.

Entering the city where Lady Gwell certainly had eyes was too dangerous to be considered. Especially when a passing word to a stranger on the street could very well get them killed, murdered to prevent any risk that word of magic outside the Lady Sorcerer's control might further contaminate Ilara.

Even from the window in Mara's hideaway, the swarms of soldiers and guards surrounding the library, docks, soldiers' barracks, and healers' hall all screamed of the futility of attempting to sneak word of Ronya's army to any council members.

Searching for information on the missing children from Ian Ayres had struck a similar end.

Action required reaching Ilara. Entering Ilara promised death.

Lady Gwell knows us too well. She knows we need help. The snake will have set traps for us all.

There is always a path forward, Allora whispered. *You're a Karron. Find it.*

Mara set the list of unusable options aside and looked back to the map of Ilara.

A letter sent under the seal of Lord Karron. Sure to grab the recipient's attention.

And get them killed.

"It's not that hard." Asher's voice carried from the hearth room.

A muffled reply came a moment later.

"We need Lord Nevon's records." Elver took Mara's list. "It's his ships that carry women to Ian Ayres. It's got to be his ships that take the older children away."

"I spent years on ships that weren't under the Sailors Guild," Tham said. "It's more likely to be an unguilded ship that moves the older children. A secret like that wouldn't stay silent long on the docks."

"Hmm." Elver frowned. "I'd been working on that thought for an hour."

"There are options we haven't considered," Tham said.

"The sorcerers don't need ships to cross the sea?" Elver said.

"Magic stands against magic." Tham met Mara's gaze. "If we can't warn the Guilds—"

"Stay down!" Asher shouted.

Mara dug her fingers into the dirt, resisting the urge to scream.

"That one is never nice," Elver said.

"—we can look for a way to help them fight," Tham said.

"Look for a way?" Elver frowned.

"Hope from wild magic outside of the white mountains." Mara let herself shift closer to Tham, pressing her leg against his, letting that touch promise she hadn't slipped into madness. "We've never found anything we could twist into a weapon against the Daeduris, let alone Ronya."

"But if someone else has?" Tham let the question linger, tearing itself into a thousand warnings Mara had learned to always heed.

"Someone who?" Elver asked.

A store of maps worth execution. A vow to the people she cherished most to never share their secrets while the sorcerers tormented Ilbrea.

My mother's tomb protects our secrets to keep us alive, Allora said. *If Ilara falls, who of us will survive to fear the sorcerers?*

"It's been days," Tham said. "If the Ice Walkers took the children after the battle at Ian Ayres, they could be halfway to the white mountains by now."

"Further than that," Elver said.

"And that's how it's done," Asher cackled.

"You're right." Mara took Tham's hand. "If we can't think of anything else, we'll go after nightfall."

"Go where?" Elver said.

"Not far," Mara said. "We'll be back before dawn."

"I'll come along," Elver said.

"No," Mara said too quickly. "You need to stay with the children. Please."

"If you think you can find the boulder in dark..." Elver tutted and shook his head.

"Boulder?" Mara asked.

"To dig up the ice ring we took from Ture Kian's hand after I cut it off so you can use the ring's magic to stage an attack on the gate as a subtle warning of the frozen hell to come," Elver said.

"We're not attacking our own people," Tham said.

"Even if it's a nice, small attack and we try not to hurt anyone?" Elver said. "Wouldn't help with finding the children. Might help save the city."

"They'd blame the Lady Sorcerer." Mara shut her eyes, spinning through the hopeless plans again.

"What a braidicky dead end to have tunneled into." Elver

nodded. "If you won't attack the gate with ice, we're as useless as a spoon in a butcher's shop."

"We're stuck for now," Mara said. "We just have to find the right—"

"Slip of information that opens a thousand new possibilities? Quite wise." Elver looked toward the tunnels as the sound of sniffled crying approached. "That won't do."

"Blinkers," Mara said before the boy had stepped into view, "you're all right."

"Don't lie," Elver whispered.

Blinkers sank to the ground in the niche's doorway. Blood dripped from the poor boy's nose and bottom lip, but it was the defeated sag to his shoulders that tugged at Mara's heart.

"Asher again?" Mara opened her bundle of food pilfered from the palace's kitchen, pulling out the cloth-wrapped jar of preserves she'd stolen the night before.

"I said deadish." Blinkers's rapidly swelling nose muddied his words. "I promise I did."

"Hmm," Elver said. "What else have you done to earn the monster's wrath?"

"Elver," Mara whispered the warning as she unwrapped the jar and passed the clean cloth to the poor boy.

"Head back a bit." Tham knelt beside Blinkers. "Once the bleeding stops, we'll see to the rest."

"Quite right. Think to the future, focus on vengeance," Elver said. "Is it just your nose and lip the beast wounded?"

"Don't encourage violence among the children, Elver." Mara flipped her list of impossibilities upside down on the trunk, hiding their soul-wearying words, though she knew the boy couldn't read. "Whatever Asher's done, I'm sure Brady's idea of justice will be far worse."

"'Tis us who must see to justice." Elver stood, rolling his shoulders back as though loosening for a fight.

"Please don't make things worse." Mara pushed herself to her feet. Tingles filled her legs from sitting on the floor accomplishing nothing for hours.

"One of us must accept Brady's mantle as ruler of the horde," Elver said. "She won't be back for hours. No, days. I think days is closer."

"Back?" Mara's voice, even her heartbeat, remained unnervingly calm. "What do you mean, Elver?"

"You're a better monster keeper than me." Elver sat down, leaning against the dirt wall. "You may be the queen of the terrors. Careful not to let Asher bite you. She draws blood."

"Elver, what do you mean Brady won't be back?" Mara said.

"I didn't tell her," Blinkers wailed, choking on his blood and tears. "Don't let Asher think I told her."

"Told me what?" Mara said.

Blinkers leapt to his feet and fled back toward Asher's clutches.

"Elver!" Mara said.

"I tied a rope around her and dropped her out the window," Elver said.

"What?" Mara's calm snapped away.

"I thought convincing her to go through the window would be difficult, but she was quite willing," Elver said. "It was the actual lowering her down that gave me trouble."

"You put a child out the window?" Mara ran toward the hearth room.

"Once the other beasts started helping on the rope, we got her down safely." Elver chased after her.

The children froze as soon as Mara ran into view. Even Asher had the sense not to test Mara's panicked fury.

The waxed fabric over the window had been tucked back in place well enough Mara hadn't noticed it had been moved. But the rope in the corner—she should have seen the rope in the corner, still tied to the anchor she had placed years ago.

"Where did she go?" Mara said. "How exactly do you plan on getting Brady back?"

Elver frowned. "Best to not speak definitively with such ice on the wind."

Asher coughed a laugh.

"Why?" Tham's single word silenced her.

Elver's frown deepened. "The least worst choice must sometimes be taken."

Mara shut her eyes, taking a breath, forcing calm back into her voice. "Will Brady be returning to be hauled back up the cliffs tonight?"

Elver lifted Bevvy from her stump-made stool, claiming the seat for himself.

"Elver!"

"The screeching gets too loud for the whispers to make sense." Elver sighed. "But we've only one window, so I'm quite certain I flung the child in the right direction."

Mara turned to Tham, resting her forehead on his shoulder, grateful for the comfort of his arms enveloping her as she added finding a child who'd never entered a city to the list of hopeless feats Dudia had laid before them.

36

ADRIAL

The scratch of pens on parchment filled the too-bright corridor, as though rats had already clawed their way into the walls, hunting for dead to feast upon.

The scribes at the desks lining the right side of the hall only nodded to Adrial as he passed. Even the few apprentices who'd been granted places at the end of the row didn't stand to bow. Their desks had been shoved too close to the wall, trapping the scribes as they labored, keeping a wide enough path for guards to charge down the corridor when an attack on the library finally came.

If.

If *the library is attacked.*

Innocent tilk had been slaughtered beyond the northern gate.

It hadn't been Ena's work, that much Adrial knew in his soul.

Ena wouldn't, couldn't have allowed common folk to be killed, not even to breach the city walls.

But if it wasn't the Black Bloods. If the Sorcerers Guild had attacked…

Then it is when.

When an attack on the library finally came, the guards would need to be able to respond quickly.

Reinstating the restriction forbidding scribes from entering rooms with windows had been Lord Gareth's immediate response to the attack at the northern gate. Head Guard Friel had thankfully learned from their previous confinement and prepared strict rules for the placement of scribes' desks, requiring clear paths for the guards' use.

"May Dudia protect his children of parchment and ink."

Adrial reached the door at the very end of the row. A note had been tacked to the wood.

Office of the Head Scribe.

The Lord Scribe's office has been moved two doors east of the scribes' gallery.

Work assignments will be issued from the eastern library subsection below the northern stacks.

Adrial shut his eyes for a moment, shoving all his doubts and fears behind the title at the top of the page.

The Head Scribe of Ilara could not let panic outweigh reason.

Not now. Not with so many arrangements to be made before…

A rapturous, terrified joy radiated through Adrial's chest.

Before he held Ena again. Before he slept by her side.

Before he finally met the child they'd suffered through so much to protect.

Heat burned in Adrial's eyes as he opened the door of his temporary office.

A jolt of panic froze him in place.

My last office as a Guilded scribe.

He waited for grief to wash over him. The wave didn't come. His knees didn't tremble as he shut the door, closing himself into his final office as the Head Scribe of Ilara.

A dozen lanterns fought the darkness in the windowless room, beaming from every spare surface the space offered.

Someone had placed the page of Princess Illia's vellum he'd been laboring over on the worktable crammed against the far wall. They'd brought his inks as well, organizing the pigments by hue.

"Too dangerous for scribes to be near the windows, and my service to Ilbrea is making a pretty book for a princess." He dug his knuckles into his eyes.

Let Tammin calm the scribes. Let them look to her for strength.

He guided his thoughts away from trials, and violence, and Ilara.

A forest at the beginning of spring with the barest hints of new life beginning to appear. Two men locked in battle, the trees around them scarred by their blades. A different scene than the one half-finished on his desk, but an image he could bear to create while hiding, waiting for demons to descend.

He shifted the incomplete page to the far side of his work-space, setting a blank sheet of parchment in its place.

"Head Scribe."

Adrial whirled toward the whisper, banging his hip against the desk, gasping as the ink jars knocked together with a sound too close to disaster for a Guilded scribe.

"Aw oo ah ight, sir?" Tege stepped out of the corner, her hands pressed over her mouth muddying her words.

"Fine." Adrial bent over the desk, peering between the jars of ink, searching for any hint of a crack or leak from their glass.

"I'm sorry, sir," Tege whispered.

"Nothing to worry over." Adrial gave Tege the most comforting smile he could as he leaned against the wall, easing his weight off his good hip, which now held the subtle pounding of what promised to be an impressively large bruise.

Tege managed to move her hands away from her mouth

enough to dig her fingers into her cheeks. "I tried to say it quietly so I wouldn't startle you, Head Scribe."

"Your stealth succeeded."

"Sorry."

"You've done nothing wrong. I'm just a bit overtired."

"Oh." Tege glanced to the door handle. "Right. If you're tired, I should go. I should have a cot brought in for you."

The girl didn't move.

"There's no need to send for a cot," Adrial said. "A few minutes' rest would be much appreciated, but I haven't time. Thank you."

Tege kept staring at the doorknob.

"Is there something you need?"

She nodded. "But if you're tired, I really should go."

"You've said as much." Giving in to his pain, Adrial sank into his chair. "What's wrong, Tege?"

"I was only trying to help sir, so please don't be angry." The words tumbled from her mouth as she let go of her face to grip her apron. "It's only, I heard the whispers in the kitchen from the guards who'd come in for warmth and food, and I know how the library works. The whispers will spread through the staff and straight to the scribes and even the shadows will have heard by breakfast tomorrow, and I didn't want that, so I found Taddy and he agreed. He was going to be the one to come tell you, but I was too afraid to stay in case she bit again."

"Bit?"

"I…" Tege puffed out her cheeks as she let out a long breath, displaying the half-moon indents her nails had left in her face. "Can I please take you to Taddy, sir?"

The desperation in the girl's eyes swept any lingering sense of duty to the vellum away. "Where is Taddy?"

"I'm supposed to ask you to please promise you won't be angry."

"Where is Taddy, Tege?"

"This way, sir." Tege bobbed a curtsy and opened the door, ducking her chin as she stepped out into the corridor.

Grateful for the moment of privacy, Adrial forced himself to his feet, not keeping his pain from his face as he allowed himself one breath to wallow in anger at his sad excuse for a body.

Squaring his shoulders, he stepped back out into the corridor, focusing on the battle to hide his limp, and pain, and fatigue as he followed Tege back down the long line of scribes to a narrow wooden door and a steep set of steps.

Dudia, forgive me my self-pity when true horrors haunt Ilara.

He took the stairs one at a time, not trusting his bad leg to hold his weight as he stepped down.

Tege stopped every few stairs to turn back and watch Adrial, gripping her apron all the while, twisting the fabric into a tight ball as splotches of red bloomed on her cheeks.

"My apologies," Adrial said as he reached the bottom step.

"Please don't, sir." Tege waved for Adrial to follow as she ducked around the corner and into a narrow corridor. "It's only, I really do like my job, sir. Even more now I'm helping with the books." Tege led him past a row of old wooden doors with well-worn handles. "I love the library, and with the city how it is, there's no decent work that isn't already taken."

"Then it's a good thing you have a job here."

"I know." Tege stopped just before the corridor met another, even narrower passage. She turned to Adrial, tears filling her wide eyes. "Please remember how grateful I am for good work and don't get rid of me, sir."

She knocked on the nearest door.

"Tege, why would—"

The door burst open, and Taddy leapt into the hall, slamming the door shut behind him.

He leaned against the wood as though trying to trap an animal.

"Did she get you?" Tege searched Taddy's hands before checking both his ears.

"She found the apples in the barrels. I don't know what blessing Dudia put in apples, but she's been more interested in eating than threatening to tear my tongue and eyes out."

"Good," Tege said as Adrial said, "What?"

"Sir." Sweat dripped down Taddy's red face, the sheen highlighting the purple, swollen patches on his cheek, chin, and bottom lip. "As soon as Tege told me, I knew something had to be done. I thought I'd find her a nice corner to wait in, maybe bring her a cup of tea and a roll. But the bitey imp won't listen. I couldn't keep her from trying to find you. Took both of us to get her in here."

"Taddy." Adrial spoke above Taddy's pants. "Who have you closed in the pantry?"

"A girl, sir," Taddy said. "Came to the library gate demanding to see you."

"Why?" Adrial said.

"She said she'd come all the way from Ian Ayres. Shouted at the guards that she wouldn't leave until she'd seen Adrial Ayres, and you'd be, well"—Tege glanced to Taddy—"I, well, won't repeat her exactly, sir, but that you'd be very, very grateful if they let her in and she'd potentially remove their inside mushy bits if they refused."

"Then whispers started. It was the guards first. Then Tege heard, and she told me, and I knew we couldn't let that girl keep shouting about Ian Ayres," Taddy said.

Ian Ayres.

The words dragged talons of unshakable fear through the long-quarantined shadows of Adrial's mind. But, shimmering around the black, a gleam of unquestionable truth stopped panic from stealing his breath.

Ena had never set foot on the demon's island. Lily's lungs had never been tainted by the stench of the children's house.

"—after everything you've been through," Tege said. "Sir."

"The foul-brained getches—sorry for the language sir, but by the dirt on my boots they deserve it—I heard them saying she's yours, sir," Taddy said. "That—well, that Ena wasn't the first woman you'd seen sent to Ian Ayres."

A void swallowed every useful thought in Adrial's head.

"But I don't believe it, sir," Taddy said. "There's no resemblance, and she's too old to be your daughter. Well, probably too old. I'd guess at least few years too old. You'd have been younger than me.

"That's not to say it's impossible." Red devoured Taddy's face. He kept his gaze locked on Adrial, his eyes growing wider every second, as though certain any glance in Tege's direction would instantly end his life in an unspeakably horrific manner. "I've heard other apprentices talk, and if their stories are true—"

"Taddy." Adrial raised a hand, wrenching his mind out of its befuddled daze to spare the poor boy from his own tongue. "Whatever the girl's age, there is no chance of her being mine."

Taddy's shoulders sagged. "Good. That's good."

"Has the girl said why she believes I could possibly be her father?" Adrial laced his fingers together in a sad imitation of feigning calm at his desk.

"She hasn't said anything about being yours," Tege said. "Not to me anyway. I only heard that from the getches in the kitchen stirring whispers."

"The girl just demands to see you and threatens to hurt everyone else," Taddy said. "Or kill them. She does often mention murder."

Adrial stared at the door, picturing a wild beast worthy of Tege and Taddy's fear crouching inside the pantry waiting to attack. Teeth bared, ready to bite, and kick, and claw, and whatever else Ian Ayres had demanded as payment for surviving another day.

"Open the door," Adrial said.

"Sir—"

"The door, Taddy."

Taking a breath as though plunging into the sea, Taddy leapt away from the door and pivoted to face it, planting himself in front of Adrial.

"Careful," Tege whispered as Taddy reached for the handle.

"We've brought the head scribe." Taddy tossed open the door. "You will not be allowed to threaten him."

"I'll do what I like, soft-kneed letch."

An apple soared through the door, striking Taddy in the face.

Taddy stumbled back. "You're a beast."

Adrial took Taddy's shoulders, pivoting him out of the way as another apple soared past Adrial's ear.

Taddy or Tege had left a lantern sitting on the pantry floor.

The *beast* hadn't bothered hiding in the shadows.

The child leaned against an open barrel, apple cores scattered at her feet, her well-made, too-large coat tented around her hiding everything but her patched-together boots.

She stared at Adrial as she reached behind her head, grabbing another apple.

"I've been told you're looking for me." Adrial stepped closer to the door, keeping his hands slightly raised, enough to give him a hope of protecting his face from flying fruit.

"You're the head scribe?" The girl bit into her new apple.

"I am."

The girl kept staring at Adrial as she chewed. "You're Adrial Ayres?"

"Yes."

"Can't be."

"Yes he is!" Taddy took a single step toward the door before Tege grabbed his wrist, yanking him back.

"You'd never have made it five winters on the bastards' island without ending up stacked in a grave." She took another bite.

Sick pressed up into Adrial's throat. The talons of fear dug deeper into his mind, piercing the shadows, giving pinpricks of freedom to the long-banished nightmares.

A girl carried out, still breathing as the matrons laid her beside her grave. She'd be dead before daybreak. The matrons didn't want the trouble of moving her in the dark.

The buzz of the flies as they gathered on the wounds covering a boy's back.

The matrons forgot where they'd buried the girl. They opened the grave too soon.

Worms still feasted on the girl's face when they tossed the boy's corpse on top of her, burying them along with the flies that just wouldn't leave him in peace.

"Sir?" Taddy reached for Adrial's arm.

"I'm fine, Taddy," Adrial said.

The girl snorted a laugh.

"I was born on Ian Ayres," Adrial said. "I spent my childhood in that hell."

"Why aren't you scarred up?" the girl said.

"Robes hide wounds well."

"Why'd you keep the shit island as your name?"

"I didn't choose to."

"Who made you?"

"The scribe who registered me when I arrived in Ilara. He offered no other option for a child of Ian Ayres."

"Braidic sodding letch." The girl dropped her latest apple core at her feet.

"I've grown accustomed to the name." Adrial eased into the pantry. "May I ask your name?"

"How did you escape the island?"

"I was rescued. How did you get here?"

"Why didn't you take all the other bastards with you when you got out?"

"I couldn't have." Adrial gripped the doorjamb, steadying

himself as he sank down to sit on the floor. "And, if I'm to be fully honest, I think I would have been too afraid to try."

"'Course you would have. You're in a big library with a fancy robe while there's a rat taint's worth of us stuck on the island. Only a chivving coward would hole up here and forget where he came from."

"I've never forgotten."

"Just like knowing there are blue-toed babes dying every snow?"

The girl grabbed an apple core and hurled it at Adrial's head.

He ducked aside, dodging the blow.

"Don't you dare," Taddy growled.

"It's all right, Taddy," Adrial said. "When I left Ian Ayres, I was furious, too. I arrived in Ilara and couldn't believe how many people there were. Thousands upon thousands of them. Enough grownups to give each child on Ian Ayres a dozen families.

"But they'd left us cold and hungry in the middle of the sea. I wanted to scream at every person I met, shout the names of the ones I'd watched buried, loud enough even Dudia would hear. I was even angry at the man who'd rescued me, until I began to understand how life away from Ian Ayres really works."

"That sounds like festered chivving shit," the girl said.

Taddy sucked in a sharp breath.

"It is," Adrial said. "But the terrible truth of Ilbrea is that something being wrong, or even evil, doesn't mean it can be stopped. Not by a Lord Map Maker, let alone a head scribe. Ian Ayres exists under the King's command with the Lady Sorcerer's support. To end the travesty of that island would require the agreement of the King, which won't happen with the Lady Sorcerer in his ear.

"That leaves the hateful option of slow progress. Becoming a scribe, earning my place as head scribe so I will have a seat on the Guilds Council. There I can at least be sure the children of Ian Ayres aren't forgotten. I can become the voice in the ear of the

King's heir, helping to teach our next leader to rule with mercy. That is the best way I can help."

"It's shit."

"Everything else is just unheard screams."

The girl reached back, grabbing another apple. "I like you better than your friends."

"Which friends?"

"Fancy. Having more than one set." The girl shoved the apple into her coat pocket and reached back for another.

"If you'd like something other than apples to eat, that can be arranged," Adrial said.

"Meat?" the girl said.

"Of course." Adrial attempted a soothing smile. "While we put a plate together for you, can you tell me your name and why you're here?"

"You're nice." The girl chewed her lips. "Your pair of rats aren't too bad, either."

Tege hushed over Taddy's, "You ungrateful—"

"I don't think you deserve terrible deaths," the girl said.

"That's meant to be nice, right?" Tege whispered.

"If I tell you what I've come to say now, you've got to swear on your own asses you won't get all fussed up and forget to bring my meat," the girl said.

"I swear," Adrial said.

"Better mean it." She tucked another apple into her pocket. "There's an ice army coming from the north. Mara and Tham think the frozen slitches are marching on Ilara. The sorcerers all chivving well know about the ice queen and her deadish army because the braidic letches tried to torch all the bastards in the battle at Ian Ayres. From what I've seen so far, I'd like to watch most Ilbreans die on ice-made blades. But I need your help, and since I was nice and told you about the deadish coming to murder you, you've got to help me find the missing bastards from Ian Ayres. Fair for fair, Sir Scribe Slitch."

The girl grinned and ripped a massive bite from a new apple.

37

NIKO

Danu lifted the well-polished teapot, her hands steady as she filled her own cup. She held the pot toward Niko, offering to fill his cup as well.

He couldn't bring himself to nod as she held his gaze.

Not a hint of loathing in her eyes. No fear or murder.

She let Niko flounder for a moment, drowning as he tried to comprehend whatever stone in her blood let her look at him without fear or, at the very least, loathing filling her eyes.

Fire, yes. Bravery, yes.

A growing hint of humor. Yes.

She let him see more of her than she'd allowed since they'd left the stronghold, as though sleeping beside Niko had brought some unfathomable kind of comfort that let the edges of her armor melt.

Secrets can weigh heavier than a bloody fate. Ena's voice echoed Danu's calm.

Not this fate! Niko shouted back.

Danu filled his cup, her hands still steady, then set the pot aside.

"Thank you," Niko said. Foolish, horrible, hateful—a terrible chivving thing to say. He caught her hand. "For the tea."

"I know." Danu gave his fingers the slightest squeeze before sliding her hand from his.

Mael dragged the teapot toward himself, letting the metal rumble on the wooden top of the kitchen table.

"You're sure you're Black Bloods?" Kyley leaned back in her chair, crossing her arms over her chest.

"I'm not." Niko speared a piece of breakfast meat, pretending he'd be able to eat it.

"Aren't you, Solcha?" Mael said.

"I'm Ilbrean." Niko set his fork aside. "Not even the evil of the Brien Elder can steal that."

Pain ripped across Niko's back. He planted his hands on the table, leaning forward as he held Mael's glare.

The pain sliced deeper.

"I've suddenly found myself unable to pretend your precious Bryana didn't spend weeks torturing me," Niko said.

The pain shifted, surging toward his lungs.

"Weeks of torment with magic and blades"—Niko pressed on as the warmth of blood trailed down his back—"before deciding to call me Solcha and parade me in front of the Brien like a trained dog. I wonder if Cillian and Lorna would find that to be an interesting—"

Niko's lungs spasmed.

"Enough!" Danu slammed her hands against the table, knocking her teacup over.

The liquid spread across the surface, darkening the well-scrubbed wood.

"So that's the point in keeping Black Bloods around." Kyley grinned. "Entertainment."

Mael shifted his glare to the girl.

"Do you know you look confused when you're trying to be scary?" Kyley asked. "Adorable really, but don't waste your big angry glare on me. A Black Blood would be a chivving fool to so much as raise their voice to me. I live under Nora's protection."

"Are you shouting for fun, or are we having a tiff?" A girl with long black hair flowing down her back swept into the kitchen. "I can never tell."

"She's the one who shouted." Kyley pointed at Danu. "But he's the slitch in the middle." She pointed to Mael. "The bull's too stompish for our kitchen."

"The big one's the problem? How utterly expected." The girl chose a rag from the stack by the stove. She passed the cloth to Danu then looked to Mael. Her lips curved into a smile as different from Kyley's still growing grin as silk from a thorn. "Try not cause any fuss. Nora's locked herself in her study, and she does loathe distractions."

It almost looked as though Mael meant it when he gave the girl a nod. "Apologies."

"Make it up to me by answering the door?" The girl slid into the seat beside Mael. "There are so many horrors lurking around us, I don't even know what I should fear is knocking."

She reached for Mael, her fingers grazing the back of his hand just before a knock pounded on the kitchen door.

Mael yanked his fingers from the girl's reach.

"You don't mind, do you?" She refilled Danu's cup. "I feel so helpless knowing monsters might attack at any moment."

Mael pushed away from the table. "Ice and paun aren't things to be feared." He gripped the hilt of his dagger. "A blade through the heart drops beasts of every kind."

"A blade?" Fear tightened the girl's voice as she looked to Kyley.

Kyley stuck out her tongue before flinching as though the recipient of a sharp kick to the shin.

The girl widened her eyes at Kyley, biting her lips together, hiding her smile as Mael opened the door.

"Back to your cage, dog." Ena spoke from behind the mass of

Mael. "Beasts have no business opening the doors of Nora's home."

"Ena." Niko stood, swallowing the sour that rose in his throat as blood trailed all the way down to his lower back.

"Would you like me to move you out of my way?" Ena asked.

Mael stepped aside.

"A trueborn clinging to a blade like a babe's blanket." Ena stepped inside, shutting and locking the door behind her. "Have you ever been in a battle, Brien? Or do you prefer inflicting pain over actually fighting for your chivving cause?"

Kyley laughed, her glee cutting off with another sharp flinch.

The other girl flinched in the same way a moment later.

Ena stepped around Mael, ignoring his tightening grip on his blade, her gaze fixed on Niko in a way that hollowed out and doubled his fear simultaneously. "A passage north of the wall a horse can manage. Does it exist?"

"The gate," Niko said. "At least, that's the only way I know of."

Ena shut her eyes, her hands curling into fists as though she, too, longed to reach for her blades.

"The tunnel I know would never fit anything bigger than a person, and the cliffs around the Map Master's palace are a tough climb. Without the switchbacks leading up on the city side of the estate, only a goat would have any luck descending on four legs."

"Rowan, fetch Nora," Ena said.

The girl, Rowan, ran from the room, the grace in her movement still teasing perfection despite the worry that had stolen her coy smile.

Ena pulled her hair over her shoulder, weaving it into a tight braid.

"If you could get a ship," Niko said. "The ports north of the city—"

"Not enough time."

Nora pushed through the kitchen door, Rowan on her heels.

"The deadly ice the common folk spoke of," Ena said. "It's not a band of murderers on a spree or foreign magic coming south on a storm. There's an army marching for Ilara."

"Army?" Niko said. "What army? From Wyrain?"

"Wyrain would have had to come through the mountains," Nora said. "They'd never have made it this close to winter."

"That they came from the north is as far as I know." Ena pulled a folded bit of parchment from her pocket.

"Where under the stars could a northern army have come from?" Nora said. "It's not ours."

"Ours either," Danu said.

"Did the hovel dwellers of Whitend sharpen sticks?" Kyley said.

"All I know came from a child," Ena said. "The head scribe burned the blacksmith's use as a messenger to send word. He wouldn't have done it unless his fear was real."

"An army of ice soldiers murdered the families of the people at the northern gate," Niko said, "and now they're marching on Ilara?"

"Best to assume a horde's coming until we can prove it's not." Ena held the paper out to Nora. "If the common folk from the gate fled south on foot, the ice army can't be far behind."

"Ena Ryeland, don't you dare think of running toward a battle." Nora stayed planted by the kitchen door.

"I'm not. But I'm not fleeing Ilara, either. Not while my husband is here." Ena crossed to Nora. She lifted Nora's hand and placed the letter on her palm. "Please, Nora. If the gods are sending demons to Ilara, she needs to know why I stayed."

Nora tucked the letter into her pocket.

"Send word to Frason's Glenn." Ena strode toward the back door. "And stay inside."

"Wait!" Niko's shout froze everyone in the kitchen, even Ena. "Where are you going?"

Ena looked back. "Nowhere you'll follow."

"I need a moment." Niko's heel caught on his chair, knocking it aside as he ran to the door, squeezing himself between Ena and escape.

"Have you not been listening?" Kyley said. "The people who were shouting about murdering ice weren't actually exaggerating about Death sweeping down from the north."

"Exactly why I need a moment." Niko held Ena's gaze, willing her not to shove him away from the door and storm outside to go boldly be the Solcha the Black Bloods cherished. "Please, Ena."

"Nora, is your parlor clear?" Ena said.

"Dining room," Nora said.

Ena held Niko's gaze for one more moment, sending a warning echoing through his soul that promised he needn't wait for the ice to arrive, Ena would be quite willing to introduce him to Death without any help from the army coming from only Dudia knew where.

She nodded for Niko to follow and headed for the door. Mael waited for Ena to pass before stepping into Niko's path.

"Down dog," Ena said without looking back. "You needn't drool on Niko's boots."

"I'm sure you don't mind." Rowan threaded her arm through Mael's. "I feel such a fool for asking, but I've only ever heard of trueborn. Is it only that beautiful black stone you can control, or does your magic work on…every kind of rock?"

Nora held the door open, nodding for Ena and Niko to flee while Rowan batted her hazel eyes at Mael.

Niko kept right on Ena's heels, close enough to follow along by her apron string, if Solcha ever wore such a thing.

Sod your chivving pride.

As soon as they'd entered the dining room, Niko closed the door behind them and leaned against it, as though he'd have a stone's chance of swimming if he actually tried to keep Ena from leaving.

"Tell me what you want, or go back to the kitchen." Ena had

something worse than anger in her eyes as she watched Niko mouth like a fish.

Not pity or fear, either.

Darkness.

Still, calm darkness, like the breath before a terrible storm.

Or Death's steady hand before her blade strikes.

"Now, Niko," Ena said.

"I have to kill Mael." The words felt cold on Niko's tongue. "I need your help."

Ena laid her hand on the hilt of her knife as she stepped close enough to whisper. "What in your foolish paun head—"

"Bryana gave him orders," Niko said. "Either I die or Danu does."

Ena shut her eyes. "Chivving, demon-spawned Brien."

"You said you poisoned the last—well second to last—Lady Healer. You could do the same to Mael."

Her eyes flew open. "I'm not harming a trueborn. Not while my daughter is anywhere near the eastern mountains."

"But I could do the actual poisoning."

"And Bryana's first thought would fly to me," Ena said. "Lily is safe, but I'll not risk the Brien seeking vengeance. I can't."

"Of course." Niko couldn't make himself nod. "I understand. Lily has to be protected."

"Even if you managed to kill Mael, Bryana wouldn't give up on whatever evil made her order your death."

"But it could buy us time," Niko said. "It's only Mael who marked Danu's back. If I could convince her to run—"

"A Black Blood won't abandon the mountains. Even if the clans weren't at war and Ilbrea weren't a threat, you'd never convince her."

"I have to try. If it doesn't work, I'll throw myself on an ice-made blade." Niko pushed away from the door. His hand didn't tremble as he reached for the handle, as though accepting his fate had taught his soul a wisp of the calm darkness that led the true Solcha through the unending black over and over again.

He'd only managed to open the door an inch when Solcha pressed her hand to the wood, snapping the door shut. "Tell Danu to keep you both alive."

A spark of something too painfully close to hope flared, fracturing the calm. "Ena, thank you."

"I didn't say I'd help. I said don't die." She yanked the door open. "It was your Mara and Tham who brought word of the ice walker army."

"Mara and Tham?" Niko began to push the door closed.

Ena stopped him with a glare.

"Are they in Ilara?" Niko whispered. "Have you seen them? Their journey was meant to push deeper into the white mountains. If they found an army with ice magic, it must have been there. What else did Dudia lead them to?"

"Survive long enough to ask them." Ena strode out of the room.

"You've got to know something." Niko chased her back to the kitchen.

"Keep Danu and Niko here." Ena stopped just inside the door, taking Nora's hand. "I need them out of danger."

"Of course. They're welcome here, and so are you." Nora kissed Ena's hand. "You could stay here with me. This home is protected. We can wait for the paun to greet whatever monsters attack. Please, Ena, let this be someone else's battle."

Ena kissed Nora's cheek and slid her hand free. "Lock them in if you have to."

"That brightens my morning," Kyley said.

"You can't lock us in," Danu said.

"I promise we can," Kyley said.

"A Karron is the best currency we have. We can't afford to lose it." Ena paused beside the back door. "May we meet again in a land of freedom."

"May our freedom be worth the cost."

38

ALLORA

The edges of the ink blurred on the mist-dampened page, giving Allora's words the look of something the sky itself wished to scrub away.

She watched the ink spread with interest rather than shame. Even if by some miracle her letters reached Adrial, he wouldn't mind. Even his scribe's heart would forgive the imperfect script as his friend scrawled all the words she longed to speak.

If she could just reach the city or have Adrial brought to the palace.

Don't wish him trapped beside you.

Allora set her pen down, letting her mind sink back into the gray, misty evening.

A gardener and a man in the clothes of a kitchen hand labored together, clearing out the garden beds nearest Allora's favored balcony.

The gardener knelt in the mud, showing his helper what to do. The kitchen man spent several moments nodding before joining the gardener on the ground, taking on the work that should have been done by other hands.

But most of the gardeners had been on the city side of the

bridge when the sorcerers tore the stones apart, barring many of the staff from the palace.

A pity, the whispers in the walls said, they'd been left in the city with no way to return to the royal grounds.

Wise for the servants to spread such lies when any fool would bargain with their gods for a single chance at freedom.

The mist strengthened into a pattering rain that struck the shield protecting Allora with a high tink, as though the canopy were cast of thin metal rather than magic. A burst of wind rustled through the trees.

Only a hint of its chill reached Allora's skin.

Both men working below pulled up the collars of their coats, ducking their heads against the rain, continuing their labor though none of their clothes seemed made of thick enough fabric to withstand the cold wet.

"Gillien." Allora didn't flinch as the sorcerer stepped out of the back corner of the balcony, placing herself in Allora's line of sight. "Have a guard ask the gardeners to come in out of the rain and find work that can be done someplace warm. The grounds can wait until the storm has passed."

"That's very kind of you, Allora." Gillien stepped back out of view.

"Please don't call the lowest consideration kind," Allora said. "I never want to sink into believing that to be the most our world can offer."

The balcony door opened and closed.

Allora returned to her writing.

I am the worst of all beasts, and I can't even find the decency to despise myself. I fear Ilbrea's King has gone mad, and my life is better for it.

The door opened and closed as Gillien returned.

Brannon won't enter any space with windows. He wholly refuses, traveling from room to room through the servants' passages rather than face an open corridor.

I can hear him storming through the walls, tracing his movement by the rumble of his guards' boots. He insists on being accompanied by dozens of men even in the narrow passages.

I've heard he sleeps with guards surrounding his bed. I haven't seen it myself. I haven't slept beside him in days. He spends his nights in the den I prepared him.

Had I known how much time he'd spend locked in his hole, I would have provided a better stocked bookcase. Though I don't know if proper stimulation could slow his mind's spiral into chaos. Or, honestly, what form his madness takes at all.

I haven't so much as caught sight of him since I learned I only need keep to windowed spaces to avoid him.

The sound of the rain against Gillien's shield gained a sharper edge, as though the drops had begun to freeze with the darker clouds that overtook the dusk.

"A light please, Gillien," Allora said.

The shield above Allora began to glow. Sparks fluttered across the surface, rain drops sizzling in their heat as golden light surrounded Allora, kissing her face as though spring had finally won the day.

"Would the light burn me?" Allora asked. "If I touched it?"

Gillien stepped back into her line of sight. "Not burn, no. Though it would sting."

"Like a wasp?"

"More like a healer's tonic on a deep scrape."

"Sorcerers allow healers near their wounds?"

"In my phase of youthful defiance."

"A healer's aid?" Allora looked up at Gillien. "Such rebellious actions. I'm surprised they let you near the Queen."

"Indeed." Gillien gave Allora a sly smile. "A strict matron would be better suited."

"Do not breathe a word of that notion to the Lady Sorcerer." Allora pointed her pen at Gillien. "If she sends a wretched hag to torment me, I'll go as mad as the King."

Gillien's smile faded. "The King's reason is intact."

"Either the demons Brannon fears were born in his mind, or he's abandoned his people while true danger stalks Ilara."

"Allora—"

"Do not feed me the platitude that he is siding with the sorcerers because the other Guilds turned against them. If he will not fight to regain control of the Guilds, a King of sound mind would at least not abandon his own people to the Guilds he's declared his enemy."

"I pray Dudia will keep the King's choices so simple."

"Better to pray the people do not condemn their King. If he should ever let us out of this cage."

Gillien furrowed her brow. "As you say, Allora."

Her conciliatory tone tensed Allora's spine.

"If you can manage the storm, I'll dine out here this evening." Allora dipped her pen into her ink.

"I am happy to shelter you."

"Then please send word to Illia that she may join me. The poor girl needs to come out of her room before she becomes a mirror of her brother." Allora paused, waiting for Gillien to defend the King's metamorphosis into a mole. The sorcerer stayed silent. "Thank you, Gillien."

The door opened and closed again, granting Allora a precious moment of solitude.

Whatever eyes watched her from the shadows had a perfect view of her in Gillien's light, but even the façade of isolation lifted a hint of the weight that made it so hard for her lungs to fill.

Perhaps tomorrow Gillien would allow her to walk the

grounds, winding through the trees where the illusion of freedom might be even more complete.

She returned her pen to the parchment.

I fear what is happening beyond the palace walls. I wish I could do more than hope better men than Ilbrea's King are helping the people flounder through whatever hell Brannon has caused.

Perhaps now the people will see my husband as the monster we both know him to be.

Allora set her pen aside and stood, holding the parchment above her head, letting the sparks from Gillien's shield singe her words.

The edge of the paper caught fire.

She set the page on the marble of the balcony floor and watched her sedition burn.

Soon, Adrial whispered. *We'll be together soon.*

"Not soon enough." Allora settled back into her chair. She smoothed her skirts and closed the lid of her ink.

A streak of movement yanked her gaze to the sky.

A bird with a fluttering white tail dove toward the palace, the beauty of its flight startling against the deep gray of the stormy twilight.

But the bird was large, much too large.

"Gillien!" Allora screamed as the white tail—no not tail, fabric—fell away from the beast.

The bird twisted, soaring up into the sky as a second bird took its place, dropping something dark from its talons.

"Gillien!"

The white fabric fell too fast, dragged down by the gruesome form tied to its end, missing the rail of Allora's balcony by feet before striking the ground with a soul-rending crunch.

Allora lunged toward the balcony rail as the door slammed open behind her with a crash of breaking glass.

The second form fell beside the first.

Men—the twisted bodies of two men lay on the path below.

Allora's mind wouldn't allow her to deny the reality of the corpses.

But the banner tied to one of the men. The colors and make of their clothes.

An unnatural force cinched around Allora's waist, dragging her back.

She gripped the railing, ignoring the pain of her nails tearing as they ripped across the stone, needing another moment to force her mind into understanding.

A banner with the Wyrainian royal crest. Two men in Wyrainian colors, dead on the ground, their bodies broken after falling from the sky.

A screech rent the night. Massive birds. Seven—no twelve—flying toward Ilara.

The force yanked her from the rail, tossing her through the balcony door.

Arms caught her before she could fall.

"Gillien!" She shoved away from the one who held her, turning toward the open door in time to watch the sorcerer leap over the balcony rail.

A guard slammed the door shut, shattering more of the glass panes.

An arm wrapped around Allora's waist, ready to lift her.

Allora drove her elbow back and twisted free.

"We have to go, Your Majesty." Kenrick reached for her, ready to spirit her away to her stone cell.

"The city." Allora darted past him, grabbing his arm, yanking him down the hall. "The birds. They're flying toward the city."

She tossed open the door to the nearest south-facing room.

The lights in the parlor hadn't been lit, leaving the curtains as a silhouetted border framing the dark sky above Ilara.

She bolted toward the window, the torn tips of her fingers leaving blood on the sill as she shoved it open.

"Your Majesty." Kenrick grabbed her, lifting her away from the middle of the window, pinning her against the curtains. He reached up to close the window.

"I want to see." Allora grabbed his hand. "I have to see."

He tightened his arm around her waist, using the weight of his body to lock her against the wall as the first of the birds dove toward the city.

The plague of beasts screeched their bloodlust as they followed.

She locked her fingers through his, binding herself to his promised safety as the screams of her people breached the palace walls.

39

ADRIAL

The light glinting off the blade seemed to mock Adrial as he weighed the knife in his hand.

Made for use in a kitchen rather than a fight, the worn wood of the handle felt hefty enough to imply reliable use, though what exactly he hoped to accomplish with the weapon, he didn't know. Ian Ayres-born reflexes allowed him to dodge an apple, but fighting a proper, armed, most likely magical opponent?

He'd be dead in a minute if he was lucky enough to be granted a quick death.

But—the but that made him grab the napkin from his dinner tray to be folded into a sad sheath—if demons born of ice or the Sorcerers Guild themselves decided to attack the library and Adrial did die in the fight, he needed a weapon in his hand when they found his body. He needed everyone to know he'd fought with every ounce of his being to survive. He needed the story of his struggle to be bold enough to reach Ena, so she would never doubt that he did not greet his end gently, but fought Death himself for a hope of a life with her and Lily.

"You'd do as well pinning a note that reads *I tried* to the front of your robes." He propped his foot on the edge of his cot and slid the weapon into his boot. "You're a fool, Adrial Ayres."

The rigidity of the blade locked his ankle at an odd angle.

He lowered his foot, putting weight onto that leg.

Though the wrapped knife didn't cut him, the pressure of the metal digging into his ankle bone hinted of a swiftly blooming bruise.

He took the four steps the length of his office allowed. The hidden blade made it harder to hide his limp, but not impossible.

"If the library is attacked, you needn't bother hiding your limp. You've got to think."

Not about ways to defend the library—there was nothing the guards hadn't already done to prepare for an attack.

Not about if Tege had gotten word of the ice army to Ena.

Not about if Ena had sought shelter as he'd begged her to.

Leaving the knife in his boot, Adrial sat at his desk, returning to the list he'd been staring at since he'd run out of frantic ideas of how he might prepare Ilara for an army he couldn't warn the Guilds was coming.

Doubt rolled a wave of nausea through Adrial.

"There is nothing more to be done." He straightened the cuffs of his robes.

But Lord Kearney could send scouting parties north.

Parties the sorcerers would surely slaughter before they found any hint of wild magic.

"Even the Sorcerers Guild can't hide an army marching toward us. Not unless they defeat the frozen beasts themselves."

Adrial tipped his head back, staring at the base of the lamp hanging above him.

If the sorcerers attacked the ice army, drove them out of Ilbrea before anyone in Ilara even knew there was a threat...

You could spare them that much gratitude, Mara whispered. *We've enough reasons to loathe them. Seeing a glimmer of good bears no threat to their certain villainy.*

You're wrong, Adrial shouted back.

It was gratitude for the sorcerers' aid that had begun their path to power over Ilbrea.

The sorcerers' welcome upon their victorious return from the battles against the invaders in the south—Adrial added the scene to his list, the twelfth entry he'd managed.

When he left the library, if Lord Gareth didn't destroy Adrial's pages to rid the Scribes Guild of a traitor's work, Adrial wanted Tammin to have a guide for the rest of the vellum. At least Adrial hoped it would be Tammin to take over the task he had failed to finish.

The creation of the deep ravine around the royal palace needed to be included in the vellum as well, so Princess Illia's children might learn never to trust the protection of snakes.

Adrial reached down, itching the place where the hilt of the blade dug into his skin.

A sound, like metal shrieking against glass, grazed the edge of Adrial's thoughts, speeding his heart as though the ghosts of battles yet to come sought to torment him.

It would be Tammin's duty to add the battle for Ilara if the worst should come. If the city should burn, she would need nearly all the deep orange ink Ena had left behind.

Adrial would never again need to ration inks, no matter where Ena led him. She'd be there, collecting plants, smelling of flowers. He only had to survive long enough for Ena to find a way out of the library, out of Ilara, that his ruined body could manage.

The rumble of footsteps raced down the corridor, dousing Adrial's distracting spark of joy.

"To your shelters!" a voice shouted.

Bam. Bam. Bam.

Pounding rattled Adrial's door just before a guard flung it open. "Head Scribe, we have to get you to your shelter."

Adrial had already been wrenched through the doorway before the guard finished speaking.

Seven guards had run to fetch him, leaving anyone who tried to flee the other way to be rammed against the wall as the head scribe passed.

An ear-splitting screech pierced the stone of the library, carrying over the voices of the panicked scribes.

The noise didn't stop as more cries joined the din.

"What is that?" Adrial shouted over the chaos.

"I don't know, sir," a guard said. "An order came to get you to safety. The runner didn't say why."

He didn't resist as two of the guards gripped him under his arms, propelling him down the steps to the scribes' gallery far more quickly than Adrial could have managed on his own.

A crash shook the library roof.

Adrial peered up through the rain of dust, trusting the guards to guide him as he watched three cracks spread across the ceiling.

"We need to take him to the basement," one of Adrial's guards said.

Adrial tried to twist toward the familiar voice.

"That's not the order," another guard shouted back.

"The order is to protect the head scribe!" The first guard—Bradford, Braddock, Adrial's mind couldn't focus enough to recall—dodged into Adrial's path, shunting Adrial's pack aside as a skull-sized chunk of the ceiling crashed down between two fleeing scribes. "It's too dangerous up here."

Adrial's guards veered around the sprinkle of tumbling rubble, ignoring Braddock. Not stopping to help the terrified scribes, they ran Adrial through the gallery door, not slowing until they'd reached the platform at the far end of the room.

The two guards holding Adrial lifted him up, setting him on his feet and passing him to another set of guards, who hauled him to the back corner of the raised level where a cluster of scribes surrounded Lord Gareth.

Screams echoed from the corridor as a larger section of the ceiling fell, striking a scribe on the shoulder.

The scribe fell, blood blooming on their white robes.

Adrial jerked away from his guards as instinct screamed for him to help. Another set of hands grabbed on to him, holding him in place.

"Everyone else in!" A guard ran to the injured scribe.

The scribe screamed as the guard dragged them through the door into the gallery just before it slammed shut.

Four guards slid a long bar of metal-reinforced wood through the brackets of the door, locking the rest of the scribes out.

"We have to move them to the cellars."

"There's no escape from down there. If an attack—"

"The attack is coming from above."

"Sir!"

Guards formed a line in front of the door, their weapons drawn as they waited for an enemy to burst through the metal and wood they hoped would protect them.

"—separate them."

"We follow our orders."

"Sir."

"—weren't planning for an attack from above."

A rumble of destruction carried through the door. The platform trembled.

A sharp blow banged pain into Adrial's arm. "Sir."

"Let go." A guard shoved Taddy back, but Taddy clung to Adrial's sleeve.

"I'm his apprentice!" Taddy shouted up at the guard. "I'm taking him to his chair!"

Adrial sidestepped, the knife in his boot digging into his ankle as he placed himself between the guard and Taddy.

"I don't need a chair," Adrial said.

"Please, sir." Panic widened Taddy's eyes. He leaned his weight back, yanking on Adrial.

White-hot pain shot from Adrial's knee to his shoulder as he stumbled, the sharp burst clearing Adrial's mind enough to see what Taddy was dragging him toward.

An empty chair waited ten feet from the Lord Scribe, and sitting beside it—Brady, dressed in apprentice's robes far too large for her, the white sleeves long enough to almost cover the half-eaten apple in her hand.

Lord Gareth hadn't noticed the intruder. He sat with his hands in his lap, his gaze fixed on the door, his lips moving as though he were whispering under the chaos around him.

Adrial managed one step toward the Lord Scribe before Taddy steered him to the empty chair.

"I'm sorry, sir," Taddy said. "I didn't know what else to do. Tege still isn't back—"

"How long—"

An inhuman shriek sliced through the door.

"We need to move them," Guard Braddock shouted over the screams of the scribes.

"Apple?" Brady pulled an apple from her pocket, holding it up to Adrial.

"Get them into the pantry," Braddock said, "at least the Lord and head scribe."

"We're not trapping them," another guard shouted back.

"I couldn't leave her." Taddy yanked the apple from Brady and shoved it into his pocket, the hysteria in his eyes growing with every glance to Lord Gareth as though the Lord Scribe were the threat, not whatever had made the guards locked outside the door scream with such terror.

Bam.

Terrified cries covered Taddy's words as something rammed into the door.

Bam.

"I'm taking them." Braddock grabbed Adrial's arm, jerking him to his feet.

Bam.

The bar across the door cracked.

"Grab the Lord Scribe." Braddock gripped another guard's shoulder. "We're going."

"Taddy!" Adrial shouted. "Taddy!"

Bam.

"Move the scribes to the lower stacks." The order came from near the door. "All of them to the stacks. Now!"

"Chivving finally." Braddock pivoted toward the door on the northeastern side of the hall.

Fifty scribes ran in the same direction, packing into a tight scrum at the narrow servants' door.

"I'm here, sir." Taddy dragged Brady by the shoulder of her robe, making her follow as he kept pace beside Adrial.

Bam! Crack.

"Take her, and go," Adrial said. "Any exit you can, run."

"Step aside for the Lord Scribe!" the guard leading Lord Gareth shouted. "I have the Lord Scribe!"

Some scribes tried to move out of the way, shoving against those who still fought to reach the door.

Crack!

The door at the front of the hall shattered as it burst open, blasting the guards with metal and wood, battering them back before the monster even charged.

Red dripped from the mouth of the sparkling white beast, spattering across the floor as it whipped its head toward the nearest guard.

With a form like a wolf painted by nightmares—larger than a man, claws like a monstrous cat, and footlong fangs—the monster leapt with horrifying strength, tearing through the guard's neck before he could scream.

"Taddy, run!" Adrial shouted one more time as three more horrors charged into the hall.

Like men lost to a frozen battlefield, their bodies and clothes torn and bloody, their skin the icy blue-white of frozen wraiths, the three warriors attacked the guards in the monster's wake.

"Lord Gareth."

Adrial's mind clung to the shout as the guards nearest the platform charged into the fight.

"Lord Gareth!"

Braddock switched directions, hauling Adrial away from the other scribes toward a pantry on the far side of the platform.

"Taddy!" Adrial shouted.

The wolf tore through another guard, even as four men attacked the beast with their swords.

"Move. Everyone move!"

A guard drove his sword through an ice warrior's—a deadish's—gut.

The thing didn't seem to notice as it sliced its bloody blade across the guard's throat. A spray of red coated the warrior, covering its nose, its mouth—the creature simply pushed the slain man away and rounded on its next opponent, the dead guard's blade still lodged just below its lungs.

"Lord Gareth. My Lord!" The terror in the shout didn't pierce Adrial's panic as the wolf tossed aside a guard and leapt toward the platform.

A sword plunged into the beast's side, the guard wielding it crashing his own body into the monster, slowing the wolf's attack.

The beast staggered sideways but didn't fall. Ignoring the guard as he twisted the blade free, the wolf lunged for the platform. Not toward Adrial, toward the fleeing scribes.

No!

Adrial couldn't scream as Braddock slammed him behind a pillar, knocking the air from Adrial's lungs as he pinned him out of sight.

A howl, high and piercing, echoed through the hall.

"Get into the pantry. Bolt the door," Braddock said. "Do not open that chivving door or make any noise before a scribes' guard comes for you."

Braddock gripped Adrial's shoulder, shoving him toward the pantry.

Taddy reached the closed door first, tossing it open, shoving Brady inside.

A flash of red caught the corner of Adrial's eye.

He leapt sideways, landing hard, dropping down to his knees before his momentum had slowed. Pain blurred his vision, muddying his view of the deadish as it slashed its sword again, barely missing Adrial as he tossed himself back, crashing to the floor.

Braddock drove his blade through the icy demon's back.

The monster didn't slow.

Adrial rolled to his side, grabbing for the hilt of the knife in his boot.

Braddock yanked his sword free, pivoting his blade aside, tackling the demon as it lunged at Adrial.

"Sir!" Taddy dove toward Adrial as both the guard and the demon landed on top of him.

Adrial gasped, trapped beneath the weight of the pair.

The demon twisted, reaching for Adrial's throat. The thing's eyes moved as though it could see as it gripped Adrial's collar, lifting his neck closer to its gnashing teeth.

But there was nothing behind its pale blue eyes.

No hatred. No fear. No life.

Deadish.

Braddock grabbed the thing by its neck, tossing it backward, away from Adrial.

"Knife!" Taddy leapt toward the monster. "Knife! Knife! Knife!"

"Taddy, run." Adrial rolled onto his front, trying to scramble to his feet. "Get into the—"

Taddy dropped to his knees, Adrial's kitchen knife in hand.

He screamed as he plunged the blade into the demon's skull, his battle cry growing as he stabbed again, and again, and again.

"Corner it!" The shout came from the front of the hall. "Close in. Close in."

The deadish went still.

Taddy kept stabbing.

Something close to a cheer came from the corridor outside the hall.

"He's done," Braddock said. "Son, he's done."

Taddy didn't seem to hear.

"Sweep the corridors!"

"We need help here."

Braddock gripped Taddy's wrist. "You stopped him. All right?"

"Send a runner for healers!"

"You did well." Braddock held on until Taddy dropped the blade.

"Where's the head scribe?" a voice shouted over the rest. "Where is the head scribe!"

"Here," Adrial called.

"I have him." Braddock pushed himself off the slain demon to stand.

Taddy had slashed through the monster's face, but where there should have been blood spilling from the terrible wounds, the gashes were clean, displaying the layers of white, pink, and faded red crystals within.

Adrial managed to rise to his knees. His whole body shook, protesting every movement as he tried to stand.

Four guards ran to stop right in front of him.

One dropped to his knee, placing his face level with Adrial's. "Are you hurt, sir?"

"No. But, if you could?" Adrial reached for the guard, the trembling of his hand not easing as the guard helped him to his feet. "The library, is it secure?"

"We don't know yet, sir," the guard said. "We need to move you to safety."

Two guards gripped Adrial under his arms, whisking him away from the abomination Dudia had allowed to enter the library.

The body of the hell-born wolf lay on its side. Two guards held the lifeless beast down while a third hacked at its neck with his sword.

One of the guards didn't seem to know he was standing in a smear of blood.

Adrial didn't know who the blood had come from. Too many lay on the ground. Six scribes not moving. Four still clinging to life. More fallen guards lay among them.

So much blood from so quick an attack.

"Get them away from the breach in the roof." The shouted order came from a guard with his hand pressed to a wound on his side.

"He needs help." Adrial tried to turn toward the injured man.

The guards controlling him kept pushing him forward, toward the door the scribes had tried to flee through before.

A cluster of scribes huddled to one side of the door, none of them moving to run toward safety.

"Everyone out, now!" The wounded guard stormed toward the breached gallery door.

"The head scribe," a familiar voice shouted, "where is he? We're not going without him."

Tammin broke free from the other scribes, the tears streaming down her face quickening as she caught sight of Adrial. Her left arm hung limp at her side, and the same side of her face had already begun to swell.

"I tried to clear a path for him." Tammin's words cracked in her throat. "We tried to help him. I'm sorry. I'm so sorry."

"Who?" Adrial pulled against his guards. "Tammin, who?"

Tammin choked on a sob.

Adrial rammed his elbows sideways, striking his guards hard enough to buy a second of freedom, shoving his way into the pack of scribes before his guards could grab hold again.

Lord Gareth lay on the ground. His eyes closed. His hands placed at his sides and robes smoothed out all the way down to his ankles.

There was no blood on his robes or skin. Nothing to hint the elderly scribe hadn't lain down for a nap.

"How?" The salt of Adrial's tears tainted his lips.

"Everyone move, now!"

"He collapsed," Tammin said. "It was so quick. He just—just fell."

"Now means now!"

Guards shoved the scribes through the narrow door, forcing them to safety.

Adrial's guards gripped him under his arms again, herding him after the others.

"Stop," Adrial said. "We can't leave him. I said stop!"

The guards hesitated.

"We will not leave the Lord Scribe here. I can walk on my own. You two carry his—" The word caught in Adrial's throat. "Him."

The two guards stepped away from Adrial, turning toward Lord Gareth, grabbing back on to Adrial a moment later as a thunder of footsteps raced toward the scribes' gallery.

Twenty scribes, all of them apprentices, bolted through the shattered door.

The screaming began when the first of them spotted the headless guard right in the center of the hall.

Three guards ran toward the apprentices, trying to hurry them past the dead and wounded toward the path the other scribes had taken.

"The sorcerers sent wolves and demons into our home." Braddock took the place of the guard on Adrial's right. "We were attacked by godsforsaken magic."

Behind the apprentices, something flickered in the shadows. A glinting blade in the bloody hand of Death's worldly companion.

The specter vanished as the guards passed.

"Sheltering under the stacks won't work for long," Braddock said. "The monsters tore through the roof, I'd wager they can tear through floors as well. The beasts get wise and attack the great room, it would be easy work to cut off your only escape."

The last of the apprentices disappeared through the narrow door.

Adrial obeyed as a guard steered him after them.

"I know safer places we can send the apprentices," Braddock said. "I beg you, Lord Scribe. Their fate is in your hands."

A flicker in the darkness caught Adrial's eye as the specter returned.

The guards drove Adrial into the passage before he could ask the wraith what path spared the most innocents from their master's wretched embrace.

40

ENA

The calm of Death's approach settled over my skin before I heard the birds' first cry. The sound came from the north, out of view from my perch where I watched the library, counting the guards over and over, searching the streets for any hint of attack.

"Sodding, sheep-shitting demons." Marlo backed away from the north-facing window. "The chivving ice monsters have beasts that can fly."

I ventured three steps from my post, enough to see out Marlo's window.

Two massive beasts flew toward the library, their figures misshapen shadows until they'd almost reached the white stone building.

Birds, like falcons born of a hateful god, carried wolves in their talons, while four men rode on each of their backs.

I darted back to my window, watching as the first falcon dove into the library courtyard.

The guards on the street yanked open the gate, racing to save their fellows who'd been trapped with the beasts.

The second bird dropped its wolf onto the library roof and landed beside it. The falcon dug in its talons, piercing the roof, then beat its massive wings, taking flight, ripping a section of the eaves away. The wolf tore its claws into the hole the bird had made.

I brushed my fingers across the daggers sheathed at my hips as I ran toward the stairs.

"Ena." Marlo chased after me. "Those are true monsters out there. Not demons wearing the guise of man."

"How do you kill that kind of beast?" Alane followed behind as I ran to the second floor.

"Tear out its heart," I said. "It'll kill a croilach."

"Ena, please don't go charging into a beast-ravaged paun den," Marlo said.

I didn't bother answering as I reached the first floor and bolted straight for the door.

Attie and Kace flanked the window, watching the library gate.

A guard charged past, sword still in hand as he abandoned his duty.

"Don't follow me." I flung open the door, letting the screams from the courtyard draw me toward the fight.

Not him.

They don't get to have him.

Another guard passed me as he fled.

Coward. Useless slitching coward.

I wanted to scream at him, blame the chivving guard for whatever danger the scribe faced. But I couldn't find fault for him as I finally caught sight of the frozen demons.

The four ice-wrought warriors fought near the gate, slicing their way through the guards to reach the street. Behind them, the falcon tore through any flesh it could reach, slashing through men, tossing corpses aside.

"Chivving useless paun." Marlo plowed past me, forcing a path between the guards.

Alane followed right behind him.

I dodged in before Attie and Kace.

My shoulders rammed into the guards as we broke through their ranks.

Drawing my blades, I forced my thoughts away from my fear for the lives of those who fought beside me.

Marlo and Alane both cut left, heading for the icy beast who had his sword through the neck of a guard. Marlo slashed his sword low, striking the ankles of the icy demon.

Two guards charged the deadish on the right, driving him back toward the falcon.

I followed their path, letting them draw the bird's eye before bolting around behind her.

A blood-soaked maw greeted me.

I dove forward. Pain ripped across the top of my head as I drove my dagger into the wolf's paw.

The cold stone ground scraped across my cheek as I rolled sideways, getting behind the monster's claws as I twisted up onto my knees and drove my second dagger into the deadly place where the beast's leg met its ribs.

The blood that should have spurted out when I wrenched my blade free didn't come.

I scrambled out from under the monster, running toward the library door as it thrashed against another's blow.

A bellow of rage came from behind me.

I glanced over my shoulder.

Attie had driven his blade high into the wolf's flank. He skidded to the ground on his knees, dragging his sword toward the center of the wolf's gut.

Protect my loyal friends.

I sent my prayer to any god who could hear through the chaos as I threw open the door to the library.

Four guards blocked the steps.

I tightened my grip on my remaining dagger.

"You're hurt." One of the guards leapt forward, grabbing my elbow. Fear wrinkled his brow as he looped his arm around my waist, half-carrying me up the stairs as the door slammed shut behind us. "You shouldn't have been out there."

"The scribes, where are they?" I tipped my face away from him. Red clouded my vision as blood dripped into my eye.

"Everyone's been sent to their shelter locations. Can you make it to the cellars with the staff?"

"I'll be fine." I picked up my pace, running free from his grip.

Pallets had been laid out in the long corridor of scribes' quarters. Their carefully folded blankets hadn't been disturbed by a stampede of terrified scribes.

Wherever the guards had sent them, it wasn't in this portion of the library—a gift as it gave me only one direction to run.

The crack of splintering wood cut through the screams of the fight.

A guard limped toward me, gripping a wound in his side placed well enough to be fatal.

"Go back. Run." He met my gaze, the terror in his eyes sharpening as I neared. He stumbled to the wall, his blood-slicked hand fumbling for the hilt of a sword he'd already lost. "Gods protect me from Death's wraith. I beg you—I'm begging, please not her. I am not evil. Spare me from her vengeance. I'm sorry—"

The guard's desperate pleas followed me to the stairs that led down to the scribes' gallery.

The ceiling at the bottom of the steps had collapsed, leaving blood-stained rubble strewn before the shattered door.

An icy demon fought two guards in the center of the wide corridor, but the other three demons and the wolf had charged into the scribes' gallery.

I couldn't spot the falcon.

At the bottom of the steps, I cut to the side, bolting around the fight in the corridor.

Right ahead, four guards attacked the wolf at once, hacking at the beast.

"Behind you!"

I whirled around at the shout, ducking low just before a blade would have struck my neck.

I dodged sideways, slicing my blade across the front of the deadish's thigh, cutting deep before ripping my dagger free to dodge again.

The demon's stance wobbled, his torn leg unsteady beneath him.

I sprinted toward the scribes' gallery, hoping I'd injured the demon enough for the guards to end the monster.

Guards surrounded a cluster of scribes packed around a door on the far side of the room. Some of the scribes had formed a row just behind the guards, as though ready to fight the demons without a single chivving weapon among them.

Tammin had taken a place at the center of the line.

The wolf leapt toward the scribes.

No. Not him. Not him.

Tammin would be beside him. Tammin wouldn't leave the head scribe.

I shoved my dagger into its sheath and grabbed a sword from a headless corpse as I raced toward the wolf.

A guard stabbed the beast, throwing his weight into the blow, trying to knock the monster over.

The wolf stumbled, howling as it tossed the guard aside.

The guard lost hold of his sword as he fell, skidding across the floor.

The icy deadish nearest him spotted the easy prey.

It lunged toward the guard, stabbing its blood-stained sword for the guard's gut.

The guard rolled just before the blade struck, screaming as the demon's sword sliced along his side.

I swung my own blade, slashing deep into the deadish's arm, cutting through the muscles that kept a living man's hand moving.

The demon's sword tumbled from its grip. The fiend didn't

try to pick up its weapon before it lunged at me, reaching for my throat.

I sank my sword into its gut, throwing my weight into the blow as the guard had done with the wolf.

The deadish grabbed my arm with its still-moving hand as it tripped back, yanking me down as it crashed to the floor.

The beast gripped my neck.

A kind of cold I'd never felt before seized my throat, cutting off my air.

"Corner it. Close in. Close in!"

The demon seemed to smile as it squeezed harder.

I pulled my dagger from the sheath at my hip and sank the blade into the fiend's heart.

Its grip didn't loosen.

A blade slashed in front of me, slicing off the beast's head.

The deadish's hands fell limp at its sides as it toppled away from me.

Gasping for breath, I stood, wrenching my sword from the fiend as I turned to find another foe.

The clang of metal on metal had stopped, leaving only the cries of the wounded and terrified.

The guard I'd saved leaned against the nearest pillar as he sank to the ground, pale and sweating from returning the favor.

"Stay down and keep pressing on it." I stepped to the guard's side, sheltering behind a pillar as I scanned the dead and wounded on the floor.

You cannot take him.

Two of the white-robed dead were too mauled to be recognized.

Not him. He belongs with me.

I will tear down the sky if you take him.

"Where's the head scribe?" a voice shouted. "Where is the head scribe!"

I will not let you take him.

You cannot have him.

Dark fury flooded my soul in the moment before he called, "Here!"

A sob pummeled my chest.

"I have him." The shout came from the far side of the hall.

Guards raced that way.

The wounded guard grabbed my foot. "Ena? It's you, isn't it? You're the head scribe's wife."

"If she's alive, you can't be." I slid my foot free.

Two guards gripped the head scribe under his arms, moving him as though he couldn't stand on his own.

Blood stained his robes, but in smears from others, not dark patches from his own wounds.

Tammin ran toward him, her whole frame shaking with tears.

I couldn't hear her words, but she didn't try to grab for the head scribe, didn't stare in horror at any hurt I couldn't see.

He elbowed free of his guards, shoving his way into the cluster of scribes.

My heart forgot how to beat as the scribes closed in around him, blocking him from my sight.

"Did you send the monsters here to punish the library for letting you suffer?" the wounded guard asked.

"I have no monsters at my command." The faint sting of a lie felt bitter on my tongue.

"Now means now!" a guard shouted at the lingering scribes as he and a few of his less bloody fellows shunted the scribes toward the servants' door.

"Stop." Adrial followed behind the horde, guards gripping his arms again. "We can't leave him. I said stop!"

"Why would the Lady Sorcerer send monsters?" the wounded guard said. "We're just a library."

The guards let go of the head scribe, turning back toward the dead scattered on the floor.

"The Sorcerers Guild isn't the only evil stalking Ilbrea," I said.

A thunder of footsteps ran toward the scribes' gallery.

"What does that mean?" the wounded guard said.

I pressed myself behind the pillar as the footsteps reached the shattered door.

"If you have a family, get them out of the city." I spoke under a fresh round of terrified screams. "Go south, as far as you can manage. Bribe your way out of Ilara if you have to."

The footsteps and screaming neared.

I slid to the corner of the pillar, praying the shadows would be enough to hide me as I watched the scribes pass.

Apprentices. Children, none of them much older than Taddy, their young faces filled with fright and grief as the guards made them hurry past the monstrous wolf that had invaded their home.

My husband watched the children from the other side of their flock, a kind of bottomless fear on his face that could only be born from terror for the fate of others.

I slipped back around the side of the pillar as the last of the guards passed.

A ship to ferry the apprentices out of Ilara. It would take a near miracle, but the Black Bloods had managed worse.

Seeing the children to the docks would give the head scribe a reason to leave the library. We'd put the apprentices safely on their ship but have a boat of our own waiting. We'd sail south, far enough to hide him from the Guilds and he'd never set foot near the hell of Ilara again.

The noise of the apprentices faded, letting me hear the man's words. "I know safer places we can send the apprentices."

I peered around the corner.

A guard faced Adrial, the pair of them standing beside the perfectly placed corpse of Lord Gareth.

My lungs grew cold as something in my chest began to fray.

"I beg you, Lord Scribe. Their fate is in your hands." The guard's words ripped the tear deeper.

The freezing pain in my chest wrapped around my throat as though the icy demon still tried to choke me.

I couldn't push my scream past the cold.

Not him. Not him!

I tried to step forward. The wounded guard grabbed my wrist, yanking me back.

"If I can't know Ena Ayres is alive, neither can they." He kept his hold on me as the guards led my husband away, ready to wrap their new Lord Scribe in a duty I couldn't make him forget, setting him in front of monsters I am not strong enough to fight.

The Guilds of Ilbrea series continues with Falcon and Song.

Uncover the mysterious past of Ena Ayres in the *Ena of Ilbrea* series.
Turn the page for a sneak peek of book one, *Ember and Stone*.

The crack of the whip sent the birds scattering into the sky. They cawed their displeasure at the violence of the men below as they flew over the village and to the mountains beyond.

The whip cracked again.

Aaron did well. He didn't start to moan until the fourth lash. By the seventh, he screamed in earnest.

No one had given him a belt to bite down on. There hadn't been time when the soldiers hauled him from his house and tied him to the post in the square.

I clutched the little wooden box of salve hidden in my pocket, letting the corners bite deep into my palm.

The soldier passed forty lashes, not caring that Aaron's back had already turned to pulp.

I squeezed my way to the back of the crowd, unwilling to watch Aaron's blood stain the packed dirt.

Behind the rest of the villagers, children cowered in their mother's skirts, hiding from the horrors the Guilds' soldiers brought with them.

I didn't know how many strokes Aaron had been sentenced

to. I didn't want to know. I made myself stop counting how many times the whip sliced his back.

Bida, Aaron's wife, wept on the edge of the crowd. When his screams stopped, hers grew louder.

The women around Bida held her back, keeping her out of reach of the soldiers.

My stomach stung with the urge to offer comfort as she watched her husband being beaten by the men in black uniforms. But, with the salve tucked in my pocket, hiding in the back was safest.

I couldn't give Bida the box unless Aaron survived. Spring hadn't fully arrived, and the plants Lily needed to make more salves still hadn't bloomed. The tiny portion of the stuff hidden in my pocket was worth more than someone's life, especially if that person wasn't going to survive even with Lily's help.

Lily's orders had been clear—wait and see if Aaron made it through. Give Bida the salve if he did. If he didn't, come back home and hide the wooden box under the floorboards for the next poor soul who might need it.

Aaron fell to the ground. Blood leaked from a gash under his arm.

The soldier raised his whip again.

I sank farther into the shadows, trying to comfort myself with the beautiful lie that I could never be tied to the post in the village square, though I knew the salve clutched in my hand would see me whipped at the post as quickly as whatever offense the soldiers had decided Aaron had committed.

When my fingers had gone numb from gripping the box, the soldier stopped brandishing his whip and turned to face the crowd.

"We did not come here to torment you," the soldier said. "We came here to protect Ilbrea. We came here to protect the Guilds. We are here to provide peace to all the people of this great country.

This man committed a crime, and he has been punished. Do not think me cruel for upholding the law." He wrapped the bloody whip around his hand and led the other nine soldiers out of the square.

Ten soldiers. It had only taken ten of them to walk into our village and drag Aaron from his home. Ten men to tie him to the post and leave us all helpless as they beat a man who'd lived among us all his life.

The soldiers disappeared, and the crowd shifted in toward Aaron. I couldn't hear him crying or moaning over the angry mutters of the crowd.

His wife knelt by his side, wailing.

I wound my way forward, ignoring the stench of fear that surrounded the villagers.

Aaron lay on the ground, his hands still tied around the post. His back had been flayed open by the whip. His flesh looked more like something for a butcher to deal with than an illegal healer like me.

I knelt by his side, pressing my fingers to his neck to feel for a pulse.

Nothing.

I wiped my fingers on the cleanest part of Aaron's shirt I could find and weaved my way back out of the crowd, still clutching the box of salve in my hand.

Carrion birds gathered on the rooftops near the square, scenting the fresh blood in the air. They didn't know Aaron wouldn't be food for them. The villagers of Harane had yet to fall so low as to leave our own out as a feast for the birds.

There was no joy in the spring sun as I walked toward Lily's house on the eastern edge of the village.

I passed by the tavern, which had already filled with men who didn't mind we hadn't reached midday. I didn't blame them for hiding in there. If they could find somewhere away from the torment of the soldiers, better on them for seizing it. I only hoped there weren't any soldiers laughing inside the tavern's walls.

I followed the familiar path home. Along our one, wide dirt road, past the few shops Harane had to offer, to the edge of the village where only fields and pastures stood between us and the forest that reached up the eastern mountains' slopes.

It didn't take long to reach the worn wooden house with the one giant tree towering out front. It didn't take long to reach anywhere in the tiny village of Harane.

Part of me hated knowing every person who lived nearby. Part of me wished the village were smaller. Then maybe we'd fall off the Guilds' maps entirely.

As it was, the Guilds only came when they wanted to collect our taxes, to steal our men to fight their wars, or to find some other sick pleasure in inflicting agony on people who wanted nothing more than to survive. Or if their business brought them far enough south on the mountain road they had to pass through our home on their way to torment someone else.

I allowed myself a moment to breathe before facing Lily. I blinked away the images of Aaron covered in blood and shoved them into a dark corner with the rest of the wretched things it was better not to ponder.

Lily barely glanced up as I swung open the gate and stepped into the back garden. Dirt covered her hands and skirt. Her shoulders were hunched from the hours spent planting our summer garden. She never allowed me to help with the task. Everything had to be carefully planned, keeping the vegetables toward the outermost edges. Hiding the plants she could be hanged for in the center, where soldiers were less likely to spot the things she grew to protect the people of our village. The people the soldiers were so eager to hurt.

"Did he make it?" Lily stretched her shoulders back and brushed the dirt off her weathered hands.

I held the wooden box out as my response. Blood stained the

corners. It wasn't Aaron's blood. It was mine. Cuts marked my hand where I'd squeezed the box too tightly.

Lily glared at my palm. "You'd better go in and wrap your hand. If you let it get infected, I'll have to treat you with the salve, and you know we're running out."

I tucked the box back into my pocket and went inside, not bothering to argue that I could heal from a tiny cut. I didn't want to look into Lily's wrinkled face and see the glimmer of pity in her eyes.

The inside of the house smelled of herbs and dried flowers. Their familiar scent did nothing to drive the stench of blood and fear from my nose.

A pot hung over the stove, waiting with whatever Lily had made for breakfast.

My stomach churned at the thought of eating. I needed to get out. Out of the village, away from the soldiers.

I pulled up the loose floorboard by the stove and tucked the salve in between the other boxes, tins, and vials. I grabbed my bag off the long, wooden table and shoved a piece of bread and a waterskin into it for later. I didn't bother grabbing a coat or shawl. I didn't care about getting cold.

I have to get out.

I was back through the door and in the garden a minute later. Lily didn't even look up from her work. "If you're running into the forest, you had better come back with something good."

"I will," I said. "I'll bring you back all sorts of wonderful things. Just make sure you save some dinner for me."

I didn't need to ask her to save me food. In all the years I'd lived with her, Lily had never let me go hungry. But she was afraid I would run away into the forest and never return. Or maybe it was me that feared I might disappear into the trees and never come back. Either way, I felt myself relax as I stepped out of the garden and turned my feet toward the forest.

ABOUT THE AUTHOR

Megan O'Russell is the author of several Young Adult series that invite readers to escape into worlds of adventure. From *Girl of Glass*, which blends dystopian darkness with the heart-pounding danger of vampires, to *Ena of Ilbrea*, which draws readers into an epic world of magic and assassins.

With the *Girl of Glass* series, *The Tethering* series, *The Chronicles of Maggie Trent*, *The Tale of Bryant Adams*, the *Ena of Ilbrea* series, and several more projects planned, there are always exciting new books on the horizon. To be the first to hear about new releases, free short stories, and giveaways, sign up for Megan's newsletter by visiting the following:

https://www.meganorussell.com/book-signup.

Originally from Upstate New York, Megan is a professional musical theatre performer whose work has taken her across North America. Her chronic wanderlust has led her from Alaska to Thailand and many places in between. Wanting to travel has fostered Megan's love of books that allow her to visit countless new worlds from her favorite reading nook. Megan is also a lyricist and playwright. Information on her theatrical works can be found at RussellCompositions.com.

She would be thrilled to chat with you on Facebook or

Twitter @MeganORussell, elated if you'd visit her website MeganORussell.com, and over the moon if you'd like the pictures of her adventures on Instagram @ORussellMegan.

Ice and Sky

Feather and Flame

Guilds of Ilbrea

Inker and Crown

Myth and Storm

Viper and Steel

Tower and Grave

Siege and Sparrow

Falcon and Song

Heart of Smoke

Heart of Smoke

Soul of Glass

Eye of Stone

Ash of Ages

Fracture Pact

The Cursebound Thief

The Oathbound Blade

The Bloodbound Knight

The Fatebound Wraith

Sorcerers of Ilbrea

Spell and Secret